ISBN 979-8-9932131-0-1 (Paperback)
ISBN 979-8-9932131-1-8 (eBook)

Library of Congress Cataloging in Publication Number
2025922566

Cover art by Leeahd Goldberg • leeahd.com
in collaboration with Chase Gordon • chasegordondesign.com
and Cryssy Cheung • cryssycheung.com

Author photo by Rebecca Cain

FIREBUG

A novel by
Risa Patterson

PROLOGUE

OLIVIA MADDEN STARED OUT the windshield as streaks of rain turned the traffic lights into blurry kaleidoscopes. Daddy muttered to himself in the driver's seat, a muscle bulging in his jaw. Olivia sank further in her seat and wrapped her arms in a tight hug around her sinking stomach.

Daddy played cards with his friends every week, even though it always made him angry. He was extra cross today because Mommy was supposed to pick her up from her friend's house, but sometimes Mommy drank too much to stay awake. Olivia tugged on the seatbelt digging into her neck. Daddy was supposed to have gotten her car seat out of the trunk and buckled her into it, but Daddy, whose breath stank like Mommy's hairspray when he'd buckled her in, was so mad she didn't point this out.

The creaky windshield wipers did their best to clear the heavy raindrops. Olivia's hand found the edge of the brown duct tape her father had used to patch up a hole in the leather seat. She couldn't reach the tape from her car seat, but now, it was right next to her. She fingered the edge, longing to peel it back.

"Don't tell your mother I'm driving without the car seat," Daddy suddenly shouted.

Startled, Olivia jerked her hand back to her lap. A familiar sign passed outside—they were almost home. Almost safe.

Green light washed over the car as they sped through an intersection. They drifted too far to one side until Daddy jerked the wheel the other way, making the whole car sway as a furious honk trailed them.

Olivia looked back at the duct tape. Maybe if she could move it without touching it, she wouldn't get in trouble. She concentrated, imagining the duct tape unfurling from the seat all on its own. Of course, it didn't budge. She reached out to trace the rippled texture again. She could just lift it a little bit. She'd put it right back…

She pulled, and the tape came away easier than she'd expected, revealing the gaping hole.

Daddy glanced over his shoulder, face red. "Olivia, what did I tell you about messing with that tape?" He turned back to the road, stomping on the gas.

Olivia struggled to push the tape back in place, but it wouldn't stick anymore.

Daddy glanced back again. "What did I *just* say?"

The raindrops on the windshield turned yellow, then red. A blinding white light illuminated Olivia's window.

Tires screeched. Olivia screamed.

Then her side of the car turned into a jaw of metal and glass, biting down.

PART I

1

ARACHNE SCRATCHED HER SCALP. Tiny spiders poured out of her dark hair, tickling her shoulders. She peered across the blasted hellscape at the massive golden throne at its center. It lay empty, as it had for centuries. As she watched, a wandering soul, dwarfed by the size of the throne, approached it and inspected the words etched into its gleaming base. Arachne whispered the words, long since memorized, as the hapless soul read:

> *"Your sins have condemned you to the Underworld, but you have not sinned so greatly as to burn. One of you will be granted the opportunity to return to the world of the living and set things right. The portal to redemption lies at the end of one of these passageways, meant for one soul for all of time."*

The soul looked up from the inscription and took in the space surrounding him: impossibly huge walls sweeping up to meet a cavernous, rocky ceiling half a galaxy away. Countless holes in the distant, ashen walls ranged in size from that of a foxhole to chasms the size of small moons. Arachne chuckled to herself as the soul broke into a run. It might take him decades, or centuries, or even millennia, but sooner or later, he would learn the folly of his haste and give up his search. If he were lucky, he'd do so before he got lost in the nearly infinite network of branching tunnels.

Her chuckle turned into gagging as a large spider crawled up her throat. She opened her mouth and let it crawl down her neck to feed upon the smaller spiders streaming down her chest. Once, she'd have screamed and rent her flesh in revulsion, but by now, her curse had become as much a part of her as her olive skin or her long, thick hair, which neither grew nor could be shorn. She took a deep breath and closed her eyes, initiating her search in the world of the living.

Shards of visions flooded her mind's eye—the damp hollow of a basement doorjamb, a sun-baked brick wall, the rustling leaves of a bush speckled with droplets from a recent rain. Arachne launched her attention from one image to the next, the strange sense of tingling at His presence growing with each vision. He was close by.

"Where are you?" she murmured, searching, seeking, as the crackling sensation of His energy grew stronger...

Ah. There He was.

All of the other fragments of images behind her eyes faded into darkness as she funneled her attention into the multiple eyes of a wolf spider perched on the branch of a tree a half-dozen strides from where He was walking. He looked much different than He had when Arachne had first arrived in the Underworld to find Him sitting atop His throne. He had been almost painful to behold, gorgeous as sin itself. His earthly countenance held no comparison; it couldn't, or mortals would weep at the sight of Him. He looked for all the world like a moderately attractive middle-aged man out for a late morning stroll through a neighborhood full of landscaped hedges and green lawns glistening with rain from a recent storm…but Arachne knew better. He was up to mischief.

The hairs on her wolf spider's legs prickled at His approach. Arachne waited until He was beneath the tree, then shot tension into the spider's legs so it leapt from its branch onto the white linen of His shoulder.

"Hello, Hades," Arachne said.

Though she was unfathomably far away in wherever the Underworld actually existed, Hades turned and smiled at the spider on His shoulder. "Hello, Arachne. I was wondering when you were going to find me again."

"As if you didn't know."

Hades's grin deepened. "I foresee events in the world of the living. I find no advantage in doing so for the dead."

Hades fell silent as a child on a bicycle wobbled past, chased by a speed-walking woman. Arachne turned the spider's multiple eyes on Hades's hands as the woman passed. Would he place a condom in her purse to instigate trouble with her spouse? Or perhaps steal her keys? But Hades let her pass without incident. He wasn't here for her.

Plastic blue-and-red signs peppered many of the yards, advertising DEWEY COATES FOR GOVERNOR. Coates's challenger Will Harvey had fewer devotees.

Hades made His way up the driveway of a particularly nice house. Its mailbox read *Coates*.

"Sabotaging a good man's gubernatorial run, are we?" Arachne asked.

Hades didn't respond. He plucked a muddy set of boots from the porch, tucked them under His arm, and kept moving. A block later, Hades removed his shoes and pulled on the mud-caked boots. He trudged through a sodden stretch of yard, leaving deep tracks, and planted both feet outside the back window of a quaint white house with forest-green shutters. Satisfied, He returned to the first house, ditched the boots, pulled his own shoes back on, and slipped away.

Arachne winced as a spider bit into the soft flesh of her armpit. "What's going to happen next?"

"Dewey Coates will be charged with a murder taking place in that house in three...two...one."

A faint bang rippled the hairs on her spider's legs.

"He'll be acquitted," Hades added, "but the damage will be done. His political career, ruined. His marriage, finished. He'll kill himself in five years with the handgun he keeps in a shoebox in his closet." Hades sighed and ran a hand over His face. "I tell you, Arachne, this used to be harder."

"Not as fun without a sparring partner?"

"It certainly was a more interesting game of chess."

Arachne laughed dryly. "Interesting is one word for it." When she'd been alive, there had been a thriving coterie of gods possessing all sorts of attributes: jealousy, bravery, vanity, rage. She'd made the mistake of crossing one. Hence her curse: spiders. Erupting from her skin, biting her, crawling over every inch of her body, for all eternity. The only upside to her curse was that over time, she discovered if she concentrated, she could see through the eyes of the spiders in the world of the living. She observed humanity, learned their languages, witnessed wars and festivals and storms. Civilizations rose and fell; empires spawned and burned. Over the centuries, she'd even managed to exert her will enough to control the earthbound spiders, though she'd had no luck doing the same for the spiders in what she'd come to think of as Hell.

The goddess who cursed Arachne suffocated on her own obsolescence millennia ago, along with all the other gods, choked into nonexistence one by one as human life smothered the planet. Perhaps the last to go was the entity Hades called the Old One, the predecessor of all the other gods, who had fallen silent millennia ago. Hades claimed He didn't know if the Old One was dead, withdrawn into the realms above, or in a kind of deep cosmic slumber.

Now, as far as Arachne could tell, only the Lord of Death remained. He had many names, but she called Him by the name she'd known when she was alive.

Arachne pried a wriggling spider from underneath her eyelid. "Is it really a game at all, without the Old One to play against?"

Hades shrugged. "It's the only game I know."

"We could play," said Arachne.

"You and me?" Hades raised an eyebrow. "You'd find yourself at quite a disadvantage, Arachne. You've become adept at manipulating your terrestrial spiders, but you can't influence the mortals like the Old One used to."

Arachne chewed her lip. "Well, you usually select your own targets. You stalk them like a lion hunting the weakest gazelle, going for the easy kill. So…what if I picked one?"

Hades scoffed. "Without the Old One balancing things out, they're all weak."

"You're saying no matter who I pick, you could make them fall?"

He grinned. "I could whisper madness into their mind, and they would take their own life as surely as a leaf falling from a dead tree."

Arachne stared up at Him for a moment through the eyes of her spider. "What if you couldn't infiltrate their mind?"

Hades tilted His head. "Interesting. What do I win, should I succeed?"

"What could I offer you, beyond the satisfaction of claiming an otherwise pure soul?"

He paused. "And if I fail?"

"If you fail..." Hundreds of baby spiders burrowed into Arachne's ear canal. She ground her teeth in agony.

"Yes, Arachne?"

She clawed a finger into her ear. "If you fail, then you release me!" Arachne shrieked.

The pain in the depths of her ear disappeared.

"Release you," Hades repeated. Arachne looked at Him and recoiled. Flames filled His eyes. It looked like His mind was on fire. "Now *that* would be a game."

With a soft *foomph*, the fire extinguished. Tendrils of smoke rose like tears from the corners of His eyes. The smoke twisted upwards until it disappeared into the idyllic blue sky.

2

"THERE IS NOTHING IN this world you cannot accomplish if you put your mind to it."

Olivia Madden's eyes fell to the program on her armrest, finding her name on the list of forty-seven graduates at UC Boulder who'd gone through hell and back to earn their Master's degrees in Chemical Engineering.

The commencement speaker's amplified voice competed with the buzz of the fluorescent lights overhead. "Each of you are here because you possess a talent. Intelligence, creativity, determination. Talents like these are a gift from God. As it says in Romans: 'Having gifts that differ according to the grace given to us, let us use them: if prophecy, in proportion to our faith.'"

Olivia stared at the printed program. Energy gathered, like a ball of light behind her eyes.

"Your talent is your gift. Do not squander it."

The hairs on her forearms rose. She directed her energy toward the program, probing it mentally, feeling the weight and shape with her mind. *Move*, she thought. *Move, just a little bit—*

"It must have been God working in the lab until four in the morning," whispered Milo Madrigal from the seat behind her, breaking her focus.

Olivia glanced over her shoulder and grinned. "Hush."

"It must have been God who cleaned the rat shit out of the cages."

"Milo, you're not funny."

"You think I can't tell when you're smiling?"

Blindness didn't stop Milo from being one of the most perceptive people Olivia had ever met. In the first class they shared, he'd arrived before and left after everyone else, so it had taken her weeks to notice the expandable cane he kept in his backpack. When she told him later that she thought he wore sunglasses because he was hungover, he had laughed and asked, "Who says I'm not?"

"The real world can be unforgiving," continued the speaker. "But remember—no matter where your future careers take you, your faith is your most valuable asset. It will be with you wherever you go."

Olivia sighed and returned her attention to the program. The mental energy she'd summoned was gone. Not that it mattered; ever since she was a little girl, she'd tried to move things with her mind. It never worked.

In her dreams, it was different. In dreams, Olivia moved objects with the simple flex of a mental muscle. Sometimes, she could even fly.

As the speaker droned on about God, Olivia gazed around the room. She was one of the lucky few in her graduating class with a job lined up. In a few days, she'd start work at Fisher Biotech in Austin. The small but growing company produced a meal-substitution liquid called Nosh. She'd flown to the headquarters for an interview a few months ago and been offered a Research Associate position on the spot. The pay wasn't much, but she was grateful for the opportunity.

Milo nudged Olivia's folding chair forward, producing a harsh scraping sound. Olivia stifled a laugh with her palm.

She was going to miss seeing him so regularly. Milo had scored a job too, as a Materials Engineer at a startup in Salt Lake City. Part of her was sad about the impending distance, but another part of her was relieved not to be in the same dating pool anymore. Years ago, she and Milo had dated briefly, but something hadn't clicked. He was confident and charming, with dark features, long eyelashes, and a shaggy mop of hair that lent him the effortless good looks of a surfer, but she couldn't bring herself to feel the way he did about her. Dating Milo felt as wrong as her attempts at telekinesis felt right.

Life would be so much easier if she could switch those convictions.

When the graduation ceremony ended, Olivia hugged Milo goodbye and found her mother, Betty, in the crowd of assembled parents. Betty's cheeks shone with tears, bouquets of crumpled tissues peeking from her pockets. "I'm so proud of you, Liv."

Tears stung Olivia's eyes as she hugged her mother. She was sure other parents were proud too, but her mother's words really meant something. The years following the car accident that broke Olivia's wrist had been harrowing. Her father's injuries had sent him spiraling into addiction to pain pills and booze, his chronic pain fueling a burning rage that he took out on his wife and daughter. Things could have easily gone in another direction for Olivia and her mother if he hadn't died a few years after the crash. The tattoo on her wrist was a grim reminder of that.

Olivia shook the thought away. "Thanks, Mom."

"I can't believe you're flying out tomorrow." Her mother wiped away tears. "Promise you'll visit?"

"All the time," Olivia assured her.

"Good. Now let's go home. I've got so much food to feed you, you'll still be full by the time you get to Austin."

3

"Her? With the red hair?"

Arachne studied Olivia through the eyes of a spider on the back of a folding chair. She was tall and willowy, somewhere in her mid-twenties. Her hair, cascading in unruly waves over her shoulders, was a rich, glowing copper. Her green eyes sparkled as she hid a smile behind her hand at her friend's joke. Arachne caught a glimpse of a colorful flame tattoo on her wrist.

"Yes. Her."

Hades was hundreds of miles away, lying in a cot in an abandoned building, but He could see Olivia through Arachne's mind.

"You can pick anyone," He reminded her, turning to another spider she had perched on His shoulder. "An eighty-year-old saint with one foot in the grave. A child with a terminal illness. The Pope."

"The Pope is sinking like a lead weight, and you know it."

Hades smiled. "May I ask why you've chosen this particular lamb to lead to the slaughter?"

"I don't know," said Arachne, though that wasn't exactly true. Olivia Madden wasn't religious, and she didn't strike Arachne as being particularly selfless, yet there was a magnetism to her. Something about her *crackled*. Arachne wondered if Hades was aware of this too—she saw the world through a spider darkly, but who knew how *He* saw it?

"In the days before the Old One fell silent, we waged battles over far purer souls than her," Hades replied. "She might seem like a sweetheart, but she's got a temper."

"So accept the wager."

"You aren't allowed to torment or kill her with your spiders, you know," Hades added. "Bite her with a black widow or anything like that. Her or anyone else involved in her downfall."

"And you can't drive her mad by placing thoughts in her mind."

Hades grinned, and Arachne suddenly remembered how hideously ancient He was, that He only looked like a man when it suited Him. "I won't need to. Olivia Madden..." He drew the name out, flames flickering in the recesses of His pupils. "Hang on a moment. This kind of wager requires personal attention." Hades rose from His cot, walked behind a pillar, and disappeared, sending Arachne's spider on His shoulder tumbling to the ground.

Arachne fiddled with a spider on the back of her neck, waiting. Finally, a rumbling sound shook the pebbles at her feet. Arachne stood from her vantage point on a rocky bluff and made her way toward His throne.

The sound grew louder as she approached, as if an enormous being were hurtling toward her, some ancient creature of claw and cunning, born before time, who would laugh the stars into darkness at the end of it.

The thunder reached a fever pitch, then fell silent as He stepped through an invisible doorway beside His throne that He alone could see, looking more beautiful than any human who had ever walked the Earth.

Terror and fascination warred in Arachne's chest as she approached Him. It was unfair for one so sinister to be so gorgeous. He was twice the size of a mortal man, so He loomed over her, kind smile clashing with the wicked light in His eyes.

In a voice that could lure sailors to a rocky death, He said, "Our wager ends with her in the realms above, or in my grasp. If you win, I will show you the way to the doorway that leads to the world of the living. If I win, you will understand what Hell really is." His hand glowed as He held it out. "For the soul of Olivia Madden."

"For my freedom," Arachne answered.

Hades nodded.

Arachne reached for His hand. As she did, the energy surrounding Him shifted from enticing to sickening. All at once, her mind rioted with her earthly deeds: meals she'd eaten, things she'd stolen, people she'd loved. Every lie she'd ever told danced across her tongue like water skittering over a hot pan. She felt aroused and nauseated and savage.

His massive hand clutched hers. It was a vice, a branding iron, a shackle. Arachne fell silent, even as her mind screamed and thrashed for release. All existence narrowed to His hand—the hand that had dragged billions of souls to their doom.

Innumerable realities exploded in her mind's eye, each one branching into countless more, until finally a lightning bolt shot down into a single timeline, cruel jaws gnashing down where it struck.

Arachne reeled backward as He released her hand. Every spider on her body tucked its legs and dropped to the ground, surrounding her with a dark wreath of death.

When Arachne looked up, panting and terrified, He was gone.

4

Azrael Hatch woke to a cold hand clutching his wrist. Another hand settled over his mouth. His dream broke into shards of darkness that reshaped into a shadow pinning him to the bed.

A voice whispered: "Shh, it's me."

Lila.

Azrael made out her shape in the darkness. A thin band of moonlight shone across her pale hair. He felt her eyes on him, soft and dark as the eyes of the deer roaming the surrounding woods. The stiff cotton of her nightclothes brushed against his arm. Her smell washed over him, a mixture of sleep and sweat, dulcet as the caramels Father Clark brought the children from the farmer's market, and clean as the lavender soap the mothers made.

Azrael shot a glance to his half-brother Elijah, asleep in the next bed. The other sons of the Colony slept in rows of bunk beds in the barracks next door. Azrael and Elijah would have been forced to sleep there, too, along with dozens of snoring and farting boys not yet old enough to be Fathers, if not for the privilege of being the only two children of the Prophet, Henry Hatch.

Lila squeezed Azrael's wrist until his bones creaked. Urgency flashed in her eyes.

Azrael moved her other hand away from his mouth and whispered, "What is it?"

Lila leaned close, silk strands of hair brushing his face. "I am with child."

The words, so soft they were almost subliminal, echoed through Azrael's mind. The Prophet's intended wife. Pregnant. Panic rose like bile in his throat.

Being the eldest son of the Prophet had gotten Azrael out of so many scrapes he'd lost count. There was the time Azrael had gotten drunk on Father Clark's hidden stash of whiskey (his father hadn't spoken to him for a month), and the time he'd nearly burned down the main hall while he was playing with matches (his father had denounced him before the Colony as a "firebug"). Hell, he'd even gotten caught in the act of hiding a nest of spiders in Elijah's bedsheets, and even then, he'd just been lashed and not exiled.

But now Azrael was as good as dead. When the Prophet declared his intention to wed Lila, he'd announced to the Colony that God had told him Lila—his fifth wife—would be the one to finally bear him the "quiver" of children he was destined to beget. So far, the Prophet's other four wives had only borne him two sons: Azrael and Elijah. Azrael had never known his mother—she'd died giving birth to him, if the Prophet was to be believed. Azrael didn't even know her name. Lucille had borne the Prophet's only other child, Elijah, and so far, additional attempts to impregnate her had proved fruitless. The Prophet maintained that his lack of progeny was the fault of his wives, but Azrael wasn't so sure.

If Lila had been intended for one of the Fathers, Azrael may have stood a chance. But like a fool, he'd become enamored with the young woman who was to be wedded to the Prophet himself. The only reason Lila wasn't married already was that the Prophet always wed his wives on the first day of spring, which was months away.

If Azrael were lucky, when the truth of Lila's pregnancy came out, he'd be exiled.

If he were unlucky, Robert Grayburn would kill him.

For at least as long as Azrael had been alive, Grayburn had whispered the Colony's secrets in the Prophet's ear, frightened the mothers with his cold, grinning menace, and exposed the Fathers for the sycophants they were. Grayburn towered over the other men of the Colony, the Prophet included, with broad shoulders and a square jaw that seemed to be permanently clenched. He wasn't considered a "Father" because, despite having two wives and at least twice as many mistresses, he had no children. Despite this mark of shame, Grayburn's place of power within the Colony remained as immutable a fact as the Prophet's leadership.

Azrael had long sensed that Grayburn harbored a particular loathing for him, a seething rage barely held at bay, and now that Azrael's rebellion against his father had crossed an irrevocable line, there was nothing standing between him and Grayburn's wrath.

"Are you sure?" Azrael whispered. "We were so careful…"

Lila moved Azrael's hand to her belly. It was taut and round. She wasn't showing through her clothes yet, but that would change in another month or so.

Lila's lips grazed his ear. "We have to run away."

Azrael swallowed, his head spinning. "They'd find us," he whispered.

Lila's pale face floated in the moonlight. She looked so young, a child afraid of the monsters under her bed. "You know where the train station is."

Azrael had tried to run away the summer of the previous year, when the Prophet had caught him stealing cash from his desk drawer. Azrael had broken out of his father's grasp and ran south as quickly as his feet could carry him. Azrael's knowledge about what lay beyond the Colony property was limited—the Prophet forbade cell phone access to anybody except himself, Robert Grayburn, and Father Clark, who sold goods at the Farmer's Market and handled the Colony's finances. Azrael had gathered from sneaking glances at the cell phones whenever he could that the Colony was in Eland, Texas, and that they were a hundred miles from a city called Austin.

He also knew that when the Fathers came and went from the compound, they always turned south when the dirt road connected with pavement. Azrael had made it as far as a nearby train station when Robert Grayburn and Father Clark caught up with him. Azrael had seen Father Clark first and turned to bolt in the opposite direction in time to see Robert Grayburn's gleaming metal baseball bat swiftly growing in his vision. There was darkness after that, until Azrael regained consciousness back at the Colony.

Azrael whispered, "Even if I could find the station again, they'll track us down."

"Not if we leave in the middle of the night. We could be on a train before they realize we're gone."

Azrael's mind raced. "You could tell the Prophet it's Grayburn's baby."

Lila rolled her eyes. "If Grayburn could bear children, the Colony would be crawling with bastards. You're not listening. We need to *leave*."

Elijah shifted under his sheets.

Azrael held his breath, staring at his devout half-brother. If Elijah woke to find Lila in their room, he'd betray Azrael faster than you could say "Holy Ghost." Though Azrael was the eldest son, the Prophet had declared early on that Elijah was his true heir. Azrael recalled his father's words from years ago with perfect clarity: "Azrael, you have the potential to be a true leader, but at every opportunity, I have watched you choose wickedness instead."

Azrael couldn't deny that Elijah was better suited to follow in the Prophet's footsteps. To Elijah, their father's word was gospel. If the boy stayed here, he'd become the same kind of monster their father was. But if he left...

Azrael locked eyes with Lila. "There's a way we can all get out of this. You, me, and Elijah."

Her eyes widened. "Elijah? But—"

"Lila, he's my brother. I can't abandon him."

Lila looked over at Elijah. "How are we going to get him out, too?"

"I'll leave first," Azrael whispered. "I'll find a safe place for us, and I'll come back for you."

"Azrael, you can't leave me here."

"I have to. It's the only way I can get us all free. I'll leave tonight—any longer and we risk someone realizing you're with child. When they wake to find I'm gone, you'll tell them that's Elijah's baby in your belly."

Lila's nose wrinkled in disgust. "But...he can't be older than thirteen—"

Azrael gripped her shoulders. "Tell them...tell them I fell in love with you, but you chose my brother instead. Tell them when you confessed your affair to me, I was overcome with jealousy, and I ran into the woods. Tell them you think I'll come back once I have time to process things. It may buy me some time."

Lila's lower lip trembled. "Azrael...if I do that, the Prophet will declare me a Shamed Woman, and Elijah will be exiled."

"Exactly," Azrael whispered. "He's the golden child, the one chosen to lead once our father is dead. They won't hurt him—not any worse than he's been hurt before, anyway—but they'll cast him out. That's how I get all three of us out of here." Azrael quietly slid open his nightstand drawer. He lifted the drawer's false bottom and showed Lila the cash he'd been secreting away from the Prophet's coffers. "Give this to Elijah before he leaves."

"I—how—"

"Find a way." Azrael removed a few bills from the stack and handed the rest to Lila.

A tear slipped down Lila's pale cheek. "Where will you go?"

Azrael reached into the drawer and pulled out a silver pin bearing a five-pointed star. It had fallen off the coat of one of the newcomers who had come to the Colony gates last year. Stamped into the star was the stately image of a building and the words AUSTIN, TX.

"Give this pin to Elijah and tell him to go to Austin and find this building," Azrael rasped, his hand trembling. "I'll be there at sunset every day. When I'm sure I've set up a life we can safely hide in, I'll come back for you."

"How will I—"

"I'll tie a red ribbon to the big oak tree south of the compound. The day you see it, meet me there at midnight, and we'll run away and never come back."

Lila studied the pin, her breaths coming quick and shallow. "Come before the baby does. I won't bear a child in this place."

"I will. I promise. Now get back to your room before they realize you're missing."

"I love you," Lila whispered.

"I love you, too," Azrael said, though the terror singing in his veins felt like the Prophet's love—sick and full of fear.

Lila kissed him. The beating of her heart was a ticking clock, every heartbeat nourishing the child growing in her belly. Then she slipped away, and the room was silent other than Elijah's breathing.

Azrael dressed quietly and stashed the cash left over from what he'd given Lila in his pocket. He picked up the only pair of shoes he owned at the door and spared one last look at Elijah. If Azrael believed in God, he'd send up a prayer that he could get Lila and Elijah safely out of here, somewhere Lila could bear his child in peace, where his half-brother wouldn't follow in his father's footsteps. But God wasn't real, so Azrael was the best they had.

"See you soon, brother," he whispered, and fled.

5

AFTER WEEKS OF SEARCHING, Arachne found Hades up above, on a moving train. He'd taken the form of a man with kind gray eyes and a few days' growth of beard. She got the impression, as she crept her spider along the windowsill toward Him, that the only reason she'd found Him was because He wanted to be found.

"There you are," she said.

Hades reached into His pocket, pulled out a cell phone, and pressed it to His ear. "Oh, hello, dear. Good to hear from you again."

"Why are you here?" Arachne asked. "I'd expected to find you closer to Olivia than this."

Hades grinned and lowered His voice. "There's a young man on this train who will influence the woman you've selected as my prey. He's about a dozen seats ahead of me, with dark hair and torn-up clothes."

Arachne found another spider on the train and trundled it closer until she was next to the young man in question. He wore frayed pants and a white shirt streaked with dirt. His arms sported tiny scratches, as if he'd been running through thick underbrush. He looked as if he hadn't bathed in days, though he was handsome, in a feral way. He ran his fingers through his dark hair and stared out at the passing landscape with bright amber eyes.

"What's his name?"

"His name is Azrael Hatch, but he will change that soon. He's fleeing from a life in a cult called the Colony, but he won't escape it for long."

Arachne furrowed her brow. "How will he influence Olivia?"

"Oh, now, I wouldn't want to spoil anything," Hades said, raising His voice so both of her spiders could hear Him. "I think that's something you can find out for yourself at the library."

"At the *library*?" Arachne asked.

"Yes, the Austin Public Library," Hades said.

Azrael cocked his head, clearly listening.

"Anything you want to know about Austin, you'll find it there," Hades said. "It's a few blocks from the train station. I can meet you there."

Azrael's eyes widened. He peered over the back of his seat to see who'd spoken, then settled back down, hands fidgeting in his lap. His eyes fell to something stuffed between the train seats, and he pulled out a book of matches. He inspected it, finding it nearly full, and shoved it into his pocket as the train rumbled on.

"So it begins," Arachne sighed.

Hades's smile widened. "See you soon."

6

"OLIVIA?"

Olivia looked up from her library book. One of her coworkers—a pretty blonde woman whose name she couldn't recall—was staring over at her from between two bookshelves, a stack of books cradled in her arms. Olivia's coworker smiled at her expectantly, and something about the dimples that formed under her sun-kissed cheeks helped Olivia remember her name.

"Nancy, hello!"

"I thought that was you!" Nancy beamed. "Mind if I join you?"

Olivia smiled at Nancy's drawl. Listening to Nancy talk felt like the conversational equivalent of eating comfort food. "Sure, pull up a chair."

Nancy grunted as she set down her books. "Thanks. What're you reading?"

"*Still Life with Woodpecker*. Someone at the park recommended it to me. It's been a pretty fun read so far."

"I'm sure it's more fun than what I'm trying to suss out."

Olivia eyed Nancy's tower of books. "And what is that?"

"Well," Nancy said, making the word two syllables—*way-oll*—"you know how Dan at work is a bit of a misogynist prick?"

After a moment of shock, Olivia laughed loud enough to elicit a withering glance from a bespectacled man the next table over.

"Pardon my language, but you've noticed it too, right?" Nancy asked.

Olivia leaned in conspiratorially, relieved to finally have someone to vent to about this. "The other day, I was cleaning some of the dishes other folks had left behind in the office kitchen sink, and Dan walked in said, 'Well, aren't you the happy homemaker?'"

"Jail," hissed Nancy. *Jay-oll.* "What did you do?"

"I stopped what I was doing and walked away," Olivia said. "I haven't cleaned anything but my own dishes since."

Nancy grinned. "Good for you. That man is all hat and no cattle. That's why I'm looking through these books. We're trying to adjust the arginine-to-lysine ratio in Nosh without altering the taste, and I've got an idea I think will work. I just need to sort out the details, and then figure out a way to present it to Dan on Monday that makes him think it's his idea." Nancy pulled the top book from her pile. "Now, don't judge me. If I tell him what to do, he'll fight me on it, and we're less than a month out from starting human trials, so we don't have time for that. I'd rather get this right than get recognition for being right."

Olivia peered at the book. "Why would he fight your idea?"

"Because he thinks I'm a spoiled rich girl."

"You're rich?" As soon as the words were out of her mouth, Olivia clocked how Nancy's blonde hair shone in the sunlight streaming through the library window, like she'd just sauntered over from the set of a shampoo commercial.

Nancy's outfit was casual but effortlessly chic, from her cream-colored cable-knit sweater to her boots made of real leather. Her baby-pink nails looked like something out of an influencer video, and she smelled ever-so-slightly of lilacs.

Olivia became aware of her own elbow sticking out of the tattered hole in the sleeve of her denim jacket and her threadbare bargain bin T-shirt. She tucked an unruly lock of hair behind her ear and dug her fingers into her palms to hide her chipped red nail polish.

Nancy flipped through the pages of her book. "You didn't know? I thought everyone at work did. You ever hear of Samuel Bell?"

"No."

"He was my great-grandfather. He made a fortune in the oil business about seventy years ago, and my grandparents and parents made smart investments, and here I am. Nancy Bell, oil heiress."

Olivia whistled. "Holy shit. How rich are you?"

Nancy's dimples deepened in apparent delight at Olivia's directness. "Rich enough that I put a fake name on my resume and didn't tell Fisher Biotech who I really was until after I got hired."

"You didn't want them to hire you just because you were an heiress?"

"Oh, *hay-ull* no. They definitely wouldn't have hired me if they'd known. Look at me. Blonde hair, big boobs, southern drawl. Add a trust fund, and you get a whole lot of people thinking I'm a vapid, entitled rich kid. I was born lucky, but I wasn't born stupid. My brothers have had an easier time with it. Turns out, if you're rich, white, and male, it doesn't matter if you're the next Einstein or dumber than a box of rocks." Nancy pulled a handful of colored Post-it notes out of her pocket and arrayed them on the table. "I don't mean to act like I wasn't handed a lot. I got my education paid for and more privilege than any person should rightfully have. But I still come off as a dumb blonde until proven otherwise."

Olivia smiled. "Not to me."

Nancy's laugh was husky and genuine. "Well, that's a relief. What about you? I hear you moved here from Colorado?"

"Yeah, Denver," Olivia said.

"Oh, Denver's lovely! Did you grow up there?"

Olivia nodded. "I was born there a few months after my parents' high school graduation."

Nancy's bright blue eyes widened. "Preggers right out of high school! They still together?"

Olivia caught herself picking at a hangnail and forced herself to stop. "They were, until my dad died when I was ten."

Nancy's hand flew to her mouth. "Oh, honey, I'm so sorry. What happened?"

The truth came blurting out before Olivia could stop herself. "He was a firefighter. A burning building collapsed with him in it."

"Oh, Olivia. Oh my God."

Olivia's cheeks burned. Why the hell was she spilling her guts to her coworker like this? There was something familiar about Nancy, as if they'd known each other for years—or maybe it was just Nancy's naturally disarming southern charm. "It's okay. It was rough, but it was a long time ago."

Nancy reached for Olivia's hand and held it. Her grip was soft and firm. "Do you want to talk about it? Or take a hand squeeze and change the subject?"

The tension in Olivia's shoulders unwound slightly. "Thanks for asking. Let's not dwell on it for now."

"Right." Nancy gave her hand a brief squeeze. "You getting settled into Austin okay?"

"Yeah, actually. I'm renting a cute one-bedroom house that was somehow in my price range. It's got hardwood floors, lots of natural light, and bay windows in the bedroom. Every twenty minutes or so, there's a passing train that kind of shakes the place, but I've always liked trains, so it doesn't bother me. And everyone here's been so friendly."

"Austin's a great city," Nancy agreed. "It gets even better when you know the underground spots. I'd be happy to show you."

Behind Nancy, a young man climbed the stairs to the library's second floor. He had dark, disheveled hair, sharp features, and wore an ill-fitting white T-shirt and ragged gray slacks with mud stains on the cuffs. If Nancy had strolled into the library from a shampoo commercial, this young man—who might have been anywhere from late teens to early twenties—looked as if he'd crawled out of a hole in the woods. The way he scanned the room made Olivia think of a wild animal. The flame tattoo on the inside of her wrist itched as heat spread through her chest.

Nancy had asked Olivia something. "Sorry, what?"

"I asked what you thought of Fisher Biotech so far."

The young man disappeared into the bookshelves.

"I'm...uh...I'm really enjoying it."

"It's not too bad, huh? First start-up I worked for, the founder was a lunatic. It was my first gig out of school, so it took me a while to realize how toxic it was. People quitting without explanation, tyrannical micro-management, the whole nine. I lasted eight months, which was more than most. The company tanked soon after. I hopped between a couple of other gigs before landing at Fisher."

"I'm glad to hear that," Olivia said. "This is my first job outside of academia other than working in food service, so I didn't have much of a reference."

"Don't get me wrong, Dan's a moron. Nobody would blame you for setting the building on fire when he made that 'happy homemaker' comment." Nancy's eyes rolled under her perfectly shaped brows. "But overall, it's a pretty good place to work."

Olivia smiled. "I do feel lucky."

Nancy leaned in. "Hon, don't let this go to your head, but luck ain't got nothing to do with it. People know value when they see it. It's the mark of good leaders to surround themselves with people who are smarter than they are."

"Really?"

"I'm not blowing smoke up your skirt. You've got a bright future ahead of you. We're lucky to have *you*."

"Holy cats, Nancy." Warmth spread across Olivia's face. "Thank you."

Nancy waved a hand in the air. "Don't mention it. Now—can I ask an uncouth question?"

"I really wish you would," Olivia said.

"Are you a natural redhead?"

Olivia touched the unkempt waves of her hair self-consciously. "Yeah...it's natural. A little too natural, at the moment."

"Nonsense, it's gorgeous," Nancy said. "I'd do anything for that kind of curl and body. I've always wanted to try dyeing my hair red. Never had the guts to go with anything other than slightly lighter blonde, though."

"Well, on behalf of redheads everywhere, I think you'd make a great one."

Nancy grinned. "Well, now that I've got an endorsement, I guess I'll have to do it one of these days."

Olivia smiled back. "Do you want any help finding something in those books? I was just killing time reading this."

"Oh, doll, I'd love that. Here—look through this book for a mention of the biomarkers in lysine and arginine. Let me know when you find something."

Olivia searched through the book for a few minutes when a sudden movement caught her eye: the young man from earlier, hastening down the steps and out the front door of the library. A chill cascaded down her back. She was positive she'd never seen this young man before in her life, but watching him, she felt something eerily close to recognition.

7

Azrael Hatch followed the roads in the map he'd torn out of the library book until he reached the Capitol building, which looked just as it had on the star pin. The building glowed in the setting sun. A flurry of dry leaves rustled past him. The sunset lit up the clouds like molten gold, the city unfurling itself to the edges of the sprawling horizon, inconceivably vast, alive with sparkling lights.

Azrael's stomach growled. He walked around until he found a hot dog stand, bought three hot dogs, and devoured them. It wasn't until he'd finished the last one that he realized there were toppings he could have put on them. It would be a while before he possessed anything approaching street smarts.

As darkness fell, Azrael sat in the grassy field outside the Capitol building and counted the money he had left over. After his train ticket, a change of clothes, and a few bites to eat, there was little left. His exhaustion deepened as the food settled into his belly. He curled up on a bench and drifted off to sleep wondering what he and Lila would name their child.

He awoke some hours later to the wind cutting through his clothes. His jaw ached where it had been pressed against the cold metal of the bench. He drew his knees into his chest, teeth clacking against each other.

After willing his stiff limbs to move, Azrael rose, trembling, and searched for a source of warmth in the baleful glow of the streetlights. He came across a full trash can and used one of his matches to light the edge of a newspaper sticking out of it. He added leaves and twigs until he got a fire crackling. The smell of the melting plastic trash bag scorched his nostrils, but he covered his nose with his wrist and piled more branches into the bin. Slowly, feeling returned to his fingers, and his shivering subsided.

Azrael had fallen asleep on his feet when he woke to the sound of someone shouting.

"Hey! Hey you, what are you doing?"

Azrael froze. A man stood silhouetted next to an idling car maybe forty feet away. Azrael didn't have the energy to outrun him.

"I was cold," he explained.

The man approached slowly. "I'm a volunteer firefighter. You're not in trouble, but we've got to put that fire out. I'm sorry to do this to you, but it might be better if you weren't around when the other—"

The man stopped in his tracks when he stepped up to the flickering light of the fire.

"Azrael? Azrael Hatch?"

Azrael tensed. No one in this city should have any idea who he was, and yet there was something familiar about the man's sad brown eyes, lanky limbs, and hunched shoulders…

Azrael's jaw dropped. "Warren Young?"

"Oh my God, it is you," Warren said. "Were you exiled?"

"I ran away," Azrael said, "like you."

"Is that what they told you I did?" Warren's eyes darted toward the sound of sirens. "Come on, get in the car."

Azrael hesitated. Warren Young had run away from the Colony after he'd been caught raping Melinda Coleman, one of the daughters intended for Robert Grayburn. His name hadn't been spoken in the Colony since.

The sirens grew louder. A gust of wind chilled Azrael's bones.

"Azrael, come on, you don't want to be here when they show up."

Azrael sprinted for Warren's car and climbed inside, grateful for the warmth that blasted from the heaters as Warren sped away from the fire.

"Thank you," Azrael said.

"Don't thank me yet," Warren Young said, frowning. "You're putting me in a lot of danger, coming here. Does anyone know you're in Austin?"

Azrael thought about the pin he'd given to Lila. "No. Not a chance."

A beat of silence stretched between them.

"Why did you run away?"

Azrael closed his eyes. Lila's panicked breath on his skin in the night. Her terrified heartbeat.

"Because the Prophet is a monster," Azrael responded.

Flashing lights in the rearview mirror lit up Warren's eyes. "Kid, you ain't kidding."

WARREN PARKED HIS CAR a half block away from a Shell gas station. Azrael followed Warren down a dimly lit brick alley until they stood before a green door, paint peeling away to reveal bands of rust. Warren opened the door and gestured for Azrael to enter. A long hallway opened into a dark living room. The smell inside the apartment, sweat and plaster, was a relief after the dumpster stink of the alley.

Warren flipped on a few lights. "Want anything to drink? Tea? Coffee?"

"Got any booze?" Azrael asked.

"Not since I got sober."

"Water, then."

Warren retrieved two glasses and filled them with tap water. He handed one to Azrael and held his own aloft.

Warren said, "Here, hold yours up too. This is called a toast. To freedom." Warren touched his glass to Azrael's. "Now you drink. It's bad luck not to drink after a toast."

Azrael gulped down his water. "The Prophet told everyone you escaped before he could confront you for...sleeping with one of the intended mothers. Is that really what happened?"

Warren Young refilled Azrael's glass and handed it back to him. "No. That's not what happened." Warren's eyes glazed over as he stared far beyond the walls of his apartment. "I was just a kid when my parents joined the Colony. My dad was in crippling gambling debt, and the Colony offered him an escape. He was exiled for his alleged 'sins' less than a year later. I remember my mom being really sad and distant once my dad was gone. That winter, she took her own life." He shot a dark glare at Azrael. "At least, that's what I was told."

Azrael swallowed, his throat suddenly dry.

"I didn't want to remain at the Colony, but I had nowhere else to go, and no way of reaching anybody on the outside. For years, I gave into despair, but then I started to talk to one of the daughters, Melinda." Warren's expression brightened a little as he continued.

"Melinda was a year or two younger than me. She and her older brother Mark had come to the Colony under similar circumstances as I had. Their mother just packed her things and disappeared one day, and their father turned to the Colony for support, but ended up in exile. Mark followed him months later, leaving her alone—just like me."

Azrael frowned. Exiles weren't unheard of in the Colony, but what Warren described far exceeded the frequency he was used to. "What was the reason for their exiles?"

Warren gave a cold laugh. "Sometimes the Prophet stated a reason, and sometimes he didn't. It wasn't until I was in the outside world that I realized the real reason. The fathers wanted multiple wives, and they couldn't have that with an equal distribution of the sexes."

Azrael blinked. How had he never noticed that the Prophet only ever exiled boys and men? He stared at his water glass, feeling stupid.

"By the time we were teenagers, I'd fallen in love with Melinda," Warren said. "Believe me when I tell you, I've never in my life been more relieved than when she said she loved me back. We weren't alone anymore."

Warren set down his glass and wrung his hands. "We kept it a secret, of course. Then, when she was fourteen, the Prophet announced Melinda was to marry Robert Grayburn. You may remember that, actually. I think you'd have been about ten years old."

Azrael nodded. Melinda had looked so small standing next to Grayburn, like she could have been his daughter instead of his intended wife.

Warren looked at Azrael, his eyes glassy with tears. "I felt so helpless and scared. I can only imagine how she must have felt. We talked about taking our own lives, and might have if we didn't believe suicide would send us straight to Hell. One night, out of desperation as much as attraction, we made love, and Elijah's mother Lucille caught us in the act. I didn't have time to get my pants back on before she returned with

Robert Grayburn, who knocked me unconscious with that metal baseball bat."

Azrael flinched, remembering the same bat connecting with his skull.

"I woke up locked inside the dining hall's walk-in freezer," Warren said. "I almost couldn't get up because the blood had frozen my head to the floor. I shouted for help and fought to stay warm, but after a few hours, I gave into the cold and sat down in the corner to sleep."

Warren took a deep breath, looking gaunt in the wan yellow glow of the overhead kitchen lights. "I'm not sure how long I lay there before the door opened and someone dragged me out of the freezer. I pretended to be dead, but I cracked an eye open and saw it was Robert Grayburn. He dragged me through the back door and into the woods by my shirt collar for what felt like an eternity."

Warren shuddered and blew out a breath before carrying on.

"The second he let go, I leapt to my feet and ran. My legs burned like they were on fire, and I could barely put one foot in front of the other. Robert chased after me, and if it weren't for his bad leg, he would have caught me for sure. I heard him shout that if I ever came back to the Colony, I'd be dead."

Azrael forced his jaw to unclench.

"I kept running until I hit civilization. I made my way to Austin and found work as a dishwasher, making money under the table. Those first few years, all of my spare money went to booze."

"How long have you been gone?" Azrael asked. "Seven years?"

"Eight. Sober for three of them." Warren sighed. "I work for a moving company now, and signed up to be a volunteer firefighter. Working on becoming a real firefighter someday." Warren looked up at Azrael. "Is Melinda still at the Colony?"

"She is."

"Did she marry Robert Grayburn?"

"No. She never took a husband."

Warren's shoulders sagged. "Thank God for that."

Azrael avoided eye contact. The truth was, after Melinda had been caught lying with Warren, the Prophet declared her a Shamed Woman, unfit for marriage to Robert Grayburn or to anyone else. She stayed at the Colony because she had nowhere else to go, but her life was a hollow one. She would never marry nor become a mother.

A deep weariness infused Azrael's bones. "Can I stay here tonight?"

Warren eyed him suspiciously. "You're sure no one is going to come looking for you?"

Azrael thought of Elijah, his faithful fool of a brother who needed to be saved from himself. With any luck, Lila's lie would send him to Austin, and soon.

"Trust me, they're glad I'm gone," Azrael said. "No one's looking for me."

Warren nodded, satisfied. "I've got a spare room. It's not much, but there's a bed and a nightstand for clothes when you're able to buy some. You're welcome to stay here as long as you need to get your feet under you. The real world can be rough, but trust me, it's a lot better than living under the Prophet's thumb."

8

"Do you know why you're here, Elijah?"

Elijah stood on the parapet before the assembled members of the Colony. He trembled as he scanned the stony eyes of the faces peering up at him in the morning chill. Robert Grayburn ushered Lila Monroe to the front of the crowd.

"I'll ask again," the Prophet said. "Do you know why you're here?"

Elijah had been accused by his father of wrongdoing before, but this felt different. It might have something to do with Azrael's disappearance two weeks ago, but what role could he have had in that?

"No," Elijah said.

The Prophet's eyes were as icy cold as Elijah's feet. "You stand accused of a terrible crime, Elijah. Do you have anything to say for yourself?"

"I...I don't know what you mean."

The Prophet pointed at Lila Monroe. A gust of wind swept pale hair across her face. Her dark eyes glared up at Elijah, her hands resting on her belly.

"What have you done?" the Prophet asked. "Tell the truth." Elijah winced as the Prophet's hand touched his cheek. "Did you lay with Lila?"

Tears fractured his father's ruddy face into shards. His father's white hair, streaked with a few remaining locks of black, turned into a smudge of ash. His hazel eyes shone like coins at the bottom of a river.

"No," Elijah said.

"Elijah, I've told you a thousand times what happens to liars when they leave this world. I want you to think on that before you answer this question. Is that your child growing in Lila's belly?"

"No, Father."

The Prophet slapped him. Pain flashed across Elijah's cheek, hot as shame itself.

"Father, it was not me!"

The Prophet's voice was heavy with disgust. "Do you understand what you've done? Lila was meant to be united with me in God's love, and now she will forever be shamed, because of you."

"Father, I swear on my love for you—"

The Prophet struck him again. Elijah tasted blood.

"You were meant to lead, Elijah. You were meant to be Prophet, to be the voice of God to the Colony as I have been. But now you must leave our midst forever."

"Please, I am innocent, you must believe me—"

"Elijah, it pains me to say this more than you can imagine, but you've given me no choice. You are hereby exiled from the Colony for the rest of your days." The Prophet gripped Elijah's collar and lowered his voice to a whisper. "And if you ever tell anyone who you are, or where you came from, the world will come crashing down on our home with the fury of Satan himself, so you keep your mouth shut, you understand?"

"Wait," Lila said, stepping forward.

The Prophet's lips drew back from his teeth. "Speak, child."

"Let him take this," Lila said, holding out a Bible.

Elijah recognized it as the Bible the Prophet had given him when he was five years old, when he'd announced that Elijah was destined to lead the Colony in his wake. "So he can repent of his sins."

A murmur rippled through the Colony. Robert Grayburn glared at Elijah like a wolf staring down its prey.

"Elijah, take the Bible," the Prophet said.

Elijah descended the steps of the parapet in a dream. He'd never walk up those steps again. Not to deliver a sermon, or officiate a wedding, or to address the Colony as their new Prophet after his father passed. The remainder of his mortal life was doomed. His immortal soul was forfeit. He was to join the sinful ranks of the rest of the world, out in the cold. The Prophet had turned his back on him. He may as well have blacked out the sun.

Lila stepped toward Elijah and leaned in close as she pressed the Bible into his hands.

"Lila..." Elijah pleaded.

Lila leaned in close. Her breath was warm on his frigid ear as she whispered one word: "Run."

Elijah's dread culminated in a rabbity panic, and he sprinted into the woods, Bible pressed to his chest.

Elijah ran for hours, sobbing, stumbling at length upon a set of train tracks. He walked along the tracks for miles, arriving finally at a station, where he took a seat and opened his Bible to find a hollow carved into the pages.

Inside was a note from Lila, a bundle of cash, and a five-pointed silver star.

9

Azrael pulled the matchbook from his pocket, touched a match's red-tipped head to the sandpaper strip, and flicked it. Flame burst against his thumb. Fire blackened the head of the match and traveled down toward the base. He shook it out before it got there.

Azrael looked away from the Capitol building and closed his eyes. The setting sun warmed his back, a gentle breeze lifting his hair. He felt nothing but lightness. Was this how it felt to be condemned eternally? He had half a mind to return to the Colony and tell his father's followers what damnation felt like: a smothering blanket torn away, allowing him at last to breathe.

Azrael stretched out the ache in his muscles. Even the soreness felt sweet, a thing earned rather than endured. Warren had gotten him a job with the moving company he worked for, and the exchange of manual labor for money was intoxicating. Azrael had worked for the Prophet for free his whole life; now his labor bought him anything he wanted. Clothes, shoes, cigarettes, booze (which he had to get someone else to buy), meals so flavorful they made his eyes roll back in his head. He'd purchased a pair of headphones as well, so he could listen to the deliciously secular music on Warren's old laptop at full volume.

Warren had urged Azrael to work under a false name. "No one's going to think twice about a name like 'Warren Young,' but 'Azrael Hatch?' That might raise some eyebrows. I don't care what it is. Just stay away from anything biblical."

Azrael had gone to a nearby coffee shop, looked through a newspaper, and found what he was looking for under the 'Obituaries' section: Randall Cheshire. Randall's photograph depicted a man with a long face and a thin mouth. The man's eyes stared out like beacons from the grainy print.

"Randall Cheshire," Azrael had told Warren when he got home.

"Cheshire, like the cat?"

"Like what cat?"

Warren had pulled up a photo on his phone and showed Azrael. "The Cheshire Cat."

Azrael had taken in the cartoon cat's manic grin. "Yeah, like that."

"That's hardly a normal name."

"It's not biblical."

Warren had shrugged. "Fair point. Nice to meet you, Randall."

Azrael popped another match into flame, lit a cigarette, and drew in a deep, dizzying drag. Warren didn't know where Azrael went every day at dusk after they'd finished up their moving work for the day. If he'd had any idea Azrael was sneaking off to the Texas State Capitol to wait for his God-fearing little brother...

Still, Azrael figured he could convince Warren to let Elijah stay. The Prophet didn't come looking for exiles once they were gone. But Lila? If Azrael brought the Prophet's pregnant bride-to-be into his house, Warren would kick all of them out on their asses.

Azrael needed a plan, some way of getting Lila somewhere safe, and that meant saving up enough money to get a place of his own. He snuffed out his cigarette and took in a lungful of fragrant evening air. Another day, another sunset, with no sign of his brother. Disappointment mingled with relief. His brother's absence certainly meant tomorrow would be an easier day.

It would be easier if you never went back for Lila, either.

The wicked notion capered in the back of his mind. Azrael shivered. Abandoning Lila to a life alone at the Colony was too cruel a thought to contemplate. He had to go back for her.

He had to go back for his child.

Azrael stood up and brushed himself off. Time to go home and drink away the poisonous thoughts in his head.

"Azrael?"

Azrael's head snapped up. Elijah stood in the dim glow of a streetlight at the edge of the square, grasping a Bible to his chest. The hollow under his right eye sported the dark crescent of a bruise.

Azrael approached him. "Elijah—"

Elijah hurled the five-pointed star at him. It hit Azrael's chest and clinked to the sidewalk. "How could you?"

Azrael's throat tightened. "You must hate me, but—"

"Do you have any idea what you've done?"

Two people sitting on a nearby bench looked up from their phones.

"Not now, Elijah."

"It wasn't enough to damn yourself. You had to damn me and Lila, too!"

"Stop it," Azrael said. "Do you want these people to find out who we are?"

"I don't care what these people think. They're going to Hell, same as us! You've damned us! You've—"

Azrael slapped him. Elijah recoiled and regarded him with tear-brimmed eyes.

Azrael said, "I'm sorry. Come on, let's go talk about this somewhere else. I've got a safe place for us to stay. It's warm. There's food and water."

Elijah's eyes darkened. "I'm not going anywhere with you."

"Then why did you come here?"

His face crumpled. "I was scared...I didn't know where else to go..."

Azrael softened his voice. "Hush, brother. I know you've been through hell."

A tear slipped into the bruise under Elijah's eye. "Not yet I haven't, but Hell's coming for both of us, thanks to you."

Sighing, Azrael took off his coat and slung it over his brother's shoulders. "Can I feed you in the meantime?"

Elijah slumped in defeat and put his arms through the holes. Azrael picked the pin up off the ground and stuffed it into his pocket.

"Come on, home's not far away, and there's a familiar face there."

10

IT HADN'T TAKEN ARACHNE long to infiltrate Warren Young's apartment with her spies. Lucky for her, there was no lack of bugs for the spiders to feast on inside the apartment's grubby walls.

The buzz of the microwave rippled through the fine hairs of the jumping spider clinging to the underside of the kitchen counter. Warren stood at the counter, staring dully at the freezer meal spinning in the microwave window, when Azrael walked into the living room with Elijah. Warren peered out from the kitchen. "Who is..." His eyes widened. "Is that...Elijah Hatch?"

"Warren—" Azrael began.

"I thought you said no one knew you were here!"

Azrael held up his palms. "No one else does!"

"Then how did he find us?" Warren's voice held a tinge of panic.

"I gave him a pin with the Texas State Capitol on it. No one else saw it."

"No one else?" Warren demanded.

Arachne watched through the eyes of a house spider suspended from a gossamer thread in the hallway as Azrael pinched the back of Elijah's arm.

"No one else," Elijah said, his gray eyes flashing with anger.

"Do you have any idea how dangerous it is for me to have both of the Prophet's sons under my roof? What's going to happen if anyone comes looking for you?"

"They won't—"

"They'll kill me. Grayburn already tried."

Elijah said, "You defiled the woman who would have been his wife."

Warren's hands clenched into fists. "I fell in love with a young woman who was going to be forced to marry a man twice her age."

"You deprived her of her chastity," Elijah spat. "She will live out the rest of her days under a shroud of shame because of you."

"Get him out of here. Now!"

Azrael said, "Warren, listen—he just got kicked out of the only home he's ever known. He's scared, and he doesn't have anywhere else to go. Neither of us do. And no one is going to come looking for us. I swear it."

Down below, Arachne scoffed. "Liar."

Warren jabbed a finger at Azrael. "If I get any inkling that someone's looking for either of you, and I mean anything, from someone sitting in a car outside this alley, to someone coming around the fire station asking about me, a bad feeling in my gut—you're gone. Understand?"

Azrael nodded. "I'm saving up money as fast as I can so we can get our own place."

"You might want to stop drinking so much whiskey, then," Warren said, storming into his room and slamming the door.

The microwave beeped three times and went silent.

Elijah scowled. "Azrael, we're staying in the house of a rapist."

"He's no more a rapist than you are," Azrael said. "And stop calling me Azrael. My name is Randall Cheshire now. Don't ever call me by my old name again. Not in public, not here, not anywhere. You'll have to pick a fake name, too."

Angry tears streamed down Elijah's cheeks. "I don't want to."

"If anyone hears the last name Hatch, it might make it easier for the Prophet to track us down," Azrael said. "If we're going to stay safe, we've got to play things close to the vest."

"What does that mean?"

"It's a poker saying."

"Azrael, you've been playing *poker*?"

Azrael rolled his eyes. "I saw it on TV. And what did I say about calling me by that name?"

"I'm sorry..."

"You're sorry, what?"

"I'm sorry, *Randall*."

"Randall Cheshire," Randall said slowly. "Don't forget it." He handed Elijah the same newspaper he'd found his new name in. "You can find a name somewhere in here while I make you some dinner."

Elijah slumped onto the couch, close enough to one of Arachne's spiders for her pedipalps to smell the fear emanating from his pores. She read along with him as he flipped through the paper. *Fisher Biotech "Nosh" Human Trials Underway*, one headline read. Elijah paused on that page, then looked up at Randall.

"Fisher," Elijah said. "I'll be Elijah Fisher, like the passage in the Bible where Jesus calls his disciples to be fishers of men."

Randall shrugged. "We'll have to check with Warren because Elijah's biblical, but as long as you're not a Hatch, I think it will work."

Steam filled the room as Randall boiled water and prepared spaghetti. Warren's dinner remained untouched in the microwave.

Elijah didn't say a word until he finished his spaghetti.

"I'll never forgive you for this," he said.

Randall picked up their plates. "I thought the God father was peddling was pretty big on the whole forgiveness thing."

Elijah turned away. "Never."

11

"Psst—coffee?"

Olivia looked up from reading a participant survey and saw Nancy holding two mugs of coffee by the laboratory door. She set her clipboard down and accepted the steaming mug. "Sweet nectar. Thank you."

"You're welcome, and don't call me Sweet Nectar." Nancy winked.

Olivia snorted. "Jesus, give me a chance to swallow before you say something funny."

Nancy beamed a smile at her. "Don't call me Jesus, either."

Olivia grinned. She and Nancy wore identical lab coats, apart from their names embroidered in navy blue on the chests, yet Nancy looked radiant in hers, and Olivia looked like a gangly kid playing doctor. Olivia may have felt self-conscious about this, but damned if Nancy didn't have a way of setting her at ease.

They sipped their coffees, the scent of which mingled with the astringent cleaning solutions used to keep the lab clean, watching the bustling activity. Centrifuges whirred, fellow scientists pipetted blood into test tubes, interns took notes. Olivia and Nancy had both been in the laboratory past midnight the night before, labeling and refrigerating hundreds of blood samples from paid participants trying out Nosh as a way to lose weight.

"How are you holding up?" Olivia asked.

"If I could generate energy from tossing and turning, I could power my whole neighborhood," Nancy said. "I can't believe how fast all of this is happening. I mean, the Nosh formula is as solid as we can get it, but giving it to actual humans…I just hope it works."

"It's going to work," Olivia assured her.

Nancy sighed and nodded. "I hope you're right. I'll be glad when it's done and out there. Thanks for working late with me last night."

"Happy to. It's not like I have much of a life outside of work anyway."

"Oh, that reminds me!" Nancy said. "Would you be interested in going on a blind date?"

Olivia blinked. "I mean…maybe?"

"I ran into a guy I know from high school the other day. His name's Harrison. Apparently, he got out of a long-term relationship a few months ago. He's on the sensitive side, but in a good way. Like a poet."

Olivia crinkled her nose. "I've dated a few of those."

"Ha! Want me to set you two up?"

"If he's such a catch, why aren't you dating him?"

"He's cute, just not my type. Come on, what's the worst that can happen?"

Olivia shrugged. "Okay, put us in touch."

"Ooh, I love matchmaking. I'll send him your number. Now, let's get back to work."

Olivia set aside her coffee and followed Nancy into the lab. What was the worst that could happen, indeed?

12

RANDALL SMILED AS HE walked down a darkened sidewalk, drawing a deep drag from his cigarette. He'd seen a house earlier in the day as he and Warren carted people's belongings around town, and he'd decided on the spot that he needed to return to explore it. It had looked old, abandoned, and he'd had the strange sensation that it was reaching out for him.

Randall wasn't so stupid as to steal from the moving company's clientele, but he was developing a sixth sense for places he could slip into, carry off an item or two, and walk out without anyone seeing a thing. Every item he didn't need to pay for was a step closer to getting a place of his own where he, Elijah, and Lila could live safely.

Randall flicked his cigarette into the grass and approached the wrought iron fence surrounding the house. A brisk wind whispered through the barren trees in the yard. A weathered FOR SALE sign lay face-up on the lawn. Randall parted the ivy choking the fence, revealing a stone sign carved with the name: MOLOCH. A flicker of déjà vu went through him like a chill, and then it was gone. He let the ivy fall back into place, gripped the fence, and hoisted himself into the yard.

Knee-high grass brushed his legs as he crept toward the house. He tried the door latch, but it was locked, as were all the windows. While circling the house, he spotted a cellar door hidden behind an overgrown bush, secured with a rusted lock. He found a shovel, brushed it free of cobwebs, and brought the business end of it down on the lock, which cracked open and tumbled to the ground.

The cellar door squealed like an injured animal as he opened it. Randall slipped inside and struck a match in the darkness. The flame revealed a stone cellar with a pile of musty blankets, a broken lightbulb hanging from the ceiling, and the ruins of an old rocking chair. A glint of glass behind the rocking chair turned out to be a half-full handle of whiskey. Randall shook out his match and screwed off the cap. He took a swig, gasped for air, and then took another. He hadn't been drinking booze since Elijah's arrival, and the warmth spreading through his chest felt like reuniting with an old lover.

On the ground floor, Randall approached an intricately carved stone fireplace that dominated the far end of a long, narrow room, illuminated by the skeletal blue light of the moon. He lit another match and held it up to the stone, captivated by the way the shadows danced away from the light. Sculpted cherubs cavorted through a flowing veil, their stone eyes rolling like those of a panicked horse. If there had been roaring fire in the belly of the fireplace, it would have looked as if these innocents were roasting over the flames.

Randall made his way upstairs, where a spiral staircase ascended into a nook that might have once been a children's playroom. He spotted an odd texture on the wall through the moth-eaten holes in a hanging tapestry. He pulled the tapestry aside to reveal a small door, which opened up to a dark crawl space. He crept inside and found the crawl space led up to the house's attic, which contained a collection of old paintings and mirrors. Tucked away in a corner of the attic lay dozens of canisters of film reels. Randall tucked one of the canisters under his arm and climbed back down through the crawl space.

After exploring every inch of the place, alternating between moonlight and matchlight, Randall concluded he'd never seen a house so beautiful. Maybe he could find a way to bring Elijah here. Maybe he could show him the outside world wasn't a wicked, depraved place—or at least that wasn't all it was. There was beauty in it that could never exist within the cold, concrete structures of the Colony.

And Lila...

Randall sighed. In his early days in Austin, he'd thought of Lila all the time. How far along she was in her pregnancy, how frightened and lonely she must be. Now, when his thoughts turned to her, they were weighed down by the despair of what her arrival would mean. If he went to save Lila too early, they'd have no place to go, but if he went back for her too late...

A floorboard creaked somewhere in the house.

Randall froze, waiting for another sound to follow. When there was none, he checked his watch and saw with a shock that he'd been in the house for over an hour.

He let himself out the front door, leaving it unlocked so the next explorer would have an easier time getting in. As he closed it, he registered movement near the door handle.

An enormous black spider crept toward him, staring up at him as if wondering what he was up to.

"Hello, darling," said Randall. He opened his film canister and brushed the spider into it.

13

"You're a what whisperer?" asked Olivia.

"A cat whisperer," said Harrison.

Olivia stared at him across the table, grateful the clamor in the sushi restaurant was loud enough that nobody else could hear their conversation. "What does that mean?"

"Well, you know how there are horse whisperers? I gather from your expression the concept is new to you."

"No, no, horse whisperer, right. I'm following."

Harrison took a sip of his hot sake. "I can do that, except with cats."

"That's...interesting. What do you tell them to do?"

"Oh, you know, to be calm when they're frightened or upset. To go into a different room. Nothing crazy." Harrison smiled. "The thing with cats is they don't do anything they don't already want to do, even when they understand what you're saying."

"If they only do what they want to do, then what's the point of talking to them?"

Harrison peered at the upper left corner of the restaurant, as if searching for the patience to explain something to a child. "It's not about *controlling* the cats. It's about *communicating* with them."

"Oh." Olivia coughed into her hand. "Excuse me, I'm going to use the restroom."

Olivia fled into one of the bathroom stalls, pulled out her phone, and texted Nancy.

Nancy!

After a few seconds, ellipses appeared, and then: *He's cute, right?*

Olivia rolled her eyes. Harrison was good-looking in a nerdy kind of way she would be totally into if he wasn't a pseudo-intellectual whack job. She texted back: *He just told me he's a cat whisperer!*

Another set of ellipses. *A WHAT?*

Olivia texted: *I went to the bathroom to see if I could find a window to climb out of.*

The ellipses appeared, disappeared, returned. *What I'm hearing is, don't quit my day job to become a matchmaker.*

Olivia snort-laughed. She sent a laughing emoji, then, *I've got to go. I'll tell you more tomorrow.*

When Olivia returned to the table, their sushi had arrived, along with another carafe of sake.

"I waited for you to start eating," announced Harrison.

"Thanks," said Olivia. She took a bite of her food. "Oh, this sashimi is delicious. Here, try some."

Harrison leaned away from her. "No, no thank you. I don't eat food off other people's plates."

Olivia raised an eyebrow. "Oh, no problem. More for me."

"Mhmm."

Her cheeks flushed with frustration. She searched for a neutral conversation topic. "I saw something interesting on my walk over here."

"Oh?"

"I was walking through this quiet neighborhood and all of a sudden I smelled smoke," said Olivia. "Someone's cigarette had started a fire in the grass by the sidewalk. I had to run over and stomp it out."

Harrison shook his head. "Smokers are terrible people."

Olivia gave up. The only time he'd been remotely engaged was when he told her about his cat-whispering skills, and Olivia wasn't sure she could revisit that subject with a straight face.

When the check came, Harrison put down enough money to cover half of it. Olivia paid for the remainder plus tip. "I have to be honest," said Harrison, as they walked toward the door. "I'm relieved you paid for your half of the check. I really lose respect for women when they expect men to pay for them."

Olivia forced a smile. She would have happily paid for the meal in its entirety if it meant it would end. At least the date had gone as poorly for him as it had for her. "Well, Harrison, it was nice meeting you."

"Nice meeting you too. Let's do this again sometime," Harrison said, and leaned in for a kiss.

Olivia was too surprised to recoil, and his lips connected with hers. She pulled away and forced herself not to break into a run. Did he really think the date went well? What would a *bad* date look like for him?

"How are you getting home?" he asked.

"I walked here," Olivia said. Was it possible that her date possessed an absolute lack of chivalry? Could she be so lucky?

"Let me walk you home," said Harrison. "You never know what kind of weirdos you'll encounter out there."

Olivia winced. "That would be great."

"LOOK, THAT'S WHERE THE fire was," Olivia said, pointing to a black circle in the grass. "You can still smell the smoke."

"God, they should tear some of these houses down," Harrison said. "Look, the worst one's coming up in front of us. It's dragging down the property value of the entire neighborhood."

"Is that right?"

"Yeah, it's the old Moloch house."

"Moloch house?"

"Yeah, see for yourself."

Olivia stopped in her tracks. She'd been distracted by the fire earlier, so she'd hurried past the house without looking. All three stories of the Moloch family's house leaned into the moonlight like a person bracing against a strong wind. Some of the wooden slats had come undone and hung from the house's facade like crooked teeth. The barren branches of the trees in the yard clawed toward the house. Long, swaying grass choked the walkway to the door.

"Wow."

"I know, what a wreck," said Harrison. "The last living family member died a few years back, and the house is in such a state of disrepair that the estate has basically given up trying to sell it."

Olivia stepped up to the gate. "I'm going to explore it."

His eyebrows shot up. "You're what?"

"I said, I'm going to explore it," she repeated.

"What on earth for?"

Excitement stirred in her belly. "Look at it! You said it's empty, right? Abandoned?"

"Yes, but it's falling apart. It's not safe."

Olivia ignored him, pushing the iron gate open and stepping into the yard.

"Some people would call what you're doing breaking and entering," Harrison said.

Olivia looked at him over the fence. "If you're too scared to join me, you can go home."

Harrison muttered something under his breath and joined her. "We won't be able to get in."

"Not with that attitude."

Olivia's fingers stretched almost to the doorknob when she spotted a huge spider perched on the knob. She jumped back, and her other hand touched something sticky—an enormous spider web spanning half the porch. She shrieked through gritted teeth and wiped her hands on her sides.

"Jesus," said Harrison. "What are you doing?"

"Is there a spider on me? Did one get on me?"

"You're good," Harrison said, laughing. "Nothing's on you."

"It's not funny. I'm terrified of spiders."

"I can see that. Can we go now?"

Olivia glared at Harrison with enough ferocity that he fell back a step. "Harrison, could you please do something useful and get that spider away from the door handle?"

The humor dropped away from his face. "Sure." He walked up to the door and brushed at the spider, which skittered away and disappeared into a crack. He walked away. "You have fun with that."

Olivia watched Harrison open the gate and leave without looking back. "Finally," she whispered.

Olivia discovered several other spiders lurking in the door frame, and a few smaller ones crawling across its surface. The entire porch was teeming with them, but she couldn't turn back. She had to at least try to get in...

The door handle turned in her grip. She held her breath, stepped inside, and closed the door behind her. She looked around and let out a low whistle.

Moonlight illuminated a dusty, ornate parlor. The breeze outside made the house feel like it was whispering. Olivia wandered the moonlit halls of the house, stopping occasionally to inspect an old tapestry, an intricately carved fireplace, a rust-covered cleaver in one of the kitchen drawers. A family of rats in the kitchen scurried away when her cell phone flashlight turned their way.

Olivia was on the second floor when she looked up and saw a trapdoor in the ceiling. She stacked some old wooden crates on top of each other, climbed on top, and shoved the trap door as hard as she could. The door swung open and slammed down on the other side, kicking up a cloud of dust.

Olivia hooked one of her elbows up onto the attic floorboards and jumped to get more purchase, accidentally kicking the top crate to the floor. She coughed as dust tickled her lungs, kicking air, and then hefted herself the rest of the way into the attic. A moment later, she lay in the thick layer of dust on the attic floor, panting.

She rose and flipped the trapdoor closed as her cell phone flashlight painted the small, stuffy attic with a pale delta of light. She took her time, exploring framed portraits of stone-faced men, women, and children, a threadbare Turkish rug that looked centuries old, and a taxidermied opossum snarling at her with one remaining marble eye. She wiped dust from a cracked full-length mirror and saw her reflection smiling back at her.

Between her exertion and the daytime heat trapped in the attic, Olivia was sweating profusely. She'd seen enough at any rate—time to get out of this house before she got caught trespassing.

She turned toward the trapdoor and froze.

Tendrils of smoke rose through the cracks. She pressed her hand to the trapdoor. It was warm. An instant later she registered a dull, orange light glowing through the slats.

The walls closed in on her. She'd trapped herself in the highest room of a bone-dry house, and it was on fire. It would go up like a box of matches. Her only exit was already growing too hot to touch.

Olivia looked at her own terrified reflection in the mirror and knew she was going to die.

14

Elijah Fisher struggled awake from a drowning dream.

He lay in the semi-darkness of the living room, panting, trying to shake the feeling he was sinking into the freezing depths of a dead lake. He turned on the light and opened his Bible to Ephesians, a book deep enough into the Bible to survive the furrow Lila had whittled into the pages.

Elijah's heart was still hammering in his chest when Randall threw open the front door. It banged against the wall like a gunshot.

"Randall! You frightened me."

"Unintended, brother," said Randall, closing the door. He held a cylindrical object under his arm. "I've just been to the most marvelous house on Person Street. It was abandoned, and had crawl spaces, a massive fireplace, even secret passages."

Elijah frowned. "You're drunk."

"I found something else, too. A gift for you."

Elijah cast a glance towards Warren's closed bedroom door. "Keep your voice down, or you'll wake Warren."

"Come here, hold out your hand." Randall leaned close enough for the smell of cigarette smoke to prickle Elijah's nostrils.

"Randall, if this is a trick…"

"Your hand, brother," said Randall.

Elijah extended his hand, and Randall brushed it with his fingertips. Elijah looked down at an enormous black spider perched on his palm. The spider took two steps toward his wrist before Elijah's reflexes caught up with his fear. He shrieked and shook his hand like it was on fire. The spider fell to the floor and skittered under the couch.

Randall laughed. "Tell me she's not the biggest spider you've ever seen."

Elijah screeched, "God above, Azrael!"

Randall took hold of Elijah's collar. "What did you call me?"

"I—"

"What's my name, brother?" Randall demanded, drawing Elijah close, breath reeking of whiskey. "Tell me. I want to hear you say it."

"Randall, you raving fool," Elijah shot back.

Randall's gold eyes burned into Elijah's. "I thought I heard you call me something else."

Warren emerged from his bedroom, bleary-eyed.

"I told him to be quiet," blurted Elijah. "I told him not to wake you."

"I got a call," said Warren. "There's a fire on Person Street."

Randall stiffened. "A fire?"

"Some old house going up," said Warren, pulling on his shoes. "It's probably already too late to save it. We just need to keep the blaze contained."

"Can we come with you?" asked Randall.

"Did you say the house was on Person Street?" Elijah asked Randall.

"Yeah, near the graveyard," Warren said, not realizing Elijah wasn't talking to him.

Not a word, Randall mouthed to his brother.

"What have you done?" whispered Elijah.

"Did you say you wanted to come?" Warren asked from the hallway.

"We don't have anything else going on tonight," Randall responded, not moving his eyes from Elijah's.

"You can come, just stay out of the way, okay? Come on, let's go."

ELIJAH GLARED OUT THE truck window as they drove. The sky stretched out above them: a dark, starless void. Azrael—Randall—had told him the stars were harder to see in the city because of light pollution, but Elijah knew the real reason. They'd been snuffed out by the world of iniquity Randall had thrust them into.

When they turned onto Person Street, Warren pointed above the tree line. "See that pillar of smoke? That house is going to be nothing but ashes by morning."

Elijah coughed as wind carried smoke into the truck's air vents.

"Anything we can do to help?" Randall asked.

"No. Stay back."

When the house rolled into sight, Elijah gasped. The entire front side of a three-story house was ablaze. The heat of it felt like a sunburn, even through the window.

Warren parked his truck and leapt out, joining the half dozen firefighters standing outside the fence. A hose sent an enormous white arc of water up and into the house, to little effect.

Randall climbed out of the truck and made his way toward the firefighters.

"Warren said to stay out of the way!" shouted Elijah.

"Have you ever seen anything so beautiful in all your life?" Randall asked. "It's like watching God take back one of His creations."

"It isn't like watching *God* do anything."

"Jesus!" one of the firefighters shouted. He pointed up at the top floor of the house.

Elijah followed his line of sight and gaped in horror. A board broke and fell from the third-floor window, and then another. A slender arm reached out from the gap created in the boards. Elijah made out a mane of wild red hair framing a woman's pale face as she tried in vain to fit between the iron bars.

"There's someone up there!" Warren shouted.

"Get the life net," howled the other firefighter to the men on the truck.

"There are bars in the window!" Warren protested. "She can't get out!" He started to run towards the blaze but the firefighters on either side of him grabbed his arms.

"Young, the house is about to collapse!"

A window on the ground floor shattered from the heat.

"We've got to help her!" Warren shouted, fighting the men holding him back.

Randall looked back at Elijah, who saw something in his brother's eyes he'd never seen before. It wasn't fear, or compassion, but something else that, for a few seconds, changed his brother's face into a shape Elijah didn't recognize.

Randall turned on his heels, launched over the fence, and ran toward the house.

15

OLIVIA PRIED AND KICKED away the remaining planks of wood from the attic window, but it didn't matter. The window was barred. She was trapped.

The trapdoor poured smoke into the attic. Heat pressed in on her on all sides. She looked down into the yard—one of the firefighters was struggling to break free from a few men holding him back. She tried to take a breath, but all the oxygen had been sucked out of the air.

Olivia remembered what her father had told her about most fire-related deaths: people usually died of smoke inhalation rather than the fire itself. She needed to get as far from the smoke as possible. She ran to the far corner of the attic and lay on the floor, chest heaving. The heat was on her like a lion, its teeth bright and steely on her flesh. Olivia thought of her mother, how devastated she'd be, losing both her husband and her daughter to the same fate. She hoped she could forgive her. Olivia coughed, her lungs spasming and burning, growing dizzy, letting her mind drift away...

A movement in her periphery caught her attention, and she watched the Turkish rug lift into the air. An odd calm settled over her. Had she finally been able to summon the ability to lift things with her mind? Was her pineal gland releasing a burst of chemicals into her dying brain, unleashing the telekinesis that evaded her before?

Shame no one's here to see it, she thought.

The rug flipped over to reveal a young man's face. He appeared to be in his late teens, with hazel eyes and black hair. He wore a plain white T-shirt streaked with soot. A swell of recognition hit her: he was the young man she'd seen in the library weeks ago. It was a powerful hallucination, and a convincing one, except for the eyes, which looked too bright to be real.

The young man reached out and grabbed her hand. "Come on, follow me!"

Olivia allowed him to pull her forward, moving in a kind of dream, and saw he'd gotten into the attic through a hidden trapdoor.

He planted his feet on the floor below. "Drop down!"

Olivia leapt into the trapdoor and fell into the young man's arms. She sucked in a breath of cooler air. He pulled the Turkish rug down after her and tucked it under his arm.

"Stay close," he said, gripping her hand. "Take a deep breath and hold it as long as you can." They emerged into a bedroom full of smoke. Olivia followed blindly behind him, eyes burning as he led her through a hallway and down a flight of stairs.

Heat hit her like a slap to the face—a blazing inferno had enveloped the base of the staircase. Olivia tried to back away, but the young man held her fast.

"Jump on three," he said. "One...two...three!"

He threw the rug forward. Olivia's stomach lurched as she leapt from the second stair, landing beside him on the rug, flames roaring around them on all sides.

"Jump!" he shouted, and they leapt toward the wall of fire.

They collapsed on the other side, and Olivia felt his hands on her, patting out the flames on her hair and clothes. He grabbed her hand, hoisted her to her feet, and ran.

"We're almost out! Keep going!"

Olivia tried to tear her hand away from his. "We can't get out that way!"

"Trust me!" he shouted, wrenching her down the basement stairs. "It's the only way out!"

He drew her through the smoke-filled basement and shoved open a cellar door, producing a dark, clear rectangle of outside air. The house roared as if in fury at losing its quarry as he swept her up in his arms, climbed out of the cellar door, and ran from the house.

He collapsed when they reached the waiting line of firefighters. Olivia tumbled to the ground, coughing uncontrollably.

"You're okay, you're okay," a firefighter said. Over his shoulder, he added, "Get some oxygen over here, now!"

Olivia's skin felt tight and hot from the burning inferno. An oxygen mask appeared over her mouth. Cool air filled her lungs.

The man who had saved her lay on the ground beside her. Smoke rose from his clothes in ribbons. He wasn't moving.

"I'm fine!" Olivia shouted into her oxygen mask. "Help him, please! Help him!"

Strong hands restrained her. She felt lightheaded, as if she was tipping backward. She watched the flames consume the attic as darkness claimed her.

16

"T HAT WAS CHEATING," A RACHNE SAID.

Hades chuckled. "It was not."

"You started the fire and made Azrael think he did it."

Hades lounged in the branches of a tree a safe distance away from the remains of the Moloch house, watching the firefighters sift through the ashes. His face looked different than it had the last time He had disguised Himself as a human—older, gaunter. The overcast sky above Him grew incrementally lighter with the dawn. Arachne's spiders filled the branches around Him.

"What if you'd killed her?"

"Then she would have died a pure soul, and I would have lost our bet. But I didn't."

Hades had done other things to orchestrate Olivia and Azrael meeting—making sure Azrael and Warren worked at a moving job in the right neighborhood, booking up reservations in other restaurants so that Olivia and Harrison chose one that would lead them past the Moloch house. For every trick Arachne saw, there were likely a dozen she didn't.

Arachne said, "And now that they've met, his wickedness will lead her astray."

"No," said Hades. "It's his virtue that will make her fall."

She scoffed. "She's going to have to dig pretty deep to find virtue in that one."

"Love makes for a strong shovel."

Arachne couldn't argue with that. "She's going to be in an awful lot of trouble when she wakes up. The firefighters think she started the fire."

"She's not going to be in trouble until I want her to be," Hades said.

"Oh yes? How are you going to sidestep that?"

"In case of fire," Hades grinned, "make more fire."

17

OLIVIA OPENED HER EYES.

She was in a hospital room. She winced as she saw the IV needle taped to the back of her hand, connected to a tube leading to a hanging bag of clear fluid. She was dressed in a hospital gown. Her skin was warm to the touch and her throat felt like it had been scrubbed with a bottle brush. She smelled burning hair, but her wild tangles seemed mostly intact, give or take a few matted patches. The clock on the wall read 7:37 a.m.

She wasn't alone—a boy with pinched features watched her from a nearby chair, his hands fidgeting in his lap. He looked to be about thirteen years old, pale and thin, with eyes the slate gray of an ocean under storm.

"Hi," Olivia croaked.

"Hi," the boy said.

"What's your name?"

He hesitated. "Elijah Fisher."

"It's nice to meet you, Elijah. I'm Olivia."

Elijah resembled the young man who saved her from the fire—the same sharp jawline, the eyebrows like inverted Vs. "Do you know who saved me?"

Elijah nodded. "He's my brother."

"Is he all right?" Olivia asked.

Elijah pointed at the curtain drawn by her bedside. "He's right there."

Olivia pulled the curtain aside, and a fever flashed across her skin.

The young man who'd saved her lay asleep in the next bed. He looked older than he'd appeared in the fire, maybe close to her age. Black hair fell across his forehead in a swath, and a bandage covered one of his ears. His face was round, with well-defined cheekbones, pale skin, and flushed cheeks. His nose was slightly snubbed, the flesh around his eyes the color of varnished copper. Eyebrows arched over his closed eyes like the wings of a dark bird.

Elijah rose from his chair, scraping it against the floor, and left the room.

Her rescuer's eyelids fluttered. He coughed, stretched under his sheets, and turned toward her.

They stared at each other as the sounds of the hospital hummed around them.

"I've seen you before," Olivia said. Her cheeks prickled with heat, as if she'd admitted to an infatuation.

The young man stiffened. "You've seen me? Where?"

"At the library, a few weeks ago."

"Oh."

"What's your name?"

His answer seemed to rush out. "Randall Cheshire."

"The kid who was in here a second ago said he was your brother. Elijah Fisher?"

"Half-brother," Randall said. "What's your name?"

"Olivia." She looked at his bandaged ear. "Are you all right?"

"I'm fine," he said. "You?"

Olivia nodded. "I think so. Thank you for saving me. I'd be dead if you hadn't come in after me."

Randall's eyes dropped away.

"Are you a firefighter?" Olivia asked.

Randall smiled, exposing crooked front teeth and sharp canines. "My roommate Warren's the firefighter. Well, a volunteer one, anyway. I came along for the ride with him to see the fire. I'm more of a firebug than a firefighter myself."

Olivia's breath caught in her throat. "My dad used to call me Firebug." Olivia showed Randall the tattoo on the inside of her wrist, the delicate burst of flame.

Randall's eyes widened. "So did mine."

Olivia's cheeks felt hot enough that she wondered if she'd been more badly burned than she realized. "Really?"

"Really. I've got a scar instead of a tattoo, though." He showed her a snarl of pale scar tissue on the back of his forearm in the shape of a crooked grin. "Playing with matches."

"Oh good, you're awake," said a voice from the doorway. A nurse peered in, two police officers at her side. "Is it all right if these officers ask you a few questions while I check your vitals?" she asked.

Olivia's palms went cool with sweat as Harrison's words came back to her: *Some people would call what you're doing breaking and entering.*

Advice Milo had given her in college echoed in her mind as well: *Never talk to cops. Anything you say will only hurt you, never help you.*

"Yes, of course," Olivia said. The words came out before she could stop herself. Her stomach sank as the nurse and the two officers entered the room. She remembered the flame tattoo on her wrist in time to hide it from sight. The nurse went about checking vitals as the officers asked her questions.

It didn't take long for Olivia to understand how an interrogation could lead to a false confession. She knew full well she hadn't done anything to start a fire, yet found herself wondering if it were possible she *had* caused the fire. Her voice shook as she told the officers about the cigarette fire she'd put out a few hours before entering the house, which the younger of the two officers jotted down in a notebook. She apologized for entering the house and told them the front door was unlocked, and she'd just wanted to take a look around.

The older officer's radio crackled to life. "Dispatch controller Romeo Charlie 11 on duty, Delta Bravo 425, are you receiving?"

"Keep her talking," muttered the older officer as he stepped away. In the hallway, Olivia heard him respond, "Delta Bravo 425 receiving."

"We've got another 451 on Person Street. Suspect on foot, officers in pursuit."

Olivia locked eyes with the officer in the room with her. She wasn't terribly well-versed on her police radio codes, but she was an avid reader, and she knew what 451 meant.

"One moment, ma'am," the younger officer said, joining his partner in the hallway.

"Same MO?" she heard the older officer ask.

A pause on the radio. "Yes. Suspect was last seen heading in the direction of St. David's."

St. David's. Olivia had a feeling she'd just learned the name of the hospital she was in.

A whispered conversation transpired between the officers in the hallway. The older officer leaned in the doorway, his face flushed bright pink from his collar to his cap. "Thank you for your help, ma'am, we'll be in touch if we need more information."

Stunned, Olivia listened to the squeaks of the officers' shoes as they hurried down the hallway. She locked eyes with Randall, who was breathing more heavily than she was.

"That was a lucky break," Randall murmured.

Olivia let out a slow, shaky breath. "You're telling me."

Olivia's heartbeat was on its way back to normal when Elijah returned with a man in tow. Olivia guessed the man was around her age, although his receding hairline, troubled eyes, and hunched posture made him seem older. He stared at the starched white sheets covering her legs as if summoning the courage to make eye contact.

"Hi," Olivia said. "Who are you?"

"I'm Warren. I was at the fire."

Recognition dawned on her. "You tried to come in after me."

"You saw me?"

Olivia nodded. "You would have run in if they hadn't stopped you. Thank you."

Warren raised his eyes to meet hers for a few seconds before looking away again. "I'm just glad you're okay."

"So, you know each other?" asked Olivia, gesturing to Randall.

Warren cut a glance at Randall. "Yes. The three of us go way back."

"Sorry to interrupt, but you two need to fill out some paperwork," the nurse said, handing tablets to Olivia and Randall. "I understand neither of you have any health insurance information on your persons, so just fill these forms out to the best of your ability, and we can sort out the details later. Once that's done, you're free to go." The nurse hesitated, then added, "There are some reporters outside the hospital. They might want to ask you some questions about the fire and the dramatic rescue. Do you have any interest in talking to them?"

"Absolutely not," Olivia and Randall said in unison.

The nurse nodded. "I thought so. There's a side exit we can send you through when you leave so they won't bother you. Oh, and the nurse on shift before me told me he threw away the clothes you came in with. They were pretty burned up. I could probably find some clothes in the lost and found for you to wear home, too."

"That would be great, thank you," said Olivia. For some reason, the banality of the paperwork made what had thus far seemed like a bizarre nightmare into something real. The words on the form blurred as she found herself fighting back tears. She wanted more than anything else to go home and process how close she'd come to suffering to the same fate as her father.

Like father, like daughter, Olivia thought, and shivered.

18

A FEW HOURS LATER, Arachne's spiders watched as Olivia, Randall, Elijah, and Warren exited the hospital through the loading dock area, hurrying through the parking lot to avoid being noticed by the press milling around the front entrance. Across town, Hades had led the police down a narrow side street. Hades turned a corner and vanished steps away from a stunned man dressed the same as Him. The police officers rounded the corner and arrested the hapless man on the spot.

Down below, Arachne spat out a scrabbling wolf spider. "Poor bastard."

Once they were safely away from the hospital, Warren asked Olivia, "Can I give you a ride home?"

"Thanks," Olivia said, "but my house isn't that far away, and I could use the walk to process what happened."

Warren took in a breath. "Well...then, can I take you out to dinner sometime?"

Olivia blinked. "Oh...um..."

Warren smiled bashfully. "Listen...it's just that I didn't want to let you walk away without asking. It doesn't have to be anything more than a friendly dinner."

Arachne watched Olivia size Warren up, considering. Olivia glanced over at Randall, who shifted a toothpick from one side of his mouth to the other with a flick of his tongue. From the tiny eyes of a jumping spider yards away, Arachne watched her blush.

Olivia said, "Uh…okay! I don't see why not."

Warren's smile widened. "How does next Saturday at seven sound?"

"I'm free. That sounds great."

Warren handed her a note. "Here's my phone number and address. If you want, we can meet at my place—there's a Thai restaurant down the street, they've got a drunken noodle that'll put hair on your chest."

Olivia smiled. "All right."

Warren fidgeted. "Thanks. I'll see you then."

"Okay, see you. And thanks again. To all of you."

Randall shot Olivia a smile as they parted ways. Arachne felt a flash of energy pass between the two of them, rippling through her spider like an invisible shock wave.

"What the hell was that?" Arachne whispered.

As Randall passed near Arachne's spider, she realized he didn't have a toothpick in his mouth at all. He was gnawing on the business end of a match head.

19

OLIVIA'S DREAM DESCENDED ON her like a creature of wind and flame. In the dream, she was once more trapped inside the burning house, but there was no heat, no fear. She floated down the hall, toes grazing the floor.

Randall stood at the end of the hallway, staring at her with ember-bright eyes. He wore a faded shirt featuring a tropical sunset and plaid pajama shorts.

Olivia floated toward him. Randall watched her approach with fear and fascination. She lifted her hand in greeting, and he lifted his. She waved her arms, and he did the same. As she watched, his face changed, dark lashes softening, cheeks breaking out in freckles, black hair rolling out into long copper locks. Olivia froze when she realized she was looking into a reflection identical to her own.

Except the eyes: the eyes staring back at her were full of fire.

Olivia opened her eyes, and her bedroom materialized around her. She rolled away from the band of afternoon sunlight falling across her face and curled into a cool, dark pocket of her sheets. The intensity of the dream tingled on her skin...or maybe it was the burn from her brush with death.

Everything rushed back in, and she started shaking. If Randall hadn't been outside...if there hadn't been a way out...if they'd been in the house a few seconds longer...

Had it been like that for her father when he died? Realization, terror, acceptance...then instead of rescue, darkness?

When the tears came, they soaked her sheets. Every time she thought she was finished, another vision of her death flashed before her eyes, and she started weeping all over again.

A knock fell on her door. Olivia pulled herself together and answered it.

Nancy stood on her stoop, wide-eyed. "I'm sorry to come over unannounced, but you stopped answering my texts, and...oh Jesus, have you been crying? What happened?"

Olivia burst into tears and fell into Nancy's arms.

"Oh, honey," Nancy said into her hair. "Do you need me to hire a hit man to kill Harrison? I've got a crazy uncle who probably already knows one."

Olivia laughed and shook her head.

"Okay, hon. Tell me all about it."

Olivia sat Nancy down and told her about the night before. Nancy gasped and pressed her hands to her mouth. She screamed when Olivia showed her where her hair had been singed, and by the time Olivia finished, Nancy was in tears.

"Oh, Olivia, I'm so sorry."

"It's all right," Olivia shrugged. "I'm okay."

"*Are* you okay?" Nancy asked.

Olivia considered her response. "If I'm being honest, I've got a ways to go before I get to okay. I fell asleep as soon as I got home, and I dreamed I was in a burning house again, and I woke up shaking and sobbing...but it's not like this is unfamiliar territory for me."

"What do you mean?"

She chewed her lip. "When my dad died, I had nightmares every night for months."

"Oh, of course, hon," Nancy said.

"No...I dreamed I was the one who made the fire. That I was the one who killed him."

"Oh, honey." Nancy winced. "How horrible. It's bad enough grieving without blaming yourself for something that had nothing to do with you."

"Yeah," said Olivia, unable to meet Nancy's eyes. She stopped herself from saying something she would regret. "Anyway...I'm going to be all right. It's a lot to process, is all."

"Dang," Nancy said. "Talk about a bad date, huh?"

"You're not kidding. Oh—I left out the part where I'm going to go on a date with a volunteer firefighter who's friends with the guy who saved me."

Nancy's eyes widened. "Way to make some damn *lemonade*. Is he cute?"

"He seems...nice."

"That bad, huh?"

Olivia laughed. "He's alright-looking, just seems kind of awkward. He'd have come in for me if one of the other firefighters hadn't stopped him. I feel like getting dinner with him is a fair response."

Nancy drew in air through her teeth. "What's the worst that could happen, right?"

20

"Hello?" Warren said into the phone. "No, I...I mean, yes...aw fuck, I'll be right there."

Elijah scowled at Warren's cursing. Randall had picked up the habit as well. The words felt like splinters pushed into his flesh.

Warren flew out of his room, throwing on gear, gloves grasped in one hand. There must have been a fire, and judging by his haste, a bad one.

"Elijah, listen, Olivia's going to get here soon. Can you tell her something for me?"

"What?"

"Tell her I've been called away to a fire. Make sure she's comfortable, give her some tea or a snack. Just don't let her leave. I'll be back as soon as I can."

"Okay," Elijah said as Warren dashed outside.

Elijah returned his attention to his Bible. He was deep in a New Testament list of *begats* when Randall burst into the apartment.

Elijah jumped. "Good Lord, Randall—"

Randall swept past him into Warren's room. "Is he gone?"

"Warren?"

"No, the Holy Ghost. Yes, Warren."

"There was a fire. He just left."

Randall grinned at the same moment the smell of kerosene tingled Elijah's nostrils.

"Randall...what have you done?"

"I have no idea what you're talking about."

"You knew...you knew he had a date with her..."

There was a knock at the door.

"Just get her in here and make yourself scarce." Randall disappeared into his room.

"Randall!" snapped Elijah.

The knocks came again. A wave of fury crashed over Elijah. If he said nothing, he was as guilty as Randall. Yet—if he told Warren, he and Randall would be banished again, with no hope of finding a safe place to stay.

Elijah hurried to the front door and opened it to find Olivia halfway down the alley.

"Olivia!"

She turned. "Elijah!"

"Warren had to go. There was a fire."

"Oh, I see."

"He'll be right back," Elijah assured her.

"Are you sure?"

Elijah forced a smile. "By the time he gets there they'll probably tell him to turn around and go home. I was actually about to run to the store, so if you want you can wait for him here. Make yourself at home!"

Olivia hesitated. "Oh, um...sure. I will, thanks."

When Olivia brushed past him to go inside, Elijah caught the faintest whiff of burning hair. His smile faded into a scowl as he closed the door. He hurried away, seething with helpless rage.

21

THE SUDDEN DARKNESS INSIDE the apartment made Olivia feel like she was entering a cave. The air inside smelled of dust and smoke, and a dry, earthy tone, like the cedar closet in her mother's basement. Another smell she couldn't place made her think of camping.

Her heartbeat was loud in her ears. Instinct warned her against spending another moment in this place, but Elijah seemed so earnest, and she wanted more than anything else to get this date over with.

She emerged from the hallway into a dim living room torn from the pages of *Young Male's Apartment Weekly*. It wasn't filthy, but it wasn't clean, either. She set her purse on the coffee table and inspected a Bible left open on the couch. Odd...there was a hollow carved into the first hundred or so pages...

A tinny noise broke through her thoughts. It was coming from the room beside her. Olivia crept toward the open door. It was music, so faint she could barely hear it.

Randall's face appeared in the doorway. He yanked down his headphones around his neck. "Olivia!"

Olivia's heart leapt into her throat. "Randall! I'm sorry. I thought...I didn't know you were home..."

"It's okay. I didn't mean to scare you," said Randall. He was wearing a red T-shirt with a faded graphic and dark gray pajama pants. "You're here for your date with Warren, right?"

"Yeah. Elijah said he was called away to a fire."

Randall shrugged. "Happens. How have you been?"

Olivia hovered on the verge of telling Randall about her dream—and how she'd floated toward him in a burning house. She shook the thought away. "Honestly, I'm still processing how crazy it was that we got out alive. A part of me doesn't believe it's over."

"I know the feeling." Randall grinned, flashing his crooked teeth.

What would it feel like to kiss him?

Olivia shook the thought away and pointed to the tinny sounds coming from his wireless headphones. "What are you listening to?"

"PJ Harvey." He placed the headphones over Olivia's ears.

A discordant guitar riff swallowed all outside noise. The singer's voice shuddered against Olivia's ears like a bad grudge.

Randall's eyes moved over her face. *What do you think?* his lips asked.

Olivia nodded her approval, her eyes not leaving his. She was the same height as him, and this close, she saw how the green flecks made his hazel eyes look golden, made them glow like lanterns in the low light. She moved to take off the headphones, but Randall stopped her, his fingers brushing against her wrist.

This is the best part, Randall's lips said.

The music made Olivia feel dizzy, disoriented. The steady pressure of Randall's calloused fingers on her wrist sparked a bright ember to life in her chest. Without thinking, she took hold of his hand, twining her fingers into his. His pulse ticked in time with her pounding heart.

The part of her that knew she was insane to walk into this apartment in the first place told her to run, to get away from this strange man with the mischievous smile who chewed on matchsticks, to run out into the alley and never look back.

Another part of her knew she had wanted this to happen since Randall saved her from the fire.

Olivia closed her eyes and kissed him.

Randall drew in a deep breath as their lips touched, then he clutched her hair and parted her lips with his tongue. The kiss was a bonfire, blazing all the way to her toes and back. Music jarred in her ears. When she opened her eyes, Randall was staring at her with the intensity of a bird of prey. His hands moved down to her waist, grasping the fabric of her dress. He waited for her to either break away or give in to what he knew she was feeling. In her mind's eye, Olivia watched a saner version of herself push him away and walk out the door.

With a distinct sensation of forsaking reason, she fell into Randall's arms, kicking the bedroom door closed behind her.

As they kissed, Olivia caught flashes of Randall's dimly lit room. A small red lamp cast a pool of light, illuminating the knickknack-covered walls with a rosy hue. A small, ornate terrarium rested on a table by the bed, though she couldn't see anything living in it. A coral pink curtain hung over the room's sole window, and a fragrant band of smoke rose from a glowing incense stick on a glossy black dresser.

When the PJ Harvey song in her ears faded to silence, Olivia took off the headphones and set them on the dresser. "Where did you find all this stuff? It's beautiful."

"Warren and I work for a moving company," Randall said. "You wouldn't believe the kinds of things people throw away."

Randall drew Olivia close, tilted her head back, and kissed her throat. Olivia drew in a sharp breath. The soft heat of his lips on her skin made her feel like she'd never really been touched before. When his other hand drifted downward, she lifted the hem of her dress, reveling in the sensation of the same hands that had wrenched her from the fire gripping her exposed thighs. Christ, he was so *strong*. His crow-black hair brushed the side of her face as his lips trailed up her jawline. Olivia swooned at his scent—heady and sweet, reminiscent of the smell emanating from the pages of a library book, mingled with a faint trace of smoke.

"I haven't stopped thinking about you since the fire," Randall said.

Her cheeks flushed with fever. "I haven't either."

She pulled Randall's face to hers and kissed him, losing herself in the taste of him. He pulled ever-so-slightly on the handful of hair grasped in his fingers, and the sensation in her scalp sent pleasurable chills down to her toes.

His breath was hot against her earlobe as he asked, "Is that okay?"

"Yes," Olivia said breathlessly. The urgent stiffness inside Randall's pajama pants pressed against her thigh. She took in a breath with every intention of telling Randall that they needed to stop, that she barely knew him, that she wasn't about to sleep with a man before he'd even taken her on a date.

Instead, she heard herself ask: "Do you have any condoms?"

22

ARACHNE THOUGHT RANDALL WOULD kill the spider he'd found at the Moloch house, but instead, he acquired a terrarium from an estate sale and turned the spider into a pet. He named her Lilith and fed her insects he found around the apartment. Arachne was used to having to hide her spies in nooks and corners, but with Lilith, she was granted a front row seat.

"Any what?" Randall asked.

"Condoms," Olivia repeated.

Arachne watched a quick calculation play out behind Randall's eyes: he needed to find out what a condom was as soon as possible.

"No," Randall said. "Do you?"

"No, I—"

They startled in unison at the sound of the front door opening. Floorboards creaked in the hallway.

"Warren," Randall whispered.

From a jumping spider tucked under one of the couch cushions, Arachne watched as Warren took in the scene in the living room. Olivia's purse, abandoned on the table. Randall's bedroom door, closed. The heavy silence in the air.

Jealousy heaped over Warren like handfuls of earth thumping onto a grave. He stalked into his bedroom and slammed the door.

"Shit," whispered Olivia. "If I hadn't left my purse in the living room, I'd climb out the window."

"Well, I don't want to pretend this didn't happen. Do you?"

Olivia paused, then shook her head. She happened to look over Randall's shoulder, making direct eye contact with Lilith in the terrarium.

"Is that a spider?"

Randall smiled. "Yeah, that's Lilith."

Olivia shuddered. "I have a thing about spiders."

"Oh, don't worry. She can't get out," Randall said.

Olivia blinked as if coming out of a trance. She straightened her dress and attempted to smooth out her hair. "I should go."

"I want to see you again," Randall said.

Olivia stopped in the middle of reaching for the door. "I...I don't know if that's a good idea."

"Look, here's my number," Randall said. He jotted down the number for his prepaid phone on a notebook on his dresser, tore out the page, and extended it to her. "Call me anytime."

Olivia looked down at the number, apprehension flickering across her features. "I don't know anything about you. You could be a murderer."

"I promise not to murder you if you call me." Randall's face fell as he realized what he'd said. "I mean...I won't murder you either way. I just want to get to know you."

Olivia's cheeks flushed. "I'll think about it." She slipped away, shaking her head as she walked to her car.

Oh, little girl, thought Arachne. *I know a fly in a web when I see one, and you're as trapped as they come.*

23

Olivia held out a whole week after her first delirious encounter with Randall, going practically out of her mind with unrequited lust, before she broke down and texted his number. She told him she wanted to slow things down and get to know each other better before they engaged in any more physical contact. He agreed, and they set a date for him to pick her up to go get dinner.

Randall barely crossed over her threshold before several things happened in quick succession: Olivia leaned in to give him a friendly peck on the cheek but instead found herself kissing him passionately, pressing her body against his, and running her fingers through his dark hair. Randall closed the door behind him and thrust Olivia against the wall, lifting her dress, grasping at her with the desperation of a drowning man. Olivia yanked down her panties with the same frantic urgency, Randall pulled on a condom, and then he was inside her, and she felt the way she had in the dream—drawn to him as helplessly as a moth to a flame, beyond caring if her wings burned.

After that, it was all Olivia could do to focus on her work or hold a conversation without her mind turning toward the strange man who'd ignited something so bright inside her it was frightening. She had told Nancy about it but hadn't mentioned anything to her mother or Milo yet, other than telling them a strange young man had rescued her from a house fire. She felt conspiratorial about Randall, as if their relationship were an exquisite secret she ought to hide for as long as possible before letting the rest of the world in.

Weeks into their relationship, Olivia received a voicemail from Milo. She hit *play* and stared ruefully at her phone.

"Olivia, it's Milo. I haven't heard from you in a while, and I just wanted to make sure everything was all right. Um…call me, okay?"

Olivia sighed. She had to tell him.

She clicked Milo's grinning picture on her phone.

Milo answered on the second ring. "She lives!"

"I do indeed!" Olivia tried her best to sound natural. "How are you?"

"I've been pretty good. Work's going well and I've been going to a lot of shows lately. How are you?"

"I've been good. I…I've started seeing someone."

"That's great! What's he like?"

"He's…well…remember the guy who saved me from the fire? Randall?"

"Him?" asked Milo.

"Yes, we've been spending a lot of time together," said Olivia. "I guess we're a couple now."

"I thought you said he was younger," Milo said, laughing incredulously. "You made it seem like he was a teenager."

"He's five years younger than me," Olivia admitted. "He turns twenty-one next month, a few weeks before my birthday."

"Olivia—"

"Okay, he's on the young side, but things are going well. I don't notice the age difference."

The truth was, there were enough unusual things about Randall that his youth hardly registered. He seemed to have watched so few movies and TV shows that she'd stopped asking if he'd seen something. The first time she took him to a movie theater, he stopped in the entry, stunned by the size of the screen. Even stranger, he had next to no knowledge of history, math, or literature. It was as if he'd sprung out fully formed from the earth like some sort of Greek legend just in time to rescue her from the house fire.

When Olivia had asked Randall how it was he was so disconnected from these things, he told her he was raised in a large, religious family in the country, and had only recently moved to the city, bringing his thirteen-year-old half-brother with him. Olivia didn't ask many questions about this, as his past seemed an unwelcome place for him to dwell.

Despite these peculiarities, Randall was whip-smart, funny, and sexually ravenous. Every time he touched her, it was like he was discovering her body for the first time. On their last date, he'd told her, "I've never met anyone like you before. You light up whatever room you're in. I just can't believe I get to be with you."

Olivia might have been scared by the ferocity of her passion if she weren't so consumed with the ecstasy of it.

"Huh," Milo said. "Well…if you're happy, I'm happy."

"I am happy," Olivia said.

"I guess I have news for you too, then."

"What?"

"I bought a plane ticket to visit you on your birthday. I was going to surprise you and take you to dinner and maybe a show. I hadn't planned it out much further than showing up on your doorstep."

"Milo! I'd love to see you! And I really don't have any plans. We could go get dinner somewhere."

"You're sure I won't be a third wheel?"

"Not at all! I'll invite my friend Nancy. I want you two to meet each other anyway. She's awesome."

"Well...that sounds great, Liv. I'll send you my itinerary."

"I'm glad you're coming down. I—"

"I actually have to go. You caught me in the middle of a work thing."

"Oh," said Olivia. "Of course. I'll talk to you soon, Milo."

"Sure. Good hearing from you, kiddo," Milo said, and hung up.

24

Arachne, whispered a voice at her ear.

Arachne leapt to her feet, a shower of spiders falling from her hair. She was alone, which meant...

"You."

Me, it snickered. *Me, me, me.*

Arachne couldn't see it, but she could *feel* it, close as a dream upon waking. "Fuck off, Agon." she said. She hated it, hated all of them—demons sprouting like weeds from the muck of human misery.

And deprive myself of your company? Agon crooned, materializing in front of her.

Arachne forced herself not to recoil. Its features resembled that of a bat who'd encountered a blast of radioactivity. Jowls swung on either side of its rotting maw of a mouth, which bristled with dozens of filthy tusks. Gaping eye sockets glittered at her with liquid malevolence. She hoped its existence was as painful as it looked.

Rumor is you've got a wager going, Agon thought at her.

"You've really got nothing better to do than chatter amongst yourselves like housewives?" asked Arachne. "Don't you have a mortal to possess?"

Why, just yesterday I drove a young mother to madness, said Agon. *She drowned her three children in a bathtub before putting the barrel of a gun in her mouth. She's here with us now.* It grinned, mottled skin drawing back in curtains from the horns crowding its mouth. *I've been far from idle. And you didn't answer my question.*

Arachne frowned. "What business is it of yours?"

A cold knot formed in her stomach as Agon drew close. Hades forbade demons from tormenting the souls on this plane of Hell physically, much to the demons' consternation. They enjoyed afflicting her in ways other than physical, of course.

Agon plucked a spider from her hair and began to remove its legs. *Then it's true. The terms of your wager, should you win—it is your release, is it not?*

A spider scrambled out of Arachne's ear canal and crawled down her neck. "What else?"

You do know that He exists outside of the flow of time, don't you? Agon asked. *That's why He's able to influence the lives of the living so easily. He wouldn't have made this wager if He was going to lose.*

Arachne shivered, thinking of the paroxysm of realities she'd glimpsed when she'd shaken His hand to seal their wager. "Well, it's too late to back out now."

Agon leaned in close. The smell billowing out of its throat was cruelty itself. The spider on her neck folded in its legs and perished. *In that case, I'd keep an eye on the Colony if I were you,* Agon snarled.

Then Agon was gone, the stench of its breath fading slowly away.

Arachne shivered as a wave of apprehension coursed through her. She took a deep, shaky breath, roused the hundreds of spiders hiding in the woods around the Colony, and sent them skittering into its walls.

25

RANDALL CHESHIRE OPENED HIS apartment door to find Olivia grinning ear to ear.

"Happy birthday!" Olivia said.

"Thanks, Firebug." Randall hugged her, nuzzling her neck, drinking in the scent of her. Three months into their relationship, he still felt pleasure rocking from head to toe whenever they touched.

"Ready to go?" Olivia asked.

Unless she was spending the night, Olivia didn't like lingering at Randall's apartment longer than was necessary. Warren's sulking wasn't as bad as it had been at the beginning, but his presence put a damper on things. Elijah, with his irritable disposition, wasn't much fun to be around, either.

"All packed." Randall patted a backpack slung over his shoulder. "Do we need to pick up anything on the way?"

"Just some ice. We're good on food and drinks for the night." Olivia took Randall's hand as they walked to her car. "I can't believe you've never been camping before!"

"Wasn't really a thing where I grew up," Randall said.

Olivia nodded, as if accepting this as yet another stitch in the tapestry of Randall's oppressive, God-fearing childhood. "Well, I think you're going to enjoy it. Especially the s'mores."

"The what?" Randall asked.

Olivia smiled. "You'll see."

Olivia drove her car into the woods, parked at the plot of land she'd reserved, and taught Randall how to set up a tent. They walked around the park until they dripped with sweat, then cooled down in the shallows of a fast-moving river. When the sun grew low in the sky, Randall proved himself adept at starting a fire, and they ate charred hot dogs and drank ice-cold beers by a crackling campfire.

When it grew dark, Randall asked, "When do I find out what a s'more is?"

"How does right now sound?" Olivia speared a marshmallow on the end of a sharpened stick. "Hold it over the fire, near the embers." She went to prep the rest of the ingredients.

The marshmallow swelled and browned. "How do you know when it's done?"

Olivia looked over her shoulder. "Catching on fire is a pretty good indication."

Randall jumped. His marshmallow was alight. "Ah, fuck. Is that bad?"

Olivia blew his flaming marshmallow out. "Nope. I actually prefer it that way. Hold it still." She sandwiched the singed, fluffy marshmallow between two graham cracker squares and a chocolate bar, slid it free of the stick, and held it out to him. "Enjoy!"

Randall inspected the s'more, smelled it, then took a bite. His eyes widened at the burst of sticky sweetness in his mouth. "Holy shit."

"Right?" Olivia grinned.

Randall finished off his s'more, leaned close to Olivia, and kissed her. "Thank you," he said. Olivia's cheeks flushed. He loved making her blush.

Olivia made a s'more for herself, and Randall helped himself to another, and they washed them down with the last dregs of their beers.

He caressed her leg with sticky fingers. "Bed?"

Olivia nodded eagerly. She climbed inside the tent and clicked on the fairy lights she'd strung up. They helped each other out of their clothes, smelling of smoke and sugar and sweat.

"Oh," Olivia said, "I almost forgot. I have a birthday gift for you."

"I thought this camping trip was my birthday gift," Randall said, his chest warming as he traced his fingers up the velvet softness of her inner thigh.

"I made something for you." Olivia pulled a box out of her pack, wrapped in pink and purple paper that sparkled in the camping lights. "Happy Birthday."

Randall looked at the gift for a few seconds. He removed the wrapping paper gingerly, sprinkling flecks of glitter on the tent floor. He opened the box and stared at what was inside.

It was a piece of wood with an artistic image carefully burned into the surface, featuring two arms to the elbow, one emerging from the top and the other from the bottom. The top arm was masculine, with a mark burned across the back of it in the shape of a crooked grin; the bottom arm was delicate and feminine, with flames on the wrist. Randall's scar and Olivia's fire tattoo, arranged in a yin and yang, with a tiny heart burned in the space between them. The richly varnished wood smelled sweeter than the s'mores.

"I took a wood burning class," Olivia said. "What do you think?"

The dark lines of the wood burning blurred as Randall's eyes filled with tears.

"Oh, hon, are you all right?" Olivia asked.

A tear spattered onto the wood. "Would you believe this is the first birthday gift anyone's ever given me?"

Olivia embraced him as hot tears streamed down his cheeks.

In that moment, warm and safe in her arms, her smell more like home than any place he'd ever known, Randall wanted to tell Olivia everything. His real name, where he came from, the pregnant lover he left behind. Olivia would never hide anything from him. She deserved the truth.

But when he looked into her eyes, a steely bolt of fear stayed his tongue. "I love it," he said. He added softly, heart hammering in his chest: "I love you, Firebug."

Olivia's eyes sparkled in the fairy lights. "I love you, too."

They made love, and Randall allowed the last remaining tethers of his life before Olivia to slip away. Olivia would still love him if she knew the truth about where he came from, or his real name, but there was no way in hell she would accept that he'd left his pregnant lover behind with the monsters who raised him. And if she left him, Randall would inherit a barren, bleak future—the sort of godless world outside the Colony the Prophet had warned of all those years. It would be a worse fate than if he had been killed for impregnating Lila before he'd escaped.

When they were done, lying panting beside each other, Olivia said, "Sometimes, I wish I could stop time in its tracks when I'm with you. I know eventually we're going to have to put our clothes on, pack up this tent, and go back to our jobs, but I want this moment to last as long as it can."

"It's funny," said Randall, "I was thinking the opposite. Being with you makes me excited about the future. I've started talking to Warren about becoming a firefighter, so I can help people the way you're going to help people with

Nosh. I'd never have thought I was capable of that sort of thing, but you make me feel like I can do anything. You make me want to be the best possible version of myself." He nestled close, laying his head on her shoulder. "I really don't know what I'd have become if I hadn't met you."

Olivia kissed his cheek. "I think you'll make an incredible firefighter." She clicked the lights off. "Now let's get some sleep so we can do the whole future thing together."

Randall gazed at Olivia for a while in the moonlit darkness before closing his eyes as well. The only possible way he was going to have a future with Olivia was to think of the Colony as a nightmare from which he'd woken up.

He had to hope Lila would find her own way out.

26

LILA MONROE GAZED UP at the cracked plaster ceiling over her bed. The smell of rain drifted through the open window on a sweltering breeze along with the rumblings of a summer storm. Her sheets clung to her, damp with sweat. She shifted to the other side of the bed, grunting with the effort of hauling her massive belly along with her. Her baby kicked her ribs in protest.

The Prophet had moved her into a private room, which was a mercy, because the Colony considered Lila a Shamed Woman. Nobody had spoken a word to her since Elijah had been exiled. She was more or less prepared for the changes her body was going through, having seen some of the other mothers endure pregnancies, but there was a profound lone-liness in not being able to talk to anyone about it. Each day stretched into an eternity of isolation, and each sunset that came and went with no red ribbon on the oak tree drove a cold spike further into her heart.

Tonight, her pillow was damp with tears as well as sweat. All the false hope she'd carried with her along with her growing child collapsed under an avalanche of despair. Azrael wasn't coming back, which meant one of two things: either something terrible had happened to him in the outside world, or he didn't care enough about her to come back. She wasn't sure which actuality was more devastating.

In a flicker of lightning, Lila saw a spider in the corner of the room, dark as the cracks splitting the plaster walls. She had the unsettling impression the spider was staring at her. A few seconds later, the roll of thunder was accompanied by another noise—the whining creak of her bedroom door opening. A dark shape hulked into the room, floorboards creaking as he approached. Lila's limbs went leaden with dread. There was no stopping what was coming next.

Henry Hatch crept toward her bed. Lila smelled him before he touched her—sweat mingling with the animal urgency radiating from him in waves. He'd declared Lila unfit for marriage, but that didn't mean he'd stopped lusting after her. Hot tears spilled down her cheeks. She could cry out for help, but to whom? The Prophet's authority was absolute.

As Hatch reached for her in the dark, Lila cried out at a terrible pain in her gut. It grew stronger, tightening like a noose, radiating to her lower back, culminating in an awful, glassy cramp, then breaking like a wave.

"No," Lila moaned. Not here. Not now.

Hatch recoiled. "What is it?"

"No, no…it's too early…not yet…"

Hatch turned on her bedside lamp and looked her over. "The baby is coming, Lila."

The next contraction was worse. Steel hands gripped her insides, and an elbow dug into the small of her back until she thought she was going to pass out. Just when she couldn't stand it anymore, the pain crested and withdrew. When she opened her eyes, Hatch was gone, and three mothers were at her side. One of them wiped sweat from her forehead with a wet cloth.

In her mind, Lila went somewhere else. She went to a place where she and her baby were safe, where men like Henry Hatch couldn't lay their wretched, groping hands on her. She tried to imagine Azrael with her, but he was nowhere to be found, even in her imagination.

Time lost meaning. Its passage was marked by waves of agony, each coming harder and faster than the last. Something was wrong. She felt it deep in her body.

"I need a hospital," she told the mothers. Lila only had the faintest idea of what a hospital actually was, but she'd heard other mothers beg for it in the past.

"Blasphemy," one of them spat.

"Trust in God's will," said another.

Hours of pain. Screams for mercy, unheeded.

Lila at last bore down, and her baby emerged slick with blood, the umbilical cord wrapped around his neck. He was blue-faced and still.

Lila's heart stopped. She choked back a cry at the brittle silence. The mothers unraveled the cord and set to slapping him. It seemed like they were barely trying. They wanted her bastard son to die.

"Give him to me!" Lila screamed.

The mother who'd been languidly slapping her baby handed the child to Lila.

Lila pressed against her baby's ribcage. She breathed air into his tiny lips, fighting against unconsciousness herself. Her thighs were slick from the flow of blood leaving her body, and she prayed that if her baby died, she would, too.

Lila was slipping into darkness when the baby in her arms wailed. His tiny, wrinkled face turned from blue to pink. He howled as if he'd fought against death itself and emerged from battle uttering a war cry.

Lila looked with wonder into her child's face. She was a mother. "Welcome to the world, Cade."

Cade stopped crying and stared at her.

In the last seconds before unconsciousness, Lila looked into her son's eyes and saw Azrael's bright eyes staring back at her.

27

"Happy Birthday," whispered Randall.

Olivia squinted in the early morning brightness of his bedroom. "What time is it?"

"A little after seven. I have something for you."

"Why are you awake?" Olivia pulled the sheets over her head. "Come back to bed."

Randall placed an object on her lap. "Careful, there's a vase."

Olivia blinked and slowly pulled herself up onto her elbows. A tray of glowing, antique wood with clawed legs straddled her lap, bearing a plate with two sunny-side-up eggs, three strips of bacon, and a piece of toast smothered in crimson jam. Randall had finished off the presentation with a scarlet rose in a delicate blue vase.

Randall went back to the kitchen and returned with a fragrant cup of coffee. "You can go back to sleep if you want, Ms. Madden, but I couldn't wait."

Olivia smiled and accepted the coffee. "I've never had anyone make me breakfast in bed before." She took a bite of bacon—so crispy it was almost burned, exactly how she liked it. "This is honestly the nicest, most thoughtful birthday gift I've ever gotten."

Randall beamed. "If you're feeling up to it, after breakfast, I'd like to take you fishing on Lake Austin. We can bring whatever we catch back here, cook it, and eat lunch on the roof. We'll kill the rest of the afternoon finger-painting and watching B-horror movies." He caressed her arm. "Then we'll pick up Milo from the airport, head to the best Thai restaurant in the city, and eat with him and Nancy until they roll us out of there."

Olivia leaned in close to Randall. "You realize you've described the perfect day."

Randall's crooked, boyish smile made her weak. "I just want to make you happy."

"You make me happier than anyone has any right to be. You should be a controlled substance."

Randall carefully moved her tray and coffee to the nightstand. "There's nothing controlled about the way I feel about you."

As they made love, Randall's pet spider faced away from them, its attention elsewhere.

"Madden," said Olivia. "Party of four."

The hostess checked the list on her podium and smiled. "Follow me."

Olivia offered Milo her arm and led him to the table, Randall and Nancy following behind. Milo gave Olivia's hand a quick squeeze before he took a seat—a show of support. Olivia knew Milo could feel her heart beating faster than normal. Randall was charming, funny, and captivating, but he was also strange, otherworldly. Olivia liked that about him, but what would her best friends think?

Randall's eyes shone in the candlelight as he took his seat next to Olivia. He leaned in and whispered, "You look beautiful."

Randall had given her the day he'd promised. They'd bought a pair of bamboo fishing poles and some bait and sat for hours, sipping beers and shouting with excitement when their bobbers went under. They'd brought home four medium-sized fish, and Randall filleted, breaded, and pan-cooked them to golden perfection. Pleasantly buzzed on sunlight and beer, they climbed onto the roof and ate the fish with their bare hands, returning to Randall's room to make love and fall asleep. When they woke, Warren and Elijah had returned from a day of moving furniture (Elijah had started joining Warren on some of the less demanding moving jobs) and the four of them sat in the living room watching a terrible movie about a race of giant, mutant frogs who wreaked havoc on a small Floridian town until the hero discovered the location of their nest—a swamp full of Buick-sized tadpoles—and napalmed the bastards.

Olivia and Randall had rolled with laughter at the bad special effects and acting. Warren had even laughed at a few of the scenes. Elijah sat in sullen silence, nose buried in his Bible.

Randall had told Olivia she was beautiful three times before they left for the restaurant, and she blushed each time, as she was blushing now. She felt beautiful, and not because she'd done up her hair and put extra effort into her makeup. She'd felt just as beautiful earlier with worm guts on her hands. The simple act of being with Randall made her feel like she could fly.

"Thank you," Olivia said. "You look wonderful, too."

Their server poured water into their glasses. Milo got his bearings at the table, gingerly touching the glass and flatware in front of him. "Any dishes I should try?" he asked Olivia.

Olivia scanned the menu. "It's the usual Thai fare. I hear their Pad Thai is really good."

"Pad Thai it is," Milo said. "So, Nancy, Olivia was telling me Nosh is doing well in human trials."

Nancy looked up from her menu and beamed. "It's going better than we could have hoped. One of our participants weighed over three hundred pounds at the start of the trial, and after a few months, he's lost twenty pounds. He says it's the easiest diet he's ever been on. We've only lost three of the hundred and twenty participants so far."

"Lost? As in…" Randall drew a finger across his throat.

"Oh, Lord no!" Nancy said. "As in they dropped out of the study. They missed eating solid food, which is understandable. There's nothing we can do to replace the feeling of eating a fried chicken sandwich, or a burrito. That's why Nosh isn't for everybody—it's for people who are trying to lose weight when other avenues haven't worked. And it's not meant to be a permanent solution. Our goal is to help people get to a healthy weight and then empower them to have better eating habits moving forward."

"When's it going to be available to the public?" Milo asked.

Nancy said, "We're hoping to get FDA approval next year, so we're looking at Nosh being on the shelves soon after that."

Milo looked impressed. "That's incredible. I bet you'll get a lot of folks trying it out of curiosity. I know I will."

"If you'd like to try it, we could send you one of the seeding kits," Nancy said.

Randall asked, "Seeding kit?"

"What we'll be sending out to influencers," Nancy said. "You know, planting seeds of interest to help with brand visibility."

"Oh, right," Randall said.

Their server arrived and took their drink and food orders. Randall ordered the green curry dish, medium spicy—Olivia's recommendation since he'd expressed concern back at the apartment about not knowing what to order. "Get that and a Singha beer," she'd told him.

To Olivia's relief, after they'd placed their orders, the conversation flowed naturally, Nancy laughing at Milo's jokes, Randall asking Nancy and Milo about themselves and responding with easy wit and good humor when they asked him about himself.

The food arrived, and they dug in.

Randall looked up from his green curry. "Wow. This is incredible."

"The Pad Thai's really good, too," Milo said. Olivia caught the slightest undercurrent of wariness in Milo's tone, as if he found Randall's comment about his dish a little too enthusiastic. Olivia told herself she was imagining things, that the evening was going swimmingly.

Once he finished his Pad Thai, Milo said, "I need to visit the restroom. Olivia, could you show me where it is?"

"I have to go, too," Randall said, standing up. "I can show you."

Randall offered his elbow to Milo, like Olivia had shown him. Milo hesitated for a fraction of a second before reaching out and hooking his arm around Randall's and allowing him to lead him away.

Nancy fanned herself with the drink menu.

"Spicy bite?" Olivia asked.

"No," Nancy said. "*Milo.*"

Olivia's eyes widened in delight. "Oh, yeah. He's cute, huh?"

"You didn't tell me *how* cute. He's gorgeous."

Olivia leaned in. "Nancy Bell, do you have a crush?"

"I think I just might." The color in Nancy's cheeks deepened. "He's funny, too. You might have told me that, but I wasn't prepared for it. He's a charmer."

"Always has been," Olivia agreed. "You know…I could fake a tummy ache and ask you to give Milo a ride home so you two could have some time alone together."

"No, no! He's only in town for a few days. I don't want to monopolize his time."

"I can meet back up with him tomorrow for breakfast." Olivia grinned. "You know, when my stomach is feeling better."

"But he's here to visit you!"

"Listen, I'm good at reading him. I've been watching his body language since we got to the restaurant. He likes you, too."

A glint of hope sparkled in her eyes. "You're not just saying that?"

"Come on, Nancy. He'd be crazy not to be into you."

Nancy eyed her cautiously. "Didn't you two used to date?"

Olivia waved this away. "Years ago, and only for a few months. Believe me, if you two became an item, I would be over the moon."

Nancy gnawed on her thumbnail, considering. "I do really like him."

"Consider it your birthday gift to me," Olivia said.

"Oh, I almost forgot!" Nancy reached into her purse and held out a small red box. "Happy birthday."

Olivia opened the box and gasped. An iridescent stone lay inside, glistening with goldenrod yellow, emerald green, and blazing red, clasped in a gold setting connected to a delicate chain.

"It's a fire opal," Nancy said. "You mentioned you liked one of my rings a few months back, so I thought you might like to have the same kind of stone for yourself. What do you think?"

Olivia lifted the necklace out of the box. The flecks of color inside the opal danced in the candlelight. Knowing Nancy, this necklace probably cost more than Olivia's car. "Oh, Nancy...it's beautiful. I'm glad you've got a birthday coming up in a few months, so I have some time to think of what to get you."

Nancy scoffed. "Take me out for tacos. I like those better than jewelry, anyway." She helped Olivia clasp the necklace around her neck and they both admired it.

Tears welled in Olivia's eyes. "Thank you, Nancy. I love it. You're the best."

"Of course, love. Randall seems really great, by the way. I see what you mean about him being magnetic. He's got this devil-may-care charisma about him. No wonder you're a smitten kitten."

"I'll confess I was a little nervous about him meeting you and Milo," Olivia said. "He can be kind of eccentric."

"He's doing great," Nancy assured her. "And he's clearly crazy about you. I'm glad you found somebody who gets how great you are. Oops, here they come."

Randall led Milo back to the table and helped him find his seat. "What's this?" Randall asked, inspecting Olivia's necklace.

"It's a fire opal from Nancy. Isn't it beautiful?"

"It's incredible. I've never seen anything like it."

"It's a shifting kaleidoscope of color," Olivia told Milo. "It's stunning."

"Aw, lovely." Milo smiled. "If we're doing gifts, I brought one for you, too." He reached into his backpack and pulled out a paperback book.

Olivia read the title aloud: "*The Midnight Assassin: The Hunt for America's First Serial Killer*. Ooh, sounds fun!"

"It's about a serial killer in Austin in the late 1800s," Milo said. "I hear it's pretty interesting."

"It's right up my alley, for sure. I can't wait to start reading it." Olivia hugged Milo. "Thank you so much."

Their server arrived and cleared empty plates from the table. When he was gone, Randall said, "All right, last gift." He reached into a satchel he'd slung over the back of his chair and presented Olivia with a flat, rectangular gift wrapped in brown paper and tied with a dark red bow.

A low breath escaped Olivia's lips as she removed the wrapping. It was a collage made from sections of film strips. Olivia trailed her fingertips across the varnish holding the film in place. The texture felt both satisfying and foreboding. She inspected the sharp, tiny details of each strip—leaves lit up gold and green in a burst of sunlight; a night scene with a shining street and a shadowy figure lurking by a lamp post; a close-up of a pale woman's face, red lips slightly parted, perfect eyebrows furrowed over dark brown eyes; three different angles of a black gun held in a gnarled, grease-stained hand, the last of which showed a white flower of flame erupting from the barrel.

In the bottom corner, painted in what looked like red nail polish: *To Olivia*, along with a sketch of a smile with crooked teeth Olivia recognized as Randall's grin.

"Randall...this is amazing."

"Let me see!" Nancy said. "Oh wow...what movie is this from?"

"I don't know," Olivia said.

"I don't know either," said Randall. "I found it."

Nancy placed Milo's hand on the collage. "Feel that? What an interesting texture."

"Interesting," Milo agreed.

"Where did you find it?" asked Olivia.

"That's what makes it so special," said Randall. "It's from the Moloch house."

Olivia stared down at the collage as the tiny frozen slices of time in the film strips seemed to change. The shadowy figure standing in the moonlit street now struck her as possessing an otherworldly wickedness. The woman's dark eyes transformed into something eldritch and hungry. The gun, an instrument of senseless death. The images struck her as haunted, malignantly aware. It was as if the figures sealed beneath the clear coat of varnish had, while trapped in that glossy underworld, turned into creatures that were no longer human.

Randall touched her arm. "Olivia?"

"How did you get this from that house?" asked Olivia slowly. "It burned to the ground."

"After we left the hospital, I went back to see what was left of it," Randall said. "There were some things lying around the yard, and one of them was a film reel in its canister."

The restaurant seemed suddenly airless. "Why would you think I wanted a reminder of that place?" Olivia asked.

"It's where we met," Randall said. "I thought it would be significant to you."

Olivia felt her friends' eyes on her. She softened her voice. "Of course it's significant to me. It just took me by surprise. And...I'm actually not feeling well." She realized as she said the words that they were true.

Randall's brow lined with concern. "Oh no, what is it?"

"I don't know. Maybe something I ate."

"You do look a little pale," Randall said. "Do you want to get out of here?"

Olivia nodded. "I'm sorry, Milo, I think I need to get to a non-public bathroom, and Randall's place is ten minutes closer. Do you think you could catch a ride with Nancy back to my place?"

"Of course," Milo said. "No problem at all. If you're feeling better, maybe we can meet up for breakfast?"

"Exactly what I was thinking." Olivia smiled weakly. "I'll text you."

"Go ahead and get out of here," Nancy insisted. "Dinner's on me."

Olivia hugged Nancy and Milo and gathered her gifts together. Her head spun as she stepped out of the air conditioning and into the warm night.

"Are you okay?" Randall asked. "You look like you're about to faint."

"I'm all right," said Olivia. "Let's just get home."

HALF AN HOUR LATER, nestled in the darkness of his bedroom, Randall murmured into Olivia's ear. "I'm sorry about that gift. I wasn't thinking. Of course that was traumatic for you. I can throw it away if you want."

"I was just taken aback," Olivia said. "It's lovely, really."

"I don't ever want to do anything to hurt you," Randall said. "I love you so much."

Warmth flooded her veins. "I love you too, Randall."

"Did you have a good birthday?"

Olivia sighed contentedly. "I'm pretty confident that was the best birthday I've ever had. Milo and Nancy really liked you, by the way."

"I can't tell you how happy that makes me."

Olivia felt herself start to drift away. "You've got an early moving job tomorrow, right?"

"Mhmm," Randall nodded.

"Let's get some sleep," Olivia said.

Randall kissed her gently on the lips. Love swelled to fill the spaces where doubt may have otherwise thrived as Olivia slipped into a dreamless sleep.

28

ONE OF THE BENEFITS of Arachne's curse was being able to watch multiple events unfold at the same time. As Olivia and Azrael—or Randall, as he was calling himself—celebrated Olivia's birthday by fishing, dining with friends, and falling asleep in each other's arms, Arachne witnessed the downfall of the Colony.

When Lila woke in the dark, misty hours before dawn, she found Cade sleeping in a bassinet by her bed. She stared down at him for a few minutes, swaying on her feet, then bundled him up in a blanket and fled into the woods.

Arachne shifted her viewpoint from spider to spider, hundreds of her spies witnessing Lila's flight through the trees. Arachne wrung her hands, silently urging the young woman on. Lila's escape would likely mean disaster for Olivia and Randall, but Arachne couldn't help herself. She wanted the patriarchs of the Colony to pay for their sins.

Cade began to wail as the first gray tendrils of dawn brightened the horizon. Not long after he'd started to cry, Lila staggered across a set of train tracks, and followed them until she came to a train station.

A woman in an orange railroad vest approached Lila on the platform. Arachne's spiders were too far away to hear the exchange, but Lila must have been convincing, because the woman's phone was at her ear in under a minute, and ten minutes later, police vehicles began to arrive. Arachne's spiders drew close enough to hear Lila's impassioned plea that the officers rescue the women and children trapped by a madman. Lila was ghostly pale, her dark eyes huge on her gaunt face. "Grown men are marrying children," she told them. "They're raping us and forcing us to have babies. I begged them to let me go to the hospital, but they…" Lila went gray and collapsed into the arms of the nearest officer.

By the time the sun burned the nighttime dew into a thick haze of humidity—around the time Randall and Olivia were catching their first fish—paramedics had arrived to tend to Lila and her child. The officers at the train station had ascertained the location of the compound, and a warrant was in the works.

Arachne crept one of her spies into the ambulance driving Lila and Cade to the hospital. She watched through her dozens of spiders dispersed throughout the Colony as a fleet of police vehicles descended on the compound, sirens wailing. Henry Hatch staggered out of his office and stared. All around the Prophet, mothers, fathers, and children emerged from buildings and gaped at the officers as if they'd never seen outsiders before in their life. Many of them probably hadn't.

Robert Grayburn appeared behind Hatch and grasped his arm tightly. "Lila must have gone to the police. If that's true, then they've only just learned about us. This is private property, and they can't enter without a warrant. Don't tell them anything other than asking to speak with your lawyer."

Hatch nodded and smoothed out his graying hair. "Afternoon, officers," he said amiably, revealing his teeth in a preacher's grin. "What can we do for you?"

"You can cooperate while we investigate some claims about crimes happening on your property," said an approaching officer, holding up the warrant fast-tracked from the county judge.

Hatch's smile faltered. "Well, of course. We've got nothing to hide."

Chaos ensued.

As Olivia and her friends were sitting down for dinner, officers detained dozens of Hatch's followers. Arachne's pleasure at seeing men like Henry Hatch and Robert Grayburn zip-tied and shoved into vehicles was tempered by the inevitable fallout of the terror of the innocents within the Colony gates.

The worst moment came when one of the Fathers refused to step aside from the door of the birthing barracks until three officers wrestled him to the ground, bloodying his nose and zip-tying his wrists together. Inside the barracks was a teenage girl named Patricia who'd given birth a few days prior. Patricia tearfully pleaded with the officers to leave as they grimly radioed in paramedics.

Arachne ground her teeth in sympathetic fury at the child's distress. The men of the Colony deserved everything that was coming to them, and worse.

By the time Olivia and Randall fell asleep in each other's arms, the first news van appeared at the Colony. Officers rolled up a CRIME SCENE tape barrier to keep them out, but the cameras captured plenty.

29

"THANKS FOR BEING FLEXIBLE last night," Olivia told Nancy and Milo, sitting opposite from her in the diner booth. Morning sunlight shone brightly through the windows, reflecting off the white Formica tabletop and making her friends' faces glow. The diner's TV mentioned a hurricane named Ophelia nearing the Texan coastline.

"Did you two do anything after the Thai restaurant?" Olivia asked.

Nancy's dimples deepened as she repressed a smile. "We weren't quite ready to call it a night yet, so we went to a bar a few blocks away. One of those places where they take ten minutes to make a cocktail."

Olivia locked eyes with Nancy, silently confirming that much more than a cocktail had transpired. They must have been quiet a beat too long, because Milo cleared his throat and said, "Will one of you point me to the bathroom so you have a second to talk with more than your eyes?"

Nancy's cheeks flushed.

"It's at your 6 o'clock, straight back, all-gender so there's only one door," Olivia said.

"Thanks," Milo said, and Olivia could have sworn she saw him wink behind his sunglasses. He extended his cane and clicked his way across the room.

Olivia waited for Milo to close the bathroom door. "Dish."

"Oh, we totally hooked up," Nancy said in a hushed voice. "I hope that's not weird."

Olivia's cheeks glowed with excitement. "It's not weird. It's amazing. Can I ask—"

"It was unreal. I mean…just incredible. I don't think I've ever had so much immediate chemistry with anybody ever before. Please don't tell him I said that."

"I won't," Olivia assured her. "I promise. But I'm overjoyed. Are you going to see each other again?"

Nancy looked over her shoulder. "We didn't talk about it, but I would really like to. He seems so great."

"He's a gem, and so are you. The two of you would make one hell of a couple."

"It's too bad he lives in Utah," Nancy said. "I've done the long-distance thing before. It's not fun."

"Do you want to get some more alone time with him before he heads home?"

"No, no. I don't want to impose. He's here to see you!"

"He's got two more nights here before he flies back. Maybe you two could spend some more time together on his last night in town." Olivia gestured to the weather report on the TV, barely audible over the conversations in the diner. "If this hurricane hits like they say it's going to, his flight may get canceled anyway."

"Liv—"

"Come on, I let you play matchmaker a few months ago," Olivia reminded her, grinning. "Let me do it now. I promise it won't go as poorly as my date did."

"Oh, all right. But only if he's interested."

"I find it hard to imagine he won't be. Hush, he's coming back."

Milo navigated his way back to the booth and sat down. "Are you two hearing that forecast? It sounds like Austin's going to get hit by a pretty big storm. I don't love Salt Lake City, but at least we don't have to deal with hurricanes."

"You don't love Salt Lake City?" Nancy asked. "I thought things were going well."

Milo shrugged. "Eh, it's okay overall. I'm meeting lots of nice people, but I'm struggling to build deeper connections. My job's all right, but I'm not feeling passionate about it."

"All the more reason for you to visit Austin more often," Olivia said, winking at Nancy.

"Or move here," Milo said.

Olivia and Nancy gasped.

"Do you mean that?" Olivia asked.

Milo grinned. "I've been thinking about it. There's really not much keeping me in SLC, and hurricanes aside, Austin seems pretty great."

Olivia said, "I can't tell you how happy it would make me if you lived here."

"There's even a company I'd like to work for here. It's just a matter of—" Milo stopped talking and tilted his head.

Olivia strained to hear what Milo was hearing. There was nothing—just the murmur of conversation and the drone of the news station. "What is it?"

"Listen—the news."

Olivia made out a few muted syllables. "I can't hear it. What's going on?"

"There was a raid on a compound in Eland, Texas," said Milo. "A cult got busted there yesterday."

Olivia's flesh prickled. "A cult?"

"Yeah. They're saying a young woman carrying an infant walked onto a nearby train platform and said she was forced to give birth at the compound."

Nancy pressed her hand to her mouth. "Holy shit."

Milo listened. "They got her to the hospital. She and the baby are both stable."

"Thank God for that," Olivia said.

"The cult was called 'the Colony,'" Milo said.

Nancy shuddered. "Ugh, 'Colony' makes me think of ants. Or bees. A hive mind."

"There were over two hundred people in the compound. Some were pregnant girls in their early teens."

The diner grew quiet as more heads turned toward the TV. One of the servers turned the volume up. The banner read, *Cult Leader Arrested in Eland, TX.*

"How far is Eland from Austin?" Olivia asked.

A nearby man said: "Not far enough."

On screen, women and children marched as if headed for the gallows. One pregnant girl who looked no older than fourteen sobbed and staggered forward, her blue cotton dress stained with mud. Some of the women appeared to be singing or chanting, their faces pale and stoic.

"They don't look like they're being liberated," Olivia said.

"That's because they're brainwashed," Milo said.

Nancy shook her head. "This is nuts."

A clip played on the TV: a ruddy-faced man with white-streaked hair being thrust into a police car. The man's mugshot materialized on screen above the chyron: *Henry Hatch arrested on suspicion of sex trafficking and forced labor.*

Olivia stared at Henry Hatch. There was something familiar about his eyes...

"All right, who had the bacon and eggs combo?"

Olivia accepted her plate of food from the server, staring down at the undercooked bacon and overcooked eggs.

"Olivia...I've had something on my mind since last night," Milo said. "I'm sure it's nothing, but Nancy and I talked about it, and we thought it was worth mentioning."

Olivia hid a smile. Milo already using the word "we" seemed like a good sign for her friends' romance, even if she was pretty sure they were about to gang up on her.

"What is it?"

"It's about that gift Randall got you. He said he found the film canister in the ashes of the house you were in."

"Yeah?"

"Have you ever seen what happens when a film reel gets stuck in front of the projector lamp? It bubbles and melts in seconds. Those film canisters aren't insulated against heat. If there was a reel anywhere near the fire, the film inside would have been destroyed in seconds."

"What are you saying?" Olivia asked.

"We don't think Randall's being dishonest," Nancy rushed to say, "but he might not be telling you the whole truth, either."

All at once, the smell of her scrambled eggs turned Olivia's stomach. "Why would he lie to me about that?"

"I don't know," Milo said. "Just...something to think about."

"Yeah, okay," Olivia said. She turned around to look at Henry Hatch again, but the news had switched to a commercial.

30

RANDALL STARED AT THE mugshot on Warren's phone, propped up on the kitchen counter. His father's face stared back at him.

"I don't believe it," Randall whispered. "They got the bastard."

Elijah turned his tear-filled eyes on Randall. "Don't talk about our father like that."

Randall watched as his father's mugshot cross-faded into Robert Grayburn's. Randall shivered. Grayburn's eyes gleamed as if he was delighted at the chance to play a new kind of game. White text scrolled across a red bar at the bottom of the screen: *HURRICANE OPHELIA TO MAKE LANDFALL IN TEXAS BY EVENING.*

Warren paced in front of the couch like a caged animal, the morning light coming through the living room's sole window casting dark shadows under his eyes. He ran his hands through his hair as if scouring something dirty from his scalp.

Randall checked the time. "We'd better go," he told Warren. "We're going to be late for work."

Warren gaped at Randall as if he'd lost his mind. "Who cares about work? The Fathers will suspect we went to the authorities. They'll stop at nothing to find us now."

Randall scoffed. "And how exactly are they going to do that?"

"You're sure there's nothing you could have done to lead them here? Nothing at all?"

"Nothing," Randall insisted. "As far as they know, the Hatch children fell off the earth the moment we set foot outside of the Colony."

"We may as well have," said Elijah, angry tears spilling down his cheeks. "Why is this happening? What crime did the Prophet commit?"

"He's been brainwashing men and women, and marrying children," snapped Randall.

Elijah shot a defiant look at Randall. "Was Lila a child when you made a Shamed Woman of her?"

Warren stopped pacing. "Who's Lila?"

Randall glared at his half-brother. *Shut up, for both our sakes.*

Warren approached them in the kitchen. "Elijah, who is Lila?"

The truth came out of Elijah in a torrent: "Lila Munroe. Randall got her pregnant. It's why he ran away. He told her we'd go back for her, but he lied, and now she's brought the entire Colony crashing down because of it. And you'd better believe the first chance she gets, she's going to try and find us."

Rage darkened Warren's features. "Out. Both of you. Get out. Now."

Randall's anger at Elijah vanished all at once, replaced by a cool, calm feeling enveloping him in a soothing wave. A slow smile spread across his face. "We're not leaving."

A bitter edge sharpened Warren's voice. "I'm done risking my life to let you live here rent-free, parading the one woman I've felt anything for since Melinda in front of me—"

"The woman who'd be dead if not for me?" Randall asked.

Elijah muttered something.

"What was that?" asked Warren.

Elijah took a deep breath. "I said, there would never have been a fire if it hadn't been for Randall."

Warren's eyes widened. The dim yellow glow of the overhead kitchen light cast a wan sickle-shape in his eyes as he turned toward Randall. "You started the fire at the Moloch house?"

Randall said, "If you're going to start blaming me for every fire in Austin, then you'd better thank me for keeping your firefighting friends employed."

A muscle in Warren's cheek twitched as he drew close to Randall. "I want you to look me in the eye and tell me you didn't start the fire that almost killed Olivia."

"You're just angry because I was the one who saved her."

Warren's hands balled into fists. "Get the hell out of my apartment."

Randall smiled. "You're forgetting I'm not the only one with secrets. You've created a life for yourself here. A job, a place to live, a good reputation. It would be a shame if your firefighting buddies found out about where you really came from."

Warren's face twisted into an ugly shape. "I won't live under the same roof as you."

"Fine by me." Randall gestured to the door.

"This is my *home*, Randall."

"If you stay here," Randall said, "I'll step forward, and testify against my father. All three of us will face whatever threat that brings. But if you leave right now, no one will ever know who you really are. You can live out the rest of your life as a normal person. You have my word."

A vein pulsed in Warren's forehead. It occurred to Randall that Warren might hit him. It wouldn't change anything. He still held the winning hand.

Warren reached past Randall and grabbed his phone off the counter. He stalked down the hallway, jangled his keys from the hook, and slammed the door behind him.

Elijah stared daggers at Randall. "What have you done?"

Randall kept his voice even. "Despite your best attempts at sabotage, I've ensured our safety. And now you get to move from a couch to the main bedroom. I imagine Warren will be back for his things once he's had a chance to cool down and think things over. He's had to start over before. He can do it again."

"This is wrong, Randall," Elijah said, his bottom lip quivering with fury.

"This is the beginning of things going right," Randall said. "I promise."

31

By dusk, the sky outside of Randall's apartment was split in two: one half burning a bright, febrile red illuminated by the molten remains of the sun on the horizon, the other half the slate-gray arm of the storm reaching out to clutch Austin in its iron grasp. Hurricane Ophelia, after gathering strength over the Atlantic Ocean for days, had finally hit the coast. Seaside cameras tethered to docks captured footage of wind so violent it tore apart the waves bearing the storm to shore.

Arachne watched from the eyes of a wolf spider as Olivia pulled up outside of Randall's apartment. The nearby Shell sign cast a dull yellow light onto the deserted street. A thick haze clung to the streets as Olivia's steps echoed down the alley. She took a deep breath and knocked on Randall's door.

No one answered. Olivia tried the door and found it unlocked.

"Who's there?" Randall asked from his room.

"It's me," said Olivia.

Randall's head popped into view. "Olivia! I thought you were spending tonight with Milo."

"I was, but…Randall, we need to talk."

"Okay…come on in."

Arachne shifted her attention to the caged spider in Randall's bedroom as Olivia and Randall sat down on the edge of his bed.

Olivia wrung her hands. "Randall, were you a part of the cult that got raided in Eland?"

Randall tensed as if calculating his response. His shoulders sank. "Yes."

"Are you related to Henry Hatch?"

Randall hesitated, then said: "He's my father."

Olivia took a shaky breath. "I knew you grew up in an oppressive religious community, but…is everything they're saying about the Colony true? The underage marriage, the sexual assault, the brainwashing?"

"Yes," Randall said. "It's all true."

Olivia looked at him. "So, why wasn't it you?"

"What?"

"If all those things are true, why wasn't it you who exposed your father? Why was it a terrified young mother?"

"Good girl," Arachne whispered down below.

"There's a lot I didn't tell you about how I grew up," Randall said. "These people are dangerous. If I'd stepped forward, it would have put all of us in jeopardy. Me, Elijah, Warren, even you. When we left the Colony, we had to disappear for our own safety."

Olivia wiped tears from her eyes. "Is Randall your real name?"

Darkness swept across Randall's expression. "My name *was* Azrael Hatch."

"Azrael…"

"Olivia, please. That name feels like a noose around my neck."

"All right, Randall, how could you hide this from me?"

"I…I was terrified of you leaving me."

"Is there anything else you're not telling me?"

Randall hesitated before replying. "I don't know when my birthday is, or how old I am. I don't have a birth certificate or a social security number. I don't even know who my mother was. All my father ever told me was that she died giving birth to me. Anytime I asked about her, everyone in the Colony refused to answer." His eyes went glassy with tears. "If I hadn't run away and gotten Elijah out too, one of us would have been the new Prophet when our father died—probably Elijah, given that he worshiped the ground our father walked on. I tried to run away last year, and they beat me senseless and brought me back. I ran away again a few months before I met you, and I've spent every day since looking over my shoulder, praying they aren't coming to find me. You think what they're reporting on the news sounds bad? That's barely scratching the surface. I could tell you hundreds of horror stories about where I came from, but none of it matters. It's all in the past. If you'd been raised by a man like my father, you'd want to bury it, too."

Olivia looked over at Randall's pet spider Lilith, and for a few moments, Arachne felt like Olivia could see straight through to Hell.

"I never told you about my dad," Olivia said in a low voice.

Randall's gaze darted about, searching for the memory. "You told me he was a firefighter who died in a fire."

"I never told you I wanted him to die."

Randall drew in a deep breath. "Go on."

"When you tell people what your dad did for a living, and that he died in a fire, everyone assumes he's a hero. They also assume you don't talk about him because it's too painful." Olivia took a deep breath. "I haven't told anyone about this, not even Milo."

Arachne crept Lilith as close as the confines of her cage allowed.

"My dad got my mom pregnant their senior year of high school," Olivia said. "They got married right after high school graduation, and a few months later, I was born. I'm not sure when he started beating her, but my first memory is him knocking her out of her seat at the dinner table. I remember feeling scared and ashamed, but not surprised.

"As the years went on, my mom made it clear that what was happening in our house was a shameful family secret— both the abuse, and how much she and my father drank. I wasn't allowed to tell anybody what was going on. If I did, Dad would lose his job, and we'd lose the house. I'd be taken away and given to strangers. I lay awake at night, terrified my dad would hurt my mom badly enough for someone to notice."

"Did he hurt you?" Randall asked.

Olivia traced a finger over the flame tattoo on her wrist. "Feel here."

Randall did, following a curve of scar tissue amidst the warm swells of color. "I didn't realize this was covering a scar," he said softly. "What did he do?"

"He was drunk driving with me in the back seat. He ran a red light and a pickup truck T-boned our car. The impact made my wrist bone break through the skin. I was five years old."

Randall held her hand as she continued.

"Things got really bad after that. He hit me sometimes, usually because I talked back to him or defended my mom. That's why he called me 'Firebug'—because of my temper. The night before he died, a few weeks after my tenth birthday, I told him I wished he was dead, and he slapped me so hard my feet left the ground. When three firefighters came to our house the next evening with their helmets in their hands, I knew my wish had come true. Mom collapsed on the floor and wept, but I knew she was crying from relief. I made myself cry too, but I didn't feel sad. I felt powerful. I wanted him to die, and he did."

Olivia looked at her wrist. "I acted out a lot in my teenage years. I was resentful of my mom for not standing up to my dad when he was alive, and for drinking herself into a stupor every night after he was gone. I got into a lot of fights at school, got suspended a few times. My sleep got really messed up, and I started sleepwalking. Once, I sleepwalked halfway down the block and came home to find I was locked out. My mom was passed out drunk and no amount of banging on the door would wake her up, so I broke a window to get back inside. In the morning, she accused me of sneaking out on purpose, and grounded me for a month. I was around fifteen when I used a fake ID to get this tattoo. My mom was furious when she saw it, and we argued back and forth for a few minutes before I stormed out. When I came back home, I found Mom collapsed in the bathroom in a pool of blood. She'd hit her head on the toilet and had been lying on the floor long enough for most of the blood to dry. Thankfully, she was still breathing, and she made a full recovery in the hospital.

"She went into a program of recovery after that. Eventually, she was well enough to get a job working at a diner and started going to night school. By the time I graduated high school, she was working as a junior developer at a small tech company." Olivia sniffed. "She and I kind of both pulled our lives together around the same time."

Randall stared at her for a few heartbeats. "What was your father's name?"

"George," Olivia said.

"Wouldn't you give anything to never have to say his name again?" Randall asked.

Olivia looked at him with eyes brimming with tears. "Yes."

Randall kissed her. Fresh tears rolled down Olivia's cheeks as Randall pulled her close.

"No more secrets, okay?" Olivia breathed.

"No more secrets," Randall promised.

Arachne watched through Lilith as Azrael and Olivia made love and fell asleep.

Down below, Arachne scowled. Azrael had more than just a storm headed his way.

32

OLIVIA WOKE AT DAWN to what sounded like a volley of stones pelting Randall's window. She sat up, parted the drapes, and watched the street go white with hopping chunks of ice.

The tall, glowing Shell sign of the nearby gas station rocked in the wind as dark clouds roiled low in the sky. A flash of white light lit up the block, and a split second later, a peal of thunder shook the building.

"Good morning," Randall said, kissing Olivia under her jawline. The hair on the back of her neck stood up. She felt the way she did in her telekinesis dreams.

A knock fell on Randall's bedroom door. Randall waited for Olivia to fumble her pajamas on. "Come in," he said.

Elijah opened the door and stood wide-eyed in the doorway. He'd already outgrown the pajamas Randall bought him a few months ago, and his stomach and ankles were exposed.

"This is bad," Elijah said.

"It's just a patorm, Elijah," Randall said, rising from bed and stepping into his sweatpants. "We'll be fine."

"The TV's saying there are tornadoes."

"Go hide in the closet if you're nervous."

Elijah paled with anger and walked away. Olivia heard the hallway closet door close a few seconds later.

A voice announced from the television: "An F3 tornado is moving toward the city center of Austin."

Outside, the hail stopped and turned into a deluge of rain. The wind howled like a wounded creature. Olivia reached for Randall's hand, felt his pulse racing in time with hers. "Maybe we should get in the closet, too."

"Don't let Elijah scare you," said Randall.

"I'm not scared, it's just—"

Randall's window lit up in a blinding flash as a lightning bolt struck the Shell sign. A deafening *CRACK!* rattled the building.

"Ka-*POW!*" shouted Randall, laughing. "I've never seen one hit so close before!"

Dazzled by the lightning bolt, Olivia looked down to see her arm hair standing up straight. "Look at my arm!"

Randall swept his fingers over the tiny, raised hairs. "Wow."

The darkened, smoking Shell sign rocked in the wind. The S had shattered, leaving HELL behind.

It was then, under the hypnotizing sway of the charred HELL sign, through sheets of rain, with Randall's fingertips brushing her arm, that Olivia spotted a person hunched and shivering beside one of the gas station pumps. It was a petite woman, by the look of the pale wrist emerging from the oversized jacket sleeve and the blonde hair hanging from the hood obscuring her face. She held a bundled-up object in her arms.

"Randall, look!"

"What? A tornado?"

"No, look! There, by the gas pump!"

Randall's fingers gripped hers like a vice. "Jesus Christ."

"I think she's holding a baby," Olivia said, breaking free of Randall's grasp and running from the room.

"Olivia!"

Elijah shouted from the closet: "What's going on?"

"There's a person out there!" Olivia yelled back, opening the front door. Propelled by a gust of wind, the door slammed into Olivia's nose. She stumbled back, dazed, and shook her head against the stars blooming in her vision. A sheet of rain soaked her in seconds. Over the howl of the wind, she heard a rumbling sound, like an oncoming train.

"Who's out there?" asked Elijah.

"No one worth risking her life over," Randall grasped Olivia's shoulders, pulling her back. "Olivia, come back inside!"

Olivia shoved Randall away and ran out into the alley.

33

Lila Monroe huddled next to the gas pump, barely sheltered by the overhang groaning and shifting in the wind. Rain pelted her from one direction and then the other, soaking through her coat. Cade, feverishly hot in her grasp, screamed in awful, squalling cries.

She was a fool. She'd thought she could slip away from her foster parents' house with some cash stuffed in her pocket, catch a train to Austin, and find Azrael. She'd never been to a city before and wasn't prepared for how massive it was. Her days in Austin had been marked by hunger, exhaustion, and terror. When Cade wasn't eating or sleeping, he was crying. She'd walked until her feet bled and sobbed until her throat was dry. Even if she and Cade survived the storm, she wasn't sure where her next meal was coming from.

The worst part was that somebody was following her.

Lila kept seeing the same rail-thin man with a shabby coat and a salt-and-pepper beard, lurking around corners, never far from sight. At first, Lila had suspected he was someone the Prophet sent to punish her for exposing his cult…but her gut told her this man had something else on his mind.

The night before the storm hit Austin, Lila had turned a street corner and found herself face to face with the man.

He grinned at her and winked. She'd run away as fast as her legs could carry her, Cade jostling in her arms. Later, when she lay curled up under an abandoned blanket in an alley a mile or so away, she thought she remembered seeing a spider perched on the man's shoulder. Her skin had crawled until she passed out from exhaustion.

Lila woke in the morning to the wind buffeting the filthy blanket covering her and her son. She needed to find someplace safe to hide, somewhere the angry clouds couldn't drown her in their deluge. The hail began to pelt her head and shoulders moments before she ducked under the relative safety of the canopy covering four machines that smelled like Father Clark's tractor. She curled up next to one of them and cast her eyes downward, praying the shelter would be enough to protect her child from the storm.

Please, please let him survive this, even if I don't.

A bolt of lightning tore apart the world in an explosion of light. The thunderclap was like a punch to the chest. Cade went silent for a few breaths and then shrieked louder.

The ground shook beneath her—the storm converging into a single, murderous funnel that would snuff out their lives.

Better the storm than the man following her, Lila thought bitterly.

Lila heard a splashing sound over the din of the storm and looked up to see a woman running toward her through the downpour. The woman's pink pajamas were plastered to her skin and her hair flew out behind her like coils of copper.

"There's a tornado coming!" the woman shouted, holding out her hand. "You're not safe here!"

Lila stared at the woman's outstretched hand. Could she trust her with her baby's life? Could she afford not to?

Lightning struck again, dangerously close, and thunder cracked across the gas station.

The woman yelped in fear but held her ground. "Come on!"

Lila reached out and allowed herself to be pulled to her feet.

The woman drew her out into the driving rain as the rumbling noise grew louder. Lila chanced a look over her shoulder and watched a tornado come into sight a few blocks away. The thin, gray funnel moved toward her hypnotically. Lila cast her eyes to the nest of debris where it connected with the ground, and time slowed to a crawl.

The man who'd been following her was at the base of the twisting funnel. She knew it was him, though his silhouette was utterly black, his shape cut out of the fabric of reality. He was drawing closer in pace with the storm.

Lila's hand slipped free of the woman pulling her down the alley. The wind whipped her hair around her face as she stopped and stared.

"What are you doing?" the woman shouted. "We need to get inside!"

"Do you see him?" Lila asked.

The woman followed Lila's line of sight and gasped. "Is...is that..."

The remaining four letters of the charred Shell sign broke free of their post and sailed into the sky. A shower of sparks rained down on them. Lila and the woman screamed and shielded themselves.

A voice called from the alley: "Hurry, get inside, it's coming!"

Blinded by rain and debris, Lila ran toward the voice. The rain stopped suddenly as she entered a dark hallway. The woman who'd saved her slammed the door behind her and led her into a closet, where she huddled beside her in the darkness. Her baby howled in her arms.

The rumbling grew louder. The closet door rattled on its hinges. Lila could make out somebody's hand on the doorknob, holding the door closed. Breaking glass chimed over the roar of the storm, the floor rocking under her feet like a ship at sea. A tremendous shredding and groaning sound drowned out Cade's screams.

Three distinct, heavy knocks fell on the closet door.

Then, all at once, everything stopped. The thunderous noise disappeared, replaced by the drumming of heavy rain. Through what little light shone through the bottom of the closet door, Lila saw the hand holding the doorknob start to turn it.

"Wait!" Lila said. "He's out there."

"What are you talking about?" asked a voice beside her in the darkness. He sounded familiar, like something from a dream.

"The man in the storm," said Lila.

"The *what*?"

Lila stammered, "I...I thought I saw someone."

"If anyone was out there, the sorry bastard is gone," he said, throwing open the door.

34

Olivia stared in shocked silence.

She stepped out of the closet and into the pouring rain. The building was destroyed; the closet where they'd taken cover was now the only standing structure among a jagged pile of rubble. A section of the building's roof clung to the top of the closet, making it look like one of those western rock formations with a ton of rock perched on an impossibly narrow base. It was a marvel the closet hadn't been crushed under the weight bearing down on it.

"Get out," Olivia said.

None of the closet's inhabitants moved. Elijah and Randall stared at the woman as if she'd sprouted wings.

"Get out of there!" Olivia shouted. "The closet's going to collapse."

Randall ignored her. "Lila?"

"Is that really you?" asked Elijah.

"Yes," said Lila, not taking her dark eyes from Randall.

Olivia stood watching them, soaked through by rain. "Please, you all need to get out of there right now."

The closet groaned and settled a few degrees to the side.

Lila said to Randall, "The storm led me to you."

"Is that...?" said Randall, paling as he stared at the shrieking baby in her arms.

"Yes," said Lila. "It's your son. His name is Cade."

A swell of vertigo hit Olivia as the closet tilted a few inches farther. "Your son?"

Lila stood and approached Olivia. She lifted her jacket away from the baby's face.

The baby stopped crying and looked up at Olivia. Its eyes were bright, alert, and so like Randall's—so like *Azrael's*—that it took Olivia's breath away.

A load-bearing structure inside of Olivia ripped away from its mooring. She scanned the horizon, the grim sprawl of debris obscured by curtains of driving rain. Her world, torn apart in an instant.

Azrael appeared at her side. "Listen, I can explain—"

"You lied to me."

"Olivia, please—"

The baby began to cry again. The sound filled Olivia with rage. Elijah hunched in the tilting closet, wide-eyed and trembling, like a snared rabbit.

"I knew you were hiding something," Olivia said. "I just didn't think it was *this*."

Azrael looked helplessly at the wailing child in Lila's arms. He drew close to Olivia, squeezed her hand, put his lips to her ear, and whispered: "They're my past. All I care about is my future with you."

Olivia wrenched her hand from his. A desolate, searing anger unfurled its wings in her chest.

Something deep inside of her lashed out like a whip.

With a deafening CRACK, the closet collapsed under the weight of the roof above it.

Elijah realized what was happening an instant before the walls closed in. He leapt forward, but not fast enough.

Both of his legs were inside the closet when it flattened to the ground.

The wrath that had moments ago filled Olivia's every fiber vanished. A terrible coldness rushed in to fill its place.

Elijah looked back at his legs, crushed underneath the wreckage, and let loose a scream Olivia would hear in her nightmares for the rest of her life.

AT THE HOSPITAL, GURNEYS bearing the injured and the dying lined the walls. Concussions, gashes, broken bones, punctured lungs. One woman walked in with a dinner fork jammed into her eye. The hallway echoed with moans, screams, sobs.

Olivia sighed and rubbed her eyes. Were Milo and Nancy among the injured? Or the dead? The thought was too terrible to contemplate. Her cell phone was somewhere under a pile of rubble, and she couldn't stomach the idea of standing in line to use one of the hospital's few working phones, so for the time being, she had to hope they made it out all right.

She wasn't ready to tell them what she'd learned about her lover, either.

And then there was the split second where it had looked like the dark silhouette of a man was walking with the tornado, drawing it towards her...

Olivia shook the thought away and checked the clock: almost midnight. The idea that not even a full day had passed felt like emotional whiplash. Just hours ago, she'd been in love. She'd been blind.

Randall—Azrael—had begged her not to leave him. Olivia had ignored him, telling him to go find help. Azrael had complied, climbing over debris toward the sound of sirens until he was out of sight. Olivia found a T-shirt in the rubble and used it as a tourniquet on Elijah's legs, holding his hand as his heaving breaths faded into gray-faced shock. Lila watched, holding her squalling baby, glaring at her in silence.

It had taken what felt like hours for an ambulance to arrive, and another eternity for a forklift to show up and lift the wreckage away from Elijah. Olivia got into the ambulance with Elijah and pierced Azrael with an angry stare as he stood outside the doors.

"Don't leave me," Azrael had pleaded.

"She needs you, Azrael," Olivia responded. "I don't."

The paramedics had closed the ambulance doors and Olivia held Elijah's cold, limp hand as they raced to the hospital.

"Olivia Madden?"

The doctor standing in front of her looked as tired as Olivia felt. The badge clipped to his scrubs read: COLEMAN.

"Yes?"

"You brought in Elijah Fisher, correct?"

Olivia nodded.

"Can you come with me?"

Olivia followed the doctor numbly from the waiting room. "I can't wait for us to get wherever we're going. Just tell me if he's alive or not."

"He's alive," Dr. Coleman said. "We needed to amputate both his legs below the knee, in addition to stitching up several lacerations. He's got a long road of recovery ahead of him, but he's going to survive. He came out of anesthesia about half an hour ago, and he's been moved from the PACU into his own room. I just have some questions for you." Dr.

Coleman led Olivia into a private room and gestured for her to sit. "What relation are you to Elijah?"

"I'm a...friend," said Olivia.

Dr. Coleman nodded. "I was told that he came in without any identification or health insurance information. Does he have any immediate family?"

Olivia looked down at her hands, then back at the doctor. "If I tell you something, will it be kept in confidence? There's some kind of patient-doctor confidentiality thing, right?"

"Physician-patient privilege prohibits me from using anything a patient tells me against them in a court of law, and of course there's HIPAA." Dr. Coleman glanced toward the closed door and lowered his voice. "I will tell you I think that child has been through enough, and I'm not interested in making more trouble for him."

Olivia let out a slow breath. "His name isn't Elijah Fisher. It's Elijah Hatch. He's the son of the cult leader Henry Hatch, the one who just got arrested. He's been in hiding since he escaped the Colony earlier this year."

Dr. Coleman eyed her seriously. "That explains some of the things he said as he was getting prepped for surgery. How do you know him?"

"I was dating someone who was helping him."

"Did you live with him?" asked Dr. Coleman.

"No."

"Is his caretaker available?"

Olivia's chest tightened. "His caretaker was his brother, but I don't know if he's going to be able to help him anymore."

"Do you know how old he is?"

"I don't know. I don't think he does, either. I would guess between twelve and fourteen."

"I've got to report this to a social worker," Dr. Coleman said gently.

Olivia swallowed. "If you do, you have to make sure they keep his identity quiet."

A concerned line appeared in Dr. Coleman's forehead. "Why?"

"Because he's in danger. He knows what went on in the Colony, and now that Henry Hatch has been exposed, Elijah's a liability."

"Well, he's going to have to deal with years of physical and occupational therapy. He's going to have to trust the system to keep him safe."

Olivia ran her fingers through her hair. She caught something stiff and pulled out a leaf. "Can I see him?"

Dr. Coleman nodded. "Follow me."

Olivia followed the doctor down a series of hallways, the din of the hospital fading away as they walked. Her nose prickled at the antiseptic scents of gauze and ammonia. Dr. Coleman turned a corner and led Olivia into Elijah's room.

Olivia approached the bed, staring at the empty space where the lower half of Elijah's legs should have been. His face was ashen, his lips softly parted, eyes closed. His arms were hooked to a half-dozen tubes. A faint beeping sound kept time with his pulse.

"Elijah," said Dr. Coleman. "You have a visitor."

Elijah's eyes opened and focused blearily on Olivia.

Olivia's breath caught in her throat. "Hi, Elijah."

Elijah's lips trembled and his eyes glazed with tears. "They took my legs."

The rasp in his voice made Olivia want to cry. She reached for his hand and squeezed it. "I know everything seems hopeless now, but I promise it's not. Everything's going to be okay. Is there anything I can do for you? Anything I can get you?"

Elijah's eyes widened. "Can you get my Bible?"

"I'm not sure I—" Olivia began, thinking of the pile of rubble that used to be Azrael's apartment. Then she thought of the anger she'd felt right before Elijah's legs were crushed. How it felt like she'd been the one to bring the closet crashing down.

Olivia sighed. "I'll try."

Elijah's monitor beeped faster as his pulse accelerated. "You have to find it. It's all I have left…"

Dr. Coleman fiddled with something on the machines by Elijah's bed, and Elijah closed his eyes, his breathing slowing.

"Let's let him rest," Dr. Coleman said quietly, leading Olivia into the hallway.

Olivia took a deep breath and let it out shakily. "What now?"

"I'll reach out to a social worker and inform them of the situation so they can determine next steps. As a heads up, based on what you told me, they may decide to put him in protective custody."

"What does that entail?" Olivia asked.

"He'd be moved somewhere secure. It's possible they wouldn't tell us where for safety reasons."

"Oh," Olivia said. A profound weariness settled over her.

"Go home and get some sleep," Dr. Coleman said. "One of us ought to."

Olivia walked for over an hour to get back to her house, which had been mercifully untouched by the storm. She'd lost her house keys along with everything else, so she climbed through her bedroom window, peeled herself out of her filthy pajamas, and chucked the collage Azrael had given her in the trash.

35

ARACHNE PEERED UP AT Hades from the eyes of the spider resting on His shoulder. He took a drag from a cigarette in the smoking area outside the hospital where Elijah was recovering. A gust of wind lifted a graying lock of hair from His forehead. He squinted up at the glow of the streetlights as storm clouds roiled low overhead and a gale of rain swept across the parking lot.

"Something happened when the closet came crashing down on Elijah, didn't it?" Arachne asked. Down in Hell, she shivered as a cluster of spiders climbed her spine. "It felt like...I don't know how to describe it. Like something *snapped*."

Hades blew out a jet of smoke through a crooked grin.

"Why are you here?" Arachne asked Him.

Hades took another pull from His cigarette. "You have eyes in Elijah's room, yes?"

Arachne shifted her attention to the single spider she'd been able to trundle into Elijah's recovery room. "Yes."

"Watch."

Arachne waited, and at length, Dr. Coleman walked into Elijah's room and stood by his bed, staring at him. The hairs on Arachne's spider's legs stood on end.

"What's he doing?"

"He's trying to sort out how he can get Elijah out of the hospital without getting caught," Hades said.

"Why?"

"Because Dr. Mark Coleman is an exiled son of the Colony, too. He's Melinda's older brother."

"Melinda...the girl Warren fell in love with? The one who'd have married Grayburn if Hatch hadn't deemed her a Shamed Woman?"

"The very same," Hades said. He nodded to a passing pedestrian who shot Him a sidelong glance. "When Mark Coleman was seven years old, his mother packed a bag and left, leaving Mark and his little sister Melinda in the care of their alcoholic father. Bereft and seeking direction, Mark's father took him and his sister Melinda to the Colony. Mark may have lived at the Colony indefinitely if he hadn't witnessed Robert Grayburn dragging a body into the woods when he was ten years old. When Mark went to the Prophet and told him what he'd seen, Henry Hatch declared he was to be exiled for blasphemy. Mark ran into the woods, barely escaping Grayburn chasing after him."

Arachne crept her spider closer to Dr. Coleman, trying to imagine him as a frightened little boy. "What happened then?"

Hades watched as a woman cradling a broken wrist hurried past him into the hospital. "Mark Coleman was homeless for a few months before finding his way into the foster care system, where he was shifted from foster to foster until he reached adulthood. A kind-hearted guidance counselor helped Mark apply for a student loan so that he could attend a good college, which in turn led him to pursue a career in medicine. He's kept to himself his entire adult life—a few acquaintances, but no real friends, and no lovers. He's considered calling the police many times over the years to tell them the truth about the Colony, but he's not certain he even remembers what he saw correctly, or if the leadership of the Colony would allow themselves and their followers to be taken alive if the authorities closed in."

"I don't remember seeing a 'Father Coleman' at the Colony," Arachne said. "What happened to Mark's father?"

Hades snuffed out His cigarette against His shoe and flicked it into a nearby bush. "Mark's father was caught stealing from Father Clark's stash of whiskey a few years after Mark was exiled. Robert Grayburn strangled him in the pantry and buried his body in the woods." Hades wiped His hands on His pants and strode into the hospital. "When Dr. Coleman saw the news of the raid on the Colony, he scoured the coverage in vain for any mention of Melinda. He called the police, but they said they couldn't divulge the names of any of the victims. He had begun to despair that his sister was alive, until he learned one of his patients was Henry Hatch's banished son, and saw an opportunity."

"An opportunity to do what?"

Hades strolled through the metal detector and past security. "To use Elijah to get back to Melinda."

"How?"

"He figures if he can contact Colony leadership and tell them that he can get Elijah back to them, they'll agree to let him see his sister again, if she's still alive. It's why he told Olivia Elijah was going to be taken into protective custody—he planted that seed, so if Olivia returns to find Elijah gone, she won't raise many questions."

Arachne watched Dr. Coleman gnaw on his fingernail as he stared at the slow rise and fall of Elijah's chest in the beeping stillness of his hospital room. "How's he going to get him out without getting caught?"

"He wouldn't have much luck without my involvement, I'll tell you that much," Hades said, reaching out to yank down the handle on a fire alarm.

Bright lights strobed and a flat, strident horn blasted from speakers lining the corridor. Hades kept walking as all around Him, nurses leapt into action and patients covered their ears.

In Elijah's room, Dr. Coleman startled, looking around.

"That's your plan?" Arachne scoffed. "Pulling the fire alarm?"

Hades picked up the pace. A pair of nurses hustled past Him toward where He'd pulled the alarm. Hades reached out and brushed His fingers over a sensor at the end of a hallway. It beeped, allowing Him to slip into the adjacent door.

Lights flashed and alarms blared as Hades strode up to three large yellow machines, each bearing a CAT logo. "The power grid is about to go down for this whole side of Austin," Hades said. "This hospital has backup generators, but when those fail, it will be necessary to move dozens of patients to a nearby hospital. Power failure in three...two..."

The halogen lights above the generators flickered to darkness. A metallic click sounded from inside the generators and the massive machines growled to life. The lights above came back on just as Hades punched His hand into the machine and pulled out a handful of wires and cables. The generator threw off a cough of smoke and rumbled into silence. He walked over and did the same to the second, and the third.

The room went dark other than the flashing strobes of the fire alarm.

Moments later, a series of dim lights—presumably battery-operated—lit up the room in a dull orange glow.

Hades winked at Arachne's spider, took a step to the left, and disappeared.

Over the next several minutes, the hospital descended into bedlam. "The gennies aren't coming on," shouted a nurse outside Elijah's room. Arachne watched as nurses and doctors wheeled critically injured patients on gurneys out to ambulances to transfer them to a nearby hospital while technicians worked furiously to fix the generators. Arachne counted at least three patients who passed away before an ambulance could ferry them to another hospital. Her lips thinned with cold anger at the senseless collateral damage caused by Hades's meddling.

In the midst of this mayhem, Dr. Coleman collected opioids, antinausea meds, hospital gowns, catheter bags, antibiotics, saline, and several doses of ketamine. He returned to Elijah's room and injected him with a healthy dose of ketamine, then loaded Elijah onto a wheelchair along with the pilfered supplies stuffed into Elijah's bag with the rest of his belongings. He typed something into the battery-powered med cart in Elijah's room—Arachne guessed a transfer to another hospital—then wheeled Elijah out into the hall.

Dr. Coleman froze as a red-faced hospital security guard hustled past down the hall, holding his breath as he headed toward the loading dock. Dr. Coleman shot a glance at one of the security cameras as he passed, and Arachne could feel him praying it had shut off.

When he was sure nobody was watching, Dr. Coleman rolled Elijah's wheelchair out the loading dock doors and into the dark, stormy parking lot. Arachne watched through a series of spiders nestled in the trees as he hurried through the parked cars, opened the back door of his car, and hefted Elijah inside—an undertaking made easier by the lack of

Elijah's legs below the knee. By the time Dr. Coleman was finished, he was drenched from the downpour.

He ran back to the hospital, rushed into the staff changing room, traded his wet scrubs for street clothes, and grabbed a few things out of his locker.

"Hey, Dr. Coleman!"

Dr. Coleman froze as he saw a nurse approaching him, her face heavy with exhaustion. "Dr. Coleman, where are you going? We need help in—"

Mark stopped her. "I need to go home. I just found out my mother was killed in the storm."

The nurse blanched. "Oh, Mark...oh no..."

Mark hurried away before she asked any questions. Arachne thought about what Hades had said about Mark's mother abandoning him when he was young...for all Mark knew, his story about his mother being dead might have been true.

36

MARK COLEMAN PULLED OUT of the hospital parking lot with his heart in this throat. He felt dizzy, dislocated from reality. He forced himself to take slow, deep breaths as he drove. He wasn't going to get pulled over. There was no reason for anyone to suspect Elijah wasn't on his way to another hospital, not with everything thrown into chaos by the power outage.

When Mark parked outside his apartment, the rain had stopped, and the night was calm and still. Mark scanned the complex. How many of his neighbors had security cameras? It didn't matter, he assured himself. His neighbors wouldn't check the footage unless they had a reason to.

Mark reached between the seats and prodded Elijah's shoulder. "Elijah, wake up."

Other than the slow rise and fall of his chest, Elijah was still.

Mark took a shaky breath. He had to be fast.

Mark crept to his front door, unlocked it quietly, and pushed it open. He slunk around to the passenger side of his car and dragged Elijah out of the backseat by his shoulders. Elijah's body seemed to have grown heavier on the drive home. Mark thought his heart was going to hammer through his chest as he carried Elijah up the steps to his apartment and laid him gingerly on his bed.

Mark waited for his heartbeat to return to something closer to normal before going to retrieve the supplies and wheelchair from the trunk. He changed Elijah into a clean hospital gown, scrubbed him down with a warm cloth, administered a catheter, hung a saline bag, treated his wounds, and returned to the room with a microwave meal to find Elijah looking around the room in confusion.

Mark set the microwave meal down on his dresser. "Hello, Elijah."

Elijah blinked as if trying to sort out if he were awake or dreaming. "Who are you? Where am I?"

"My name is Dr. Mark Coleman," Mark said. "I was exiled from the Colony, like you. This is my apartment."

Elijah grunted with pain. "Ah...my legs..."

"Oh, hang on," Mark said, carefully injecting a small amount of morphine into Elijah's saline drip.

Elijah sighed as the drug took effect. "I don't understand."

"You want to be reunited with your family, right?" Mark asked, checking Elijah's pulse. "I'm sure they're worried about you. If you'd stayed at the hospital, I'm not sure you'd have ever seen them again."

Elijah blinked heavily as his pulse slowed. "My family?"

"I'm going to get you back to them. Your father's being held without bail right now, but I'm going to contact the other Fathers of the Colony so you can be reunited."

"Reunited?" Elijah drew each syllable out slowly. "You mean I'm going home?"

Mark looked at Elijah sadly. If Elijah hadn't already seen the news of the raid, now wasn't the time to tell him. "Yes, Elijah. You're going home."

37

By the time Olivia returned to the site where Azrael's apartment used to be, some of the rubble had already been cleared away. She recognized some items in the wreckage as Azrael's—a painting, a section of his bedspread, his bathtub, cracked in half. She expected to feel pain at seeing these items, or regret, or fury—but she felt nothing. It was like looking at the remnants of a dream. About a dozen folks with thick gloves and resolute expressions stomped across the wreckage, tossing items into the dumpsters and the back of trucks.

Olivia searched through the debris for what seemed like a long time. At one point she stopped, dazed, forgetting what she was looking for. Elijah's Bible. Of course.

She was close to giving up when she saw something small and brown sticking out of the scorched and S-less "HELL" sign that once glowed above the Shell station. She climbed over a pile of concrete and broken glass to get to it.

The tornado shot the Bible like a holy bullet into the E of the ruined sign. She pulled it out, opened the cover, and read the handwritten note on the first page.

To my son, destined to lead. -HH

Olivia closed the Bible and shuddered.

"Well," she muttered. "Got your Bible, Elijah. Let's see if I still have a car."

As it turned out, her car was right where she left it. Her first thought, approaching it from behind, was that it might not be as bad as she'd feared. Then she came around to the front. It looked like a cannonball had been fired through her windshield.

Maybe it wasn't totaled—after all, it was just broken glass and a few banged-up seats. She peered into the back seat window to see which object had done the damage, and froze.

Lodged in the cushions of her backseat were the mangled remains of the terrarium that had adorned Randall's bedroom nightstand. The one that contained his pet spider, Lilith.

Olivia backed away from her car. That spider was in it somewhere. She knew it. Roaming the lacerated remains of her vehicle like a walking curse.

"Nope," said Olivia. She didn't care what her insurance company said. She wasn't ever driving that car again.

WHEN OLIVIA ARRIVED BACK at the hospital, she went to Elijah's room and found the bed empty.

Trembling, Olivia approached the receptionist's desk. "I'm here to see Elijah Fisher," she said. "Can you tell me where he is?"

The weary nurse clicked on her keyboard. "I'm not seeing a patient by that name."

"I visited him yesterday. He was in that room, but there's someone else there now."

"He must have been discharged, then," the nurse said, checking her watch.

"But he—" Olivia stopped when it hit her. Vanishing into thin air was exactly what people did when entering protective custody. Whatever social worker got assigned to Elijah's case must have decided he wasn't safe in Austin and moved him somewhere else. Somewhere Henry Hatch's followers wouldn't find him.

Olivia looked down at Elijah's Bible. She wouldn't get a chance to give it to Elijah after all, but at least he'd be safe. She could hold onto it for him in case he ever resurfaced.

"Is there a phone I can use?" Olivia asked the nurse.

The nurse pointed, and Olivia called the two phone numbers she had memorized: her mother and Milo. Her mother had, of course, been beside herself with worry and blubbered through Olivia's reassurances that she was all right. Milo sounded so relieved he was almost angry. "We drove to your place, but you weren't there, so we looked for you at Randall's place, but it had been completely leveled... we've been driving around visiting all the hospitals, but you hadn't been checked in anywhere. We've been losing our minds." Milo's voice broke. Olivia heard Nancy crying in the background. "Holy shit, Olivia. We're so glad you're okay. What happened? Where are you calling from?"

"St. David's Hospital," Olivia said.

"We're getting in the car right now," Milo said. "Should we meet you at the hospital or at your house?"

"Meet me at the hospital," Olivia said. She thought of her car—smashed in by Lilith's terrarium—and tears pricked the corners of her eyes. "My car is totaled. I could use a ride home and I really need to talk to you and Nancy about what happened with Randall—"

Olivia's next words were choked out by a bout of sobs.

38

It took Mark two days to get in touch with one of the lawyers representing the Colony, and another day for his phone to ring with an unfamiliar number.

Mark closed the door to the bedroom where Elijah was sleeping and scurried into his dim, cramped kitchen. "Hello?"

"Is this Mark Coleman?"

Mark's throat tightened. He'd told the lawyer he needed to speak with Lucille Hatch, Elijah's mother. Based on his conversations with Elijah, talking to his mother seemed the best plan if he were to convince them to accept Elijah back into the fold. Instead, the heavy slab of a man's voice—one Mark recognized—was on the line.

"Yes, this is he."

"Mark, this is Robert Grayburn. I understand you've been trying to reach us—specifically to contact one of the mothers. The sole reason for this phone call is to let you know that if you do not desist, we will sue you for harassment. This will be your only warning."

"I have Elijah," Mark blurted.

The line went silent for several seconds. Mark's throat clicked as he swallowed dryly.

Grayburn asked, "What do you mean, you *have* Elijah?"

"He suffered a serious injury in Hurricane Ophelia. I was one of the doctors taking care of him at the hospital. I was able to check him out without anyone realizing who he was. He's recovering at my place now."

Another pause. Some muttering too low to make out. Mark thought he heard a woman's voice and prayed it was Lucille's. "Do you have any proof you're telling the truth?" Grayburn asked.

"He's got a birthmark on his hip," Mark said. "If you're in contact with Lucille, she can confirm—"

"I used to change the boy's diapers. I know the birthmark. What's your address?"

Mark told him. A few agonizing seconds passed.

"Does the boy know the extent of your sins?" Grayburn asked quietly.

It took the kitchen wall pressing against Mark's back for him to realize he was retreating backwards. "He knows I was exiled from the Colony for telling lies."

"This doesn't change anything," Grayburn growled.

"Please," Mark blurted, "can you let me know if Melinda is all right—"

The line went dead. Mark slid down the wall until his butt hit the tile, catching his breath. *You misunderstood,* he reminded himself for the thousandth time. *Grayburn was dragging a deer into the woods, not a man's body. You need to remember that if you want to ever see your sister or father again.*

Mark didn't think he'd be able to sleep, but he must have slipped off, because he jerked awake on his couch to a knock on the door. He took a deep breath, unclasped the chain lock, and opened the door.

A diminutive woman bearing a striking resemblance to Elijah stood outside, flanked by two men Mark recognized immediately.

The man on the left was Father Clark, though he'd gained fifty pounds around his midsection, his hairline had retreated halfway across his skull, and his mustache bristled with white hairs. The pink scrawl of burst blood vessels on his nose meant Father Clark's alcoholism remained in full swing, which meant he was still responsible for the Colony's finances, and thus too valuable to exile.

The man to Lucille's right was Robert Grayburn. Time had broadened his shoulders and thickened his eyebrows, his freshly-shaved jaw glinting in the blue glow of the streetlight like a shovel set to dig deep into the earth. Grayburn leaned on a white cane with a gold grip—an upgrade from the one he'd used when Mark last saw him. He seemed to have grown taller, as well, though that didn't make sense, because he was in his twenties when Mark had accused him of...

"Hello, Mark," said Robert Grayburn.

Grayburn reached past Lucille and stretched his hand into Mark's doorway. All the moisture retreated from Mark's mouth and reappeared in his gut.

It never happened, Mark reminded himself as his hand disappeared into Grayburn's grasp. *You made it up.*

"Yes, Robert Grayburn. And F-Father Clark," Mark stammered, shaking Father Clark's hand as well. "And Lucille..."

Lucille Hatch ignored his outstretched hand and pushed past him into his apartment. "Where is he?"

"In the bedroom. I've been sleeping on the couch," Mark added hastily. He opened the bedroom door and flipped on the cold overhead light, revealing Elijah's sleeping form. Even under the three blankets Mark had piled over him, it was clear his legs ended at the knee.

Lucille Hatch released a cry and fell to her knees beside the bed, brushing the hair back from Elijah's forehead. Tears streamed down her cheeks. She stared at the shape of the bed sheets before burying her face in the hollow of her son's neck. "Oh, Elijah—"

Father Clark frowned. "You didn't tell us the extent of his injuries."

Mark Coleman quailed. "I...the—"

"The blind sometimes see better than those with sight," Robert Grayburn said. "Perhaps it will be a child without legs who will allow us to walk free."

Elijah's eyes fluttered open. He looked around the room, finally focusing his eyes on the woman beside him. "Mother?"

Lucille clasped Elijah's hand. "I'm here, Elijah. I'm here."

"Why?" Elijah croaked.

"We're here," said Robert Grayburn, "because the Prophet is being held without bail. Until he's absolved of the allegations against him, the Colony needs a leader."

Elijah's eyes went glassy with tears. "But I...I was exiled."

"The Colony now knows the truth about who fathered Lila's child," Father Clark told him. "The baby's resemblance to Azrael was undeniable."

Elijah turned to Mark. "And what of *your* exile?"

Mark looked to Lucille for an answer, too frightened to look at Robert Grayburn. He'd told Elijah the truth, or enough of it—that he had been exiled for a false accusation and had since repented.

"We think that should be up to you, Elijah," Father Clark said.

Elijah considered this. "How many years has it been?"

"Fifteen," Mark said.

"I lived in exile for less than a year," Elijah said, "and it was the darkest time of my life. I cannot imagine the hell you have gone through."

Mark swallowed and nodded.

Elijah looked up at his mother. "The cruelty of this world has made exiles of us all, but I understand my purpose now. Why I was tested, and why I was cast out. It will now be my mission to save us, to return us to the light."

Lucille Hatch let out a sob, her shoulders shaking as she held her son. Father Clark and Robert Grayburn shared an inscrutable look.

Elijah turned to Mark. "You, Mark Coleman, will be the first to be saved."

39

LILA CLUTCHED AZRAEL'S FILTHY, calloused hand. Her hand was pale and small in his, and just as dirty. It had been five days since they'd showered at a makeshift storm shelter, and she smelled the brine of her sweat mingling with Azrael's. A siren howled a few blocks away, setting her nerves on edge. Cade slept, nestled in a scarf tied around Azrael's neck, his face visible so passers-by could connect the battered cardboard sign reading *PLEASE HELP US FEED OUR BABY* with a flesh-and-blood child. The pink crocheted hat placed upside-down in front of them collected more cash that way.

Today had been a good money day. They'd accumulated enough to get a hot meal and a room for the night. Lila scratched at the rime of scum at the base of her scalp. Their future was uncertain, but she could cling at least to the promise of a shower. That, and the fact that the man who had been following her—the man who had drawn the storm to her—seemed to have disappeared.

Azrael sat beside her, his back against the hot brick wall, staring off into the distance. Plenty of other things could be on his mind—the storm that almost killed them, the destruction of his home, his half-brother's life-threatening injury, or that Elijah had apparently checked himself out of the hospital and vanished without a trace—but Lila knew none of these things were the reason behind his distant expression.

It was her—Olivia.

The very thought of her made Lila feel like she was sinking her teeth into a rancid peach. Azrael had been seduced by the kind of woman the Prophet was always warning the sons of the Colony about. Olivia had gotten her claws in him and tried to tear their family apart. Azrael had chosen his family—thank whatever God existed for that—but Lila could tell Azrael's addiction to Olivia still coursed through his veins.

Lila squeezed Azrael's hand, eliciting a tired smile on his dirt-streaked face, which faded as soon as he turned away.

Her ears pricked at the sound of another siren, closer this time. A horn blasted alongside it.

Azrael's nostrils flared. "Do you smell that?"

"Oh, no. Does he need to be changed again already?"

"No," said Azrael. "Smoke. Don't you smell it?"

Lila sniffed the air. "Someone's burning leaves."

Cade stirred and began making grunting noises, which meant they had about fifteen seconds to get him pressed to one of her breasts before he started screaming. Azrael hoisted him out of the sling and handed him to Lila. She lifted her shirt and affixed her son to her aching nipple.

"As soon as I'm done feeding him, we should find a place to spend the night," Lila said.

"I think the motel we passed this morning would be best. There was a restaurant next door—"

"That's not leaves," Azrael said, looking up. "It's a house fire."

Lila followed his line of sight and saw dark smoke smudging the pale blue sky.

Cade unlatched from her breast, and Lila switched him over to the other side. Azrael had told her about his dreams to one day become a firefighter, but now wasn't the time for him to live out that fantasy. "Don't even think about it."

"They might need help."

"I thought you said we needed to lay low until the trial. That fire's going to be teeming with people."

"You're right." Azrael's eyes darted from side to side. "You stay here with Cade. I'll go check it out."

"No, Azrael—" Lila protested, but he was already on his feet.

"I can't just stay here and do nothing. I'll be back."

Lila watched, stunned, as Azrael disappeared around the corner.

Cade broke away from her breast and started to cry. Lila rose, stuffing the cash-filled hat into her bag along with Cade's last three diapers. She tucked the cardboard sign under one arm, cradled Cade in the other, and walked toward the sound of sirens. With each step, the back of her shoe scraped against a blister on her heel. Her back ached from sleeping on the ground. Cade's screaming yanked like a fishhook at her insides.

The smell of smoke grew stronger, and a block later the blaze came into view. Lila stood, dazzled. Cade stopped crying and stared as well. Flames consumed the top two floors of a five-story apartment building, surrounded by firetrucks, dozens of firefighters, and a crowd of onlookers. A fire hose arced a high white plume of water over the flames, and a dark pillar of smoke billowed skyward.

Lila scanned the scene and spotted Azrael speaking to one of the firefighters. Every tendon in her body went taut with rage as she stormed toward him.

"Azrael."

Azrael's eyes widened. "Lila—it's not safe for you and Cade to be this close."

Lila pulled him away from the firefighter. "It's not safe for any of us to be here."

"There may be people in there," Azrael argued.

"Azrael, I don't care who's in that building—they're not your family. We are. If you don't come with me right now, then you'll never see me or your son again. Do you understand? You've got to choose between our world and theirs."

Lila walked away, Cade bundled against her chest, the heat of the fire at her back. The noise and smell of the fire faded. She thought of Lot's wife, turned into a pillar of salt for the sin of looking back. She would not be weak. Azrael was either following her or he wasn't.

She walked for several blocks, averting her eyes as a police car screamed past. She'd stopped to wait at a crosswalk when she became aware of a person standing beside her.

A hand brushed against hers.

Lila grasped Azrael's hand, hard.

40

Elijah Hatch peered from backstage at his new empire: a few dozen followers fidgeting and whispering in their seats in a small theater that smelled of dust and stale popcorn. Father Clark had rented this venue for the evening, thirty miles outside of Austin, bordered by acres of forest, hoping that they'd be remote enough that the media would not catch on about their gathering. Elijah frowned at the mottled red carpet, lit by the dim light emerging from cracked opal sconces on walls of peeling gold paint. Father Clark's plan to avoid media attention seemed to have worked, though Elijah wished his tenure as Prophet could have had a more auspicious beginning.

Elijah forced himself to not scratch the itch buried in the ripples of flesh where his stitches had been removed. He felt a deeper, prickling sensation where his toes used to be. Mark Coleman had warned him about this. He called it "phantom limb."

"Why so few?" Elijah asked Father Clark, standing beside him in the shadows.

Father Clark knelt so he was level with Elijah. Elijah's lip curled at the sour smell of bourbon trapped in the whiskers of Father Clark's mustache. "We are being investigated, and some of the mothers are afraid of their children being taken from them. More followers will join us in time as the media's scrutiny fades further."

Elijah nodded. "All right. I'm ready."

Father Clark wheeled Elijah to the center of the narrow stage, then took his seat in the front row.

Elijah turned his chair to face what remained of his father's followers—fewer than thirty souls. The bright stage lights drew sweat from his temples. The theater was so quiet he heard his heartbeat in his ears.

"Children of the Colony," said Elijah. "I look out at you now and see a people who have suffered greatly."

A murmur of agreement rose from the crowd.

"I have suffered as well." Elijah looked down at his legs, the seams of his pant legs sewn up to hide his healing stumps. "But perhaps *suffered* isn't the right word. I've been tested. And I think we all remember another who was tested."

Elijah made out a few nodding heads at the edges of the dazzling light.

"And we remember by whom he was tested."

"Yes, sir," said a voice near the front.

"Now you, too, have been cast out into a world of sin, depravity, and lies. You feel, as I felt, the flames of its vice on your skin. You grieve, as I grieved, the loss of the Colony. We cannot go back to the way things were. But we can build something new." Elijah shielded his eyes from the light. "Mark Coleman, please stand up."

A man near the back rose.

"I understand that Mark Coleman was exiled because of a false accusation. As I forgive the Colony for its false accusation against me, I compel you to forgive Mark."

The theater filled with whispers. Elijah didn't understand exactly why Mark had been exiled—both Mark and Robert

Grayburn had refused to answer when pressed for details—but it didn't matter. Elijah needed to make it clear as early as possible: his word was as immutable as his father's.

Elijah's voice echoed over the mutters of dissent: "If there are any among you who doubt that, in the event of my father's incarceration, I will be the one to lead us down the narrow path to the paradise of the next life, then I beseech you to leave now and never return."

The room fell silent.

"Mark Coleman, you may be seated, as a worthy acolyte." Elijah spread his arms, as he'd watched his father do countless times. "Your loyalty will be rewarded, in this life and the next."

"Amen!" cried someone near the front—his mother, Lucille.

Elijah smiled at his mother. "We shall rebuild our kingdom, my brothers and sisters, and the world will fall to its knees in awe of our radiance."

The crowd erupted in a cheer.

Tears stung the corners of Elijah's eyes. He was home.

41

Arachne watched through her many spiders in the theater's backstage room as Robert Grayburn shuffled down the hall, leaning on his cane with every other step. He peered into the room, finding Mark Coleman repacking Elijah's medical supplies into a bag.

"Mark," Grayburn said.

Mark whirled around. "Yes?"

"Can I give you a ride back to your apartment?" Robert Grayburn asked.

"What about Elijah?"

"You said he was well enough to travel, so we're moving him to the house where Father Clark and his family are staying. We decided it was best to keep him near his people."

"I...well..."

"Come on, Mark. If you will indeed be joining us once again, this will give us a chance to bury the hatchet, so to speak."

"I'm sorry f-for..." Mark stammered. "I was a kid. I didn't know what I was talking about."

Robert Grayburn smiled. "Apology accepted. Let's get you home."

Arachne's spiders bristled and squirmed. "Say no, you idiot!"

Mark hid his trembling hands behind the bag of medical supplies. "Yes, that would be fine." He hesitated, as if summoning resolve. "I'd like to see Melinda and my father soon, if that's all right. I understand why they couldn't come tonight, but..."

"Of course," Robert Grayburn said. "I've told them you've returned to us. They're looking forward to seeing you, too. We may be able to arrange a meeting as soon as tomorrow."

This was a lie, too. At Grayburn's insistence, Melinda had not been informed of her brother's return, nor allowed to attend the meeting. Mark had also not been told of his father's "exile."

The hope in Mark's eyes was painful. "Tomorrow? Oh, that would be wonderful."

Robert Grayburn smiled. "Come on, my car's around back."

"No!" Arachne shouted. "Get the hell out of there!"

Mark finished packing the medical bag and followed Grayburn toward the back exit. Mark stepped outside, saying, "I can't wait to see Melinda. I thought about her every day—"

Arachne's spiders rounded the corner in time to watch Robert Grayburn pull a box cutter from his back pocket and draw it across Mark's throat.

Mark Coleman gurgled and clawed at the darkness spouting from his neck. Robert Grayburn tipped his victim's head back and dragged him into the woods. He emerged from the trees several minutes later, wearing a different shirt and pants, carrying Mark's medical bag. Grayburn turned on the hose attached to the building and washed blood from his shoes and cane until the water ran clear.

THE NEXT MORNING, ARACHNE watched as Elijah woke in Father Clark's guest room to Robert Grayburn redressing his wounds.

"Where's Mark?" Elijah asked.

Robert Grayburn sighed. "It pains me to tell you this, Elijah, but Mark Coleman assaulted one of the mothers last night after your sermon."

Elijah's jaw dropped. "What? How?"

"I walked in on him forcing himself onto her backstage. I hauled him off her, but he ran, and I wasn't able to catch him. If we're lucky, we won't be seeing him again."

The color drained from Elijah's face. "But...I absolved him..."

"He used you," Robert Grayburn said. "He only brought you back to us so we'd accept him back into the fold. He was never a believer. He was a predator."

Elijah nodded slowly. "Which of the mothers was it?"

"She made me promise not to reveal her identity."

Arachne slapped a palm to her forehead, narrowly missing a black widow burrowing its way into her hair. "You're not really buying this, are you?" she shouted at Elijah.

Elijah thought a few beats, then asked, "If Mark Coleman reaches out to us, will you please let me know?"

"Of course."

"Can you send Father Clark in?"

Robert Grayburn nodded and left.

Father Clark appeared in the doorway. "Yes, Elijah?"

"What is our financial situation?"

Father Clark sighed and rubbed his temples. "Your father's assets have been seized by the state. That includes the Colony, as you knew it—property and housing and all. Every bank account in your father's name is inaccessible at the moment." The corners of his mustache twitched up as he grinned: "Luckily, I created a secret account not even your father was aware of, so that if the Colony were ever disbanded, we would have options. It will take me some time to access these funds without detection, but once I'm able to, our resources will be considerable."

"Excellent news," Elijah said. Good enough news that it seemed to balance out Mark Coleman's departure, Arachne noted wryly. "Please let me know when you're able to do that."

42

"HENRY HATCH, THE MAN *known to his followers as the 'Prophet,' is on trial today for multiple counts of sex trafficking, child molestation, racketeering, and forced labor conspiracy. Hatch's wives and followers will testify on his behalf. Hatch's son, as well as the young woman who came forward to expose him in August of last year, will be the prosecution's key witnesses."*

Olivia clutched her knees to her chest. Nancy nestled next to her on the couch, staring at the TV. They'd both taken the day off work; Olivia because she wouldn't be able to focus on anything, and Nancy because she knew Olivia needed support.

In the months since the storm had ripped a hole in her life, Olivia had wavered between being a zombie and a wreck. She had hoped Henry Hatch's trial would bring her some closure, but that hope was shattered when she discovered that Azrael and Lila had resurfaced from wherever they'd been hiding to testify at his father's trial.

A preening blonde newswoman named Sherry Prince was reporting from the courthouse. Her equally groomed counterpart, Chuck Wagoner, asked Sherry the same questions

Olivia had already heard a half dozen times from his swivel chair in the newsroom.

"Now, it's been reported Henry Hatch had as many as five wives, is that correct?"

"That's right, Chuck. It appears that in the Colony, men married multiple women, many of whom were minors, which brings us back to Azrael Hatch and Lila Monroe, and the importance of their testimony in the prosecution's case. To date, all evidence against Hatch is circumstantial. Everything hinges on what these two will expose during the trial."

"Thanks, Sherry. We'll check back in with you soon."

Nancy muted the volume and put her hand on Olivia's shoulder. "You okay? You look a little green around the gills."

"I'm all right." Olivia rubbed her eyes. "I didn't sleep much last night."

"Do you want to turn this off?"

"No," Olivia sighed. "I think I need to see it."

Nancy nodded. "Then I'm going to order some pizza. We're going to need a lot of cheese and carbs if we're going to make it through this in one piece."

"Thanks, Nancy."

When the pizza arrived an hour later, there was no sign of Henry Hatch. Olivia forced herself to eat two slices as Sherry and Chuck chased their tired repartee around the ring another handful of times.

Olivia was returning from the bathroom when she heard Sherry say, "It seems that Henry Hatch, the self-described 'Prophet' of the polygamist cult known as the Colony, has just pulled up to the courthouse." Sherry's heels clacked on the sidewalk as she joined the crowd of reporters. "He is joined by his lawyers."

The camera tilted up.

Olivia took in a breath and held it. There he was—the Prophet, Henry Hatch.

Hatch smiled and waved at the gathered reporters as if they were fawning fans. The glimmering confidence in his eyes said this whole thing was a temporary indignity which he would soon overcome—that he was not a dangerous psychopath, but a misunderstood messiah. He walked into the courthouse as if he didn't have a care in the world.

Olivia shuddered, looking at Hatch's eyes. They gleamed, but without warmth.

"I see the resemblance," Nancy said softly. She winced at Olivia's expression. "Sorry."

"No, you're right," Olivia said in a low voice. "I see it, too."

Sherry Prince rambled: "He's—okay, he's walking toward the courthouse now—he looks confident—he's followed by his two lawyers and—and another car pulled up, and it looks like a man is getting out—yes, this is Robert Grayburn, one of Henry Hatch's followers, here to testify—and a van is pulling up now, and getting out are three—four—five women— wearing the traditional clothing of the Colony mothers—the youngest looks to be no older than a teenager—"

"You know how sharks can't stop swimming, or they'll die?" asked Nancy. "I think that woman thinks the same thing would happen to her if she stopped talking."

Henry Hatch and his followers disappeared from sight and the camera returned to Sherry. "At any moment, Azrael and Lila will arrive—oh, I believe this is them!"

Nancy reached for Olivia's hand. Olivia took it and squeezed.

"If you're just joining us," said Sherry, "Lila Monroe and Azrael Hatch, key witnesses against Henry Hatch, have arrived. The trial will begin shortly, and Channel Six

News will be here, giving you moment-to-moment reports of what transpires."

Olivia, plunging through layers of numbness, watched her lover walk toward the courthouse, hand in hand with the mother of his child, black hair slicked back from his forehead. He and Lila were both dressed up in nice clothes. His baby was nowhere to be seen. Olivia was grateful for that, at least.

Off-camera, Sherry babbled on: "Neither father nor son look as if they know the meaning of the word defeat. It will be interesting to see who will prevail."

Nancy scoffed. "Ugh, like they're rival sport teams."

Sherry's painted face gave way to the same hand soap commercial that had already played a dozen times. Olivia put her head in her hands.

"When do you think Elijah's going to show up?" Nancy asked. "Didn't you say he was in witness protection or something for the trial?"

"I don't know. I guess they're keeping him under wraps until it's his turn to testify."

"I don't think it works like that," Nancy said. "I'm pretty sure if Elijah were going to be a witness, we'd know by now."

An uneasy feeling grew in Olivia's gut. Her phone buzzed with a text from Milo. *How you holding up?*

"God bless that man," Nancy murmured, seeing the text. "I'm so glad he'll be moving here soon."

"Me too," Olivia said, responding to Milo's text with a line of queasy emojis.

He sent back a heart, and she replied with the same.

Nancy hugged her. "I know this is hard, but look at it this way—at least none of these vultures knows who you are. You got royally fucked over, but you get to walk away from it without a circus. Trust me, everything's harder when the world has its eyes on you."

Olivia nodded. "Thanks, Nancy. I hadn't thought about that. This would definitely be worse if people like Sherry Prince had any idea I existed."

"One hundred percent. And in no time at all, Henry Hatch will go to prison, and then you can move on with your life."

"Here's hoping," Olivia said.

43

ARACHNE WAS USED TO the kind of carnival currently unfolding at the courthouse. Times changed, but people didn't. Humanity would always be drawn to tragedy like ants to sugar. It didn't take her spies long to spot Hades in the back of the courtroom, in the form of a man whose face was the same drab beige as His suit. She nestled a spider into the crease of His tie and waited for the drama to unfold.

One by one, the mothers of the Colony came forward to defend their leader as they all received the same questions. Did the Prophet, or any of the men in the Colony, sleep with underage women? Were any women or children forced into arranged marriages? Were any of the members of the Colony abused, intimidated, or mistreated?

The muted refrain from the plain, frightened women was either "No," or "Not to my knowledge."

Robert Grayburn's testimony on the Prophet's behalf was more convincing than the mothers', nearly as charismatic as the Prophet himself. Arachne could see through Grayburn's smile, though, which failed to reach his eyes—he didn't care who was in charge, Henry or Elijah, as long as he was able to retain his spot as their second-hand man.

A few days into the trial, it was Lila's turn to speak. Lila placed one hand on the Bible and raised the other, promised to tell the truth, and took a seat.

The lead prosecuting attorney approached the stand. "Miss, would you please state your name for the jury?"

"Lila Monroe."

"Can you point out Henry Hatch for the jury?"

Lila pointed at the Colony patriarch with defiance in her eyes.

"Lila, I'd like to ask you some questions about your life in the Colony, if that's all right with you."

Lila nodded.

"To your knowledge, were young women in the Colony forced to marry against their will?"

"Yes," Lila said emphatically.

It was the first of dozens of damning responses. Rape, abuse, terror, manipulation. Lila glared at Henry Hatch and divulged everything.

The defense asked her a predictable line of questions regarding her character, lingering on the part of her journey where she'd stolen a few thousand dollars' worth of jewelry from the foster parents who had taken her in following the raid, leaving out the fact that the couple had declined to press charges against her.

Then it was Azrael's turn.

Azrael answered questions about his life in the Colony and his escape from the tyranny of his father. He described finding Lila during Hurricane Ophelia and deciding to help her bring down the Colony. The defense then peppered him with questions regarding him abandoning the mother of his child, calling his accusations against his father into doubt. Azrael responded to these question with his chosen shades of the truth.

At last, after days of testimony, the prosecution and defense gave their closing arguments, and the jury retired to make their decision.

Arachne knew the faces of the jury well, and not just because of the trial. Hades was blackmailing three of them.

One was a married college professor who'd engaged in no fewer than five affairs with his students over the years—four young women and one man. Another was an architectural engineer who'd amassed a small fortune's worth of bribes from contractors eager to cut corners. The third was a pretty blonde woman who'd killed her abusive partner with a fatal dose of Rohypnol in his whiskey nightcap. All they had to do to ensure these indiscretions were never seen by another soul was to acquit Henry Hatch of all charges.

"What's going to happen once Hatch is acquitted?" Arachne asked Hades.

"Plenty," said Hades.

44

"We've gotten word that the jury has returned with a decision," Sherry Prince said. "Any moment now, we will learn Henry Hatch's verdict."

Olivia's phone buzzed beside her on the couch. Another concerned text from Nancy. Olivia had woken in the morning with a gut feeling the jury's verdict would be announced, so she'd called in sick to work. This turned out to be a self-fulfilling prophecy, as she'd felt like she'd been on the verge of throwing up all morning. Olivia responded, *I'm okay, just not feeling well.*

Hope you feel better soon, love, Nancy texted. *I'll bring you some soup after work.*

Olivia thought about telling Nancy the other reason for her unease: today was the anniversary of her father's death. If she told Nancy that, she wasn't sure if she could stop herself from telling Nancy the rest of the story—how she'd hated her father, how she was more than half-sure she'd caused his death.

Instead, she heart-reacted Nancy's offer for soup and set her phone aside. She massaged the bridge of her nose. At least, one way or another, it was almost over.

Sherry Prince pressed her finger to her ear. "I'm getting word that—yes, it's confirmed, the jury's verdict: Henry Hatch was found *not guilty* of all charges."

Olivia's hands flew to her mouth.

Not guilty.

Against all odds, the monster was walking free.

Something fierce flared to life in Olivia's chest. It grew in strength, feeding off sleepless nights and countless tears, all her shame and anger and fear culminating in a single white-hot flame.

On screen, Sherry Prince prattled away. The chattering fool didn't care what men like Hatch got away with—as long as she got her story. Sherry continued talking, but Olivia couldn't hear anything over the high, whining drone between her ears, which grew and grew—

The anger burning in Olivia's chest detonated as a savage brightness lashed from the center of her.

"It seems we may have—" Sherry said. Her face froze in a half-cocked smile. She wavered, then her eyes rolled up behind the sheen of her purple eye shadow and she dropped out of view.

The raging flame inside Olivia vanished.

The camera panned down to reveal Sherry Prince sprawled on the grass outside the courthouse. Bystanders rushed in and knelt at her side.

The camera cut back to Chuck in the studio. He stuttered through a segue that led to a cheerful paper towel commercial.

Olivia muted the television with a shaking hand. What the hell just happened?

Elijah's face appeared in her thoughts: the fear in his eyes as the closet had come crashing down. The feeling she'd been the one to make it happen.

Olivia drew her knees to her chest. Elijah…Sherry Prince…

Her father...

Olivia flipped over to another news station, which featured Hatch's motorcade, waiting for him to emerge from the courthouse.

Anger, bright as an ember, glowed back to life in her chest.

45

H*AVE YOU SEEN?* A*GON* whispered in Arachne's ear.

Arachne shied away from Agon. She'd been so absorbed in what was going on above she hadn't realized the demon had drawn close to her. "Have I seen what?"

Have you seen what the mother will do?

"Which mother?" Arachne asked.

She's taking advantage of the media's distraction.

"Who is?"

Hush, or you're going to miss it.

Arachne vaulted her attention from spider to spider. Henry Hatch and Robert Grayburn left the courthouse with their team of attorneys in tow. The spinning lights of Sherry Prince's ambulance danced across Henry Hatch's face as he waved away questions from the media. Hatch wore the contented smile of a man on the right side of justice.

When Hatch and Grayburn reached their idling town car, they shook hands with their legal representation and disappeared behind the car's sleek, tinted windows. A handful of protesters broke through the ranks, one of them cracking the rear windshield with a rock as the town car drove away. Their vehicle passed within half a block of Sherry Prince's dead body as it departed.

Arachne peered through the eyes of the brown spider on the underside of the town car's back seat, staring at Hatch and Grayburn's feet.

The car pulled to a stop at a red light.

A rush of light and air entered the car as Hatch's door swung open. A familiar set of legs stood outside: Lila.

"The hell—" Henry Hatch said.

Hatch kicked against the footwell, making a gargling sound. Dark red droplets scattered from his polished black shoes as his feet convulsed in a shuffling dance. Grayburn's feet braced against the footwell as if he was leaning against the opposite door. Lila's legs disappeared as she fled.

Shadows shifted as the driver threw the car into park and came around to Hatch's door. "Oh, shit," said the driver.

"Do something!" Robert Grayburn demanded.

The driver hollered for the police. A chorus of slamming doors and shouted commands ensued.

Rivulets of blood traced down the leather seat and dripped onto the footwell. Henry Hatch gurgled and kicked the blood-soaked fabric as gagging noises gave way to wet clicks. His kicks grew weaker, then stopped.

A police officer leaned into the car. "Jesus Christ. What happened?"

"Lila Monroe slit his throat," Grayburn barked. "She ran off that way!"

"I saw her!" Someone outside the car said. "She ran into the woods!"

"Create a perimeter," an officer ordered. "Roadblocks at one and five miles. Find her!"

Nicely done, hissed Agon. *Did you see her face?*

Arachne's throat filled with a surge of spiders. She choked them back. "No."

It was expressionless, said Agon. *Flat eyes, a born predator. She drew her blade across his throat, slow and deep. It was almost tender.*

Arachne shuddered. "I thought I'd feel more satisfaction at that man's death. This wager business is brutal. Did the Old One really participate in something as vicious as this?"

Agon chuckled. *Folly, to think of the Old One as kind.*

46

SWEAT BROKE OUT AT Elijah's temples as he read and re-read the headline on his phone. *Henry Hatch Declared Not Guilty.* His phantom pain intensified until Elijah gasped in pain. He set aside his phone and massaged the pale snarls where his legs ended. The invisible flesh of his feet burned as if dipped in fire.

You deserve to burn, Elijah thought. *You wanted your father to be found guilty. If that's not a sin, then I don't know what is.*

A knock fell at the door. "Elijah?" asked Father Clark.

"Yes?"

"Your father has been declared not guilty."

"I saw, God be praised."

"He is returning to us as we speak."

"Thank you."

A brief silence, then: "Do you wish to announce the news to your followers?"

"They're not my followers anymore," murmured Elijah.

"What?"

"Yes, I'll address them. Go and call an assembly. I will join you soon."

"Very good, Elijah," said Father Clark.

Elijah dressed and wheeled himself outside. He winced at the white, overcast sky. He would face his people one last time, and then he'd face whatever terrors his father would unleash upon him for trying to take his place.

ELIJAH TOOK A DEEP breath backstage. His legs felt beset by needles. The pain grew until tears pricked the corners of his eyes.

Elijah wheeled himself into the blinding spotlight. The buzz of the assembled crowd fell silent.

"My dear Colony," Elijah began. "It is with the deepest relief that I tell you my father, our Prophet, has been absolved of any wrongdoing, and is returning to us as I speak."

A low hum rose in the back of the theater. A bead of sweat trickled down Elijah's back.

"Had my father been found guilty," said Elijah, "I would have proudly served as your Prophet. However, the strength of the Lord has overcome the men who sought to bring my father down, and now he will return to us, victorious."

The murmuring grew louder, and unless Elijah was imagining it, it contained notes of fear. He looked down at his legs, half expecting to see them covered in wasps.

"Elijah Hatch!" came a voice from the back of the theater.

"Yes, Father Clark?"

"It's your father!"

Elijah gritted his teeth against the agony in his legs. "Has he arrived so soon?"

"No!" cried Father Clark. "Robert Grayburn contacted me with tragic news—the Prophet has been murdered!"

The theatre erupted in a collective howl of grief. Men rushed into the aisles and fell to their knees. Women gathered their children to their sides.

The pain in Elijah's missing legs vanished.

His father was dead. Elijah turned the idea over in his mind like he was inspecting a jewel. He was now the Prophet, and he would lead his people to a glorious future his father could never have imagined.

He needed to grasp hold of his followers now, or they'd slip through his fingers.

"Despair not!" Elijah cried, his voice echoing over their panicked wails. "Have you forgotten so soon the words of your Prophet? What did he teach us about despair?"

A woman's voice rose above the lamentations. "Despair is a sin!"

Elijah shaded his eyes from the light. His mother's thin, pale face turned up toward the stage. Something fragile in his heart pulled taut at the sight of her.

"And why is despair a sin?"

His mother responded in a small voice, "Because it alleges God has forsaken us."

"And what does God never do?"

"He never forsakes us!"

"He *never* forsakes us! Not in times of fear, not in times of tragedy, and not in times of grief. There is no stone out of place in His kingdom, not a thing that is not a part of His plan. So, we will mourn, we will weep, and we will grieve—but we will not despair. We will get through this as we have gotten through everything else—with faith!"

Someone in the audience shouted: "Amen!"

"Our faith will overcome!" Elijah shouted. "God is stronger than all the wickedness in the world! We will rise through the pain of our loss into glory!"

"With you, our new Prophet!" his mother cried.

"Yes!" said someone near the front. "Prophet!"

Elijah peered into the white light, fringed with the shadows of disciples calling out to him: "Prophet! Prophet!"

The Prophet was dead.

Long live the Prophet.

PART II

RUINATION

1

"TODAY MARKS THE THREE-YEAR *anniversary of the murder of cult leader Henry Hatch. Some called him a Prophet; others, a monster. A jury deemed him not guilty, and the woman accusing him of rape allegedly took his life shortly after that verdict. Three years later, so many questions remain: What has become of Hatch's followers? How was his alleged killer, Lila Monroe, able to vanish without a trace? Where are she and her suspected accomplice, Azrael Hatch, now? We may never know the answers.*

"Of course, today also marks another anniversary. Three years ago, Channel Six News lost a member of its family. A dedicated journalist known for her tireless pursuit of the truth, Sherry Prince had been a part of the Channel Six News team for seven wonderful years. Sherry was an inspiration to everyone who worked with her. Her impassioned reporting never failed to breathe life into a story, and her smiling face lit up the studio. She is survived by her loving husband, Wayne Prince, and her two daughters, Felicity and Diane. Here at Channel Six, we take comfort in knowing that, although she was taken before her time, Sherry died doing what she loved.

"Sherry Prince, you are, and always will be, greatly missed."

The studio lights dimmed around Chuck Wagoner. He receded into darkness as the camera drew away and a portrait of Sherry Prince cross-faded into view. She was beaming, as if someone off-camera was making her laugh.

Olivia's mouth went dry as she stared down at the video on her phone, dimly registering the murmur of conversation in the Fisher Biotech food hall through her earbuds. She tried to connect the woman in the picture—a young, starry-eyed journalist—to the vulgar, clownish woman she had felt such anger towards three years ago. Sherry Prince had been a mother, a wife, a friend, but Olivia hadn't thought of that. She hadn't wondered if Sherry's husband would be left to raise his two daughters alone. She hadn't thought about how many people would suffer when Sherry was taken from them.

She hadn't thought of anything but her hatred for a woman who'd had nothing to do with the crimes committed in the Colony.

Sherry Prince's photograph transitioned to two photos, side by side—Lila Monroe and Azrael Hatch, along with a phone number to call with any information regarding their whereabouts.

Azrael's bright hazel eyes burned through her phone screen. What did he look like now? Did he ever think of her? Did he really love the mother of his child?

And where the hell was he?

"Olivia, are you all right?" Nancy asked.

Olivia looked up from her phone to see Nancy approaching with a lunch tray.

Olivia paused the video and removed her earbuds from her ears. "Yeah, I'm all right. It's just…you know. One of those days."

Nancy set down her tray and took a seat beside her. "Oh, wow. Today's the day that bastard died, isn't it? It always sneaks up on me."

Nancy meant Henry Hatch, but Olivia's breath caught in her throat as she thought of her father's death, years before the Prophet.

Nancy stared down at the paused video on Olivia's phone. "I can't believe they've been on the run for three whole years."

Olivia clicked off her phone. "Tell me about it."

"With a baby and everything…oh, damn, Olivia, I'm sorry."

Olivia hadn't realized she'd been on the verge of tears until they were pouring down her cheeks. She wiped them away, hoping her other coworkers in the food hall hadn't noticed.

"Heck, I had to open my big damn mouth," Nancy said, hugging Olivia from the side.

"It's okay, it's not that." Olivia struggled to get her next words out. "I…woke up with more bites on me this morning."

"Oh no, after the heat treatment?"

Olivia nodded. There were plenty of things in her life for which she was grateful. When Nosh cleared human trials and hit the market, success stories came pouring in, with thousands of customers curbing their appetite and leveling out at a healthy weight without the risks of lap-band surgery. Olivia's mother was happy and healthy. Nancy and Milo had gotten married and were sharing a wonderful life together. She'd built a community for herself in Austin, with friends who made her laugh and held space for her when she needed it. She'd even managed to move on from the betrayal and heartbreak of finding out her lover was nothing more than a fabrication.

But all the good things in her life paled in comparison with the infestation taking over her sanity.

It had started when Olivia woke to find welts on her arm. She'd upended her mattress, and there they were: three apple-seed-sized insects, their little bodies dark with her blood. Olivia had plucked them from the mattress with a tissue and flushed them down the toilet.

In the following months, Olivia had become a refugee in her own home. She washed everything that could be laundered, dried everything on the hottest setting, placed her clothes in sealed bags. Her books, albums, knick-knacks, tax documents, and shoes all went into bags along with poison strips to kill anything inside. She bought a cover for her mattress and pillows. She threw away her wooden bed frame and replaced it with a metal one. She hired an exterminator and slept with all four posts of her bed in cups. She sprinkled diatomaceous earth around her bed like she was casting a protective spell. Most recently, Nancy had paid for a multi-thousand-dollar heat treatment that baked Olivia's entire house with the promise of killing anything living.

Still, the bites appeared.

"I don't believe it," Nancy said. "The heat treatment was guaranteed to work. I'll call them—"

"No, it's okay." Olivia shook her head. "I'm tired of fighting. At this point, I'm just going to move out and start over someplace else."

Nancy's face fell. "But you love that house."

"I know. I just can't keep doing this."

"Oh, hon. You can come stay with us if you'd like while you figure out your next move," Nancy said, rubbing Olivia's shoulders.

"Thanks, Nancy." Olivia hugged her friend, sniffling.

"Ah, geez," came a voice from behind them. Olivia turned to see her coworker Dan approaching. "Looks like it's somebody's time of the month."

Before Olivia could stop herself, it happened again.

The same thing that happened every time she'd gotten angry in the years since Hurricane Ophelia.

One victim had been a man seated behind her in a plane who kept digging his knees into her seat and saying racist things to his friend in the seat beside him. Olivia's fury had built until it glowed unbearably hot, then lashed out. An instant later, her seat rocked forward, accompanied by heavy grunting noises. A flight attendant ushered a doctor to the man's seat, where his attempts at CPR were unsuccessful. The man was dead.

"Heart attack," the doctor had said. "There was nothing anyone could do."

Another time, Olivia had been rear-ended at a busy intersection on a hot day. Her rear window burst into a thousand pieces, blue-green chunks of glass landing in her hair. Shaken, she'd gotten out of her car to see if the other motorist was okay.

The driver, an older woman, threw her car into reverse, slamming into the car behind her. When Olivia realized the woman had been attempting to drive away from the crash, anger filled her chest, and smoke filled the interior of the woman's car. The woman piled out of the car hacking and clutching her throat.

Later that same day, a mechanic at Olivia's body shop made a condescending comment about woman drivers and then promptly sliced his palm open on the broken glass on Olivia's window.

So far, she'd managed to keep these incidents separate from her work or personal life.

Until today.

Olivia stared daggers at Dan as his next step fell in a slick of spilled liquid on the food hall floor. His leg shot up into the air with an almost balletic grace as the top half of him pitched backwards. His head connected with the ground with a sharp *crack*!

"Holy shit!" Nancy rushed to his side. "Dan, are you okay?"

Olivia's anger evaporated, dread rushing in to fill the vacuum as it always did. Her gut turned to lead as blood spread in a dark puddle around Dan's head. He wasn't moving, and she couldn't tell if he was breathing.

Nancy's phone was at her ear. "Yes, my coworker fell, and he's sustained a head injury. He's unconscious and bleeding. We're in the food hall at Fisher Biotech..."

Nancy's voice faded into a dull buzz as Olivia watched her coworker's spreading blood touch Nancy's sneakers. No, no...Dan was an idiot, but he didn't deserve to die. None of them did. Not Sherry, not the man in the plane...

Olivia knelt beside Dan and held his hand. "Dan, if you can hear me, it's going to be all right," she said. "Paramedics are on their way. You're going to be okay."

THAT NIGHT, OLIVIA STOOD in her darkened living room, ears ringing as her empty house blared silence back at her. Dan was one of the lucky ones—he'd survived Olivia's wrath. He had a concussion and seven staples keeping the back of his skull closed, but he was otherwise okay. Who knew—he might think twice about making a comment about women's bodies from here on out.

Tears stung Olivia's eyes as she took a long, slow breath. It wasn't her fault. It was an accident. She hadn't been near him. Nobody in their right mind would think she'd had anything to do with hurting him.

But maybe she wasn't exactly in her right mind anymore.

She was bone-tired, but the idea of going to bed filled her with terror. That way lay nightmares, restless tossing and turning, the grim certainty she was neither safe nor alone. Worse yet, the less she was able to rest, the harder it would be to control her impulses. She'd put off her decision to move for long enough. It was time to admit she'd lost the war.

Unless...

Olivia looked down at her shaking hands, at the remnants of Dan's dried blood in the creases of her knuckles. What if she could harness whatever power was inside her to end the infestation? If she could elicit an aneurysm or heart attack in a human, wouldn't she be more than capable of snuffing out the life of an insect?

She felt crazy for considering it...but what could it hurt? If it didn't work, she was still stuck in the same awful place she was before. And it would act as a test—if it worked, then her ability to hurt things...people...might be real.

Olivia walked to the center of her living room. She pictured every nook and cranny of her house, each corner and furrow, the inner reaches of her mattress. She visualized the intricate maze through which her tormentors crawled and bred and fed. She felt their presence, the low, humming malevolence of the tiny, bloodsucking pests.

The blazing light inside her chest glowed to life.

She thought of the dread in her stomach when she found bites on her skin, feeling like she was going insane, all her anger and fear and helplessness converging in a single point of blinding light, growing too bright and hot for her to contain it—

The power burst out from her in a shock wave, emanating outwards, echoing back from the walls. Through her closed eyes, Olivia thought she saw the lights flicker on and off again.

Olivia waited until the energy around her spun itself into nothingness. She opened her eyes, half expecting to see a blast radius around her, but it was just her house, silent and dark.

Something was different, though. Olivia felt it.

She crawled into bed, closed her eyes, and was asleep in minutes.

WHEN OLIVIA WALKED OUTSIDE the next morning, she saw her next-door neighbor, an older woman named Frankie, sitting outside on her porch, sobbing into a cup of tea.

"What's wrong?" asked Olivia.

Frankie wiped her tear-streaked face. "I'm sorry, I hope I didn't wake you."

Olivia tilted her head in sympathy. "No, not at all. Are you all right?"

Frankie blew her nose into a fresh tissue. "It's Harry. He passed away last night."

Harry was Frankie's dog, a shaggy little mutt. Olivia's eyes widened. "Oh no, what happened?"

"He fell asleep in his favorite window, the one facing your house, and when I woke up this morning, he was cold and stiff."

Olivia's jaw clenched. The thing inside her hadn't been satisfied with the death of insects. It had lashed out from her house, like a tiger's claw catching the hide of an animal too close to its cage.

"It doesn't make any sense," sobbed Frankie. "He was so young."

Olivia hugged her neighbor until the shoulder of her shirt was soaked. At least now, she knew two things. The first was that her test had been a success. There would be no more bites, no more bugs. That was over.

The second was she was never going to intentionally let the thing inside of her out again.

2

"I didn't understand what compelled me to choose Olivia at first," Arachne told Agon, "but I do now."

Arachne sat, covered in her usual assortment of eight-legged pests, on the edge of a slate gray outcropping, legs dangling over the side. Arachne sensed Agon's desire to shove her off her perch emanating from it in waves.

Foul green liquid dribbled from Agon's mouth. *Oh?*

"I think Olivia already possessed some kind of ability before Hades started toying with her. It was faint, just a glimmer. That's what drew me to her, though I didn't realize it at the time. If not for our wager, I think she would have lived out the rest of her life without realizing it was even there. But Hades must have done something to unleash it, and now she's able to *do* things." Arachne sighed. "I thought maybe everything that's happened till now was a coincidence, or Hades making it *seem* like she was affecting things around her. But when she killed the bedbugs, my spiders in the house died too. I'd been using my spiders to kill off as many bedbugs as I could, and Olivia snuffed all of them out like that." Arachne snapped her fingers. "It's really happening. She's hurting people with her thoughts."

Agon said, *Yes.*

"Are there others like her?" Arachne asked.

Agon said, *Many.*

Arachne's mind flooded with visions of humanity: a Brazilian girl in the throes of puberty unknowingly sliding flower pots off a shelf twenty feet away; a middle-aged oil rig worker in the Gulf of Mexico drinking himself into a stupor every night to stave off violent visions of the future; a Vietnamese toddler conversing with an unseen presence in her bedroom; a manic young man in Wyoming backing away from the shadows of real demons as his psychosis revealed their presence to him; countless more.

If you knew how to look, you'd see them everywhere, Agon said.

Arachne shook her head as the visions dissipated. "How could I sense it in her, and not the others?"

Agon tilted its head at her. *You really can't be that stupid, can you?*

Arachne gaped when it hit her. "He let me see her power because He *wanted* me to pick her."

A grating, gurgling sound emerged from the ruin of Agon's mouth—its version of laughter. *I thought even you would have figured that out ages ago.*

Shame roiled in Arachne's stomach. "I can't believe I didn't see it."

If it's any consolation, you never had a chance. Agon shook its head, rancid jowls swinging. *The human capacity for hope is a Hell unto itself.*

Arachne coughed up an enormous, wriggling huntsman spider and spat it over the edge of the cliff. She and Agon watched it tumble through the air and smack onto the rocks below.

"Well, I suppose there's nothing to do now but wait for something terrible to happen."

Terrible things happen all the time. This will be different.

"How so?" Arachne asked.

He hasn't just unleashed her natural ability, He's amplified it. It's growing beyond its natural bounds, Agon said with a pleased hissing sound. *Only He knows what will happen next.*

3

AZRAEL HATCH PEERED UP at his apartment from the front steps, exhausted from another day of work at the docks. The work had calloused his hands, strengthened his muscles, and darkened his complexion in the driving sun. It was honest work, but most days he daydreamed about getting injured. He'd seen broken digits, busted noses, a hundred cuts ranging from mild to serious. Last week, a barrel had rolled off a forklift, shattering a man's femur. If Azrael could pick an injury for himself, a spiral fracture of the tibia would be ideal: weeks in the hospital, pain medication, physical therapy, and best of all, respite from his home life.

This was folly, of course—he was using a false name and getting paid under the table. If he were to hurt himself badly enough to go to the hospital, the best-case scenario would be crippling debt, and the worst would be them discovering his identity, and he and Lila getting caught. Odds were, they'd both go to prison for a long time.

But...would incarceration be any worse than his current captivity?

He'd cared for Lila once. There had been something *other* to her, something sharp and true, and when she looked at him with her fathomless eyes, he'd wanted nothing more than her. She was a full moon in a sky of dull, distant stars.

But then he'd met Olivia, and she was the sun. She burned with such a bright life force that it had turned his desire for Lila into a pale imitation.

The night before Henry Hatch's verdict was announced, Lila had told Azrael what she planned to do if he were acquitted. "I will leave Cade with you, catch up to Hatch's motorcade, and slit his throat. Then I'll cut through the woods to the last motel we stayed at the night before the trial started. You remember the one, a mile north of here?"

Azrael had said he did. He didn't think Lila was serious, and he certainly didn't think things were going to go the way she'd planned.

But everything had happened just as she said. Azrael had slipped away from the media circus surrounding the court-house, cradling his wailing son in his arms, and ran like the devil was on his heels until he got to the motel. Lila arrived soon after and kissed Azrael desperately, her fingers red with his father's blood.

The first weeks on the run were the worst. They were hunted like animals. They'd left Austin on foot, sticking to back roads, dodging the sounds of sirens. Azrael had sensed authorities closing in on them on the outskirts of Rockdale when a man with gray eyes and salt-and-pepper stubble suddenly stopped his car to offer them a ride. Lila hadn't wanted to get in the car, but Azrael was able to convince her they had no other choice, and the man had driven them over the state line to Hope, Arkansas, where he'd given Azrael and Lila a bundle of cash and wished them luck.

Azrael and Lila had used the cash to rent a tiny, furnished efficiency with a cockroach infestation. It was better than sleeping under an overpass, but not by much.

They'd moved a dozen times since then, to motels and apartments and shelters in Arkansas, Mississippi, and Louisiana. At five months, they'd been at their current apartment the longest: a cramped two-bedroom walk-up outside of Saint Rose, Louisiana.

A headache glowered behind Azrael's eyes as he stared up the kitchen windows. What would he be doing tonight if he had stayed with Olivia? He wouldn't be on the run, terrified and fantasizing about getting injured. Maybe he could have found a way to convince Olivia to take him back. Maybe he could have found a way to be good for her.

The sound of broken glass startled Azrael from his thoughts. He ran up the steps and found Lila in the kitchen, plucking shards of glass from the linoleum as Cade toddled toward her.

Azrael scooped up his son. "That's not safe, Button." He kissed Cade's forehead and set him on the couch. "You stay here until we get the mess cleaned up."

Cade smiled at his father. "Kay, Dad."

Azrael sighed, wishing his love for his son felt less like a shackle around his heart.

"Nice of you to come home," muttered Lila, the knees of her gray sweatpants soaking up red wine.

"Get away from there. You'll cut yourself—look, you already did."

"It's just wine."

"No, your hand."

Lila gritted her teeth as she spotted the slice on her palm. "Oh. Damn."

Azrael swept the broken glass into a pile, discarded it, and searched for any slivers he may have missed. Lila wrapped her hand in a dish towel, plucked a fresh glass from the dish drying rack, and poured the rest of the wine bottle inside.

Azrael watched her with a pang of jealousy. He hadn't had a drink in months. The kid needed one sober parent, at least.

In the living room, Cade said to his stuffed lion, "No, I don't know how glass is made."

Lila scowled at Azrael over the rim of her glass. "You think I don't see you when you're standing outside, staring up at our home?"

Cade ran up to Azrael. "Daddy!"

"Not now, Button," Azrael said.

Lila said, "Like maybe one day you're not going to come inside?"

Azrael drew an inhale through his teeth as a tiny sliver of glass went into his palm. "Lila, not in front of the kid..."

"Daddy!"

"What, Cade?" Azrael said.

"Glass is made of sand and fire!"

"That's...actually pretty close to the truth, Cade." Azrael looked up from the glass shards in his hand. "Where did you hear that? One of your TV shows?"

Cade shook his head. "Nero told me."

"Who's Nero?"

"Nero's his stuffed lion," Lila said.

"Nero, huh?" asked Azrael. "He must be a pretty smart guy. When sand gets hot enough, it melts and becomes glass. We can look it up and learn more about it if you want."

"No thanks," said Cade. "Nero, Daddy says you're right!" Cade was silent for a few seconds, then burst into screaming laughter, as if Nero had said the funniest thing he'd ever heard. Goosebumps prickled Azrael's arms.

Azrael glared at Lila. "Don't talk to me like that in front of him."

Lila took a long drink from her glass. "Hungry?"

Not really. "Yes."

"Spaghetti all right?"

"Perfect," Azrael said flatly.

THAT NIGHT, WHEN CADE was asleep and Lila lay passed out on top of the covers, Azrael turned on the TV. He ought to go to bed—he had to leave for work again in six hours—but he couldn't lie down next to Lila. Not yet.

He clicked around until he came across a news station. "Breaking news," the anchor said. "Henry Hatch's son, missing for years, has resurfaced."

Terror rocked Azrael on his heels. He'd been found. He wasn't sure how he was hearing it through the news before they'd arrested him, but it had happened at last. His running days were over. The daydream of capture, turned into a nightmare.

"It turns out," continued the anchor, "he's been hiding in plain sight all along."

Azrael's mind raced. Maybe there was time to run. Maybe they knew where he worked, but not where he lived...

"This morning, a charity located in Denver, Colorado called Fishers of Men announced that their leader, Elijah Fisher, is the son of the late Henry Hatch."

Elijah's face appeared on the TV screen. His hair was a few shades darker, his once-boyish face angular and stippled with sparse facial hair. He looked lean and strong as he wheeled up to a reporter in his wheelchair. Behind him, the foyer of an old building bustled with activity.

"We're still learning details about Fishers of Men," the voiceover explained, "but what we do know is that many known members of the Colony, the cult led by Elijah's late father Henry Hatch, are involved in this organization."

Azrael turned up the volume.

Onsite, the reporter asked Elijah, "You were living outside the Colony when your father was arrested, is that correct?"

"I was living in Austin at the time, yes," Elijah said. "Right after his arrest, I was wounded in Hurricane Ophelia, and my legs had to be removed below the knee. My family came to my aid, but they were lost, afraid, confused."

"Why did you not step forward as a witness during your father's trial?" the reporter asked.

Elijah's expression grew serious. "I'll be honest. I knew my father was innocent, but it seemed like the entire world was against him. I was young, and frightened."

"And what took place following your father's murder?"

"I knew I needed to lead my family through the devastation of his loss. As things progressed, I realized how much people outside the Colony needed to hear our message as well, so we founded Fishers of Men: a place where people can receive aid."

"And you do that using Nosh?"

"Nosh has made Fishers of Men what we are today," Elijah told her. "The first diet we know is a liquid one. It gives us all the nutrients we need to grow and thrive. All Fishers of Men is doing is allowing people to return to that simplicity. We provide people not only with sustenance, but also coats, diapers, children's toys, and countless other donated goods."

"I'll be damned," whispered Azrael. Was it true? Had Elijah turned their father's charade of faith into something good?

"And your brother, Azrael Hatch…do you have any knowledge of his whereabouts, or of Lila Monroe's? Have either of them contacted you?"

"If I knew anything about Azrael or Lila, I would tell the authorities immediately," said Elijah. "Lila took my father from me, and while I forgive her for doing so, I do believe she should be brought to justice."

The newscast moved on to another topic, and Azrael turned off the television. He walked on shaky legs into the bedroom and lay down beside Lila, his heartbeat pounding in his ears. Beside him, Lila stirred and reached for him in the dark. He shifted away from her touch.

"Why do you hate me?" Lila whispered.

As Azrael drifted off into an uneasy sleep, the feeling of Lila's touch lingering on his skin like a bad taste in his mouth, he felt the bed shaking with her quiet sobs.

4

"DAN, ARE YOU SERIOUS with that email you just sent?" Olivia fumed. "You want to *donate* Nosh to Fishers of Men?"

Dan looked up from his laptop. "Absolutely."

"Do you have any idea what kind of monsters these people are? They're child molesters. They abuse their wives. They're led by a delusional teenager who thinks he speaks directly to God."

Dan cocked his head in confusion. "I thought you said you were friends with him."

"I said I *knew* him. He wasn't a friend. He was a sullen little kid back then, but now he's turning into his father— can't you tell that from their press release?"

Dan smirked. "What I saw in their press release was a young man whose brush with death gave him a new perspective on life."

"It's not just him," Olivia said. "One of the men in the press photos is Robert Grayburn. He was Henry Hatch's right-hand man before he died. That can't be a good sign."

Dan stared at her for a moment and then shook his head. "Listen, I've looked into their organization. They haven't stepped a toe out of line since the adoption of their new name. Fishers of Men is generating a lot of good press, and it's barely going to put a dent in our profits to provide them with most of the Nosh they need free of charge."

"This isn't about press, Dan. They're a toxic cult. We shouldn't be helping them."

An impatient edge crept into his tone. "Tell you what, Olivia. If you can find anything bad on Fishers of Men, let me know, and we can examine our donation plan then."

Dan turned to retrieve his laptop bag from the table behind him, granting Olivia a glimpse of the scar tissue knitting the back of his head together, fringed by a pale strip where his hair was growing back. Olivia forced herself to walk away before she did something she regretted. She hadn't hurt anyone since she blasted her house free of bugs, and she didn't want to break that streak by hurting Dan again, whether he deserved it or not.

AN HOUR LATER, OLIVIA approached Milo and Nancy, who waited for her at an outdoor table at Celis Brewery. Nancy had decided a few days ago to pull the trigger on dyeing her hair a warm, copper red, and as Olivia had predicted, she looked more radiant than ever. Milo had let his dark hair grow out nearly to his shoulders, and between that and his sleek sunglasses, he could have passed for a celebrity in disguise.

"Hey there," Olivia said, hugging Milo.

"Oof," said Milo, wincing at her tone. "I take it the talk with Dan didn't go well?"

Nancy pulled Olivia in for a hug as well. "I caught Milo up about Fisher Biotech's Nosh donation to those screwballs. What hot garbage."

Olivia sat beside Nancy. "I feel like either I'm going crazy, or everyone else is. Is the public attention span really so short people have forgotten about what happened in the Colony? What the Fathers did to the women and children?"

"I know, hon," Nancy said. "It's some top-notch bullshit."

When the server came around, Olivia ordered a beer, then put her head in her hands and sighed.

"Are you all right?" Milo asked.

Olivia struggled to find the right words. "After Elijah vanished from the hospital and didn't show up for the trial, I thought he might have been killed. I thought maybe Azrael was right about their lives being in danger. And now, Elijah's alive and well, and I should be relieved, but it just makes my stomach hurt." Olivia sighed. "Maybe Dan's right. Maybe I just want to punish Elijah for what Azrael put me through. Maybe I'm a petty, miserable person who wants everyone else to feel as awful as I do."

Milo grinned. "Sounds far-fetched."

Olivia laughed. The tension in her shoulders unwound a bit.

Nancy said, "Look at it this way: either they're an evil cult, and people will figure it out, or they're a legitimate charitable organization, and they're really helping people. Give it time. The truth will shake out one way or the other."

Olivia blew out a slow breath and relaxed her fists. "Yeah… you're right. It's just a gut punch, you know?"

"Yeah, dude," Nancy whistled. "Weird times."

Milo asked Olivia, "Are you planning on visiting your mom for her birthday?"

"Yeah, I am."

"Doesn't she live pretty close to Fishers of Men?"

Olivia's stomach clenched. "Yeah."

"Maybe you'd get…I don't know, some kind of closure if you went and checked it out."

"Yeah," Olivia conceded. "Maybe."

"Ooh, want me to watch that cute kitten of yours while you're gone?" Nancy asked. "What was her name again?"

"Dinah," Olivia said. A few days after she'd eradicated the bedbug life from her house, she'd awoken to a mewling sound outside her bedroom window and discovered a tiny ball of fluff nestled in the grass. Olivia fell in love with her at once, and named her Dinah. The kitten had been brightening Olivia's life now that she felt safe being in her home again. "Maybe just one night. Dinah likes having someone to poke in the eye at five o'clock in the morning."

"Sure thing, doll. Just let me know when. Now, cheer up. There's a new horror movie playing at the Alamo tonight, if you'd like to join us. It's supposed to be a real gore-fest."

"A few people at the movie's premiere actually fainted," Milo added cheerfully.

Olivia managed a thin smile. "Yeah, that sounds great. Should help get my mind off the whole 'Fishers of Men' thing."

Olivia took another long drink of her beer. In the absence of anything resembling a romantic relationship in the last three years, she'd settled comfortably into her role as Nancy and Milo's third wheel. Maybe someday, somebody would come along and make her feel a fraction of the fire she'd felt with Azrael. Something real, like what Milo and Nancy had. Maybe she could let go of the invisible tether connecting her heart to Azrael's.

Maybe one day, but not today.

5

Lila checked the time. 8:30 p.m. Half an hour past Cade's bedtime, and Azrael hadn't come home yet.

"Time for bed, Button," she told Cade.

Cade's eyes filled with tears. "But Daddy—"

"I know, Cade, he's working late tonight. You'll see him in the morning," she lied. Azrael would be gone before Cade woke up, and Cade knew it.

"Daddy," Cade whimpered again.

"I know, Button, I miss him, too."

Cade screamed as Lila lifted him off his bedroom floor and deposited him in his bed.

"*DADDYYY.*"

"Yup," said Lila. "Daddy's not here right now. It's almost like he doesn't care about us."

Cade flopped onto his stomach and sobbed. Lila watched him for a few seconds, then left the room and shut the door. He'd cry himself to sleep eventually.

Azrael had grown more distant than ever since he'd learned of "Fishers of Men." He was taking on more work at the dock, pulling twelve-hour shifts, sometimes six days a week. At least, that's what he told her. Some days he came home smelling of sweat and diesel, and some days he didn't.

In Lila's more paranoid moments, she imagined Azrael was having an affair with Olivia, but she knew if that were the case, Azrael wouldn't come home at all.

The phantom of Azrael's ex-lover haunted him. Lila saw it in his eyes. She'd believed once that Azrael's obsession with Olivia would fade over time, but it hadn't.

Olivia, the specter of the better, easier life Azrael could have had. Olivia, the reason Lila drank herself to sleep every night.

Lila poured herself a glass of wine as Cade screamed. Her neighbor banged on their paper-thin wall. Lila banged back, then burst into tears. How she wished she didn't need Azrael with every fiber of her being. How wretched it felt to be so trapped, obsession and fury warring within her, wondering every night whether it would be the night he didn't come home.

Lila turned on the TV and flipped through a few fuzz-filled channels until she came across a movie. She turned the volume up to drown out Cade's cries. In the movie, the camera panned over the rolling green hills of a graveyard under a white sky. The camera zoomed in on a man and woman dressed in black, staring down at a fresh grave. The woman wiped away a tear. "Now that she's dead," she said, "we can finally be together."

The view changed to a close-up of the couple's hands hanging by their sides. The music swelled as the man grasped the woman's hand. The movie faded to black and gave way to a commercial.

Lila turned off the TV and stared blankly at her reflection in the dark screen. The line of dialogue was one of a dozen signs she'd received over the last few days. She finished off the last of the wine in her glass as Cade wailed in the next room. She pressed her palms against her ears, but she couldn't block the sound out. The air grew too thin to breathe.

Now that she's dead. The words lit up her mind like a flashing road sign. *Now that she's dead, we can finally be together.*

Now that she's dead.

Lila blinked, and she was in her bedroom shoving clothes into her backpack. She had no recollection of going into the room, nor why she'd started packing. As she stuffed spare sets of socks and underwear into her bag, the answer came to her: She couldn't stay in the apartment one more minute. If she didn't walk out the door, she was going to throw herself out the window.

Lila dug the only sharp knife they owned out of the flatware drawer and tossed it into the bag as well, along with the stash of bills Azrael didn't think she knew about, stuffed into one of his shoes in the closet.

There was a satisfaction to her departure—all those sleepless nights, worrying about whether Azrael was going to come home—and now she was the one leaving. Her head spun with a sensation too manic to be glee.

"Now that she's dead," Lila murmured, "we can finally be together."

Lila locked the apartment door behind her and descended the stairs, Cade's cries fading until all she heard was her own heartbeat thrashing in her ears like a trapped bird.

6

THE FOLLOWING MORNING, ARACHNE shifted her attention from Lila's westward bus ride to the line of people slowly filing into Fishers of Men in Denver. One by one, people entered the building and emerged holding Nosh pouches, clothing, and other supplies. Olivia filed inside, where dozens of volunteers handed out goods from long wooden tables.

When she reached the table, a petite woman with the name *Lucille* on her name tag smiled at her. "And what can we do for you, dear?"

"You can tell me where Elijah is," Olivia said evenly.

"Oh," said Lucille, "He…he's not usually able—"

"I knew him," Olivia said. "When he was exiled."

Arachne crept a spider on the wall close enough to see a flicker of fear pass over Lucille's face. "Excuse me?"

"I was there when Elijah lost his legs. I was with him in the hospital. I have something that belongs to him, and I was hoping to give it back to him."

"I see." Lucille forced a smile. "I'm sorry, I didn't get your name."

"Olivia."

"Follow me, Olivia."

Lucille led Olivia away from the crowd, up three flights of stairs, and down a long hallway. She hesitated, then knocked on the last door. "Elijah? You have a visitor."

Elijah's voice came from inside: "Come in."

Lucille opened the door, and Olivia peered inside. Elijah looked up from his desk by the window. "Olivia."

"Hi, Elijah." Olivia walked into the room.

"Mother, can you give us a moment?" Elijah asked.

"Of course," Lucille said, closing the door behind her.

Arachne's spiders found good vantage points as Olivia settled into a chair across from Elijah. He turned his wheelchair to face her, and they sat in silence for a few beats.

"Why are you here?" Elijah asked.

Olivia seemed to gather her thoughts. "When I came back to the hospital…after the storm…you were gone. It was like you'd vanished into thin air. I thought maybe you'd gone into witness protection, but when you didn't show up for your father's trial, I was scared something terrible had happened to you. What *did* happen? Where did you go?"

Elijah said, "I was discovered by a fellow exile of the Colony at the hospital. He returned me to my people. They forgave me and took me back."

"Oh, wow," Olivia said, absorbing this. "I'm just so glad you're all right."

He nodded gravely. "The road here has not been easy, but I've found a way forward in Fishers of Men."

Olivia's hands fidgeted in her lap as her eyes fell on the neatly made bed against the opposite wall. "Do you…live here?"

"I do," Elijah said. "We have several bedrooms on the second and third floors, available to whomever needs a place to rest."

Olivia nodded. "I, um, I brought you something." She pulled Elijah's Bible from her bag and held it out to him.

Elijah wheeled forward and accepted it, gray eyes widening in shock. "I can't believe you found it." He opened the cover and ran his fingers over the inscription. Arachne could make it out from her nearest spider:

To my son, destined to lead. -HH

"Thank you for this," Elijah said softly.

Olivia wrestled with her next words. "Elijah...it looks like you're doing real good here, helping feed and clothe people, but the men who served your father—men like Robert Grayburn—they've had to relinquish a lot of the power they once had, and men like that don't give up control easily. I came to see for myself what was happening here. There's only so much you can tell from the news, and—"

Elijah's gray eyes held her gaze coolly. "You want to make sure that we aren't like the Colony."

"Yes."

He sniffed. "I can assure you, things are very different. Nobody is forced to stay here, and nobody is marrying anybody against their will. Both of my wives grew up in the outside world before joining us."

Olivia was not entirely successful in hiding her shock. "Wives? Is that legal?"

"These marriages may not be recognized by the government," Elijah explained, "but we answer to a higher law than that of man. The Lord's message to us has been clear: we need to spread the gospel to as many people as possible, and that includes giving life to the next generation of believers."

"Elijah, how old are you? Seventeen?"

"Old enough to love my wives and treat them as equals in our mission."

Arachne laughed. Neither of Elijah's wives—Cathryn and Casey—were forced into marrying him at gunpoint, but to call them equals was a farce. Both women came from strict religious backgrounds and arrived at the Colony pre-brain-washed and ready to bear Elijah as many children as they could. Casey was already a few weeks pregnant, and Elijah was doing his level best to put a baby in Cathryn as well.

Another marriage had occurred the same winter Elijah married his two wives: Robert Grayburn was at last allowed to marry Melinda Coleman, whom Elijah had absolved of the event that had sullied her name. Melinda, who Arachne was sure would bolt if she had anywhere to go, had accepted Grayburn's proposal with a weak smile and sad eyes.

Olivia swallowed, looking queasy. "Do you ever talk to Warren?"

Elijah shook his head. "Azrael drove him off right before the storm hit, and he hasn't resurfaced. I wish he'd come back and join us, now that things are different. He'd have a place here."

"He'll see the news about this place soon, if he hasn't already."

"God willing," said Elijah. "It's been an incredible year so far. We're opening facilities in Omaha, Kansas City, Charlotte, and Richmond. Our followers are calling themselves 'Fishers' both because of our Fishers of Men moniker and the Nosh coming from Fisher Biotech. We're becoming what God has intended—a force for good meant for more than just a few."

Olivia's shoulders shook as she failed to conceal her shudder.

Elijah's eyes hardened. "Thank you for coming, Olivia. And please give our thanks to the leadership at Fisher Biotech for donating Nosh so generously to our cause. We're going to help a lot of people. I've got to get back to work now, but it was good seeing you. Please help yourself to some Nosh on the way out."

7

NOT SINCE LILA HAD escaped the Colony had she felt so lucid, so full of purpose. Gone was the woman who drank herself to sleep every night. The woman who tore down an empire and slashed the throat of a mad king had made her return. She'd barely slept on the series of Greyhound buses that had transported her from Saint Rose to Austin, yet she felt alert and vigilant. Tiny scratches covered her arms from scrambling through a nest of rose bushes. The pain singing to Lila from the scratches was turning her into the feral, pitiless creature who could do what needed to be done.

What was Azrael doing, this very moment? Putting Cade to sleep? Pacing the apartment, frantic with worry? Thinking of something other than Olivia for once?

Olivia's house glowed bone-white in the moonlight. Finding Olivia's address had taken some work, but she was confident this was it. Lila gripped the hilt of the knife in her pocket and brushed a lock of hair from her eyes.

Once it was done, Azrael would be free. He would return to Lila, body and soul. He would love her the way he used to. It was the only way.

Lila slunk onto Olivia's back porch and tried the door—locked. The adjacent windows were locked as well. She padded over to another window and stood on a weathered plastic chair to peer inside, and there was Olivia, bundled in covers and curled onto her side, copper hair shining in the moonlight.

Lila pushed, and the window rose from the sill a fraction of an inch. She stopped and hunkered against the house. She hadn't made much noise, but it may have been enough to wake a light sleeper. She counted to sixty and peered through the window. Olivia hadn't moved.

Lila unshouldered her backpack and set it against the outside of the house. She lifted the window open in tiny increments, ducking down each time the window made the slightest noise. When it was finally open enough to fit her body through, she climbed inside.

The distant rumble of an approaching train echoed through the night. Lila stared at Olivia's sleeping body, the slow rise and fall of her chest. When the window rattled with the train's approach, Olivia rolled over under the sheets, sighing softly.

Now.

Lila slipped the blade between Olivia's shoulder blades.

Olivia uttered a muffled cry and thrashed under the sheets. Lila stabbed the knife down again. Olivia screamed and fought, but she couldn't find purchase under the covers. Lila straddled her and brought the knife down again and again. The train thundered past, shaking the walls, as Olivia's screams turned to gurgles and the movement under the covers went still.

Lila peeled the covers back. Deep slashes marred Olivia's face beyond all recognition. Beads of blood glistened in her red hair like pearls on a necklace. Lila's stomach roiled at the sight, and at the smell of death. This wasn't like when she took the Prophet's life. That had been swift, like cutting a balloon string. This death had been no less necessary for her continued survival, but it had been brutal, nonetheless.

A mewling noise made Lila turn. A tiny kitten, hackles raised, looked up at her from the darkness beside the bed. It flattened its ears and hissed. Lila returned her gaze to Olivia's body, the sickening feeling in her gut growing deeper as the train rolled off into the distance.

Now that she's dead, we can finally be together.

A hollowness spread through Lila's chest where triumph ought to have been. She climbed off the bed, lowered herself out of the window, and closed it behind her. Head spinning, she hurried around to the side of the house, stripping out of her clothes and using the garden hose to wash the blood from her face, hair, and hands. When she dressed in the clean clothes she'd packed in her bag and checked her reflection in the window, she hardly recognized herself.

A shiver of panic shot through Lila as she stuffed her bloody clothes into her backpack.

She needed to get back to Azrael as quickly as possible.

8

"Fuck," said Arachne.

9

Cade woke to Nero, his toy lion, whispering to him.

Cade, Nero said. *Mommy is coming back.*

Cade stirred and pulled Nero close. "She is?"

Yes, Cade, Nero said. *Now go and wake your father.*

Cade rose from bed and walked into his father's room. "Wake up, Daddy," he whispered.

"Good morning, Button," Daddy murmured. "What do you want for breakfast?"

"Cupcakes?"

"Cupcakes it is."

Cade momentarily forgot about Mommy's return. "Yay, cupcakes!"

Daddy pinched the flesh between his eyebrows and checked his bedside clock. "The store's not open yet, buddy. Let's watch one of your shows until it opens, okay?"

"But I want *cupcakes*."

Daddy picked Cade up, walked into the living room, and turned on the TV. "I know, kiddo, but we've got to wait a little bit before—"

"—a horrific murder in Austin, Texas, leaves a quiet neighborhood in shock."

Azrael snapped to attention, staring at the TV.

"Daddy," whined Cade.

"Go to your room," said Azrael.

"But I want—"

"Cade, go to your room *right now*."

Cade burst into tears and ran into his bedroom, burying his face into the comfort of Nero's soft fur.

In the living room, Azrael turned up the volume. Cade stopped crying and listened.

"A warning to viewers: some of the footage you are about to see is graphic in nature. Authorities responded to a 911 call and found the victim had been stabbed to death in her bed the night before."

Daddy's voice floated through the door. "No, no..."

"The killer appears to have entered through an unlocked bedroom window. Authorities do not have any suspects yet. Investigators say that nothing of value appears to have been stolen from the residence, so they believe the murder may have been personal in nature. Out of respect for her family, the identity of this young woman has not yet been released, but we—"

The sound cut off as Daddy either turned off or muted the TV.

In the ensuing silence, Nero told Cade, *You need to leave.*

Cade sniffed. "Why?"

Your mother is coming back. You must not be here when she returns.

"I don't want to move again," Cade whined.

Nero sent Cade a picture in his mind: Mommy, arms running dark with blood in the moonlight, her face twisted into an ugly shape he hardly recognized.

You need to leave NOW, Nero demanded.

Cade's heart hammered as he approached Daddy in the living room. "Nero says we need to leave."

Daddy wiped his eyes. "I know, Button. I'm sorry I yelled at you. We'll leave in a bit."

"No," said Cade. "Not for cupcakes. Mommy's coming back."

Daddy looked at him. His eyes were as red as Mommy's when she had too many glasses of wine. "You don't want to be here when Mommy comes back?"

Cade shook his head. "Mommy's...red."

Daddy blinked. "What else did Nero say?"

"He said we have to move again."

"Okay, Button," said Daddy. He looked dazed, distant. "Let's go."

Cade packed handfuls of toys, clothes, and books into his suitcase. He packed his spare pair of shoes, though they were tight on his feet, and threw Nero in as well.

Daddy lugged his own duffel bag out of his bedroom and hunkered in front of Cade. "Remember the rules for moving? We might have to move fast, and I might call you by a name other than your real one."

Cade nodded. "I remember, Daddy."

"Okay. We'll need to walk to the train station. It's about twenty minutes away. Can you do that?"

Cade nodded.

"When we get where we're going, I'll make you cupcakes, okay?"

"Okay, Daddy." Cade smiled.

Daddy took his hand, and they walked out of the apartment.

That evening, Daddy made a phone call.

10

LILA STOOD AT THE base of her apartment steps. The streetlights flickered on, painting the front of the building a pallid orange. Her back ached from sleeping upright in bus seats. She longed for a drink, a kiss from her sweet child, the comfort of her bed.

Lila took a deep breath, climbed the steps, and entered her apartment. It was dark and cold.

"Hello?"

No answer. She was alone. Judging by the time on the oven clock, Azrael was at work. Cade must be at whatever daycare Azrael had arranged for him. Lila pushed back against a creeping feeling of unease and poured herself a glass of wine. She walked into her bedroom and felt the glass slip through her fingers.

The bedroom was in shambles: clothes flung everywhere, drawers hanging open, lamp knocked over.

Azrael and Cade were gone.

Lila collapsed to the floor and sobbed. Azrael had finally done it. He'd finally left, and taken Cade with him. She had no hope of finding them now.

When Lila found the strength to stand, she picked up her overturned glass, refilled it with wine, and gulped it down.

She poured herself another glass with shaking hands, closed her eyes, and took a deep breath. Her phone was dead. Maybe Azrael had left her a message. Maybe she could find them.

She plugged her phone into its charger. When it turned on, her fears were confirmed—no new messages from Azrael.

Lila stared at the cold glow of her phone screen. She searched for *Austin stabbing* in the news and clicked the first result.

Authorities are searching for the person responsible for the brutal murder of Austin resident Nancy Madrigal.

Lila frowned. Who the hell was Nancy Madrigal?

Nancy Madrigal was stabbed to death while house-sitting for a friend. When Madrigal didn't answer her phone after several attempts, her husband discovered her body the following day. He called the police, who detained him briefly as a suspect, but then released him when he was able to prove he'd been elsewhere at the time of the murder.

"No," said Lila. She'd killed the wrong girl. *The wrong fucking girl.*

She risked so much, and all for nothing. She killed an innocent woman, and now Azrael and Cade were gone forever.

Lila screamed and hurled her glass, shattering it against the wall. "No, no, *no!*"

Three sharp knocks on the door made her jump. "Lila Monroe?"

Lila shot to her feet. She must have left some kind of evidence behind at Olivia's house…or else, Azrael had seen the news and sent the authorities to find her.

Kill yourself. Lila shook the thought away, but it brushed against her again, like the feathers of a huge, dark wing. *Kill yourself, while you still can.*

The knocks came again, harder this time. Lila backed away from the door. She gasped at a sharp pain in her heel:

the broken glass. She stared at the dizzying edge of the glass glinting in the streetlight.

The wood around the door latch splintered. They would be inside in seconds.

Lila picked up the shard of glass, took a deep breath, and drew it across her throat.

The door slammed open an instant later. Officers swarmed her apartment.

Lila fell to her knees. There was a dull pain and the feeling of suffocation. Boots and shadows surrounded her, shouting, hands pressing to the wound on her neck. Her heartbeat grew louder and slower in her ears.

Lila said goodbye to Cade and Azrael, the only humans in the world who ever meant a thing to her. Darkness surrounded her, devouring her, giving her its final gift.

11

Olivia was finishing up dinner with her mother when Milo called.

"Hey, Milo, what's up?"

A guttural sob emerged from her phone speaker. "Olivia...Nancy's dead."

All the blood drained from Olivia's head. "What?"

"Nancy's dead. Someone stabbed her to death last night, in your bed."

The room spun and Olivia gripped the edge of the table to keep herself upright. "Milo, what are...what..."

"I called her a few times, and when she didn't answer, I went to check on her," Milo said hoarsely. "When she didn't answer the door, I let myself into your place, and I...smelled blood. I went into the bedroom, and the smell got stronger. I found her in your bed. The sheets were sticky with blood, and she was cold." His voice cracked on the last word.

Olivia hurried into her room and began packing her bag. "Where are you?"

"I'm at the police station. They questioned me. They... um, they had to take my clothes as evidence. Because of the blood."

"Jesus, Milo, oh my God."

"I have to call her parents next," said Milo. It sounded like someone was squeezing his throat. "I can't…I don't know what I'm going to tell them." His voice hitched with sobs.

"I'm coming right now," said Olivia, tears filling her eyes. "I'm coming back, okay? I'll be there by tonight."

"How did this happen? What am I going to do without her?"

"I don't know Milo. I'm sorry, I'm so sorry…"

"I have to go."

"I'll see you tonight—"

The line went dead.

When Olivia told her mother why she was crying, Betty grabbed her and pulled her close. "Oh my God, in your *bed*? Olivia, that could have been you."

Olivia's breath caught in her throat. It *should* have been her. Maybe she would have ended up just as dead as poor Nancy, but then again, maybe she could have done something. Maybe she could have unleashed whatever ability she possessed on her would-be butcher. Maybe the attacker would have dropped dead of a heart attack before he'd had the chance to finish the job.

But Nancy didn't have mind-powers. She was the kindest, funniest person Olivia had ever known. And now she was gone, the victim of a senseless, grisly attack that hadn't been intended for her.

On the flight back to Austin, Olivia couldn't stop crying. Every time she'd start to get a hold of herself, the image of Nancy bleeding to death in agony and terror filled her mind and she'd start sobbing again. She kept waiting for some sort of numbness to sweep over her, but there was no reprieve. Just fresh horror, wave after wave of it.

When she landed, she checked her phone for updates and saw that an anonymous tip had led authorities to Lila Monroe's apartment, where they found her bleeding out from a self-inflicted wound. Officers attempted to save Lila's life, but she was dead within minutes. Traces of blood on the knife found in Lila's apartment were being sent for testing, but Olivia knew in her gut that the hunt for Nancy's killer had ended.

The days that followed were the worst days of Olivia's life: the tidal wave of media coverage; soulless headlines like *OIL HEIRESS SLAIN*; reporters hounding Olivia and Milo everywhere they went; online rumors that Milo had killed his wife for the life insurance money, or that he and Olivia had been having an affair; the horrors and mundanities which fell to the living in the wake of unexpected death; Nancy's funeral, which turned into the exact kind of bloated, over-serious event Nancy had insisted her wedding not be.

After the funeral, Olivia drove Milo back to his house. Olivia's throat tightened upon walking inside—the house smelled like Nancy, the soft, vanilla linen of her impeccable clothes, light as a springtime breeze. Olivia put on an old record to cover up the vulturous thrum of reporters outside the house, poured two glasses of scotch on the rocks—the way Nancy used to drink it—and settled into the couch next to Milo.

"Are the curtains drawn?" Milo asked.

"Yes," Olivia assured him, resting her head on his shoulder.

They sat listening to the record for a few songs before Milo asked, "Olivia, why was Lila Monroe trying to kill you?"

Olivia lifted her head, finished her glass of scotch, and set it down. "I think it comes down to two possibilities. My best guess is that Lila thought I represented some kind of threat to her connection to Azrael."

"Why would she think that?" Milo asked.

Olivia pressed her lips together. "Because Azrael would have chosen me over her if I'd let him."

The needle on the record player finished out the last song and swung into the center. The ice in Milo's glass clinked as it settled against the side. The paparazzi and reporters outside had either quieted down or called it a night. Olivia's body prickled in the sudden absence of commotion for the first time in days.

"What's the other possibility?" Milo asked thickly.

Olivia swallowed, her throat tightening like a fist. "I think it's less likely, but it occurred to me that Azrael might want to hurt me for some reason. I don't think that's what this was, but I truly don't know what he's capable of, so I can't discount it as a possibility."

Milo considered this in silence for a while, then said, "What can we do to protect you, if that's true? I don't know what I would do if something happened to you, too."

Tears choked off Milo's next words, and Olivia embraced him, feeling the tremor deep in his bones. "Nothing's going to happen to me," she said. "I'm not going anywhere."

"I can't believe she's gone," Milo sobbed. "I keep thinking I'm going to wake up from this like it's a bad dream, and she's going to be in bed next to me. How am I supposed to live without her?"

"I don't know, Milo," Olivia said as tears spilled from her own eyes. "We'll get through this. Nancy would want us to keep going."

Milo nodded into the hollow of her shoulder. "I know. I just miss her so much."

"Me, too," Olivia said.

They held each other and wept as the needle gave off tiny pops and hisses from the center of the record, the hazy whispers emerging from the speakers louder than the music had been.

12

Elijah dreamed of Azrael and Lila.

He was surprised to see them together, because Lila was dead. Azrael stood at the sink in a dingy kitchen, watching the muddy water flowing through the faucet before turning clear. Lila sat on the couch in the living room with a glass of wine in her hand, her eyes red from crying. Cade wailed in the bedroom.

It would have looked like an ordinary, melancholy portrait of a family isolated by their own pain, if not for the room being on fire.

Hungry flames licked the walls, blackening white-washed plaster, rendering drapes to ash, sending smoke roiling up from charred furniture, reducing candles to dripping wax on a crooked mantle.

Azrael and Lila didn't react to the fire raging around them. Azrael washed dishes, Lila sipped her wine, and Cade screamed, as their world burned.

Azrael turned to look at him. "Elijah."

Elijah wrestled himself free of the dream, waking in his cool, moonlit bedroom, dripping with sweat, pain thrumming the tendons where his calves used to be.

Beside him, Azrael hissed: *"Elijah."*

Elijah opened his eyes and made out the shape of his brother, crouched next to his bed. A month's growth of facial hair sprouted from his brother's clenched jawline, and his hair stuck up in wild swaths. "Azrael?"

"Yes," said Azrael. "Hush, don't wake your wife."

Elijah cringed. Azrael's breath could have blistered paint from the wall. "What are you doing here?"

"I need your help, brother," said Azrael. "I'm out of money. Cade's hungry. We've got no place else to go."

Cathryn shifted beside Elijah in bed. She was a deep sleeper, but she'd wake if he raised his voice.

"How did you get in here?" Elijah hissed.

"Broke a window."

"Where's Cade?"

"Downstairs. I know you don't have food here, but you could give him Nosh—"

"I can't hide you, Azrael."

"Listen, you don't owe me anything—"

"No, you listen, for once in your life," Elijah said. "We've got a silent alarm that goes off if someone breaks in. The police will be here any minute."

Azrael's face floated like a pale moon in the darkness. "Really?"

"Really."

"Brother, I beg you," Azrael whispered. "Don't do this. If they catch me, I'll go to prison, and my son will be alone in the world."

"Not alone." Elijah said. "He'll have his uncle. The only hope you have of retaining your freedom is if you go now and leave your son with me."

Cathryn stirred. "Elijah, who's..." She saw Azrael and screamed.

Azrael cursed and vanished into the hallway.

"Sweet mercy, Elijah, was that—?"

"Azrael Hatch," said Elijah.

"Are you all right? Why is he here?"

Elijah hefted himself onto his wheelchair. "He's desperate. Call the police."

Cathryn fumbled her cell phone from the bedside table and dialed 911. "Hello, yes, I'm calling from Fishers of Men, on 888 Front Street. Azrael Hatch is here…"

Elijah left Cathryn answering the operator's questions and rolled down the hallway to the elevator. Azrael must have been at the end of his rope to come here, and out of his wits to believe Elijah's lie about the silent alarm. Elijah wasn't sure where the falsehood had come from, and decided, as the elevator ferried him to the ground floor, that it had been divine inspiration from God.

The elevator doors opened, and Elijah wheeled out, peering into the dark entryway. The foyer was silent, front door slightly ajar. He let go of a breath he'd been holding in. Azrael was gone.

Elijah wheeled into the adjoining study. "Cade?" he called softly.

A tiny face popped up from behind the couch, blond hair shining silver in the moonlight, eyes wide with fear.

"Hello, Cade. You haven't met me yet, but I'm your uncle."

Cade goggled at him. "What's an uncle?"

"I'm your father's brother. You can call me Uncle Elijah. Are you hungry?"

Cade nodded. He emerged from behind the couch, wearing a backpack and carrying a stuffed lion. Elijah lifted him onto his lap. The kid smelled like he hadn't bathed in days.

Cade looked around. "Where's Daddy?"

"Daddy had to go away for a while. This is your home, now. We're going to keep you warm, and full, and clean."

A distant siren mourned in the distance, growing closer.

Tears formed in the child's eyes. "Daddy's gone?"

"Just for a while," lied Elijah. "You'll see him again, I promise. But until then, I'm your family. Please don't cry, little one."

Cade gave a high, keening whine, one Elijah was certain would turn into a wail that would wake the building before the cops did—but then the sound stopped. Cade tilted his head, as if listening. A single tear spilled down his cheek as he smiled.

"Nero says I'll see Daddy again soon," said Cade.

13

AFTER AZRAEL FLED FISHERS of Men, Arachne lost track of him for months. She couldn't find Hades, either. Azrael wasn't a surprise—he could have been anywhere—but the only reason she couldn't find Hades was because He didn't want to be found.

As the days grew shorter and cooler, Arachne searched housing resource centers, ratty motels, and unhoused encampments, but Azrael was nowhere to be found. She kept some spiders' eyes on Olivia and Milo, but there was little to watch on that front other than heart-wrenching crying, and Olivia moving out of her house into a new apartment, unable to return to the bedroom where Nancy had been slain. Elijah's activities were only marginally more interesting and mostly concerned teaching Cade oppressive things about faith and expanding his ever-growing following of sanctimonious hypocrites.

It wasn't until October that the pull of Hades' dark magnetism tingled the fine hairs of a nest of spiders in a small bush beside an Italian cafe. Sitting nearby, there He was—a roguishly handsome patron sipping a steaming espresso.

A pair of women at a nearby table tittered to each other. Hades looked over at them and smiled. Hades didn't often indulge in the attraction mortals possessed for Him, but Arachne caught a glint in His eye as she trundled a spider closer, and guessed He was on the verge of making an exception.

Hades reached into His jacket pocket, pulled out an earpiece, and inserted it into His ear. "Well, hello there. It's good to hear from you." He tipped the women a wink, eliciting a gale of giggles. "How have you been?"

A spider tickled the roof of her mouth. Arachne swallowed it down. "Peachy. You?"

"At this moment, I'm enjoying one of the finer espressos in the world." Hades lifted His tiny white cup.

Her spider's legs rippled with the rich aroma. "I have a question for you," Arachne said.

"Shoot."

"Where is Azrael?"

Hades chuckled. "Lost sight of him, have you?"

Arachne's spider bristled in annoyance. "I haven't seen him since he fled from Fishers of Men a few months ago."

"And you're asking me to tell you his whereabouts? Why, so you can torment him and tip the scales in your favor?"

"You mean like how you're speaking to Cade through his toy lion?"

Hades raised an eyebrow and took another sip of espresso.

"You said, no whispering madness into their minds," Arachne said.

"What I'm doing to the child isn't madness. I'm merely giving him information."

"How altruistic."

Hades smirked. "Take that back."

"You're right, you don't deserve that. What you did to Nancy was horrific, even for you."

Hades lowered His voice. "The Old One has made more terrible things happen to good people than I ever have. There's a famous book with entire chapters about it."

"Is Nancy up above, at least? Someplace safe from you?"

"What?" Hades asked, pressing a finger to His earpiece.

"Hades, is she—"

"I'm sorry, you're breaking up," Hades said. "In case you can still hear me, you'll find what you're looking for in Omaha. Good luck."

"Hades!"

Hades returned His earpiece to His pocket, finished off His espresso, and prowled toward the giggling women. Arachne didn't wait around to see what He'd planned for them.

She shifted her attention to the millions of spiders in Omaha, scouring the town for any sign of Azrael. When she finally found him, she nearly didn't recognize him. He was clean shaven once more, but he'd dyed his hair light brown and wore a dark beanie, glasses with no lenses, a thick gray scarf, and a black pea coat. He was walking down a city sidewalk, carrying a brown box under his arm.

Arachne threw her gaze from one spider to the next, following his progress. As he walked, the sun disappeared behind the horizon and streetlights popped on in quick succession.

She realized where Azrael was headed a half block before he arrived: the newly opened Fishers of Men location.

Azrael scanned his surroundings to make sure nobody was around, knelt at the front door, and emptied the contents of the box through the mail slot. From the vantage point of a wolf spider inside the facility's lobby, it took Arachne a few moments to realize what she was looking at, and once she did, she released a single sharp, "Ha!"

Crickets. Hundreds of them.

Arachne watched as Azrael ditched the box and scampered three miles to the efficiency he'd apparently been living in. He ate a microwave-warmed dinner sitting on the edge of a creaky bed draped with a moth-eaten sheet, reading a newspaper in the blue band of streetlight coming in through the barred window. He'd risked much with his cricket stunt, but Arachne saw in his expression he was more emboldened than scared. She didn't need to see the words in the newspaper to know he was reading about the rising tide of Elijah's "Fisher" movement: attacks on transgender people, protests at women's health clinics, the vilification of immigrants.

Azrael panhandled enough money to catch a bus to the Fishers of Men facility in Kansas City, scrawled a snaggle-tooth grin on a brick, and threw it through the storefront's darkened window. When the Kansas City director sent Elijah a photo of the brick, he recognized it at once as Azrael's "Cheshire" grin. "It's my brother," Elijah told the authorities. "I'm sure of it."

A few weeks after vandalizing the Kansas City location, Azrael made his way to the Fishers of Men facility in Charlotte, spray-painted his signature red grin on the wall, and threw a Molotov cocktail through the window. Security cameras captured everything, and he escaped on foot.

A month later, as Azrael approached the facility in Richmond, Virginia, Arachne watched him freeze. He sensed what she already knew: the place was being watched. He started to slink away, but a pair of officers with flashlights spotted him and gave chase.

Azrael vaulted over fences and darted through thick foliage, sprinting through a parking garage and hurtling over a railing. He landed in a dark alley and crouched in the shadows, panting.

"Hey," said a nearby voice.

Arachne's nearest host, a tiny jumping spider, made out the silhouette of a young man at the end of the alley, holding the glowing cherry of a lit joint. He looked to be in his late teens, possibly early twenties.

"No way," said the young man.

"I have a knife," Azrael lied. "Get away."

"Are you running from the cops?"

Azrael straightened, sizing him up. "Yes."

"This way." The young man flicked the joint into the parking garage and sprinted away.

Azrael hesitated, then followed the young man north a few blocks before ducking behind a dumpster beside him. Red and blue lights splashed the wall as a cop car sped by.

"I'm Ray," whispered the kid.

Ray led Azrael a few blocks east and pulled a jangling set of keys from his pocket as they climbed the steps of a nondescript apartment building. Ray unlocked a door and gestured for Azrael to go inside.

Azrael stood on the steps, panting, staring up at him.

"Dude, come on. Someone'll see you," Ray said.

The swell of sirens grew closer. Azrael sighed and followed Ray inside.

14

ONCE RAY HAD CLOSED the door behind him, Azrael looked him over. Ray was tall and thin with sandy hair, and he might have had a decent smile if he'd done a better job of brushing his teeth. His fingernails had been chewed to the quick, and he wore black pants and a shirt featuring an illegible band name.

"Holy shit," said Ray. "It's really you."

Azrael's heart hammered against his sternum like it was trying to get out. So much for hoping this young punk hadn't recognized him. "Okay. What do you want?"

"What do I...want?"

"There's probably some kind of reward for information leading to my arrest," Azrael said. "I don't have any money, but I—"

Ray cut him off with laughter. "Oh, no, man. Chill out. I'm not going to turn you in. You're my hero."

"I'm your *what*?"

"Your girlfriend killed a cult leader," Ray said. "You've been evading the cops for years. And now you're striking back at your brother's fucked-up religion? Come on, man."

Azrael gaped, at a loss for words.

"If you need a place to hide, you can stay here as long as you like," Ray said. "My dad's name is on the lease, but he'll be in prison another year at least. My grandparents are paying for the place."

Azrael looked around the grimy, smoke-stained apartment into which he'd fled. Fruit flies wheeled in a drafty kitchen, and a tattered couch faced a television that was probably older than the kid standing in front of him.

"Are you thirsty?" asked Ray, checking the fridge. "I've got beer...and tap water. No food, unless you're into condiments. Oh—I could order a pizza if you're hungry. Do you like pizza?"

Azrael's mouth watered at the thought of food. "Yeah."

"Okay, I'll order some." Ray cracked open two beers and handed one to Azrael. "Sorry if I'm acting nervous. I'm not a weirdo or anything, I just can't believe Azrael Hatch is standing in my apartment."

"It's okay," said Azrael. "If anyone here is nervous, it's me. I wasn't aware I had fans."

Ray's jaw dropped open. "Dude, don't you look at the Internet?"

"To do what, check my email?"

"No...I mean...here, I'll show you." Ray pulled a laptop out from under the couch and flipped it open. He tapped a few keystrokes, hit enter, and handed it to Azrael.

Azrael scrolled through message board posts, catching a glimpse of his name every third line or so.

"You're famous," said Ray. "You're a real-life vigilante, a symbol of resistance. Everyone knows it's been you defacing the Fishers of Men facilities. And you're fucking here, in my apartment. Fuck, I can't believe it!"

Azrael's eyes widened as he scrolled. Dozens...no, hundreds of posts...thousands of comments...

"What do you want on your pizza?" Ray asked.

"Anything," mumbled Azrael, unable to tear his gaze from the laptop.

Ray tapped an order into his phone. "One large pepperoni pizza on the way."

"Thank you." Azrael looked up at Ray in disbelief. "I had no idea."

"That's just the tip of the iceberg. Folks are pissed. Those Fisher assholes are hurting a lot of innocent people."

Azrael shook his head. "My brother never was one for subtlety."

Ray gnawed at the edges of his pinky fingernail. "Can I ask you something?"

"Sure."

"Why the smile? Some people think it's a Joker thing, but my theory is it has a deeper meaning."

Azrael made himself take a slow breath and unclench his jaw. "It was my name, when I was in hiding before the Colony was raided: Randall Cheshire, like the Cheshire Cat. Plus, I've got these crooked teeth. Hence the smile."

"Randall Cheshire," Ray breathed. He switched hands to chew a hangnail on his thumb. "Holy shit. Angel's going to flip out."

Azrael snapped the laptop shut. "Who's Angel?"

"Fellow anarchist I went to high school with," Ray explained. "She's a hairstylist, but her parents are filthy rich and give her pretty much anything she asks for, so she doesn't need to work much. She's dating our dealer, Witt."

An anarchist whose parents pay her bills, Azrael thought wryly. The muscles in his shoulders tightened a few notches as a siren wailed past outside.

Ray tore a flap of skin away from his thumb with his teeth. "Oh, and Trick. Trick's a hacker. They're trans, so the shit the Fishers are pulling is personal for them. They're probably the smartest person I know. Whatever you've got planned, they can help…"

Azrael held up his hands. "Wait, wait—I don't want anybody knowing I'm here."

"Trust me, nobody's going to rat you out," Ray said. "Trick and Angel have been fighting the good fight at least as long as I have. Witt's not into this stuff as much as we are, but he's the last person who'd turn you over to the cops."

"It's not just me I'm worried about," Azrael said. "I'm a fugitive from the law. Anybody caught harboring me would be in a lot of trouble. You're just a kid. You've got your whole life ahead of you."

"A life of what?" Ray asked. "Working at a minimum-wage job? Selling drugs to high school kids until I get busted? If I get arrested for protecting you, at least it'll mean something."

Azrael's nostrils prickled at a fetid scent, and he grimaced when he realized it was coming from his shirt. He was in dire need of a long shower, a hot meal, and about twelve hours of sleep. He sighed. "How do I know I can trust you?"

Ray pulled up his sleeve to reveal a fresh tattoo on his upper arm.

Azrael's Cheshire grin signature in red ink.

"Fuck those assholes," Ray said. "Let's give 'em hell."

15

OLIVIA FELT A BUZZ and sighed as she looked down to see an incoming call from her mother.

"Hello?"

"Hey, darling! I wanted to call and wish you a happy New Year. Bernard and I were asleep by ten o'clock last night, so we missed ringing it in."

Bernard was her mother's new boyfriend. Olivia hadn't met him yet, but it seemed he was a good influence on Betty, who'd once rung in the new year by painting the bathroom wall with her vomit. "Glad you had a chill night."

"How was your night?" Betty asked.

Olivia looked around her apartment. Dust motes swirled in the thin delta of the dusky remnants of daylight coming through the living room's single window. She hadn't been able to bring herself to decorate in the six months since she moved in. Other than Dinah's cat supplies, a few essentials, a couch left behind by the previous tenant, and a kitchen table one of her neighbors had thrown out, the place was empty. She'd spent the night curled in her sleeping bag on a camping mat, scrolling her phone with a heavy feeling in her gut.

Her voice bounced back at her from bare walls. "Not so bad."

"Did you see Milo?" Betty asked.

"He had other plans," Olivia lied. If she'd gone to visit Milo for New Year's, she'd have risked being spotted by someone with a flashing camera, asking her questions about Nancy's murder. Olivia peered out her window into the walled-in alley below. It wasn't much of a view, but at least she wouldn't have to worry about someone trying to snap her picture through the curtains.

"How's work going?" Betty asked.

"Fine. They're letting me work from home."

"Oh, that's good. Anything else new?"

Dinah gave Olivia's leg an amiable head butt, and Olivia knelt to pet her. How long had it been since she touched another human being? Milo, months ago? Olivia felt the urge to sob welling in her chest. "Not really, Mom. How are things on your end?"

As her mother caught her up about her life, Olivia lay down on the floor and stared up at a water stain on her ceiling until the tears brimming in her eyes spilled down her cheeks.

"Olivia?" Betty asked after a pause. "Are you there?"

Olivia wiped her nose on her sleeve. "Yeah, sorry, Mom, I think something's up with my signal."

"Okay, well, I'll let you go. Will you please consider coming to visit me sometime soon?"

"I will, Mom. Love you."

"Love you."

Olivia hung up and stared at her reflection in her dark phone screen. A desolate, red-eyed woman Olivia didn't recognize stared back at her. She set the phone down, climbed into her sleeping bag, and closed her eyes. Sleep evaded her as thoughts chattered in her mind like frenzied monkeys. Against her better judgment, she picked up her phone and started scrolling, reading through the latest comments and messages accusing her and Milo of conspiring to have Nancy killed.

Social media had become a minefield for more reasons than personal attacks on her. Fishers of Men's cultural footprint was growing by the day. Some followers joined for the health benefits offered by a Nosh-only diet, but true devotees of Fishers of Men took things much further. "Fishers" defaced Planned Parenthoods, assaulted queer people, vandalized mosques.

A photo of Elijah scrolled into view, with Cade smiling at his side, and Olivia winced. The news of Cade resurfacing in Elijah's care had broken months ago, and yet, every time Olivia saw the kid's face, it brought her past trauma rushing into the present.

Beneath the photo, Elijah was quoted as saying: "Fishers of Men does not condone violence of any kind. These attacks are not a representation of our faith."

Olivia rolled her eyes. Elijah's tepid, dog-whistle rebukes did little to check the violence his movement instigated. Azrael was out there somewhere too, dealing with it the only way he knew how—vandalism and fire. She wished she could find satisfaction in someone giving Elijah's organization a taste of their own medicine, but it only felt destabilizing, inching civilization closer to the edge.

You could end it.

Olivia clicked off her phone and burrowed into her sleeping bag as if she could hide from the thoughts that followed. She could end Elijah Hatch's reign in an instant. She could break something in Elijah's brain as easily as snapping a twig. To date, Elijah's followers had killed at least seven people. Seven lives Olivia could have saved by ending Elijah's. How many more would have to die before killing him would be justified?

The one person she could talk to about this, Milo, had enough to deal with without Olivia revealing to him she had magic mind-powers.

A text came through from her mother, letting Olivia know her schedule and once again imploring her to visit.

Olivia sighed. It had been so long since she'd been home. Maybe returning to the one small corner of her world untouched by chaos would be good for her.

16

WHEN A KNOCK FELL on his bedroom door, Elijah hoisted himself to standing. He admired his new prosthetic legs: gleaming metal alloy, sturdy and surprisingly light, connected to his knees with cups custom-fitted to contour to his stumps. White, glossy hulls of carbon fiber curved over the shin and the calf of the legs, providing balance and flexibility.

It had taken months of punishing physical therapy for him to take his first slow, unassisted steps. Soon, he'd be able to walk with them full-time.

Elijah answered the door. "Casey, good morning."

"Good morning, Elijah. I'm sorry to bother you, but there's a man downstairs who claims to know you."

Elijah frowned. "Did he give a name?"

"Warren."

He stiffened and tried to keep his face impassive. "Warren… thank you, Casey. Please tell him I'll be right down."

Elijah smoothed back his hair. It had finally happened. Warren was ready to come back.

Elijah made his way to the elevator with the help of his cane. He leaned against the elevator's back wall, breathing heavily as floors dinged past.

The doors opened, and Elijah gasped softly as he took in Warren Young standing in the entryway. He'd lost at least twenty pounds, and his pale skin looked almost blue in the shadows.

Warren's eyes widened when he saw Elijah. "Oh my God…you're walking."

Elijah clacked his cane against his legs. "Getting stronger every day. Someday soon, when I'm sure I don't need it anymore, I'm going to burn my wheelchair in the courtyard."

A sad smile flickered across Warren's face. "That's really something."

"Are you hungry?" Elijah said. "I'm afraid I can't offer you any solid food, but we do have Nosh."

"I'm not hungry, thank you," Warren said hoarsely. "But I do need help."

Elijah gestured toward the study. "Let's talk in here. Close the door behind you."

Warren complied. "I'm sorry. I didn't know where else to go."

Elijah settled into an armchair. "What do you need?"

"I've been struggling with addiction," Warren said. "It started with booze, but then I got into harder stuff. I can't hold down a job, and I'm dead broke." His eyes brimmed with tears. "I don't know why I thought you would be able to help me, but…"

"I know why," Elijah said. "You're here so an old injustice can be set right. It's time for you to come home."

Warren sniffed. "Elijah, I'm a mess. I've only been sober a few days, and I don't know…"

"Fishers of Men is not here to help those who are whole," Elijah said. "We're here to help the lost. We have a place for you here, a room where you can rest, and I can put you in touch with an addiction counselor. You don't have to go through this alone."

Warren looked down at his trembling hands. "I don't know what to say."

Elijah softened his voice. "You helped me when I was in need. I'm honored to do the same for you now."

"What about Grayburn?"

"Robert Grayburn is a belled cat."

The tendons in Warren's neck stood out as he swallowed a knot down his throat. "Even if that were true, he's not the only one who doesn't want me here."

Elijah turned at a knock at the door. "Yes?"

The door creaked open, and Cade's tiny face poked inside. "Uncle Elijah?"

Elijah waved the boy toward him. "Come on in, Cade. I'm just talking to an old friend."

Warren's jaw dropped. "Is that…"

"Yes," Elijah said. "Azrael brought him here when he couldn't care for him anymore."

Cade goggled at Warren as he ambled toward Elijah's chair. "Who's this?"

"This is Warren," Elijah said, hefting Cade into his lap. "He once helped give me and your daddy a safe place to stay. Now he needs help, and we're going to return the favor."

Cade smiled up at Elijah. "I like when we help people."

"Me too," Elijah said. "Warren, I'll tell you the same thing I told Olivia: this is not the Colony. My father may have stood for condemnation, but here, we believe in forgiveness. All I ask is you consume only water and Nosh, and that you help with things like chores and our volunteer efforts in the community. If you can abide by that, you can stay as long as you like."

Warren shifted his gaze from Cade to Elijah. "I'll do anything to stay clean."

Elijah grasped Warren's shaking hand. "Welcome home."

17

"Is it supposed to burn?" Azrael asked.

Angel's long, dark hair brushed Azrael's shoulder as she inspected his scalp. She ran her gloved hands through his hair, massaging in gobs of nostril-stinging bleach. In his periphery, Azrael caught a glimpse of the porcelain curve of the side of her breast through the cutout sleeve of her shirt. "It's supposed to tingle. Is it tingling, or burning?"

Azrael tore his eyes away from her shirt and affixed his gaze to where Ray was divvying up lines of cocaine on a mirror on the coffee table. "Tingling, I guess."

Angel snapped off her gloves. "Let me know if it starts to burn." She sashayed from Ray's living room into the bathroom. Azrael turned away from her in time to see two of the "Cheshires," as Ray had taken to calling their little collective, also following the sway of her long black skirt. Ray returned his attention to the table when he felt Azrael's glare on him, but Witt, the lanky drug dealer who'd brought the powders, leaned forward to leer through the bathroom door as Angel washed her hands. Azrael's cheeks flushed with heat, though whether it was from jealousy or the bleach burning its way through his skull, he wasn't sure.

Trick sat cross-legged against the wall, oblivious to the haze of hormones slowly replacing the oxygen in the room. They sucked air through their vape pen and produced a massive cloud in the blue glow of their laptop screen. "Ha!"

Ray looked up from using a razor to straighten out white lines. "What?"

Trick tucked a lock of bright red hair behind their jewel-studded ear. "Remember the Fisher who posted about lining up all the f-words and taking them out with a firing squad? He's about to be doxxed from the face of the planet."

Ray grinned. "You got an address?"

"We've got an address. And now..." Trick clicked the trackpad. "Everybody does."

Beer sloshed from Witt's bottle as he pumped his fist in the air. "Hell yes!"

"Nice," Ray said, doing a celebratory line.

Of the three new recruits that had joined them, Trick had proved themselves the most useful. They'd hand-picked users from the message boards to join an encrypted "Cheshire" chat that set about finding every stitch of data they could about Fishers with a history of violence: addresses, phone numbers, social security numbers, maiden names, blood types. It would have been easy for Azrael to praise Trick for the many devastating blows they'd dealt to the Fisher movement, but at the moment, taking down Elijah's sanctimonious empire was taking a back seat to Azrael's primary goal: getting rid of Witt.

Ray passed the mirror to Witt, who plucked a metal straw from behind his ear and made the largest of the white lines disappear. "Hope they kill the fucker," Witt said, sniffing and wiping his nose with the back of his hand. Witt laughed at his own comment, revealing a dark hole where one of his incisors used to be. Witt set the mirror back on the coffee table, knowing Azrael would have declined if he'd offered.

Azrael glowered, fighting the urge to scratch his scalp. He'd bet every cent of Angel's parents' money that Witt hadn't slept the night before. His eye sockets had taken on the dark tint of a bruise, while the rims of his eyelids burned bright red. He cackled and twitched and chattered, endlessly self-assured at his own intellect and charm. The powders Witt brought made talking to Ray, who was otherwise an all right kid, practically intolerable. The way Witt acted toward Angel made Azrael's stomach turn. Possibly the only good thing about Witt was he was fond of talking about himself, which meant all Azrael had to do was listen, and wait for the right moment...

"What's up, Azrael?" Ray asked. "Something wrong?"

Azrael shook his head. "Oh, no...nothing's wrong."

Trick looked up and narrowed their eyes. "For real, what is it?"

"Oh, it's..." Azrael trailed off, feigning uncertainty. "No, it's too much."

All eyes were on him now. Angel stood in the bathroom doorway, toweling off her hands. "What?" she demanded.

Azrael sighed. "All these actions against the Fishers are great. They really are. I just wish we could land a blow they can't ignore." He paused for effect, making eye contact with everyone in the room. "I want to hit the Fishers of Men headquarters in Denver."

Trick blew out a low whistle. "That'd be a risky operation. They've got all kinds of security cameras all over the place, and I wouldn't be surprised if there's a police presence, too."

"I know." Azrael shrugged. "That's why I said it's too much. It would need to be someone who could get in and out quickly enough that there wouldn't be time for authorities to respond."

Witt peeled himself off the wall. "How quickly are we talking?"

"I'd say two or three minutes," Trick answered. "Less if they have a cruiser watching the place."

Witt's eyes flashed. "I ever tell you I got into college on a track scholarship?"

Witt had brought up his tenure as a track star no fewer than a dozen times, but Azrael paused thoughtfully, as though this were new information. "How quickly can you run a mile?"

"Fastest time was four minutes, thirty-two seconds," Witt grinned. "I bet I could still get it done in under five. Even if it were as much as six, ain't no cop in the country could catch me on foot. Also, I know how to pick locks."

Azrael was aware of this, too, but made a show of raising his eyebrows. "I wasn't being serious. It's not going to do us any good to be reckless."

"Fuck that," Witt said. "Let's hit the bastards where they live. They should be *afraid* of us."

"You'd have to lay low awhile, someplace else," Azrael said. "If you came straight back here and led them to me..."

Witt nodded enthusiastically. "Yeah, of course. I could hide out wherever you need me to."

Azrael tilted his head back at Angel. "Do we have enough cash to get Witt to Denver and set him up somewhere between Denver and here for a week or two?"

"Ha," Angel said. "Yeah, that won't be a problem."

"Trick, could you find out more information about exactly what kind of security—"

"Already on it," Trick said, clicking away.

"Witt, are you really going to do it?" Ray asked, his eyes glassy with stimulants and admiration.

"Not only am I going to do it, I'm going to get away with it," Witt boasted. He tipped a wink at Angel.

"Badass," Angel said softly.

The heat in Azrael's scalp deepened. "If you get caught—"

"I won't."

"If you get caught," Azrael said slowly, "you don't know me. You're just a punk from Virginia who wanted to make a statement."

"I got kicked out of college for dealing and went to jail for eight months," Witt said. "I could have ratted some folks out and avoided doing any time, but I didn't. Even if they do somehow catch me, there's nothing they could throw at me that would make me blab about you."

As loathsome as Witt was, Azrael believed him. For people like Witt, there were worse things than incarceration, and losing face with his fellow miscreants was one of them.

Azrael winced. "Okay, Angel, it's definitely burning now."

"One more minute, then I'll wash it out."

"I'm not kidding. I can smell my hair frying."

Angel rolled her painted eyes. "You're fine, but all right, let's go rinse."

She led Azrael into the bathroom, positioned his head under the rusty bathtub faucet, and turned the water on. "Keep your eyes closed."

Azrael gripped the edge of the tub as she massaged his scalp. He breathed out slowly through his nostrils to stop himself from moaning. It had been so long since he'd been touched in more than a passing way, especially by a beautiful woman.

"It's looking good," Angel said.

"Good," Azrael said, grateful she couldn't see how hard her massaging his scalp had gotten him. Fucking Angel would be a terrible idea, as she regarded him as something like an idol, but as soon as Witt was out of the picture, that's exactly what he planned on doing.

"All done," Angel said. "Don't move, I'll get you a towel."

Azrael clung to the side of the tub, cool water dripping down his face. Olivia would have seen right through Angel; would have immediately sensed there was nothing underneath her rebellious pretense. Or maybe Olivia would understand Azrael's attraction to Angel, his need for intimacy eclipsing his good sense. Hell, it was possible she was somewhere cheering him on in his fight against the Fishers. Was it so wrong for him to take comfort in that hypothetical?

Angel toweled off Azrael's hair and helped him up so he could look at himself in the mirror. Azrael winced at the color—bright yellow.

"I'm going to add toner next," Angel explained. "That'll get it to the kind of platinum color you're looking for."

"All right." He'd said he wanted his hair lighter, but not this light. He stared at his reflection, feeling ill, marveling at how much he looked like his father.

18

OLIVIA HOPPED ON A flight to visit her mother, her first visit home since Nancy's death. The Denver airport felt strange and unfamiliar to her when she arrived. She was a different person the last time she walked through it.

Her mother Betty waved at her madly when she came into sight. "Hi, Liv!"

When they hugged, Olivia's stomach dropped at how thin her mother was. She was close to how much she weighed when Olivia's dad was alive, back when she drank half her meals.

Olivia forced a smile. "How've you been?"

Betty caught Olivia up about her life: Bernard's promotion at work; a misogynistic coworker who'd gotten fired from her school; her efforts in canvassing for a local election her side had ended up winning; becoming one of the lead sopranos in a choir filled with women she enjoyed spending time with.

Once they were settled at home, Betty asked Olivia how she was holding up. Olivia gave her mother a reassuring amount of information, leaving out how she'd sequestered herself from the world.

"How's Milo?"

Olivia sighed. "I haven't been doing the best job of staying in touch with him. He's going through so much, and I'm not exactly in the best place to give emotional support."

Betty clasped Olivia's hand. "It's going to be okay, hon. You've got a good job, a nice new place, and friends who love you. And if you need to move back home, there's always a place here for you."

Olivia smiled weakly. "Thanks, Mom."

"Are you hungry?"

Olivia shrugged. "I could eat."

"I have just the thing." Her mother reached into a cabinet and pulled out two containers of Nosh.

Olivia stared, confused. "You've been drinking Nosh?"

"Surprise! I've been on the Nosh diet for a month, and I've already lost ten pounds!"

Olivia gave a shocked laugh. "Mom, it's meant for people who want to lose a lot of weight! You've never been anywhere near an unhealthy weight."

"Oh, come on, Olivia. You knew when you made this stuff people of all sizes would use it. I mean, there's a whole group of people downtown drinking it, and they all seem to be doing fine."

Olivia flinched before she could stop herself.

"I thought you'd be excited," her mother said. "You and Nancy worked so hard to get Nosh on the market."

"I...I'm sorry, it's just...it's hard to have positive feelings about it now that Fishers of Men is pedaling it like some kind of religion."

"I'm not into any of *that* nonsense. I mean, I buy my Nosh through them, but that's because for every ten pouches you buy, they give one to someone in need."

"Ugh, Mom..." Olivia shivered. "Fishers of Men is a cult."

"Oh, come on. There are a few nuts, yeah, but they also give out a lot of donations—blankets, clothes, house supplies. They're doing a lot for the community."

"Their leader is a messianic sociopath who doesn't care that his followers are hurting people."

"Geez." Her mother threw up her hands. "I thought you'd be happy for me!"

Olivia stood up from the table. "I need to get some air."

"Where are you going?"

"I don't know. I might head downtown."

"Nothing will be open this time of night," her mother protested.

"I need to clear my head," Olivia said. *So I don't accidentally kill you with it.*

"It's freezing out."

"I brought a coat."

"Don't you want dinner?"

"No, I'm fine. I ate on the plane."

"All right. But put on the fuzzy hat by the door before you go."

Olivia bundled herself up and started walking. She'd forgotten how cold the winters could be here. The biting chill cleared her head. Her mother wasn't the enemy. She had a new romance and wanted to slim down, was all. Olivia hadn't even told her she looked beautiful, which she did.

The downtown area, glowing under streetlights, was mostly deserted. A gentle flurry of snow fell as Olivia made her way through the quiet streets. She approached the Fishers of Men facility and inspected the sign adorning the door:

FISHERS OF MEN
ALL ARE WELCOME

Somebody with a Sharpie had added *NOT* between *ARE* and *WELCOME.*

Olivia peered through the window: shelves of Nosh pouches, a box marked *DONATIONS*, some chairs, and a receptionist's desk. The banality of it was almost as galling as the evil at the root of it.

Olivia shivered and rubbed warmth into her arms. She should head back home. Her mother would be worried about her.

She was about to turn away when she caught a flash of movement inside the Fishers of Men foyer and looked closer.

A tall, thin man, dressed in all black with a scarf wrapped over his mouth, moved along the shelves of Nosh. He slit pouches of Nosh, whisking a blade in one motion across each row, the pouches deflating as opal gallons of Nosh gushed to the floor.

The masked man was too tall to be Azrael, but a glimmer of intuition told Olivia that he was connected to him, and would have answers to the questions that had been burning through her mind for years.

Olivia banged on the window. "Hey!"

The man saw her, froze, then bolted for the back door.

Olivia sprinted down the line of storefronts. She turned a corner and saw the man running down the street like the devil was on his heels.

"Stop!" she shouted.

The man kept running.

A band of energy as thin as fishing wire shot out of her mind.

It caught the vandal around the ankles. His feet tangled and he went down hard. Olivia caught up with him and knelt beside him, yanking the scarf away from his face. His eyes fluttered, dazed by the fall.

"Who put you up to this?" Olivia asked him. "Was it Azrael Hatch?"

The man huffed clouds of breath onto the sidewalk and didn't respond.

"Listen!" Olivia hissed. "I hate the Fishers as much as you do, believe me. I just need to know if you know where Azrael is."

The man turned his head enough to make eye contact. "Suck my dick."

Footfalls approached Olivia at a run—a middle-aged man and woman who'd been walking nearby. "What's going on?" the woman asked.

Olivia gritted her teeth. She didn't want to involve strangers in this, but she didn't have time to come up with a convincing lie. "He broke into the Fishers of Men facility—"

"I'm calling the police," the woman said.

"I've got him," the man in the couple said, pinning the young man's arms.

Olivia sat down heavily, panting in the cold. The last thing she wanted was to get caught up in this mess again, but if she ran, she'd look guilty. She put her head in her hands until sirens stirred in the distance.

19

Arachne told Hades: "Don't think I don't know what you're up to."

Hades looked at her spider, dangling on a gossamer thread from a metal beam. He leaned against a wall inside a massive hangar filled with airplanes in various stages of construction. He took a bite of a sandwich and chewed. "Yes?"

"It's not really about Olivia anymore," Arachne said. "I mean, she's the chess piece you want to topple, but you're having all sorts of fun in the meantime."

Hades took another bite. "You noticed."

"You could have driven her insane in a million small ways."

"Of course."

"But you've chosen to throw everything around her into chaos instead."

"I told you, this wasn't a challenge. If it's any consolation, it's the most fun I've had in centuries."

Nearby, in the hangar, a man in coveralls stormed up the base of a raised platform and shouted at a worker riveting bolts into the side of an airplane. "Hey! Steve! What did I tell you about taking my lunch?"

The worker, presumably Steve, stopped riveting. "Huh?"

"I know you took my sandwich out of the fridge!" the first man shouted.

"Man, I didn't go near your sandwich!"

The two men traded words, then blows, until other workers rushed up to the platform to separate them.

"Don't worry, Steve will be back to work in a few minutes," Hades said. "He'll be distracted, though, and he'll do a poor job of finishing the riveting. Not so poor that anyone will notice during the inspection, but poor enough that in five years, one of the rivets will come undone mid-air and get sucked into the jet engine. The ensuing plane crash will kill ten of the plane's passengers, including a young child who'd have otherwise grown up to be the voice of a police reform movement." Hades popped the last bite of the stolen sandwich into His mouth and grinned. "It's really too bad."

Arachne said, "I can see what you're trying to do to Olivia."

"Do you, now?" He asked, licking mayonnaise from His fingers.

"Yes. And it won't work. She won't use her powers to kill Elijah."

Hades lifted an eyebrow. "Won't she?"

Arachne shook her head, spiders hanging from web strands in her hair swinging with the movement. "She won't kill Azrael, either."

"How are you so sure she hasn't already committed a hell-worthy trespass?"

"*Óso anapnéei, elpízo.* While she breathes, I hope."

"While she breathes, the world burns. Look...here."

The hangar disappeared and was replaced by the fractured image of a dozen spiders' visions. Arachne pivoted the spiders until their combined angles turned into something she could understand: a city sidewalk, bustling with late afternoon foot traffic. Arachne scouted the area for clues and concluded she was in downtown Denver.

"What am I looking at?"

"The man with the orange hat heading south."

Arachne spotted him. He was in his fifties, with pallid skin, splotchy cheeks, and icy eyes. He wore a padded coat and faded jeans and moved quickly.

"What's he going to do?" asked Arachne.

"Watch," said Hades.

20

It was a quiet day at Fishers of Men. Icy rain had rendered the city unnavigable, and they'd had few visitors. Warren enjoyed these calm moments most of all, when he could rest awhile and collect his thoughts.

He was nearing two months of living here, cleaning the facility, organizing donations, handing out Nosh to the needy, gulping down the stuff himself. It wasn't half-bad, once you got used to it. Sure, he salivated at the thought of a nice juicy cheeseburger, but there was simplicity in removing the uncertainty from what he was putting into his body. Water and Nosh. That was it.

Warren sipped at a pouch of Nosh and tried to concentrate on the book he'd selected off the shelf in the study: *Moby Dick*. He'd never been much of a reader, but days like this, when he had nothing but time, reading the classics usually proved a decent distraction from the hungry, craving voices in the cellar of his mind.

It was true that Warren's drinking had gotten him fired from a string of menial jobs since he'd parted ways with Azrael and Elijah in Austin, but he wasn't the strung-out junkie he'd told Elijah he was. For years, he'd watched with growing concern as Fishers used their religious beliefs to justify their violence and rage. At least when the Prophet ran the Colony, his tyranny didn't extend beyond the gates of the compound. Under Elijah's leadership, the toxicity of the cult had spread like a virus to the outside world.

Warren's presence couldn't bring the hate-filled juggernaut skidding to a halt, but maybe he could help nudge Elijah in the right direction. He needed to be careful—if Elijah sensed Warren were here to convince him of something, he would send him back out into the cold. But if Warren dropped small hints, here and there, maybe he could change this new Prophet's heart.

And then there was Melinda.

Weeks ago, when Elijah had assembled his followers and announced Warren was returning to their midst, Melinda locked eyes with her shoes and pressed her lips closed, her hand enveloped in the grasp of the same hand that had dragged Warren through the woods all those years ago. Grayburn had seemed to loom over her...or maybe that was merely a distortion of Warren's jealousy and fear.

Grayburn, Melinda, and his other two wives lived in a house a few blocks away from Fishers of Men. They visited headquarters a few times a week, always together. The thrill of terror Warren felt at Grayburn's presence was nothing compared to the ache of Melinda treating him more coldly than she would a stranger.

Two weeks into Warren's stay at Fishers of Men, he'd woken to a knock at his second-floor window. He'd stumbled from bed and opened the window to find Melinda clinging to the trellis outside his window. He'd thought he was dreaming until her hair brushed against his cheek as he helped her climb inside, the smell of her bringing years of memories rushing back to him. He closed the window behind her, cutting off the frigid wind piercing his clothes. She stood panting beside him for a few seconds, her hands cold as ice on his exposed hipbones, and then she pressed her warmth against him, her lips urgent on his, and he was lost in her.

After that, Melinda came to visit Warren as often as she dared. They whispered to each other in the darkness, exchanging stories about the intervening years between their youth and now, the horror and pain and loneliness. Warren told her about Grayburn trying to kill him, and Melinda told Warren of all the years Grayburn crept into her quarters to lay with her before Elijah insisted they marry.

Warren made love to Melinda, tenderly, carefully, and they talked of escaping together, one day, when they could work out a plan that wouldn't get them both killed...

Warren realized he'd been scanning the same page of *Moby Dick* for ages without reading it. He stared down at the line: *Ignorance is the parent of fear.* He looked up from the book and sighed. If he were a better person, he may have cared more about righting the wrongs the Fishers had caused than reuniting with the woman he loved.

But Melinda had yet again become his whole world.

Warren's ears pricked at the *cluh-clunk* sound of Elijah approaching. Elijah's face appeared in the doorway. "Today's the day."

"What day?" Warren asked.

"Remember what I told you your first week here?"

Warren thought back. "You said, as soon as you were sure you wouldn't need it anymore, you were going to burn your wheelchair."

Elijah smiled. "Want to come see?"

"Yes, of course."

Outside, dozens of Elijah's followers assembled in the courtyard, shivering in the fading daylight. The wheelchair was in the center of the yard, stacked with kindling. Robert

Grayburn handed Elijah a can of kerosene, and Elijah doused his wheelchair with it.

Elijah pulled a Zippo lighter from his coat pocket and held it aloft. "To miracles," he said, and tossed the lighter onto the wheelchair, igniting a blaze, throwing light and heat into the frigid dusk. Fathers, mothers, and other followers applauded at the spectacle, then huddled around the burning chair as the sky darkened overhead.

Warren shuffled his feet and blew warmth into his hands. He could have done without the pageantry. Lighting the wheelchair on fire seemed like something Azrael would have done. And besides, he wasn't so sure Elijah was ready. Their young Prophet could only walk maybe fifty yards with a cane before he needed to stop and rest.

Cade Hatch, bundled against the cold, goggled at the fire. Looking at him made Warren's skin crawl. He looked so much like his father. Elijah was already grooming the child for a life of leadership, further lessening Cade's snowball's chance in hell at being normal. His parents were two of the most messed-up people Warren had ever met, and here he was, growing up in a cult. Warren intended to do what he could to steer the kid toward normalcy, but he still got the creeps whenever Cade talked to his stuffed lion.

Melinda stood on the opposite side of the fire, her gloved hand in Robert Grayburn's grasp. Warren's eyes caught hers for an instant, then she looked away. Heat flashed across Warren's cheeks. He chanced a look at Grayburn, who was staring into the fire. Warren shivered at the blankness in the man's eyes.

The wheelchair's fake plastic leather seat popped and melted in the fire. Warren's toes went numb from the cold. How long did they have to stand here watching Elijah celebrate his freedom before it would be all right to leave?

Warren's phone buzzed in his coat pocket. He ducked away from the warmth of the fire and checked the incoming phone call: Kyle Freeman, the PR director for Fishers of Men. He answered. "What?"

Warren's mouth went dry as Kyle spoke.

"All right," Warren said. "I'll tell him."

Elijah looked up from the fire when Warren returned. "What's going on?"

"There's been a shooting," Warren said. "Here, in Denver."

Elijah's eyes narrowed. "The Cheshires?"

"No," Warren said. His eyes flicked to Melinda before he could stop himself. "No, it was one of ours."

21

OLIVIA WAS SITTING DOWN to a liquid dinner with her mother, her hands still shaking from the previous day's clash with the young vandal, when the news hit.

The TV droned on low volume, and Olivia's ears pricked at the phrase, "Fishers of Men."

Her breath caught in her throat when she read the headline on the screen as the camera panned across a building surrounded by police cars:

*DEADLY SHOOTING AT WHEELER
STREET CLINIC*

"Mom," Olivia said weakly, "isn't that where your friend Amy works?"

Her mother looked up in the middle of screwing the cap off her Nosh pouch. "Oh my God…"

Olivia turned up the volume.

"…at least nineteen confirmed dead. According to authorities, a man walked into the free clinic, drew his handgun, and opened fire on the people inside." A blonde reporter appeared on screen and continued: "Some of those in the building were able to escape—two nurses and three patients ran out through the back door of the facility unharmed. They ran into a nearby restaurant and told the people inside to call the police. When officers arrived two minutes later, they found a man standing outside of the building, arms raised, gun laid on the ground in front of him. Officers subdued the man and ran inside the building to check for survivors. Nineteen people were declared dead at the scene of the attack. Paramedics rushed twelve others to the hospital; many of these survivors are in critical condition."

"Oh my God," Betty said again.

Olivia pressed her hand to her mouth. She longed to see the man's face. Just a few seconds of live footage of the bastard, and she could end his life without batting an eye. Anger swarmed in her chest.

"The alleged shooter, who was reported to be wearing a Fishers of Men T-shirt with the words 'Killer of killers' hand-written on the back—an apparent reference to Wheeler Street Clinic's abortion services—is alive and in police custody."

Killer of killers.

The words filled Olivia with rage.

CRACK!

Betty drew in a shrieking gasp. The TV and the lights in the room went dark and Olivia gaped in horror at a diagonal fracture in the TV screen. A plume of smoke rose from the set.

Olivia heard a gagging sound and turned to see her mother clutching her throat. Her Nosh pouch had fallen to the table and was glugging out pale opal liquid.

"Mom?"

Betty's mouth was open, eyes bulging.

Olivia got behind her mother, wrapped her arms around her waist, and pulled her fists up into her mother's abdominal muscles. Her mother felt so frail in her arms. Olivia performed the motion again and again, but Betty wasn't breathing. Her mother's legs gave out and she collapsed to the floor, unresponsive.

No time to call an ambulance. They were alone, just like when her father had terrorized them.

Olivia's surroundings faded into a dull buzz. She'd finally done it. She hadn't meant to do it, but her mother had been in the blast radius of her wrath, and the evil thing in her liked hurting innocent people most of all.

They'd survived so much together, for her mother to get killed by a flash of temper that Olivia had inherited from her father...

Fuck that.

Olivia honed her mental energy to a fine point, found the blockage in her mother's throat, grasped it with the power inside of her, and pulled.

The plastic cap from the Nosh pouch flew out of her mother's throat and rolled under the couch.

Betty's inhale broke through the buzzing sound between Olivia's ears. Her mother pulled in breath after breath of air, her color cycling back to a healthy pink. Olivia hugged her mother and began to weep.

"It's okay, honey," her mother said. "I'm okay."

There was something wrong with her mother's voice. It was raspy, like wind blowing through dry leaves. Olivia wanted to believe the hoarseness would go away, but nothing she did with her powers came without a cost. She knew it in her gut—her mother's lead soprano days were over.

Olivia sobbed into her mother's shoulder. Maybe her father couldn't help being a monster any more than she could. Maybe he'd tried to be a good father and husband. Maybe he'd been trapped in the same hell she was.

But Olivia was smarter than him. She knew sometimes, the best way to love a person was to walk away.

22

ELIJAH SAT IN HIS armchair, staring at the TV. Robert Grayburn and Warren Young stood behind him. The latest: twenty-two confirmed dead. Seven in serious or critical condition. Clear signs pointing to the attack being executed in the name of Fishers of Men.

Elijah stared into the eyes of the shooter: Zachary Hale. He remembered the day Zachary came to Fishers of Men. Zachary had spiraled into depression and alcoholism after being fired from his construction job, and he'd heard from one of his cousins that Fishers of Men offered free rehabilitation services. Elijah welcomed Zachary into the fold, helped him navigate sobriety, and rekindled his dormant connection to God. Zachary had been prone to the occasional bad mood, but Elijah hadn't seen anything in his behavior that would make him believe the man was capable of opening fire on a room full of people, even if the people in question were undeniably sinners.

Elijah hit the mute button. The clamor of reporters outside the building rushed in to fill the silence. He rubbed his eyes and sighed.

Warren said, "You need to make a statement."

"I've *made* statements."

"Not for the last several…incidents, you haven't."

Elijah glared at Warren. "If you're going to start blaming me for every murder in this country—"

"Nobody's blaming you," said Warren, "but you've got to get out in front of this and denounce it in the strongest possible terms. We've got a team working on a response as we speak."

Elijah pressed his palms into his eyes. For a dizzying moment, he wondered what would happen if he came out in support of the massacre. *This man was merely doing what he had to do to stop the godless murders of unborn children.*

He shook the thought away. "When will the statement be ready?"

"Any minute," said Robert Grayburn. "It's brief. We've got a podium set up outside for you. Just read it to the press and come back inside."

On the muted TV screen, a clip Elijah had already seen from the previous day replayed—a terrified woman with short-cropped hair giving her account to a sympathetic reporter as tears streaked rivers through her makeup.

Warren answered a knock at the door and returned with a sheet of paper filled with double-spaced type. Elijah looked it over and pulled himself to standing. "All right, let's get this over with."

Elijah's legs ached as he walked into the cold, the frigid air making his old wounds feel fresh. He reached the podium, blinking in the morning light, set aside his cane, and leaned close to the array of microphones.

"I have a few things I'd like to say. This has been a dreadful occasion for me, and for my church. We've been called a 'hate group' in the wake of a tragedy that was not our doing."

Elijah paused as his eyes fell to the paper before him. "We denounce in the most unequivocal terms…" He stopped. A vein pulsed in his forehead. "The horrific actions of…"

Elijah looked at the crowd, bristling with angry protest signs.

"A hate group," he said.

Cameras clicked. Flashes strobed.

"What about the hatred the world shows me and my followers?" Elijah asked, looking into the faces of the crowd. "Ever since I was a child, the world has punished me for what I believed. And what were those beliefs? Simple morality. Right and wrong."

A few people near the back of the crowd hollered and applauded.

"The world took everything from me," Elijah said. "My home. My hope. My legs. My father. But I never stopped believing that God had a plan for me, and I stand here today as proof that God's plan for my soul is as real as my beating heart. Yet I am *hated* for my beliefs. But I know of another man hated by the leaders of his time. Jesus Christ was declared a liar and a heretic, and he was persecuted and sentenced to death. He stood up for what was right, and he was struck down for it. Our world has seen many such figures smote from the pages of history, and the story of Fishers of Men is no different. We stand for virtue, yet we are called monsters. We fight for the very *soul* of this country and are attacked as a *hate group*."

A cry came up from the crowd—a mix of boos and cheers. Elijah's cheeks flushed with heat as he gripped the edges of the podium and raised his voice over the uproar.

"But maybe we are! Maybe our efforts to save the world with love are misplaced. Maybe in a world filled with hate, love is nothing but cannon fodder. Maybe we *should* be called a hate group—because at Fishers of Men, we hate the women who kill innocent babies before they get a chance at life."

Supporters cheered. Protesters booed. Elijah's amplified voice soared over it all.

"We hate the whores who sell their bodies to the highest bidder. We hate the men who dress like women so they can molest children in public restrooms. We hate the anarchists who terrorize our fellow citizens. We hate the plague of immorality that has sunk our nation into this egregious level of sin!"

The roar of the crowd shook the podium. Police officers shoved back protesters attempting to storm the stage. Bottles of water sailed toward Elijah.

"This is not about the war our enemies wage against us," Elijah shouted. "This is about the war between justice and chaos, between virtue and vice, and yes, between good and evil. We may stand on the wrong side of our government, but we stand on the right side of history, of morality, and of God." Elijah stared out over the thrashing crowd, chest heaving. "So, fine—call us a hate group! If our efforts are being condemned by the corrupt, then maybe we are *doing something right!*"

A canister of teargas soared into the center of the thundering masses, eliciting screams of terror and rage, cresting the sea of humanity over a violent tipping point.

Elijah jumped as a hand fell on his shoulder.

"Let's get you inside," Robert Grayburn said.

Elijah allowed himself to be led back into the building, locking the door behind him, his body vibrating with righteous fury. He'd finally done it. He'd said what he really wanted to say, and God, did it feel good.

Elijah caught eyes with Warren, who stood gaping at him, horrified, as the windows rattled with the surge of the rabble outside.

Elijah grinned. Whatever came next, he was ready for it.

23

AZRAEL WAS HALF ASLEEP when he heard Trick's alarmed voice in the next room: "Holy shit."

Azrael checked the time—a few hours until dawn. He pulled on his underwear and climbed out of bed, careful not to wake Angel, who lay curled under the sheets.

Azrael crept into the living room, latching the bedroom door carefully behind him.

"Holy *shit*," Trick said thickly, releasing a cloud of vapor.

"What is it?" whispered Azrael.

"It's Ray."

Azrael passed his hand over his face. When Ray had left the night before, saying he was going to join the protest at the Fishers of Men headquarters in Denver, Azrael had advised against it, but Ray said he couldn't stand another day of watching from the sidelines. Despite Azrael's objections, Ray had been in Denver by morning.

"Was he arrested?"

Trick's face was ashen. "He's dead."

"What...how?"

"A fight broke out at the protest. It sounds like some Fishers in the crowd beat him to death with their bare hands. There are pictures."

Azrael took a few breaths. He slipped a cigarette from a pack on the coffee table and lit it. "Ray...goddamn it."

Trick stared at their laptop screen, eyes wide, bottom lip quivering.

"It's not going to help reading about it," Azrael said.

Trick snapped the laptop closed. "You're right. I...I'm going to go for a walk. Clear my head."

"Take your time."

When Trick was gone, Azrael surprised himself by bursting into tears. Ray may have been a reckless punk, but Azrael had considered him a friend. He was funny, sincere, passionate. He deserved better than a bloody death at the hands of Fisher zealots.

On top of that, Ray's death meant they couldn't stay here any longer, and Azrael had no idea where they were going to go.

Azrael knuckled tears from his eyes, snuffed out his cigarette, strode into the bathroom, and cranked the shower all the way over to hot. While he waited for the water to heat up, he looked at himself in the mirror. The flesh around his eyes was dark and coppery. He'd been sleeping a little better since he'd started fucking Angel, but still only clocked around four hours a night. He had everything he needed here—food, booze, smokes, companionship that was damn near worship—but sometimes he missed being on the run, on his own, where nobody was looking to him for answers...

Angel padded naked into the bathroom and wrapped her arms around him, her breasts warm against his back. "You're up early."

"Ray's dead," Azrael said.

Angel's heavy lashes blinked at him in the mirror. "Really?"

"Yeah."

"How?"

"The rally in Denver turned into a riot. He was outnumbered."

"Wow." Angel's soft breath raised the hairs on his neck. "Damn."

"We need to leave here as soon as possible," Azrael muttered. "Got any ideas?"

"There's a house outside of town my parents were planning on flipping. They haven't worked on it in months."

"Why aren't they working on it?"

She waved the question away. "They're being audited for tax evasion or something like that. They'll be occupied with that for the foreseeable future."

Azrael drew in a deep breath and nodded. "Okay. We'll leave as soon as Trick gets back."

"Want some company in the shower?" Angel asked, tracing her hand down his chest.

He glowered at her reflection. "I'm really not in the mood."

She slipped her hand into his underwear and stroked his erection. "Tell that to this guy."

Azrael grabbed her hand and turned to face her. "Jesus Christ, Angel. Ray was your friend. Don't you care that he's dead?"

She pressed her body against his. "He knew the risks. He died fighting for you."

He shoved her, sending her stumbling into the living room.

Her glare could have melted steel. "Fuck you." She stalked into the bedroom and slammed the door.

Azrael closed the door to the bathroom. Part of him wanted to follow Angel into the bedroom, throw her on the bed, and have his way with her. It was what she wanted him to do; she fucked like a wild animal when she was angry.

Azrael pushed the thought away, stepped out of his underwear, and stood in the shower until his skin was pink and raw, his tears mingling with the scalding water.

24

Do you see?

Arachne jerked away from the voice at her ear, gagging at the wash of foul breath that followed. "Ugh...Agon. See what?"

Olivia.

Arachne turned her attention to her dozens of spies in Olivia's apartment. Olivia lay cocooned in her sleeping bag, surrounded by a nest of tissues. Her cat Dinah slept curled in a neat circle at the foot of the sleeping bag. Other than the hum of the refrigerator in the next room, the apartment was dark and still.

It had been two weeks since Elijah's "hate speech" had ignited riots all over the country. Fishers and Cheshires clashed in the streets, each group blaming the other for the rising death toll and rampant destruction of property. Olivia hadn't left her apartment since the riots began. She had taken a leave of absence from work for mental health reasons. Arachne thought Olivia was on the verge of getting fired, but Olivia didn't seem to care. Last night, she'd scrolled her phone for hours and cried herself to sleep sometime around two in the morning.

"What is it?"

Look closer.

Arachne trundled her nearest spider from the wall to the floor, feet away from Olivia. The fine hairs on her spider's legs suddenly prickled with static electricity.

"What—" Arachne started to say, then gasped as all eight of her spider's feet lifted from the ground.

As her spider spun gently on a tilted axis, Arachne watched Olivia's sleeping bag lift off the ground. The crumpled tissues around her rose into the air, as did Dinah, who remained curled in a contented ball as she floated away from the sleeping bag. The kitchen table and chairs lifted off the ground in the next room, as did the dirty dishes in the sink.

Most of Arachne's spiders managed to cling to the walls, but a few of them floated free of their mooring, drifting through the air like dandelion seeds.

"She's doing it in her *sleep* now?"

Agon materialized nearby. *She's exhausting herself, imprisoning her abilities in her body during her waking hours, but she has so much anger in her. It must go somewhere. It's a miracle she doesn't burn her building down while she dreams.*

The tingling sensation in the air grew stronger. Dinah startled awake midair with her fur standing on end. She scrambled to find purchase, releasing a frightened mew.

Olivia grunted in her sleep and the prickling sensation in Arachne's floating spiders subsided. They drifted back down to the ground as gravity once again took hold. Dinah's paws resumed contact with the floorboards and the cat scampered into the closet to hide. The chairs and table and dishes settled back into place. Olivia's sleeping bag made gentle contact with the sleeping mat beneath her. She rolled over and sighed.

Arachne blew out a low whistle as she sent her spiders scurrying back to their hiding places. "Well, that can't be good."

25

WARREN YOUNG OPENED HIS eyes in the darkness of his bedroom, unsure if he'd dreamed of the knocking at his window or if he'd really heard it over the cries of the protesters mobbing the front of the building. He crept to the window, and there was Melinda, one hand on the trellis and the other clutching his windowsill.

Warren looked around to check if anybody had seen her, saw no one, and helped her climb in the window. Once she was safely inside and the window was shut, he whispered, "Are you crazy? The place is surrounded. You could have been attacked by one of the Cheshires—"

"I'm pregnant," Melinda blurted.

The edges of the room sharpened. Warren's pulse pounded in his throat. "Are you sure?"

"Of course I'm sure," Melinda whispered.

Warren reached out and pressed his hand to her belly.

"I'm not showing yet," she said. "But we don't have much time."

"Much time?" Warren echoed dumbly.

Her eyes flashed with panic. "Before Grayburn finds out. I think his other wives already know. They've seen me throw up."

"M-maybe Grayburn will think it's his—" he stammered.

She shook her head. "No. He's never been able to have children. If he finds out I'm pregnant, you're dead. We've got to be gone before that happens."

Warren gaped at her. "Gone?"

"We've got to leave. Now."

He paled. "We can't...the protesters, it's not safe..."

"It's not safe for us *here*," Melinda hissed, "and you've got to come with me. You're the only one who knows how to live in the outside world, and I can't raise this child on my own—"

Her voice broke, and she collapsed into Warren's arms. Warren suddenly thought of Azrael, how he must have felt when Lila told him she was pregnant: the flash of panic, the abrupt increase of lives hanging in the balance.

"All right, we'll go," Warren said. "Tomorrow. When is it safest for you to get away?"

Melinda's breath was hot on his neck. "When he's asleep."

"I'll wait for you in the park down the block from your house tomorrow night," Warren said. He lifted her face and kissed her, tasting the salt of her tears on her lips. "I'll bring enough money to get us out of town. We can figure the rest out from there."

"Promise?" Melinda asked.

"Promise."

Warren woke the next morning with his heart thudding in his chest, as if he'd been running instead of sleeping. Had there been some noise breaking through his sleep—something sharp, like a gunshot? Warren closed his eyes and took a breath, counting slowly to four before exhaling. One…two…three…four. It was a technique his addiction counselor had taught him—if he felt overwhelmed, he could breathe deeply and slowly, and if he stuck with it for a minute or two, it helped calm him down.

He became aware he was gripping his bedsheets and forced his hands to unclench. He peeled his tongue away from the roof of his mouth and relaxed his jaw. One…two…three…four. Don't think about the rioters outside. Don't think about the conversation with Melinda the night before, so impossible and terrifying he could almost convince himself it was a dream.

Warren dressed and descended the steps to the food hall, his nerves buzzing like live wires. He had never been less hungry in his life, but he forced himself to select a pouch of Nosh from the morning box and consume it along with everyone else. The voices of the protesters shook the walls in a low, angry thrum. Shattering glass—likely a bottle thrown at the building—made one young mother emit a small scream. Exhausted Fishers sipped dejectedly at the same breakfast they'd been drinking for months. Years, in some cases.

Warren's stomach clenched as Robert Grayburn prowled into the room, lupine shoulders rolling with each limping step, along with two of his three wives—Fran and Ashleigh. Warren waited for Melinda to enter as well, but there was no sign of her. Probably she needed to stay behind at the house to watch Cade, who'd been removed from the building in case the riot breached the walls of Fishers of Men.

Grayburn pulled out a container of Nosh from the satchel slung over his shoulder as his wives selected theirs from the crate at the center of the room. They pulled up their seats beside Lucille Hatch and Elijah's two wives. Elijah would normally be seated with his mother and wives, but he hadn't left his quarters since the riots began.

Warren averted his eyes as he sucked down his Nosh. Robert Grayburn hadn't come to headquarters since the "hate speech," either. Why was he here now? Was Warren imagining it, or did everyone else in the room look petrified at his unexpected presence?

When he lifted his gaze, terror crept across his flesh: Robert Grayburn was staring at him. One corner of Grayburn's mouth twitched up in a smile.

Warren returned his eyes to his nearly-empty Nosh pouch. Breathe. Just breathe.

One...two...three...four.

He pictured Melinda's face. The soft, lunar swell of her hips. The way he could tell she was smiling when she lay beside him in pitch darkness. The growing life of their child inside her. He needed to keep her safe, and the best way to do that was not to panic.

One...two...three...four.

Grayburn had probably come back to talk some sense into Elijah. Their fearless leader couldn't hide in his room forever. He had to come out and be a voice of reason to the Fishers before everything fell apart.

A tremor rocked Warren. He took in a shaky inhale and only got to three before he had to let it out again. His teeth clacked together. On the next breath, he got to two. If this was a panic attack, it was the worst he'd ever had.

Warren's stomach clenched. His heart pummeled his ribcage.

Something was wrong.

Warren looked around the room. At least a dozen of the Fishers in the food hall gripped their stomachs. He watched as the color drained from the faces of Elijah's wives, and as Lucille Hatch's hand went to her throat, gasping for breath.

Robert Grayburn's wives, Fran and Ashleigh, gagged and bent double. All around him, men, women, and children screamed and moaned and rolled their eyes back to the whites.

Warren cried out as a stabbing pain pierced his guts. He tried to stand and pitched onto the floor. Through the tears streaming from his eyes, he watched Robert Grayburn make his way past the moaning and vomiting Fishers, granting Warren a crazed smile as he walked past. Then he slipped from the room and was gone.

Warren's eyes rolled back in his head, watching bright colors flash in the darkness, thinking that Elijah had been dead wrong when he had dismissed Grayburn as a belled cat.

Grayburn was a wolf. And now there was nobody standing between Melinda and his jaws.

26

WHEN ELIJAH FIRST HEARD the screaming, he thought the sound was coming from outside. After two weeks of the unceasing din of the protest, he barely registered the screams. The uproar of the unwashed rabble, asserting their right to wickedness, was his constant companion, even in sleep. He dreamed of them pushing their way inside the building, consuming everything he'd built in flames. It was enough to drive a saint mad.

A crashing sound under his floorboards broke Elijah out of his reverie. The screams were coming from inside the building. They'd finally gotten inside. It was only a matter of time before they got past the other Fishers and came for him.

Elijah strapped on his prosthetic legs and picked up his cane by the door. If he was going to face his attackers, he wasn't going to do it cowering in his room.

He threw open the door.

Shrieks and moans of pain echoed up from downstairs. Elijah made his way down the stairs, legs trembling beneath him, and when he arrived on the ground floor, he was met with pandemonium. Mothers, fathers, and children, screaming and vomiting, seizing as if wrenched by a huge invisible hand. He saw Warren, his back arched to an excruciating degree, choking on his own vomit. His wives, Cathryn and Casey, writhed on the floor, grasping for each other, eyes rolling back to the whites, seizing as if possessed. His mother twitched and gagged, her hands contorted into talons.

Something more evil than rioters had broken through the sanctity of his home.

Moving as fast as he could, Elijah grabbed his car keys from the hook by the back door, burst into the garage, climbed into his car, settled the foot of his prosthetic leg into place, and peeled out. A few protesters saw his car emerging from the back alley and ran toward him, but he pressed down on the gas, and they leapt out of the way.

A steely claw of terror gripped Elijah's chest as he drove. He could trust no one. Nowhere was safe. It occurred to him that he'd left his cell phone behind in his bedroom—but that was for the best. Father Clark had told him that cell phones could be tracked.

He had a full tank of gas, cash in the glove compartment, and a week's supply of Nosh in the trunk.

It wasn't until he hit the highway that he knew where he needed to go.

27

AZRAEL WAS BACK IN the Moloch house fire. Floral wallpaper blackened and curled. Windows shattered in the heat as flames roared around him.

Olivia.

Flames caressed his limbs as he ran up the stairs, smoke coiling around him. He moved a smoldering chair under the attic trapdoor and climbed onto it, the chair's springs snapping under his weight. He lifted the trapdoor and peered inside.

Olivia wasn't there.

Olivia! Azrael shouted.

I'm here.

Azrael turned to see Olivia hovering a foot above the floor, long copper hair swirling around her.

Azrael, Olivia said, floating toward him.

Azrael watched in awe and terror as she drew close to him, flames flickering in the depths of her pupils.

Firebug, she whispered, and clapped her hands to the sides of his face.

Azrael screamed and bucked away from her grasp—and opened his eyes in a white room illuminated with the gentle hues of dawn. Gold-dappled leaves swayed in a breeze outside his window as birds chirped and flitted through the branches. Still trembling from the dream, Azrael turned to see Angel sleeping at his side, her pale leg tossed over the covers.

He slipped out of bed, locked himself in the bathroom, and drew a bath. When it was full, he climbed into the hot water, sank to the bottom, and stayed submerged until his lungs burned, the dream playing out behind his eyes. When he came up for air, the doorknob was jiggling.

"Azrael? You in there?" Angel asked.

"Yes."

"Let me in, I have to pee."

A muscle in his jaw twitched. "I'm in the tub."

"I could join you."

"Angel, I just got comfortable. Use the bathroom downstairs."

Silence on the other side of the door, followed by a sigh and footsteps receding down the hallway.

When the water started to cool, Azrael climbed out of the bathtub and toweled himself dry. Clattering sounds floated up from downstairs—likely Angel making breakfast. Azrael donned a fresh pair of pajama pants and made his way downstairs.

"Morning," Angel said, tending to a panful of scrambled eggs.

Azrael poured himself a cup of coffee. "Morning."

Trick looked up from their laptop with dark circles under their eyes.

"You sleep all right?" Azrael asked them.

"Like a babe in arms. You?"

Trick was lying through their teeth. They were an insomniac, same as him. Azrael picked an apple from the fruit bowl and took a bite. "Same. Any news?"

"Everything's fucked, same as yesterday," Trick said.

Smoke rose from Angel's pan of eggs. Azrael considered telling her to take the pan off the heat, but that way lay a shouting match. He took a few more bites of his apple instead.

"Umm…" Trick set their coffee down. "Azrael?"

"Yeah?"

Trick turned their laptop around. "There's a situation."

Azrael read the headline on Trick's screen.

Massive Nosh Recall After Dozens Die of Suspected Arsenic Poisoning.

Azrael set the apple down on the counter, the bites he'd eaten souring in his stomach.

Nearly thirty people at the Fishers of Men headquarters in Denver are reported to have died of arsenic poisoning. It's believed at this time that the poison was ingested due to a contaminated shipment of "Nosh," a meal-replacement substance Fishers consume in lieu of solid food. Fishers of Men has been under fire in recent weeks for its incendiary stances, leading some to believe this was an intentional attack. It's unclear now if authorities have any suspects, but some believe the anti-Fisher group the Cheshires may be involved.

Azrael scanned down the article, his eyes freezing on the line:

The ages of the dead range from 4 to 70 years old.

Four years old—Cade's age. Christ…did some maniac Cheshire kill his son? Azrael pressed his fingers into his eyes. All he wanted was for Elijah's ignorant followers to stop hurting people, but somewhere along the line, it had all gone wrong. One more fire he'd started, burning out of his control.

"What is it?" asked Angel.

"Someone poisoned a batch of Nosh," Trick said. "A bunch of Fishers in Denver are dead."

Angel's face lit up. "Do they know who did it?"

Trick scrolled through their phone. "Doesn't say. They mention the possibility that Cheshires were responsible, but I think that's just conjecture. Fisher Biotech is instituting a nationwide recall and urging its customers not to drink any Nosh until they investigate further. Jesus…"

Angel slammed her fist down on the counter. "Take that, Fisher bastards."

Azrael shot her an incredulous look. "Angel, dozens of people we don't know anything about are dead. My son might be one of them."

Angel's lip curled. "I'm sorry if your son got caught in the crossfire, but this is a war. There are going to be casualties."

"Fuck you, Angel," Azrael said.

Angel recoiled as if he'd slapped her. "You know, this is the first time you've mentioned your son. You must really miss him, to leave him with your worst enemy."

Smoke billowed from Angel's burning eggs. A hollow place in Azrael's chest ached like a bad tooth.

"Find out who the dead are," Azrael told Trick. "I'm going for a walk. And get those fucking eggs off the stove before you burn the house down."

The morning was cold and clammy. Azrael kept his orbit close to the house, making his way through the forest, turning back when the tree line grew sparse. It was unlikely anyone in this neighborhood was keeping an eye out for the underground leader of a pack of resistance fighters, but his paranoia forbade him from taking chances.

Azrael paused as he spotted a sizable spider perched in the center of a massive web. The spider looked like a weapon, its legs honed to glossy black-and-yellow barbs. He gave one of the web's strands a pluck. The spider shifted, multiple beady eyes watching him. He thought of Lilith, his pet spider that used to watch while he and Olivia made love.

Azrael walked around for another twenty minutes before he felt like he could return to the house without wanting to set it on fire. When he walked inside, the smell of burned eggs hung in the air like an unresolved argument.

Angel, sitting on a barstool at the counter, smiled at him.

A chill cascaded down Azrael's chest. Angel only smiled like that when she'd scored a point in the game she was playing in her head.

"What are you smiling at?"

Angel pursed her lips and spun around.

Azrael caught her arm. "Angel, what did you do?"

She glared at him. "Let go, you're hurting me."

He tightened his grip on her arm. "What the hell did you do?"

"You mean, what did *you* do?"

"Angel...please tell me you didn't."

Trick looked up from their laptop screen. "Oh, Jesus, Angel..."

"Say it," Azrael said. "I want to hear you say it."

Angel grinned. "I told the Cheshires the poisoning was done by none other than Azrael Hatch himself. It's only a matter of time before it turns from a rumor into news—"

Azrael slapped her.

Her head rocked back. Azrael's hand stung from the impact.

Angel lifted her eyes to meet his, touching her cheek. "I love you, Azrael, but I'm tired of your conscience getting in the way of the revolution."

28

THAT EVENING, AFTER HOURS of talking to the police, Robert Grayburn lay in his bed, scrolling through dozens of articles about the Nosh poisoning. He lingered on one photo a protester had captured of Elijah in his vehicle, speeding away from the scene of the crime.

A text came through from Father Clark: *Online sources point to Azrael Hatch taking responsibility for the Nosh poisoning. Police say they're trying to figure out how it could have happened.*

As Robert read the text, a swell of mirth welled up in his chest. He couldn't let it out here, not with his one surviving wife alternately sobbing and comforting Azrael's bastard son the next room over.

Robert's old leg injury always hurt worse when he first started moving. He winced as he limped down the hallway, pressing his palm to his lips, tears forming at the corners of his eyes. He lurched down the stairs and into the garage, settled into the driver's seat of his car, and burst into screaming laughter as soon as he slammed the door closed. He cackled until tears rolled down his cheeks, the vehicle shaking with his glee. He laughed until he thought he might go mad.

Robert remembered the day he and his mother, Cecelia, arrived at the Colony. Cecelia, who considered herself a "seeker," had sought her way through three marriages and at least as many religions by that point. Henry Hatch, then a strapping, twenty-something "Prophet" with jet black hair and penetrating hazel eyes, had ushered Cecelia into his office, suggesting Robert visit the food hall where he could get something to eat. Robert had instead crept around to the back of the building, hunkered beneath the window, and listened.

"...you mentioned on the phone there have been behavioral issues," Hatch was saying.

"Yes," Robert's mother had said, her voice wavering. "I found...graves in our backyard. At least a half dozen of them."

"Graves?"

"Small ones, for animals," his mother clarified. "I dug a few of them up, and they looked like they'd been...dissected."

The word *dissected* was too delicate a word, and she knew it. *Mutilated* would have been more accurate. Robert had been careless, not hiding them well enough.

"I asked a counselor at his high school for an assessment of his mental health, and she said Robert showed symptoms of antisocial personality disorder." Robert's mother sniffed. "He has a good heart, and I've tried to bring positive male role models into his life, but...well, you know...I haven't been very lucky in love. My first husband, Robert's father, was not a good man. You may have noticed Robert limps a bit when he walks—that's because his father broke his leg when he was five years old." Her voice cracked as she went on. "My second husband hid a raging alcohol addiction from me until after we were married. He died in a drunk driving accident when Robert was twelve. I thought my third husband was a decent man, but he never did care for Robert. I came home from work one day a few months ago and he'd left us without a word."

Listening under the window, Robert had smirked. He'd done a better job hiding the body of his latest stepfather than he had the animals.

"What your son needs," Henry Hatch had told his mother, "and what the outside world cannot offer him, is a moral compass. I can give him that." The Prophet's voice dropped into a silkier register as he added, "It's no accident his behavioral issues have led you to us as well. You, who have been unlucky in love, will find it here in abundance."

Grayburn had grimaced at this. He hoped he was mistaken in hearing undertones of lust in Hatch's tone, but sure enough, Henry married Cecelia a few months later. At last, she had everything she needed—romance and religion—in one man.

Overall, Robert had enjoyed those early days at the Colony. He didn't have to go to high school anymore, for one thing, and the Colony was surrounded by hundreds of acres of woods, so he had plenty of time between chores to explore, trap animals, and see how long their little hearts beat once they were exposed to the open air.

Within the year, the Prophet gathered the Colony together and made an announcement: Robert's mother Cecelia was pregnant with his first child. "I've prayed for this day my entire life," Hatch said happily. "I've often asked the Lord why my many attempts to be fruitful have not resulted in a child. And now I know the answer—it was always meant to be Cecelia. He has shown me that it will be not me, but my children, who will save the world, and that my child will be the Prophet who leads us forward."

Spring gave way to summer as his mother's belly swelled with each passing month. She threw up, suffered swollen feet and ankles, and barely slept—yet she glowed. She caressed her belly and murmured to it softly.

"My child will be the Prophet's first-born," she told Robert. "That means, when the Prophet dies, my baby will be the new Prophet of the Colony. He will converse with God as the Prophet does. He will be the savior of us all."

When his mother went into labor, Robert listened from his bed in the young men's barracks as her screams echoed through the Colony. He'd heard her beg to be taken to a hospital a few times, though such a request was blasphemy in the eyes of her beloved Prophet. Her screams turned into moans, which turned into silence, which was broken by a different cry, the first batch of bawling from new lungs.

The next morning, the Prophet sent for Robert to be brought into his office. Hatch tented his heavily-ringed fingers, leaned back in his leather chair, and eyed Robert from across his desk.

"Robert, I'm afraid I have terrible news. There's no easy way to say this, so I'll be plain: your mother died in child-birth, and has gone to be with the Lord in Heaven."

Robert's stomach sank. He supposed he ought to be experiencing some kind of grief, but in its place was a hollow fear that the Prophet would no longer feel obligated to keep him around, that he would be cast out into the world as an orphan.

Robert remembered himself, and contorted his face to show the kind of anguish he thought the Prophet was expecting to see.

"Before she died," Hatch went on, "she gave me the most beautiful gift I've ever received."

Robert followed Hatch's gaze across the room to a bassinet with an infant in it. The baby's eyes looked around the room, unfocused, grasping the air with its tiny fingers.

"His name is Azrael," the Prophet said. "It means 'Help of God.'"

A wave of anger crashed over Robert as he stared at Azrael. The Prophet's progeny was less than a day old, and already he had stolen something from Robert he would never get back.

"Robert...you should know that I see you for who you really are," Hatch said. "Not who you pretend to be, and not who your mother wanted you to be. I see how sharp your teeth are through the wool you've draped over yourself."

The mask of grief slipped from Robert's face. He eyed the Prophet coldly. He'd been so careful...

"The Colony is growing," the Prophet went on, "and not everyone who comes through our gates deserves to remain in our flock. I will need help culling those who are weak of spirit." The Prophet's chair creaked as he leaned forward. "God does not make mistakes, Robert. He gave you teeth for a reason. You have been sent to me to serve a higher purpose—to ensure the rot of sin is cut out like an infection before it is allowed to spread to the rest of the Colony. Are you willing to help me in this mission?"

Robert looked at the Prophet and saw his future refashioning itself in his eyes. He could remain here, have all of his needs met, including the ones his mother labeled as compulsions.

"I have one request," Robert said.

The Prophet nodded.

"I don't want Azrael to know that we shared a mother."

The Prophet narrowed his eyes. "May I ask why?"

"You took her from me. You, Azrael, the Colony. As penance for that, I want her memory to belong to me, and me alone. I don't want to hear her name mentioned here ever again. Do this for me, and I will cull the unworthy from your followers."

"Done," the Prophet had said. "I will make the announcement over supper. Nobody at the Colony will speak her name again."

In the following years, as the Colony grew, the forest swallowed body after body of the Colony's unworthy fathers and sons. A few escaped Robert's grasp, but they hadn't returned to the Colony or brought any trouble to their gates. The Prophet didn't care one way or another what happened to his male followers once they were gone, as long as the women remained.

And now, Robert had finished the job he'd started all those years ago—murdering the sly son of a bitch who slept with Melinda.

Robert had detected Warren's scent on Melinda as soon as the two began their affair; she had gone to bed smelling like lavender soap and came down to breakfast smelling of sweat and spunk. A few months later, Robert smelled vomit on Melinda's breath, and knew her washout of a lover had gotten her pregnant. He longed for the days when the solution would have been as simple as bashing Warren over the head and burying him in the woods. He needed to come up with some other way of removing Warren from the picture so he could have Melinda to himself once again.

The answer to poison the Nosh came to Robert in a vivid dream in which a man with a crooked smile drew a skull and crossbones onto a pouch of Nosh. When the man in the dream handed him the Nosh, his fingers brushed against Robert's hand, and Robert jolted awake as if he'd been electrocuted.

It took Robert a few weeks to find a man on the internet willing to sell him arsenic for cash. When Robert met the man in a midnight parking lot to exchange cash for the poison, he thought the man looked strangely like the man from his dream.

In the hours before dawn, Robert Grayburn had stolen away with one of the crates of Nosh, wearing gloves to avoid leaving prints. He opened every pouch one by one, siphoned the crushed-up poison inside, and used a knife he'd heated over the stove to reseal the plastic covers.

His plan had worked wondrously. Warren was dead, along with the rest of the Fishers in the dining hall, including two of Robert's wives, both of Elijah's wives, and the boy's simpering mother, Lucille Hatch. Elijah Hatch had fled soon after, leaving a vacuum of leadership into which Robert Grayburn was happy to step. And now, the Cheshires were taking responsibility for his act. It was all too sublime.

If evidence did happen to arise pointing to Robert as the culprit for the poisoning, his next move would be simple. Kill Melinda and Cade, and then retrieve the handgun he kept hidden on top of the refrigerator and deliver himself to the same darkness into which he'd sent so many.

Robert's phone vibrated—Father Clark calling. Robert Grayburn let the call go through to voicemail. He'd call the drunken fool back later, when he could trust himself not to laugh.

29

OLIVIA WOKE TO HER phone buzzing on the floor beside her. She reached for it from the depths of her sleeping bag and answered. "Hello?"

"Olivia!" said Milo. "I've been trying to reach you for hours. Did you have your phone off?"

"No, I was sleeping."

"Jesus, Olivia, it's 3 p.m. Were you sleeping all day?"

Yes. "No."

"You're back in Austin, right? Have you seen the news?"

Olivia stiffened. "What news?"

"A shipment of Nosh was poisoned at the Fishers of Men facility in Denver."

Olivia sat up. "What?"

"They're saying almost thirty people died from drinking it. Some Cheshires online are claiming Azrael was behind it, but there's no evidence to back that up yet. Elijah took off in his car before the police arrived, and nobody knows where he is..."

All the air left the room. "Milo, my mom drinks Nosh. I have to go...I have to call her..."

"Call me back after you talk to her," Milo said. "Please."

Olivia selected her mother's contact with numb fingers. She couldn't be dead, not from Nosh, not from something Olivia helped push out into the world...

The phone rang and rang.

Olivia dug her fingernails into her palms.

"Hello?"

Her mother's voice, still a bit raspy from when Olivia's powers had damaged her throat.

Relief flooded Olivia's veins. "Mom, thank God."

"Olivia, what is it?"

"Have you heard? About the poisoned Nosh?"

"The poisoned...what?"

"Someone poisoned a batch of Nosh in Denver. Milo just called and told me. A lot of people are dead."

"Oh, honey. I hadn't heard. Bernard and I are fine."

"And you'll throw out any Nosh you have in the house, just in case?"

"Tossed it days ago," Betty said. "Sorry to say, you lost a customer when that twerp spouted off about how he was justified in hating everyone."

Olivia let out a heavy sigh. "Thank goodness."

"Do they know who poisoned it?"

A vision of Azrael injecting poison into pouches of Nosh stopped Olivia's breath.

"I don't know," she said weakly. "I'm just glad you're okay."

"Me, too. Those poor people. How are you?"

"I'm...all right. Work's been busy." It was a half-truth. "I'm sure we'll be in damage control mode after the poisoning."

Betty's voice went low with concern. "I hadn't thought of that. Is this going to hurt your company? Or your job?"

Olivia sighed. "I honestly couldn't care less about that. If there are layoffs, I've got savings. I'll figure something out."

"Or move back home?" Half-joke, half-question.

"Yeah. Maybe." Olivia's heartbeat quickened as Milo's words echoed in her head: *Almost thirty people died.* She had to get off the phone. She didn't think she'd be able to hurt her mother over the phone, but it wasn't worth the risk. "Mom, I'm sorry, but I have to run."

"Oh—yes, sure. Have a good day, sweetie."

"Love you, Mom."

"Love you, Liv."

Olivia hung up the phone and texted Milo: *My mom is okay.*

Thank God for that, Milo sent back. Then: *I miss you. Can we catch up soon?*

Olivia put her head in her hands and sobbed. She wanted to see Milo so badly it made her chest ache, but it wasn't safe. She could feel the power within her growing, and she wasn't sure how much longer she could hold it in before it lashed out and did something horrific.

I need some more time, she sent back. *Soon, I promise.*

Olivia's body crackled like a live wire as she scrolled through articles and posts about the poisoning. Was Azrael really capable of something this terrible?

And where in the hell was Elijah?

30

Elijah closed his eyes and listened to the sounds of the forest around him. A chilly breeze filled his nostrils with the cool scent of earth. A stream burbled nearby. It was both strange and familiar being here, like visiting a place from a dream.

Elijah looked back through the trees at the abandoned buildings and dead gardens of what had once been the Colony. As a child, Elijah had spent a lot of time in these woods. Here, he could commune with God in peace. It didn't feel like running away to be here now. In a fairer world, he'd never have left this place.

Elijah took in a deep breath and let it out slowly. He scanned his surroundings—the trees swaying in the breeze, brittle leaves shifting over the dry earth—and spotted a pale object sticking out of the leaves a dozen yards away. His brow furrowed as he drew close. It was a bone, jutting a few inches out of the dark earth.

There were deer in these woods—loads of them. The Fathers used to go out with shotguns and hunt them. It only made sense that their bones littered the forest.

Still, Elijah felt better after he'd kicked the leaves to cover up the bone.

He made his way back to the compound, careful not to tread on any loose stones or jutting roots. Time had not been kind to the Colony. Vines snarled through broken windows, and one of the roofs had caved in. When Elijah walked into the dining hall, a rat bristled at him and scurried into a hole in the wall. The platform from which his father had once delivered morning prayers was covered with moss.

Elijah found a sleeping barracks with its windows and roof intact. He scavenged a few musty blankets and a pillow from the surrounding structures. Unless the weather turned significantly colder, he had everything he needed to stay here for a few days and sort out his thoughts.

He found a length of rusted pipe in the bathroom and tucked it under his bed, just in case.

Elijah drank down a pouch of Nosh and laid his head on the mildewed pillow. A light rain began to fall, the sound making him sleepy. When he closed his eyes, he saw the anguished faces of his followers—his mother, his wives, Warren, and dozens of others—as they writhed and vomited and moaned in pain from some invisible affliction.

Elijah's chest tightened as his own words echoed back at him. He'd spoken his truth—a justifiably angry response to the state of the world—and said what his father would have said in his place, but it had brought him nothing but misery, and now his followers had paid the price.

Cade's voice broke through his thoughts: *I like when we help people.*

Elijah's limbs stiffened under the threadbare sheets. He wasn't sure if his nephew was dead or alive. As far as he knew, Cade hadn't set foot in headquarters since Elijah's speech, which meant he may have been spared the same fate that claimed the rest of Elijah's followers. If his speech had led to the death of such a sweet soul, Elijah wasn't sure how he was going to recover.

Elijah opened his eyes and stared at the water stain on the ceiling, trying to picture Cade, some years older, saying the things Elijah had said to the crowd. Elijah couldn't imagine Cade hurting anyone, even if they deserved it. His heart ached as he squeezed his eyes shut and prayed that Cade was all right.

Exhaustion ferried Elijah closer to sleep, and his thoughts strayed again to the white slab of bone in the ground. The bucks in the woods got pretty big, but did they have bones like that? If he dug around the bone, what would he find? A pelvis? Ribs? The skull of someone he used to know?

It was a deer skeleton, he told himself. The forest was full of them.

"ELIJAH."

Elijah's eyes flew open. Pain flashed across his old wounds, his nonexistent toes prickling with electricity. He blinked, but there was nothing but inky darkness.

Then he heard it: the soft squelch of a foot stepping into mud outside the door.

Elijah's eyes adjusted until he could make out the shape of a woman standing in the doorway. "Who's there?" he demanded.

The woman lifted into the air and floated toward his bed.

Elijah shook his head. He was having a nightmare. He was going to wake up at any moment.

Twin points of glowing red burned where the woman's eyes should be. Her skin was pale and freckled, her hair bright copper.

Elijah's jaw dropped. "Olivia?"

"Hello, Elijah."

"Wh—what—why are you—"

"You know why," Olivia said.

Elijah remembered the length of pipe he'd stashed under his bed and reached for it. He was certain it would be gone— this was a nightmare, after all—but his fingers closed around it, and he brandished it. "Stay back!"

Olivia looked at the pipe placidly with her burning eyes. She tilted her head. Metal shrieked as the pipe bent in half, then in half again. She tilted her head the other way and the pipe clattered to the ground.

Elijah stared in horror at the twisted hunk of metal. "You're a demon. I thought it was Azrael. I thought the Devil sent him to test me, but it was you all along—"

"Enough," said Olivia.

Everything in the room lifted into the air. The bed, Elijah's prosthetic legs, a roll of toilet paper, an empty pouch of Nosh—they floated around him as if the gravity in the room had been switched off. Elijah drew in air to scream and found he couldn't breathe.

"You've talked enough." Olivia floated closer. "Now you're going to listen. You're worse than your father, and Azrael, and all the Fathers combined. You're the worst kind of monster—one who believes himself to be a victim. And it ends now."

A thrill of terror diffused into a spreading warmth that plunged him into a deep, dark pool.

Elijah's last thought before the darkness swallowed everything was of the white bone in the forest.

31

OLIVIA DREAMED OF FLYING.

She flew for miles, soaring high over a moonlit landscape. In the strange logic of dreams, she knew Elijah was back at the raided Colony compound, sensed it as clearly as if he'd shown up as a blip on her radar. As she flew, the constellations of city lights grew sparse. When it began to rain, Olivia felt by the way it peppered her that she was moving as swift as an arrow.

When Olivia arrived at the Colony, she settled to the ground. The rain-soaked mud was pliable and cold between her toes.

How many atrocities had been carried out inside these walls?

At least one more, dream-Olivia thought, and walked toward the room where Elijah was sleeping.

What happened next was a blur.

Elijah woke in terror, they exchanged words, and Olivia snapped something small and vital in his brain. She floated closer to him, inspecting him by a light coming from somewhere inside her. A line of drool spun out from his open mouth to the pillow below. His chest rose and fell in hitches. He wasn't dead, but the light in his eyes had gone out. Olivia floated outside, the night around her sweet and rich as she soared up into the air.

Olivia jerked awake to the wailing of a siren. It was so loud that for a panicked moment she thought a fire truck was going to come barreling into her bedroom. She clung to the sides of her sleeping bag until the siren faded into the distance.

Judging by the light coming in the edge of her sleeping bag, it was late morning. She shivered. The dream had felt so real. Worse, it had felt *good*. A not-insignificant part of her wanted to do exactly that—although she doubted Elijah was hiding out in the ruins of the compound from which he'd been exiled. And she doubted, as powerful as she sometimes felt, that she could pull off that kind of Wicked-Witch-of-the-West shit. There was something wrong with her, and she was doing everything she could to stop from hurting people, but she wasn't capable of *flying*.

She reached for her phone and discovered a dozen texts from Milo. She stared at the headline in the link he sent her:

Elijah Hatch Found in a Coma in Eland, Texas

Olivia emerged from her sleeping bag, looked up, and screamed.

Muddy footprints tracked across her ceiling.

32

ARACHNE WATCHED FROM A dozen tiny spiders as Olivia paced her apartment, her hair windswept from her flight through the air. Her ankles bore streaks of mud, her eyes wide with disbelief and terror. Arachne considered using her spiders to construct a web with a message in it—something like *you're not crazy*—but decided a stunt like that was liable to push Olivia over the edge.

When a knock fell on her door, Olivia froze.

"Olivia?" Milo asked through the door.

Olivia held her breath.

"I know you're there," Milo said. "I heard you walking around. Come on, let me in."

Olivia's shoulders sank. "I'm sorry, Milo, but it's not safe in here."

"It ain't a tiptoe through the tulips out here, either, Liv."

"I'm serious."

"I don't know what kind of Howard Hughes situation you've got in there, but it's gone on long enough. I'm not leaving until you let me in."

Olivia bit her lip as she approached the door. She unbolted, unlocked, and opened it. She looked Milo over. "You look good."

Milo adjusted his sunglasses and grinned. "You look terrible."

"Flattery will get you nowhere," Olivia said, and they hugged for a long time. "You want something? Some tea?"

"Tea sounds great. Show me to a chair?"

Olivia led Milo to a chair and set a kettle to boil. "All I've got is Sleepytime. I've been avoiding caffeine lately."

Milo set his cane against the table, the corners of his mouth twitching into a frown. "What's going on with you, Liv? You've been avoiding me for months. I understand if you need some time to process what happened to Nancy... believe me, I do...but I wasn't expecting you to cut me out of your life."

"Milo...I wish I could tell you. I really do."

"Then tell me."

"You'll think I'm losing it."

"I promise I won't." Milo found her hand on the table and squeezed it. "Liv...I really need you to not shut me out. I can't lose you, too."

Olivia stared at Milo for a few beats, then said, "I'm hurting people. At first, I thought I was imagining it, but it's really happening. I caused the remains of a building to crush Elijah's legs, and the newswoman who died of an aneurysm. I'm the reason Dan fell and hit his head at work. I killed all the bedbugs in my apartment and took out my next-door neighbor's dog in the process. I almost killed my mom when I got mad at the news. I could keep going."

Milo was silent.

Olivia lowered her eyes. "You think I'm crazy."

"No, I don't," Milo said gently. "You're wrong, but you're not crazy."

"So, how did all of those things happen?"

"I don't know, but I can think of a dozen more plausible explanations than you having magical mind-powers."

"I know how it sounds. But it's real. I've hurt a lot of people. Killed some of them."

"You're not hurting people," Milo assured her, keeping his voice level. "You're just afraid that you are. Have you talked to anyone else about this? Like a therapist?"

Olivia shook her head. "I don't feel safe talking about it. It lashes out of me, sometimes, and something horrible always happens when it does. I'm only telling you this now because I think I might be losing control. You know how Elijah was found unresponsive where the Colony used to be?"

"Yeah, I…wait, you think *you* did that?"

"I know I did. I dreamed about attacking him, or at least I thought it was a dream, until I woke up and…"

"And what?"

"And saw footprints on my ceiling."

Milo's brow furrowed. "What are you saying?"

"I walked through mud at the Colony to get to Elijah, and then I came back, and I must have been…I don't know… sleepwalking around on my ceiling before I went back to bed, because I found muddy footprints there this morning."

Milo took in a slow breath. Arachne waited for him to tell Olivia she needed professional help, medication, an inpatient stay somewhere where she could get her head straight.

"Are the footprints still there?" Milo asked.

"Yes."

"Show me."

Olivia hesitated, then picked up one of the kitchen chairs and led Milo into her bedroom. "Straight up from here."

Milo stood on the chair, reached up, and touched one of the footprints. He brought his fingers to his nose and smelled. Touched the ceiling again, smelled again.

"I feel it," Milo said. "I can smell it, too."

"You do?"

"Yeah. It's faint, but it smells like earth. There's no reason it should smell like that up there, unless you put mud on your ceiling to fuck with me."

Olivia smiled weakly. "Are you saying you believe me?"

Milo climbed down. "I believe you believe it. Let's start with that."

Olivia led Milo back to the kitchen, where the kettle was growling its way to a boil.

"I keep thinking, what if I left some kind of evidence behind? Fingerprints, clothing fibers, strands of hair. Something leading them back to me."

"I wouldn't worry about that. Eland is almost a hundred miles away, and I can't think of any reason you would be a suspect. Even if they dust for prints and yours show up clear as day, you've never been booked for anything, so unless they jump to some wild conclusions and bring you in for questioning, you're safe."

Milo was right, thought Arachne. The footprints Olivia left in the mud had been drowned out by rain. There were no signs of foul play, as it seemed clear Elijah had suffered something resembling an embolism. He wouldn't even have been discovered if a passing police officer hadn't spotted his vehicle parked in the woods. As Olivia and Milo spoke, Arachne's spiders watched the slow rise and fall of Elijah's chest in the hospital, where he was being kept alive by machines.

"I hope you're right," Olivia said. "But it doesn't change what's happening to me. If I'm doing it in my sleep, then I'm not in control of it."

Milo considered this. "Let's say you did find Elijah. How did you know where he was?"

"I don't know. I remember flying through the air to find him. I don't remember how I knew where to go, just that I knew I was going the right way."

"Can you do the same thing to find Azrael?"

"No, Milo, I can't. You don't understand. Anytime I do this, something bad happens. I think the only reason I didn't hurt anybody other than Elijah this time around was because he was too far from any other people."

"Let's say we get you a quarter mile from anything living, a big, abandoned parking lot or something, and you look for Azrael."

"It doesn't work that way—"

"If what you're telling me is true, you found Elijah in a dream without trying. You're telling me you can't find the person who fed thirty people a fatal dose of arsenic?"

Olivia's voice cracked. "I...I don't want to hurt anyone else."

"I want to be clear: I don't believe you're hurting people, Elijah included. I'm only saying, if you really wanted to test your theory before we pull the trigger on calling mental health professionals, you should try to find Azrael. He's responsible for the deaths of dozens of innocent people. With Elijah incapacitated, the Fishers of Men movement is crippled, and without Azrael, the Cheshires will fall apart too. If it doesn't work," Milo added, "then we'll look into getting you some help."

The kettle whistled. Olivia took it off the heat, poured water into the mugs, and added tea bags. She set the mugs on the table and guided Milo's hand to his, staring at him from between the ribbons of steam.

She'll be here with us soon, Agon whispered at Arachne's ear.

Arachne recoiled from its foul breath as it materialized beside her. "She's fighting it. She's stronger than you think."

She believes she's turning into her father, a creature of wrath and violence, Agon hissed. *Hades knew from the beginning how to use that belief to turn her against herself. Now it's only a matter of time. Don't tell me you can't feel it.*

Arachne didn't deny this—her sense of gathering momentum, of the storm around Olivia spiraling faster and faster, out of control.

There are no more chess pieces to move into place up above, Agon jeered. *The Lord of Death has returned here, to His domain, to claim her. She'll be in His claws soon.*

Arachne shivered as a family of wolf spiders climbed her legs. "It's not over yet."

From her spiders clinging to the walls of Olivia's bleak apartment, Arachne watched as Olivia reached for Milo's hand and held it.

"Okay," Olivia said. "I'll try to find Azrael."

33

OLIVIA DROVE TO THE spot she and Milo had agreed on: Walter E. Long Park, closed for landscaping. Olivia pulled up in her car at just past midnight and surveyed the dark, exposed earth and unmanned construction equipment. She texted Milo, who was waiting for her back at his house, to let him know she'd arrived.

Good luck, he sent back.

Olivia sighed, reading his text. Whatever happened next, she could cling to how good it felt to be around Milo again, to hold his hand, to feel something warm, and strong, and real. It reminded Olivia of a time when the world had made sense, when she didn't feel like a live grenade with the pin pulled out.

Olivia turned her vehicle off, scaled the fence, and made her way to the center of the abandoned park. On her way, she passed a flock of ducks sleeping on the shore by the lake. Olivia marked its position, so she could avoid passing whatever was in her mind over that spot—if she had to walk past a bunch of dead ducks on the walk back to her car, she'd go insane.

Olivia found a spot at least a quarter mile from civilization and took a seat on a grassy hill. She closed her eyes, unsure of how to start. She pictured Azrael's face—how happy he'd looked when they were dating, how haggard he'd looked on the news. She thought of his dark gravity, the way it felt like he was pulling her toward him.

Olivia spun her mental compass point, seeking, seeking…

Her awareness expanded beyond her body. It happened slowly at first, with a feeling like a pupil dilating, and then her surroundings slipped away. The grass under her fingertips, the dew on her ankles, the smells of earth and spent diesel fuel, vanishing one after another like lights turning off.

"Azrael…" she murmured. "Where are you?"

The pull on the compass point grew stronger, almost as if he *wanted* to be found. A profound weariness swelled in her chest, and she knew intuitively she was feeling what Azrael was feeling. He was tired…tired of running, tired of the company he kept, tired of his own revolution…

Olivia had always sensed madness in Azrael—it was part of why she'd fallen in love with him—but this was different. This was a desperate, foxhole madness, haunted by nightmares of flame and terror, hiding from the world, hiding from himself…

Olivia saw him—actually *saw* him—walking under the cover of nightfall into an old house with scaffolding covering its facade. The house was at the end of a cul-de-sac, down the length of a long, tree-shaded driveway. The air around him hummed with the sounds of chirping crickets and rustling leaves.

Azrael stopped at the doorway, wind ruffling his hair, which he'd dyed platinum blonde. His amber eyes narrowed, and he cocked his head as if listening. All at once, Olivia felt like *she* was being watched, that Azrael was reaching across the miles, searching for her, *feeling* her, and for one dizzying moment he looked directly at her—

The thrashing edges of her vision collapsed, and Olivia snapped back across the expanse, slamming into herself and crumpling against the dewy hill.

Olivia lay against the wet grass for a few heartbeats, and when the tears came, she curled up and sobbed.

After several minutes, she collected herself and checked her phone. Her eyes widened in shock when she saw she'd been in the park for more than two hours. She stood, stretched her legs, and walked back toward her car. She reached the lake minutes later and, heart hammering, stared at water as black and glassy as obsidian. No ducks, living or dead.

She thought of how it felt when she snapped back into her body—her spirit had raced back to her at several times the speed of sound, and when she'd landed back into herself...

Olivia looked up into the trees and screamed.

Bones, gristle, and feathers covered the branches.

Olivia ran back to her car, chest heaving with panicked breaths. She was barely able to stay on the road as she drove to Milo's house. She parked in his driveway and peered up at the door, wondering if she should go inside or never see Milo again...at least he'd be safe.

Milo appeared in his doorway. "Olivia, is that you?"

Olivia opened her car door. "Yeah, it's me."

"I've been calling you, but it kept going to voicemail. I was worried."

Olivia approached Milo, shaking uncontrollably. "It's okay. I'm okay."

"Did it work?"

"It worked," Olivia said. "But I killed a bunch of ducks."

"I've never been more relieved to hear a sentence end in 'ducks.'"

"I *hope* that's all I did."

Milo hugged her. "How did you kill the ducks?"

"I told you," Olivia said, "somebody always gets hurt. It's the cost of letting whatever's inside of me out."

Milo ushered her inside and shut the door. "You said it worked...so you found him?"

Olivia sat down and told Milo everything she'd seen in as much detail as she could remember. "I think it's somewhere on the east coast," she concluded. "Maybe North Carolina, or Virginia. I got the feeling it was pretty isolated."

"What do we do if you find it?" Milo asked.

"I don't know," Olivia said, shaking her head.

Milo sighed. "Okay, Liv. Come on, it's late. Let's get some rest."

Olivia was sure she wouldn't be able to sleep, but she slipped into darkness within minutes of her head hitting the pillow.

OLIVIA WOKE WITH A start to bright, morning light pouring through the guest room window and the sounds of Milo making breakfast. She turned on her phone and scrolled through her newsfeed. It didn't take her long to find what she was looking for—what she'd known in her gut was coming.

Eleven Die in Unhoused Encampment in Walter E. Long Metropolitan Park.

Eleven unhoused people were found dead this morning in their encampment at Walter E. Long Metropolitan Park. The park has been closed for landscaping for months, but according to park worker Patrick Haldiman, workers have been "turning a blind eye to the encampment," as the unhoused people "weren't causing anyone any trouble." The cause of the deaths is unclear, with toxicology reports pending. In a bizarre additional detail, a flock of ducks who lived in the nearby pond were also killed...

Olivia dropped her phone and pressed her fist into her lips. Bitter tears flowed down her cheeks. When Milo heard her crying and came to her, she handed him her phone and pressed play on the accompanying video.

Milo clicked her phone off. "You didn't do this."

Olivia shook her head. "Somebody always gets hurt."

"For all you know, they overdosed, or a dozen other things that aren't you having mind bullets." Milo reached for her.

Olivia backed away from him. "Milo...I need to go home. I need to be alone right now."

Milo winced. "All right. Just...don't be a stranger, okay?"

"I won't," she said, hoping it wasn't a lie.

34

Azrael stared up at the stippled ceiling of the basement guest room. The buzz of the forced air heater vibrated the creaky pullout sofa mattress beneath him. A cricket he'd given up trying to find chirped somewhere in the depths of the basement. He took in a deep breath, his nostrils prickling with the creeping scent of mildew. All he had to do was climb the stairs, make amends to Angel, and he could be sleeping on a cushioned mattress again under fragrant bed sheets with the soft sound of leaves rustling outside the window.

He closed his eyes. He'd slept in worse conditions.

Azrael contorted his body to find a comfortable position, racing thoughts keeping sleep at bay. He still didn't know whether Cade was among the poisoned or not. If he was, he wasn't sure he could ever shake the feeling he was responsible for his son's death.

When the heater clicked into silence, Azrael checked the time. 3:42 a.m. He sighed. He'd barely eaten the day before. Maybe getting some food in his belly would help him to rest. The rusty coils in the mattress screeched as he climbed out of bed. He padded up the carpeted stairs, careful to avoid the exposed staples jutting out of the gaps. The familiar cold glow of a laptop screen reflected off the windows as he reached the top of the stairs. It was a welcome sight—Trick had their thumb on the pulse of latest developments, often relaying updates to Azrael hours before the media posted them.

Bracing himself, Azrael approached the kitchen counter. He asked quietly, "Any news?"

Trick jumped like a marionette with its strings jerked. "Damn it, Azrael. Don't sneak up on me like that."

"Sorry," Azrael whispered. "I was going to try to eat something."

Trick gestured to the stove. "There's half a quesadilla I made around midnight, should still be good."

Azrael picked up the quesadilla from the pan and sat down next to Trick. The taste of the congealed cheese mingled with the syrupy cloud of Trick's vape exhales.

"They released the names of the dead a few hours ago," Trick whispered. "Cade's name wasn't on the list. He's all right."

The strength left Azrael's limbs. He'd been spending the past few days bolstering himself against the possibility that his son had been killed; the sudden relief was so strong it felt like he was coming down with the flu. He blinked back tears and forced himself to take another bite of the quesadilla. "Do you know where Cade is?"

"It's not confirmed, but best we can figure, Cade's staying with Robert Grayburn and his surviving wife, Melinda. With Henry Hatch and Elijah both out of the picture, Grayburn's stepped into a leadership role with the remaining Fishers."

Azrael nodded. That meant Cade wasn't exactly safe, because Grayburn was more chilling than even his father had been, but Azrael didn't think Grayburn was going to do anything to hurt Cade. Not with so much attention on him.

"Thank you," Azrael said quietly.

Trick's voice was muffled as they released a sickly-sweet plume of vapor. "Don't mention it."

Azrael finished his quesadilla in silence, hiding his shaking hands.

Trick said, "Someone on the message boards is claiming to be a nurse at Elijah's hospital."

Azrael looked up. "Do you think it's legit?"

Trick nodded. "I think so. He's posting anonymously, of course. He's saying Elijah is in a medical coma. His brain waves are 'significantly diminished.'"

Trick turned their laptop to show Azrael a blurry photo of Elijah lying in his hospital bed. He looked pale and lifeless, a corpse kept alive by machines.

"I didn't want this for him," Azrael said softly.

"This wasn't anything we did," Trick reminded him. "It was an embolism. They're random."

"I know," Azrael said, though it didn't feel random at all. He stared out the kitchen window at the black trees swaying against a star-studded sky. "Trick…do you think we're safe here?"

Trick's brow furrowed. "Safe as we'd be anywhere. Why do you ask?"

Azrael shook his head. "I get the feeling I'm being watched, is all. I've been going on instinct for so long it's starting to feel indistinguishable from paranoia."

"Trust me, if the cops were onto us, I'd know about it before they got here."

They sat in silence long enough for Azrael's fatigue to start to overcome his buzzing nerves. He was about to get up to go back downstairs when Trick said, "I figured out the combination to the safe in the upstairs office, by the way."

Azrael pricked up. "Yeah?"

Trick nodded, their eyes not leaving their screen as they scrolled. "It's mostly paperwork, but there's a gun in there. A Beretta. A few spare shells, too."

Azrael considered this. "Any chance you know how to use it?"

"I do, actually," Trick said. "My dad was a gun nut. Taught me all about rifles and hunting and stuff when I was little. I think he thought if he could teach me enough straight-coded habits it would stop me from being queer." They sucked in a hit from their vape and blew out a smokestack. "Want me to take the gun out and keep it somewhere more accessible?"

"No. There's no way we win in any kind of firefight if the authorities find us. Captured is better than dead." He thought for a moment, then added, "Let's not tell Angel about the gun."

Trick made a zipping gesture across their lips.

35

Olivia looked down at Milo's text on her phone.

I had a coworker help me find a few houses matching your description. Are any of these it?

A series of links followed. The fourth one Olivia clicked on was the house from her vision. She was as sure of it as she was sure of anything else that had happened to her. Below the photo was an address in Virginia.

Olivia waited a long time before she replied.

Some of these are close, but not it.

An ellipsis appeared, then Milo's response: *Dang. Want to hang out tonight?*

Olivia bit her lip. Maybe she had lost her mind. Maybe she should call in an anonymous tip. Maybe her instinct to go and confront Azrael herself was madness...

No. Everything had been leading her to this. It had to be her.

She texted Milo: *I'd love to. Come over, I'll order pizza.*

Olivia stared into the middle distance for a long time after sending the text. If she were really going to confront Azrael— and she didn't think she could stop herself from doing so—she didn't want to go without saying goodbye to Milo.

She looked down at the flame tattoo on her wrist. Time had softened its edges, but the colors remained bright. She pulled out her laptop and booked a flight arriving in Richmond the following evening. She reserved a rental car for twenty-four hours, trying to shake the feeling she wouldn't be returning it.

Olivia snapped her laptop closed and set to digging through her dresser. What did one wear when confronting one's evil ex-boyfriend? She decided on comfortable black pants and a dark gray sweatshirt, laying them out on her dresser. She hurriedly stuffed a few more things into a backpack.

A glint of color caught her eye as she was closing a drawer, and she pulled out the fire opal necklace Nancy had given her all those years ago. Tears stung Olivia's eyes. She hadn't worn the necklace since Nancy's death. It felt too painful, like a brand on her skin, a reminder of the hole Nancy's absence had burned into her life.

Olivia clasped the necklace behind her neck. Tomorrow, it would be a talisman.

Olivia felt a nudge against her leg. She looked down at Dinah, sighed, and texted her neighbor a few doors down, confirming she'd be able to come refill Dinah's food for the next few days. *I've got to leave town last-minute,* Olivia texted. *I'll let you know when I'm back.*

Her neighbor replied in the affirmative, and Milo arrived a few minutes later.

They caught up over pizza and put on a movie. Olivia clasped her hands together in her lap and forced herself to sit still. At one point, Milo reached for her, and she took his hand, laying her head on his shoulder.

"Everything okay, Liv?" Milo asked.

Olivia realized she'd let out a heavy sigh. "No, there's a whole lot that isn't okay. But I'm glad you're here."

Milo mussed her hair. "Same, friend."

When the movie was over, Olivia set Milo up with blankets and a pillow on the couch. She retired to her sleeping bag, exhaustion overcoming her. Any worries Olivia may have held about Milo not being safe here had vanished.

Whatever lay inside her was saving up its energy for Azrael.

36

ARACHNE GRASPED WHAT WAS happening when Olivia started packing.

She had to stop her. If Olivia walked—or floated—into Azrael's house, all was lost. But maybe if Olivia saw something that made her believe she shouldn't do it...maybe she could be saved.

Azrael's pet spider Lilith had died of old age a few months after Ophelia hit Austin, but many spiders like her crawled in the woods outside of Olivia's apartment. Arachne found one and sent it crawling its way inside through an air duct.

While Olivia and Milo slept, Arachne spun her silk in a huge web over Olivia's open bedroom door, making sure to build it high enough that Olivia's cat, Dinah, couldn't tear it down. Once the base of the web was complete, the spider lay down thick strands, over and over, until visible shapes formed.

"What do you think you're doing, Arachne?" Hades asked.

Arachne whirled around, as if He were standing behind her...but she was alone.

"I'm trying to stop her," Arachne said.

"You're coming dangerously close to violating the terms of our wager," Hades said, His voice emanating from the shadows around her.

"I'm not using my spider to torment her," Arachne said. "I'm using it to save her."

He chuckled. "You're not saving anyone. What happens next is inevitable."

Arachne returned her spider to spinning out strands of web. "Then why are you distracting me?"

"Not distracting. Gloating."

"You haven't won yet."

"Oh, but I will, Arachne. Nothing you write in that web of yours is going to stop that."

Arachne ignored Him, and He fell silent.

When the sun rose, sunlight struck the glossy lines of a web reading "DON'T GO" in large letters in the center of it. Arachne rested her exhausted spider in the center of the web. This would save her, the woman who could be her salvation or her doom.

Milo stirred first.

"No," Arachne said.

He rolled off the couch, groaning in the early morning light, and felt his way along the wall until he reached Olivia's doorway. His index finger touched a thick strand of Arachne's web.

"NO!" A flood of spiders emerging from Arachne's mouth turned the word into a howl.

Milo paused, then reached for the doorway, fingers pressing up against the "D" of "DON'T." He backed away. "Holy shit."

Olivia lifted her head from her pillow. "What is it?"

"There's a huge spider web across your bedroom door."

"Please," prayed Arachne. "*Please.*"

Olivia pulled her sleeping bag over her head. "Oh, no. Milo, I'm sorry to ask you to do this, but—"

"On it," Milo said, retrieving his expandable cane.

Arachne screamed and tore out her hair. Spiders poured from her eyes and clambered down her cheeks. She sent the spider at the center of her web scrambling for safety. Maybe she could get it somewhere where it could make another message...

But Milo's cane swung through the web, catching her spider up in her own silk. The message Arachne had spent all night creating was destroyed in an instant.

"I think I got it," Milo said. "You'll have to look."

Arachne watched from another host on the ceiling as Olivia walked over and inspected the spider wrapped in silk at the end of Milo's cane. "Oh my God."

"What?"

"That's the spider Azrael used to keep as a pet."

"Are you serious? That spider must have died years ago."

"If it's not the same spider, it's the same species." Olivia's voice shook. "Put your cane on the ground." She pulled on a boot from her closet.

Arachne screamed in despair as Olivia's boot came down, crushing the spider into darkness.

37

STILLNESS CAME OVER OLIVIA as her plane flew toward Azrael. Before each of her previous uses of her abilities, her energy had felt jagged, on the knife's edge of insanity. But now the power that she had repressed for years, growing stronger all the while, was burning white hot under the surface of a preternatural calm.

It was dark when she landed in Richmond. She picked up her rental car and started driving. After a few turns, she stopped looking at her map. She was close. Could Azrael feel her getting nearer, the way she felt him? Had he been dreaming of her as well?

Olivia pulled off the road when she was half a mile away. She walked into the dark forest, navigating by moonlight. The verdant, secret smells were exactly as they'd been in her vision. The trees shifted and sighed in a cool wind. She passed through a few spider webs as she walked, finding her fear of them had vanished.

Olivia emerged from the trees and looked up at the house from her vision. The house's windows glowed with a soft orange light. The wind stilled.

Every beam in the house, each stitch of fabric, the lengths of wire, the slab of kitchen counter, the three hearts beating inside—Olivia felt it all. The night she'd reduced Elijah to a beating pulse returned to her with crystal clarity. The power inside of her sparked to life. She grasped the fire opal gem Nancy had given her and closed her eyes.

The power within her expanded like a lung. She felt a *click*, and opened her eyes to see the dark, hulking shape of the house with all the lights blotted out, a shadow against the backdrop of trees and stars.

A woman's voice inside the house said, "What the fuck is this?"

Olivia's feet left the ground.

38

AZRAEL WAS LYING ON the living room couch when the lights went out. He blinked in the darkness as his eyes adjusted.

"What the fuck is this?" Angel asked from the kitchen.

"It's a power outage," Azrael said.

Trick emerged from their bedroom upstairs. "I'll check the breaker."

Azrael's first impression of what happened next was that a vehicle crashed into the house. Wood and metal shrieked, the couch bucking beneath him like an angry animal. Azrael leapt to his feet in time to see the massive front door tear free of its hinges and disappear into the moonlit night. He stared in disbelief as the door slammed down between two trees ten yards away.

"What the *fuck* was that?" Angel screamed.

Azrael gaped at the doorway as another impossible thing happened.

Olivia Madden floated through the destroyed entryway. Her long, wavy hair flowed around her face like she was underwater.

Olivia looked at the umbrella stand by the door. It burst into flames, umbrellas turning into skeletons. A spider plant hanging in the window met a similar fate, burning bright and exuding cottony smoke.

"You like fires, don't you Azrael?" Olivia asked.

A chair in the entryway flashed ablaze. Tongues of bright orange licked the wall. Olivia flicked her head toward the kitchen and the wooden cabinets exploded into crackling flame.

"I can see why," Olivia said. "It's cleansing."

Azrael couldn't move. He was dreaming. He would wake up soon.

Angel careened out of the kitchen with a knife grasped overhead. "*Get out of my house!*"

Olivia raised a hand, and Angel flew backward, slamming into the burning cabinets before falling to the ground.

Olivia floated closer, staring at Azrael, her face flickering in the growing flames. Her head snapped up, peering at the second level of the house. "If you let me finish what I'm here to do, you'll walk out of here alive."

Azrael followed Olivia's line of sight and saw Trick, their arms thrown over the second-floor railing, the gun in their hands aimed at Olivia's head. "Get out of here or I'll shoot!" Trick shouted.

Something about the panicked shrillness in Trick's voice made Azrael realize this wasn't a dream.

"Trick, Angel, get out of here!" Azrael shouted. "She's here for me. Aren't you, Olivia?"

Olivia's eyes glowed bright in the growing flames. "Yes."

Angel screamed from the kitchen, "I can't move! She's pinning me down!"

"Olivia," Azrael said breathlessly. "How...how are you doing this?"

"You've hurt a lot of people, Azrael," Olivia said.

The heat sucked air from Azrael's lungs. "I didn't kill those people, Olivia. I didn't poison the Nosh."

Olivia's glowing eyes narrowed. "Even if that's true, those deaths were reaped from the seeds you sowed."

Angel shrieked as the kitchen burned around her.

Azrael took a step toward Olivia. "I only ever wanted to stop Elijah from turning into my father. I didn't mean to start a war—"

Olivia lifted her hand, and Azrael's feet left the ground.

Trick screamed and pulled the trigger.

Time screeched to a halt.

The flames surrounding them froze in place. Angel's screams turned into subsonic, pulsing waves. The muzzle of Trick's gun flashed with a blinding flower, the bullet emerging from the barrel at a crawl. Everything but Azrael and Olivia had become trapped in time like insects in amber.

Azrael swallowed a knot in his throat as he regarded Olivia. "I dreamed about this. About you killing me. How are you going to do it?"

Olivia nodded toward Trick's bullet, droning slowly toward them like the world's deadliest hornet. "I could move you a few feet over and let that hit you."

"Anything I could say to convince you otherwise?"

"Nothing I would believe," she said, drawing close.

Icy fear twisted around his heart. "What if I told you I had a plan to make all of this right?"

"Liar," Olivia whispered.

"Olivia, listen to me—"

"Listen? I think we can do better than that."

"*Olivia—*"

Olivia clapped her hands to the sides of Azrael's face.

39

Olivia pours fire into Azrael's mind.

She dives into his thoughts, his memories, his past.

She is with Azrael as he listens from his bassinet as Henry Hatch tells a young Robert Grayburn to cull the unworthy from his flock, and as Grayburn denies Azrael the right to know they shared a mother.

She watches as Azrael toddles around the Colony, doted on by the mothers and told by the Fathers he will be called Prophet one day. As his father looms like a monster over his bed, whispering to Azrael about all the beauty and power he'll inherit.

She is with him as he plays with matches in the main hall, flames dancing first from the matchsticks, then a cloth napkin, and finally licking the walls before one of the mothers rushes in and douses the blaze with mop water. His father deems him a firebug. The term needles and emboldens him.

Time rushes by like a river, and Azrael falls for Lila, the first thing that's felt real to him in a life of lies, subservience, and loneliness.

Olivia is with him when he learns of Lila's pregnancy. She feels the brightness of his panic. She travels along with him as he flees and finds refuge, seeing through his eyes as a woman's face appears in the flames of the Moloch house. She feels his love for this woman, the strength of it—almost strong enough for him to tell her the truth.

She rides along with the storm that reunites him with the mother of his child, and sweeps through the wretched years he spends on the run, as he finds his followers, as the war against his brother rages out of his control.

All the truths he fights to hide—the fear, the loss, the pain, the boundless *pain*—

And then, hurtling into the present moment, Olivia sees through his eyes what she has become.

Her hair is a bonfire. Smoke curls from her nostrils. Her eyes are pits of flame.

Firebug.

All at once, Olivia knows what she has to do. What she should have done a long time ago.

Olivia shifts Azrael away and turns toward the oncoming bullet.

Time cracks across her like a whip.

Her heart breaks for the last time as Trick's bullet shatters her sternum.

40

ARACHNE WATCHED THROUGH HER remaining unburned spiders as Trick shot Olivia. The force of the bullet drove Olivia backward, the flames encircling her extinguishing like someone blowing out a candle. At the same instant, Azrael flew away from Olivia, hit the wall, and slumped to the ground.

Trick hurried downstairs and put another bullet between Olivia's eyes.

"Azrael!" Angel screamed. She rose from the kitchen floor and scrambled to Azrael's side. Her hair smoldered, and swaths of her face and arms were red with angry burns. "Wake up!"

"What just happened?" Trick shouted. "Who the fuck is that?"

"I don't know, but I think she killed him!" Angel sobbed.

Trick checked Azrael's pulse. "He's alive. Come on, this whole place is about to go up. Get his legs."

Angel wiped her nose with the back of her hand. Her skin was already beginning to blister. "All right."

Arachne watched as Trick and Angel hoisted Azrael off the ground and staggered outside into the cool night air.

"Where are we going?" Angel asked as they loaded Azrael into the back of the car.

"I don't know," Trick said, looking over their shoulder at the house. "Fuck me. My laptop's upstairs, but I've got my phone. We'll figure it out from the road."

They sped away into the night, house blazing behind them.

Arachne pressed her hands to her spider-filled mouth. Could it really be? Had she won? Trick had killed Olivia before she had a chance to murder Azrael, so...

Quite a spectacle.

Agon materialized next to her. Its ravaged face curled up into a snarl.

Arachne spat the squirming spiders in her mouth to the ground. "Here to congratulate me?"

Agon chuckled. The sound was like a dog coughing up gravel. *For what?*

"I won. She didn't kill Azrael."

No, Arachne. You lost.

She stiffened. "You're lying."

Then why are you still here?

Despair brought Arachne to her knees. "But...but she didn't kill Azrael..."

She moved herself into the path of the bullet. She made the choice to end her life. She burns.

Arachne muttered, "Then why do you not torment me?"

When He has her in His claws, we will, Arachne. Agon's lips peeled back to reveal the jagged knives of its teeth. *We will.*

"Where is He?"

The real question is: where is she?

PART III

DOWNFALL

1

Olivia opens her eyes.

She's sitting in the back of a car, legs dangling over the edge of the seat. The seat's leather is cracked and peeling, the filthy reams of dark brown duct tape covering the hole curling toward her. Olivia resists the urge to pull the tape away from the seat. If her father catches her messing with it, he will yell at her.

Her father sits behind the wheel, muttering to himself. Rain patters against her window like a drumroll. Olivia remembers this drive, knows what happens next. Her father will weave his way through three more intersections before turning around to shout at her for pulling at the duct tape. As he shouts, he will roll through a red light, summoning the blinding white creature that sinks its teeth into their car.

Olivia looks down at her wrist and marvels at how small it is, how smooth. She's back in her five-year-old body, seconds away from the accident that will reveal the bone buried in the meat of her wrist. All she has to do to avoid going through this pain again is stop herself from pulling at the tape.

George Madden raises his voice. "Don't tell your mother I'm driving without the car seat."

Of course. She should be in a car seat. Her mother will later scream at her father for driving without one.

Dread fills the car like an invisible gas as Olivia realizes there's nothing she can do to stop the accident from happening. After all, it has already happened.

She sits, frozen, as her father jerks the steering wheel, correcting a swerve into oncoming traffic. She's got one more intersection until the world crunches in around her.

Olivia stares at the side of her father's face, the pitted landscape of his cheek, the sparse undergrowth of his beard, the muscle clenching in his jaw. She wishes her father could see how big he is compared to her, how terrifying his anger can be.

"What did I say about messing with the tape?" he snaps.

Olivia looks down and sees her little fingers tugging at the tape. She peers into the fathomless black hole underneath. She wants to crawl inside the hole and disappear.

Olivia looks up at her father's rage-darkened face. Flecks of spittle fly from his mouth as he thunders, "What did I *just* say?"

And all at once, Olivia sees him—really sees him. He's like her—a child living in fear, powerless to free himself from it. He is too blinded by pain to see that his heart stayed small while his body grew up big. He doesn't know his own strength.

The jewels of raindrops in the windshield turn yellow.

He doesn't know his own strength.

The thought triggers a memory...except it can't be a memory, because it hasn't happened yet. It happens in the future, far beyond the incoming crash, thousands of sunsets from now, to a version of her who will allow tiny needles to bury ink deep in the flesh that's about to be torn open. This destined version of herself will develop the ability to do things with her mind. Unbelievable things.

Bright red washes over the windshield as her father hurls anger over his shoulder.

The car windows rattle. Olivia thinks of the tornado that will come for this future version of her, of the black silhouette cut out of the fabric of the world walking at the base of it. She feels its approach again now, growing closer at monstrous speed as her father rolls into the intersection.

Olivia understands as the thunderous noise grows louder: it is the man-shaped thing walking with the storm coming for her, not the colliding vehicle...which means this is not the past.

Which means she's not helpless.

Olivia clenches her fists and sends out a blast.

The windows of the car, along with every pane of glass on the block, shatter into a million pieces. The leather seat beneath her groans, the black hole in the seat ripping wider and wider, opening into a chasm.

George Madden's rage turns to terror, his face receding as Olivia tips backward into the black abyss of the hole in the seat, hurtling into darkness, the thing closing in on her swiping its claws

> *over her head*
>> *missing her*
>>> *bellowing in*
>>>> *baffled fury*

Limbs crush in on Olivia from all sides. Moans and screams fill what little air there is. Olivia gasps for breath, her bones creaking against the crush of flesh in every dimension. She fights to break free of the bodies around her, but her struggles yield nothing but pain. Her lungs burn. She's able to see what surrounds her, though there's only flesh, and no source of light. The back of a knee bends and flexes just beyond her nose, tendons straining, and Olivia considers biting it, but surely whoever this limb belongs to doesn't want to be part of this any more than she does.

She stops struggling and waits to die.

But death doesn't come. Untold bodies tear hair from her head, wrench her arms, grind at her legs. She's pretty certain she feels a mouth gnashing on her heel, though she has no way of doing anything about it. Existence is an airless, hopeless torment.

She has no memory of a time before this place. For all she knows, she has always been here, one of thousands—maybe millions—of bodies with neither a name nor a past, bereft of air and freedom and hope.

But that can't be true, or why would she suffer so?

No—there was something before this, something other than this anguish.

You're a fool. A mote of dust that imagines it was once a person.

Something is happening. The cacophony of moans turns into shrieks of pain and surprise, the sound rising like an ocean surge.

And she knows—a creature is coming for her. It plunges through the impossible number of bodies stacked in this place, coming at her like a bullet.

Anger begins to glow inside her, and she remembers. It's little more than muscle memory, but it's enough.

The living light within her cracks out of her chest with a deafening *SNAP*.

She lurches away, breaking free of the bodies around her, hurtling through emptiness just out of the reaches of the howling, wrathful thing

> *that arrives*
>
> > *a moment*
> >
> > > *too late*
> > >
> > > > *to devour her*

Existence is agony.

Olivia writhes and screams in impossible pain with no end, no bounds, no limits.

This, and only this, forever.

Fire, fire, endless fire.

Fire without, and fire within.

Fire within.

Olivia's screams are lost in the roar of flame.

She was something other than a being of pure pain, once. She was a person.

Fire within.

This phrase breaks through the insanity of her torture, not lessening it, but glowing in the white-hot embers of it.

There is a fire within her, too.

She releases it from her breast with a sob, the force of it shoving her back, away from her suffering into a cool nothingness that feels like the kisses of angels, and as her heels kick away the bright, pure pain, something lashes out for her, something different

> *than the flames,*
>
> > *a predator*
> >
> > > *snapping jaws*
> > >
> > > > *at its prey*

2

"WHAT'S HAPPENING?" ARACHNE ASKED. "Why hasn't He found her?"

She must have held onto her power when she passed over, Agon said. *She's falling through level after level of Hell. He's trying to catch her, but He always arrives too late.*

Arachne's hand—the one He'd grasped with His claw—crackled with invisible electricity. She winced and said in a low voice: "Well, I'm glad she's at least giving Him a run for His money."

There's something else, too.

"What?"

Agon showed her a vision—Elijah opening his eyes in his hospital bed.

Arachne gasped. "Elijah's awake?"

He woke up the morning after Olivia died. It seems whatever she broke in his mind repaired itself when she was gone.

Arachne found Elijah with her spiders up above. He spoke with nurses and doctors, who were clearly dumbfounded he'd woken up.

Down below, Arachne turned to Agon. "Has this ever happened before? Someone evading Him like she is?"

No, said Agon. *And she's not just falling. She's tearing holes in each version of Hell she passes through.*

"Agon...are you afraid of her?"

I don't feel fear. I am fear.

Arachne stared at its clotted, pitiless eyes.

It was lying.

3

"TRICK," ANGEL SAID, "HE'S waking up. Azrael? Can you hear me?"

Azrael nodded without opening his eyes. "Yes. My head hurts."

"Angel's got some aspirin for you," Trick said.

Azrael cracked an eye open and winced at Angel's face. Bandages covered the side of her head, neck, and part of her right arm. The reddened skin peeking out from under the bandages was shiny with salve. She moved stiffly as she held out aspirin and a glass of water.

Azrael touched the unburned side of her face. "What happened?"

"It's not as bad as it looks. Go on, take these. And drink the whole glass of water, you're probably dehydrated."

Azrael tossed back the aspirin and downed the water. He took in his surroundings: a bedroom decorated in whites, blues, and grays. A framed painting of a sailboat hung on the wall, and he smelled salt in the air.

"Where are we?" Azrael asked.

"An Airbnb near Virginia Beach," Angel said. "Trick booked it under a fake name."

Azrael rubbed his eyes. "How long have I been out?"

"About fourteen hours," Trick said.

Azrael shifted and gasped in pain. "My ankle…"

"Yeah, it's pretty swollen," Trick said. "You must have sprained it when you fell."

"Olivia—"

"She's dead," Angel assured him.

"Shot in the heart," Trick said, "and the head."

A chamber of Azrael's heart caved in, like a deep-sea vessel collapsing under staggering pressure.

"Who the hell was she?" Angel asked.

"She was someone I used to know," Azrael said thickly.

Trick asked, "How was she…doing what she did?"

Azrael closed his eyes against a swell of dizziness. "I don't know."

"Good thing I found that gun," Trick said.

Azrael's eyes flew open as the memory came back to him. Olivia had frozen time, or else sped up her and Azrael's perception to be so unspeakably fast they'd had an entire conversation in the time it took for the bullet to travel from the gun to her heart. In that time, she could have killed him a hundred different ways.

And when she grasped the sides of his head, an inferno blazing inside her eyes, his life had flashed before his eyes.

"We can't stay here long," Trick said. "Any idea what we should do next?"

"We're going to Denver," Azrael said.

Angel's dark eyebrows shot up. "Denver?"

Azrael massaged his forehead. "It's hard to explain, but before she died, Olivia looked into my past. While she was looking, I saw something from when I was a baby."

Trick and Angel exchanged a look. Trick asked, "And what was that?"

"My father telling Robert Grayburn that he wanted him to cull the unworthy from his flock. All those exiles…" Azrael shook his head. "A few of them got away, like Warren and Elijah, but I think Grayburn murdered most of them and buried them in the woods."

"If that's true," Trick said, "we don't have to go to Denver. We can send in an anonymous tip. If there are bodies buried in the woods, the police will find them."

"I'm not concerned about the bodies," Azrael croaked. "I saw something else, too…Grayburn and I had the same mother, and he made sure I never found out. It was like he blamed me for my mother dying in childbirth…it explains why he always seemed to have it out for me." Tears stung his eyes. "And now Grayburn's got my son. I've got to save him."

Angel frowned. "Why can't we call this in and have Grayburn arrested? Why do you have to go there yourself?"

"I'm pretty sure if Grayburn senses a noose closing around his neck, he's going to kill my son, and anyone else who's unlucky enough to be around him…" Azrael's eyes widened. "Holy shit, I can't believe I didn't see it. It was Grayburn. He must have been the one who poisoned the Nosh. And if he's taking out that many Fishers, that means he's already spiraling out of control…"

Angel threw back her head and laughed. "You think you can just go to Denver and grab your kid from this guy's house? You'll be caught before you get close."

"Then help me," Azrael said. "I need to get Cade away from Grayburn. I don't care what happens to me after that."

"I'm sorry, Azrael," Angel said, "but that's what you don't understand. This is bigger than you, and bigger than your son. Grayburn is the last figurehead of the Fishers, and with him out of the picture, their whole shitty operation falls apart. Who are you to say your son's life is more precious than all the people who will die if Fishers of Men is allowed to keep spreading its hate?"

Azrael was breathing through the urge to throttle her when Trick's phone pinged. They checked it, eyes widening.

"Oh my gods…he's awake."

"Who?" Azrael asked.

"Elijah. He woke up sometime last night. Our inside man sent me a photo."

Trick turned the phone around to show Azrael the photo of Elijah, pale and hollow-eyed, sitting up in his hospital bed. "Other than him being a little disoriented, they're saying it doesn't look like there's any permanent brain damage."

"Well, there you go," Angel said. "Cade will go back to living with his Uncle Elijah. Problem solved."

"Let me make myself clear," Azrael said coldly. "I'm going to Denver to get my son, with or without you."

Angel poked Azrael's swollen ankle. He screamed.

"Good luck getting there on that," she said, storming out of the room.

"Angel's right," Trick said. "Your ankle's fucked for at least a week."

"Please, Trick," Azrael panted, sweat popping out on his temples. "Help me."

Trick looked up from their phone and bit their lower lip. "I'm sorry, Azrael. If you want to go looking for your son, I'm not going to stop you, but I'm not walking into the hornet's nest with you."

4

Olivia opens her eyes.

She's on a verdant hillside overlooking a sprawling field, which leads to a distant skyline she doesn't recognize. The sun soars in a cloudless sky. The air is lush and still.

A scream sends her to her feet.

A dark gray snake with a football-sized head, thick as a telephone pole, surges toward her over the green grass, fast as a whip.

Olivia runs, casting a glance over her shoulder in time to watch the snake wrap its massive bulk around a screaming man with shaggy blond hair. There's nothing Olivia can do for him. She keeps running.

Olivia ducks into a nearby hotel. The lobby is vacant, except for a man hunkering behind a plush pink couch.

"Please, help!" Olivia says.

The man straightens and looks her over. "Just got here, huh?"

"There's a snake—"

A deafening *BANG!* cuts her off, rocking Olivia on her feet. She whirls around to see a twisted snarl of metal at the base of the elevator bay, clouds of dust emerging from the rubble.

"What the—" Olivia says. She realizes it's not dust rising out of the elevator; it's gas. Yellow gas.

"Follow me," says the man. "You can't stay in one place for long."

"What's happening?"

"You're dead," the man says, grabbing her hand and drawing her toward the door.

A screeching roar echoes through the lobby, shaking the windows. "What the hell is *that*?"

"Who knows?" The man tugs at her hand. "Pterodactyl? Dragon? An eight-headed flying baby vomiting tulips?"

Olivia tears her hand from the man's grasp. "What's *happening*?"

The man eyes the door. "You died, and this is Hell. My best guess is we're living in other people's nightmares, and they're happening all at once, on top of each other."

Olivia backs away from the yellow cloud of gas. "I'm dreaming."

The man shrugs. "I've been dreaming for years now. There's no good way of marking the passage of time here. Everything changes all the time. The only constant is that you're in danger. And you can't die, at least, not for long. Something might kill you in the most painful way possible, but you'll just boot back up somewhere else in the nightmare and start all over. No corner of this place is safe for long."

Wake up, Olivia thinks. *Wake up, wake up.*

"You might want to get out of here," the man tells her. "I haven't died from poison gas yet, but I imagine it's a pretty bad way to go."

Olivia gulped hard as tears stung her eyes. "If it's all hopeless, why are you helping me?"

"It's not easy to find company here, and newcomers tend to be the least crazy," he says. "The old-timers...people who have been here hundreds or thousands of years…they're as dangerous as the nightmares. Usually, they're not as good-looking as you are, either."

The ground rumbles with a distant explosion. Someone runs past the hotel entrance screaming.

"How do I know you're not part of it?" Olivia asks.

"You think I'm a nightmare? I'm trying to help you."

He's closing in on her, backing her into a corner. The only exits are past him or through the spreading gas, which has turned a bright, glowing green.

"You're all the same," the man says, shaking his head. "You're all the goddamn same, even here." He seizes her wrists and drives her backward, cracking her head against the wall.

Olivia passes out for a length of time, and when she returns to herself, he's hunched over her, his breath foul in her nostrils. Rough carpet scours her buttocks.

"You're all the same," he says again.

Olivia pushes him away. He deals her a dizzying blow, white stars flashing in her vision.

"So, you are part of the nightmare," Olivia says.

"Lady, you have no idea what a nightmare is."

Olivia screams for help, and the man slaps her. "If you stop fighting, you might enjoy this, you dumb bitch."

Olivia's fists close in rage. She doesn't want to get away from this man. She wants to *hurt* him.

And, suddenly, she knows she can.

She harnesses the colors blooming in her vision and gathers them into a glowing-hot ball. The man shuffles his pants down to his knees, exposing his flaccid dick.

Olivia says, "Die screaming."

The man's penis vaporizes in a spray of blood and gristle.

Olivia falls through the floor, carpet and lobby and curling smoke receding away from her, the man's screams echoing up and away, the sensation of something huge and cruel slamming into the hotel moments after she tips out of the nightmare, plummeting

head over heels
        like a body
                tumbling down
                        a rabbit hole

5

Elijah Hatch lay in the softly beeping darkness of his hospital room. His thighs and arms burned from the exertion of his physical therapy. The doctors assured him he'd be able to walk again using his prosthetic legs, but it would take time to rebuild his strength since he'd been bedridden for a few weeks. He squeezed his hand-gripper, making it to a count of ten before his strength failed and he switched hands.

He'd be able to check out of the hospital soon…but what did he have to go back to? Elijah had turned himself into a pariah, so it might not be safe for him to leave, let alone to return to a place of leadership. His mother and wives were dead, along with dozens of his followers. The Fishers of Men headquarters in Denver had been evacuated due to the Cheshire riots. Cade was alive, at least—one of Elijah's nurses confirmed that Cade's name was not among the dead—but Grayburn hadn't answered any of Elijah's calls or voicemails, so Elijah couldn't talk to him.

Once again, he'd lost everything.

Despair is a sin, he reminded himself. *God gave you another chance for a reason.*

Elijah startled at a tapping sound, quiet as a pattering of rain.

The silhouette of a man darkened his third-floor window.

Elijah's skin prickled with terror as the man slid the window open and climbed inside. He gaped when he realized who he was looking at.

"Azrael."

Azrael lingered by the window like a shadow. "Hello, brother."

"The nurses are outside," Elijah said. "I'll scream."

Azrael limped to Elijah's hospital bed. "I'm not going to hurt you. I'm here because I need your help."

Elijah stared at his brother's eyes, bright even in the dim glow of the heart monitor. "What do you want?"

"I need to rescue Cade from Grayburn," Azrael said, his breath feverish on Elijah's skin. "He's a dangerous man, Elijah. I think he's killed a lot of other people over the years, and I'm pretty sure he's the one who poisoned the Nosh."

Elijah thought of the flash of white bone in the earth. "You're lying."

Azrael shook his head. "Not about this."

"Even if I wanted to, I can't help you. I need to get my strength back after—"

"Olivia came for you, didn't she?" Azrael asked.

Elijah failed to stop his eyes from widening.

Azrael nodded. "She came for me, too. She saw things in my past I couldn't have possibly remembered...she showed me how dangerous Robert Grayburn was." Tears shone in his eyes. "And now she's dead. Burned up in the fire..."

Elijah held up his call device, thumb hovering over the button. "You're out of your mind."

Azrael slipped a piece of paper into Elijah's other hand. "I don't blame you for not trusting me, so I'll start with trusting you. This is the address where I'm going. If you don't believe me, give this to the police. They'll catch me. I'm too injured to run. But if you think I'm telling the truth, then discharge yourself and come find me there tomorrow morning."

"Azrael—"

"Cade doesn't deserve to get hurt because of how badly you and I fucked everything up," Azrael said. "Please. We've got to get him out of there."

Elijah looked at his brother, at the panic glimmering in his eyes. "Goodbye, Azrael," he said, and mashed the call button.

Azrael hobbled to the window, panting through his teeth. He climbed outside and disappeared.

A nurse entered the room. "Yes, Elijah? Are you feeling all right?"

Elijah crumpled up the piece of paper Azrael had given him in his fist.

"I'd like some water, please," he rasped.

6

Olivia opens her eyes.

There is only darkness. She sits with her knees tucked up to her chin, naked and freezing, trapped in a space no more than three feet in any dimension with rough concrete on all sides.

She doesn't allow herself to panic. There must be a way out of this. She'd have suffocated if she were truly trapped. But no matter how thoroughly she inspects the walls, moving her fingertips along the rough texture until her skin is raw, she can find no seam, no crack, no purchase.

She screams for help, but her screams go no further than the confines of her cell.

She tries to remember a time before this place, and a near-drowned memory of power returns to her.

Olivia feels a gathering sensation in her chest.

Her stone cage cracks and crumbles. Olivia is struck by the impression of a beast made of pure fury, approaching her at a terrible speed, and then she

slips sideways

       with a swell of déjà vu

            she has done this before

                  many times

7

M ILO M ADRIGAL WOKE WITH a start. He tapped his wrist, and his watch informed him it was 10:34 a.m. His head pounded as if he'd been drinking the night before. He found himself reaching for the empty place in the bed where Nancy should have been, seeking comfort for the terrible nightmare he'd had the night before.

He'd dreamed Olivia's mother had called him and told him Olivia had died in a house fire in Virginia. It was horrific, too cruel to be real...

Milo's breath quickened as he found his phone in the bed sheets and pulled up the list of recent phone calls.

The robotic voice of his phone informed him his last phone call was with Betty Madden, for seven minutes and thirty-four seconds.

Milo cried out as grief swallowed him whole.

Olivia was dead. She had lied to him about none of the houses being the right one, and she'd gone alone to confront Azrael. He'd killed her and burned down the house to destroy any evidence.

Betty's voice had been throttled by shock and devastation, her agony reverberating through the phone. She said it had taken investigators a few days to determine the identity of the body, based on the ID in the rental car parked nearby and a dental record match. Milo couldn't bear to tell Betty that Olivia was dead because of his suggestion. What good would it do? Nothing he said would take away an ounce of her mother's pain. He knew that from experience.

Milo curled into a fetal position and sobbed. His phone pinged with messages of condolences as the news of Olivia's death spread. A few local friends offered to come by, and Milo messaged back that he wasn't ready to be around people yet.

When there were no more tears, anger came. Every muscle in his body ached with the injustice that the two best people he'd ever known had been violently ripped away from him by the actions of one person: Azrael Hatch.

Milo had known Azrael was trouble the moment he'd come blazing into Olivia's life like a Molotov cocktail. If Milo had had any idea how much trouble, maybe he could have done something.

Maybe Nancy and Olivia would both still be alive.

The day crept on, and Milo forced himself to drink water and eat a handful of crackers. Around dusk, he pulled up the news and his screen reader informed him that a message—allegedly from Azrael Hatch himself—had gone out instructing Cheshires to protest at the house of the Fishers' new figurehead: Robert Grayburn. Milo checked the Cheshire message boards, which lit up with people seeking ride-shares to Denver, expressions of delight, promises of violence.

Milo sighed and switched off his phone, exhaustion overcoming him like a shroud. He went to bed and slipped into a fitful sleep.

He woke with a start to the sound of his doorbell ringing.

Milo tapped his watch, which informed him it was 5:24 a.m. His phone alerted him to dozens of missed texts and calls.

The doorbell chimed again. Likely one of his friends, visiting out of concern after Milo had dropped out of contact.

Ring. Ring.

Milo sighed and made his way to the front door, picking up his cane out of habit. He slid open the series of locks he'd paid a man to install after Nancy's death. Azrael's legacy—a grieving widower's paranoia.

Milo opened the door. "I'm sorry, I fell asleep—"

He reeled backward on his heels as two points of impact hit his chest—the stiffened fingers of somebody knocking him off balance.

Milo stumbled and nearly went down, but a lifetime of reacting quickly to unexpected objects in his surroundings snapped him out of his depression-cloud and into a cat-like awareness.

The front door slammed closed. A creaking floorboard told Milo the intruder was inside.

"Get back!" Milo lunged forward and swung his cane where he guessed the man's head would be. He missed, but the echo of his own voice told him the man was close, standing between him and the door. He sensed desperation in the man's smell—fear and sweat and at least two days without a shower.

"Get the fuck out!" Milo shouted. "Help! Someone, help!"

"Milo, I'm not going to hurt you."

Milo recognized the voice. "Holy shit."

"I'm sorry I had to come in like this," said Azrael Hatch, "but I need your help."

Milo's thoughts raced as a fresh jolt of adrenaline coursed through his veins. It would be dark in the house at this hour. As long as it stayed that way, Milo would have the upper hand.

"Don't bother trying to turn the lights on," Milo said. "They're programmed to respond to my voice." The lie came easily. Azrael wasn't a fool, but Milo wagered he didn't know how things like Alexa worked.

Azrael backed away, toward the hallway. He was limping. "I don't want to hurt you."

"Too late." Milo moved toward him, cane raised. "You hurt me plenty."

"I didn't kill Olivia," Azrael said.

"Sure, you didn't," Milo snarled.

"Do you know what she was?" Azrael asked. "What she turned into?"

Keep him talking. If he could get Azrael to back down the hallway, the acoustics would give Milo a better sense of his exact position. One good crack to the skull with his cane would take him down, and he could beat him to death after that. No jury in the world would convict him. Not after everything Azrael had done.

"I know she was going through something she couldn't explain," Milo said.

Azrael shuffled backward another step. "Listen, Milo—I know this sounds crazy, but she set the house on fire with her mind. I don't know how, but that's what happened."

Milo thought of the footprints Olivia claimed she'd found on her ceiling. The scent of earth in a place it shouldn't have been. She could have faked that, of course, but that presumed she was a liar, or insane, and Milo didn't think she was either. "If she could do all that, then how did she die?"

"When my friend Trick shot at her, she...she stopped time," Azrael said. "She looked into my past and saw my entire life.

When time sped up to normal again, she put herself in the path of the bullet."

"You left her to burn," Milo said. Anger thrashed in his chest like a second heart.

"I would have gotten her out of there if I hadn't been knocked unconscious when she threw me aside. I need you to believe me. I'm the one who saved her from the house fire, remember? Leaving her to burn is the last thing I would have wanted for her, no matter what she was at the end."

Almost to the hallway. Azrael was limping on his left leg. That's the step Milo would get him on. "I don't care," Milo said. "Get the fuck out of my house."

"I can't do that. Listen—you're the last person in this world who owes me anything—"

Now.

Milo sprang forward and swung his cane in an arc, connecting neatly with Azrael's head—his jaw, judging by the sound of his teeth clacking together. Azrael crumpled, and Milo swung the cane again, lower this time. There was a *crack* as it connected with what he suspected was Azrael's temple. Milo stepped back, in case there was any fight left in Azrael, but he was still.

Milo waited for rage to compel him to bring the cane down again and again until it broke, to snuff the life from the man who had taken so much from him. He shook with fury, but he couldn't bring himself to do it. It wasn't what Nancy would want.

Olivia, either.

He should call the police. One of the most wanted men in the country lay knocked out on his hallway floor. There was probably some kind of reward for his capture. It certainly would bring the whole nightmare full circle.

She set the house on fire with her mind.

Milo's flesh rippled with goosebumps. If Olivia had found where Azrael was by using her mind, what else was she capable of? And why had Azrael come here, rather than go to one of his hundreds of followers?

Milo's shoulders sagged. Another question was: what did he have to lose?

8

Olivia opens her eyes.

She's in a room bustling with movement and laughter as discordant music booms from speakers on either side of a cracked TV screen. Dozens of solo cups populate a coffee table, along with a mirror lined with hills of white.

It takes her a few beats to recall where she is.

She's at a party with her friends, and she's taken mushrooms.

"Hey, Liv, you okay?" a friend at her side asks.

Olivia doesn't recognize the friend, whose face is shifting like it's underwater.

"Yeah," Olivia says. "I think I just dissociated for a minute."

"Ego death," her friend says. "Pretty great, huh? Forgetting you're a human for a minute."

Olivia can't keep a thought in her head. It's hard to speak. She wants to tell her friend something is terribly wrong.

Her friend's shifting face asks her: "You all right?"

"I...I don't think I'm actually here," Olivia manages to get out.

Her friend turns to someone beside her and laughs: "She thinks she's not here."

"How many mushrooms did you eat?" the other person asks. Olivia can't place her either.

"I don't remember…"

Her friend holds up an empty plastic baggie. "You didn't eat all of this on your own, did you?"

A distant memory from a thousand years ago sends up smoke signals telling Olivia she did. She nods.

Her two friends, faces shifting into monstrous shapes, turn toward each other and make a leering, groaning sound in unison. "Oh, babe, you are in for the ride of your life. You took too muchhhhh…"

The last word stretches hideously, echoing off the walls, pouring fractals of sound into Olivia's ears, her friend's face abstracting into monstrous shapes.

"You're *not* here," one of them laughs. "You're in Hell, Olivia."

The music and conversation of the party turns into a fiendish, dissonant tangle of notes, like someone put a calliope in a rock tumbler. The word *Hell* reverberates around Olivia's melting mind, growing razor-sharp teeth, tearing into the soft flesh of her consciousness, ripping away all hope—

"Yeah, Olivia, have a nice trip," the first friend says, cackling. "Settle in, because this is *foreeever*."

The voice comes from another galaxy, echoing and bouncing off itself until it makes no sense, shooting thrills of terror down Olivia's spine, heart pounding against her chest like a creature trying to break free.

Her teeth clamp together, and she jerks back. She's having a seizure. Or dying.

You're already dead.

She's aware of an electrocuting sensation as her muscles seize, and the music and screaming conversation turns into a chorus of agony, all sensations exponentially overwhelming, everything terrible and fever-pitched and plummeting and endless...

After an untold amount of time—minutes or hours—her convulsions stop, and she lies panting on the couch. The inside of her mind is terrifying, but she's more afraid of what she'll see when she opens her eyes—the world melting away before her, showing flames and suffering for all eternity—

Olivia hears an echoing voice: "She's settling down..."

"Damn, she pissed herself."

Shame sweeps across Olivia like a blanket of needles as she senses the warm wetness on the couch beneath her...

Whose couch, genius? her mind counters. *Why can't you think of any of these people's names? Even if you were tripping balls, you'd be able to remember who you're with. You have no memory of these people, or this place, or how you got here, and that's because you're nowhere on Earth.*

An idea occurs to her: she could use her powers to get out of here.

She shakes the thought out of her mind—that way lays a massacre. She barely had control over her powers when she was sober. It's a wonder she isn't lifting every cup on the coffee table with her reeling and delirious mind. Strike that— it's a wonder she isn't tearing everyone in this room apart.

The house starts to shake. Is she imagining it? Is she *doing* it?

One wall crumbles away, revealing a fiery landscape on the other side, magma and flames and distant figures twisting in an ecstasy of pain. She has the sense of being the center of some terrible gravity—that something is rushing toward her at an impossible speed, drawn to her as if she were a dying sun—

"Don't listen to them, Olivia," the melting thing beside her says. "You just took some mushrooms. You're not dying, and you're not in Hell."

Olivia thinks she hears fear in the thing's voice. Is it afraid for her, or afraid *of* her?

"Hey, Olivia, come back to us."

The sense of *drawing* something huge toward her intensifies. It's almost here.

"This party sucks," Olivia says.

Every being in the room turns and roars at her, gnashing jaws filled with rows of sharp teeth.

Olivia pushes away at the party with all her strength.

The scream of a predator denied fills the world.

reality

        tilts away

                into

                        darkness

9

WHEN AZRAEL CAME TO, it was in Milo's darkened living room, tied to a chair with his hands bound behind his back. His head ached, the side of his face caked with blood. His eyes adjusted to the low light. Birds chirped outside and the window shades brightened with the first light of dawn.

Milo, sitting in a chair across the room, said, "Give me one good reason I shouldn't kill you and call it self-defense."

Azrael croaked out: "Because my son is in danger."

Milo raised an eyebrow. "Well. That's an interesting lie, at least."

"You know I wouldn't come here if I had any other options."

Milo stared at him for a few seconds. "Keep talking."

"How much do you know about Robert Grayburn?" Azrael asked.

"I know he was your dad's right-hand man, and that he's in charge of what's left of the Fishers now. He seems like a cold-hearted son of a bitch."

Azrael nodded. "Right on all counts, but you left out the part where he's been killing my father's followers for decades."

Milo didn't respond.

Azrael swallowed in a dry throat. "There had to be more women than men in the Colony, so men could have multiple wives. There was always an explanation for the men and boys disappearing—exiled for their sins, most of them—but it was a lie. Robert Grayburn was killing them."

Milo's chair creaked as he leaned forward. "Why would Grayburn do that?"

"Because he's a psychopath," Azrael said. "I knew he was dangerous, but I didn't know how deep it went until Olivia...showed me...the conversation between Grayburn and my father. There were acres and acres of forest around the Colony—plenty of land for him to hide bodies. And now he's got my son."

"You're lucky your son is alive at all after you poisoned the Nosh," Milo snapped.

Azrael shook his head. "No. I didn't do that, and neither did any of the Cheshires. I swear it on Olivia's life."

"If your people didn't poison the Nosh, then who did?"

"I can't prove it, but I think it was Grayburn." Azrael shifted his hands behind his back, wincing as the rope cut into his wrists. "And if he's being that brazen, that means he's losing control."

"If Robert Grayburn is so unstable, why did you tell your followers to protest at his house?"

Azrael's head snapped up. "What?"

"You sent out a message yesterday evening instructing Cheshires to stage a protest at Grayburn's house tonight. Cheshires are heading there from all over."

Azrael blinked in terror. "No...Milo, that wasn't me. It was one of the people who was hiding me, the same woman who claimed I was the one who poisoned the Nosh. She's hell-bent on taking out the Fishers at all costs, and she doesn't care if my son gets killed in the process. She's probably already called in a tip to the police to search the woods around the

Colony for bodies. If they find something, and they come for Grayburn, he won't let them take him alive."

"How do you know that?"

"Call it a gut feeling. He'll kill himself, and he'll take my son with him. I don't know how much time we have. It may already be too late."

"If all of that's true," Milo asked, "then why don't you go save your son yourself?"

"My ankle is busted," Azrael said. "I can barely walk. I can't save Cade without help."

Milo glowered at him. "Why should I believe you?"

"Trust me—if I were lying, I'd have come up with something more believable than Olivia freezing time in its tracks and showing me visions from my infancy. I'm here because I think you're a good person, and the life of an innocent child is in the balance."

Milo settled back in his chair.

"You think I'm crazy," Azrael said.

"You're crazy," Milo said, "but you might not be wrong."

The doorbell rang.

Milo cocked his head. "Expecting anyone?"

"I...told Elijah I was coming here," Azrael said.

Milo laughed. "You're telling me Elijah Hatch is standing outside that door?"

Azrael cracked his neck. "Probably not standing."

"Is he going to attack me, too?"

"You're worried about losing a fight to a double amputee?"

"You just got your ass kicked by a blind guy."

Azrael grimaced. "Fair point."

Milo approached the door. "Who's there?"

Silence.

"Who's out there?" Milo asked.

Azrael closed his eyes. *Please.*

"I'm here for Azrael," Elijah said on the other side.

Milo sighed. "I must be out of my mind."

He opened the door. From his vantage point, Azrael could see Elijah as he looked up at Milo from his wheelchair in the dim light of dawn.

"Who are you?" Elijah asked.

"I'm a friend of Olivia's," Milo said.

"I don't understand," Elijah said. "Why did Azrael tell me to come here?"

Milo gestured with his cane. "Go ahead and ask him."

Elijah squinted into the house. Azrael wished he could have waved.

"I'm right here," Azrael said. "Come on in. Milo's going to help us save Cade."

"I don't recall agreeing to that," Milo said. "Alexa, lights on."

Azrael blinked in the sudden brightness.

Elijah rolled into the room, grunting with the effort of moving his wheels, and inspected Azrael. "What happened to you?"

"I got my ass kicked by a blind guy. I take it by your showing up without a police escort that you believe me?"

Elijah glanced at Milo, then back to Azrael. "You were right about Olivia coming for me. I was at the Colony, in one of the old barracks, and she floated into the room. Everything went dark, and then I woke up in the hospital."

Azrael's chest tightened. Milo ran his hands over his face as if trying to wake himself from a bad dream.

"Before that happened, I saw something in the woods," Elijah said. "I thought it was an animal bone at first, but..." Elijah's eyes went distant, then refocused on Azrael. "I believe you. About the bodies. About Grayburn."

Azrael's shoulders dropped in relief.

"This doesn't mean that things are square between you and me," Elijah added quickly. "The only reason I'm here is because an innocent life is in danger. As soon as we get Cade someplace safe, I'm going to call the authorities on both you and Grayburn, understand?"

Azrael nodded. "I understand."

"No more running. You're done."

"Deal."

Elijah glared at him, then nodded. "All right...now how do we save Cade?"

Azrael craned his neck around. "Milo, you're an engineer, right?"

"Materials engineer, yes," Milo said.

"I found three road flares in the back of the car I stole from my followers. Could you use them to create some sort of bomb?"

Milo sighed and threw up his hands. "And we're off."

10

ROBERT GRAYBURN SIPPED HIS coffee as Melinda and Cade ate their breakfast across the table from him. Robert hadn't intended for the Nosh poisoning to lead to the return of solid food to their diets, but it had turned into a welcome side effect.

Cade was prattling about something, but Robert had gotten good at tuning the kid out. Robert scrolled through the latest news about Fishers of Men on his phone and stopped when he saw his name.

> *Protest to Occur at Fishers of Men Figurehead Robert Grayburn's House*

Robert barked out a laugh. Melinda dropped her fork, startled.

"What?" she asked.

Robert grinned. "There's going to be a protest at our house."

"A protest...when?"

"Today, apparently," Grayburn said, scrolling down. "At the order of Azrael Hatch himself, if this is to be believed."

Melinda paled. "What are we going to do?"

A muscle in Robert's jaw twitched. "We're going to stay inside and let the cops handle it. They're going to wave a bunch of signs and shout themselves hoarse and go home. Nothing we haven't dealt with before."

"I just..." Melinda began. She caught the look in Grayburn's eye, stopped herself, and nibbled at her eggs.

Melinda had been acting differently toward him after he'd taken the lives of Warren and her sister wives. Robert knew she had no proof that he'd been the one to poison the Nosh, but he saw it in her eyes, sensed the current of her resistance growing stronger. She knew.

Robert resumed reading, and Cade looked up from his scrambled eggs and said, "Uncle Elijah is out of the hospital."

Robert's hand clenched his phone. He'd known Elijah was conscious again—and had been ignoring calls from the area code Elijah's hospital was in—but assumed he'd had at least a few more days before he checked himself out. A headache pulsed in the base of his skull. "Is that right?"

Cade nodded and took a clumsy sip of orange juice.

"Where did you hear that?"

"On the radio."

At least the kid hadn't said his toy lion had told him. He hadn't mentioned Nero talking to him for days, in fact.

"Melinda, did you hear about this?"

Melinda's eyes remained on her plate. "I did."

"When did you find out about it?"

"Early this morning."

"And you didn't think to tell me?"

Defiance flashed in Melinda's eyes as she met his glare. "You told me you didn't want to hear his name in this house."

Robert thought of smashing the light from her eyes with the aluminum baseball bat he kept stashed in the nook under the stairs, and took a long, slow breath through his nose. If he killed Melinda, he'd have to kill the whelp, too.

If Elijah was out of the hospital, that meant he was headed back to Fishers of Men, which meant he was likely to try and wrest the power Robert had inherited away from him. If Robert wanted to keep things under control, it was time to remind Melinda of a few things.

"Cade, why don't you go and play in the backyard?" Robert asked.

Melinda opened her mouth to object.

"It's a lovely day," Robert said, "and the protest won't start for hours. He'll be safe."

Melinda quailed as Cade took one more bite of eggs and made the ungainly trek out the sliding glass door to the backyard.

Robert sipped his coffee, staring over the edge of the mug at Melinda. "I'm not sure how I can express more clearly that you are not to speak to me like that in front of the boy."

The tines of Melinda's fork clinked against her plate. "I don't know what you're—"

Robert moved quickly, his chair scraping behind him, producing a sound like a baying dog. His hand was around Melinda's throat before she had a chance to scream. He drove her backwards, slamming her against the refrigerator, sending a shower of magnets clattering to the ground.

"I feed you. I shelter you. I keep you safe," Grayburn whispered into her ear. "Do you have any idea how meticulously protected you are? How easily all of this could fall apart?"

Melinda grasped at his knuckles, tears streaming down her reddening cheeks. Her eyes bulged as he tightened his grip.

"Melinda...you're all I've got. I need you to be on my side. I need for us to be a team."

Melinda's lips purpled, then went blue.

He released her. She screamed in a breath, then bent double coughing.

Robert smoothed his hair and rolled his shoulders back as he watched his wife hack and sob. He'd told her more times than he could count that he had deep connections with the Denver police, and that she would find no sympathy there, should she tell anybody what was happening to her. Melinda either believed the lie, or was too terrified to test it, or else she'd have gone to them by now.

"Clean yourself up. I'll go watch Cade," Grayburn offered. "I promise he'll be inside before anybody shows up."

Melinda ran upstairs, weeping. When she was gone, Grayburn forced his fists to unclench and returned to the kitchen table to finish off his coffee, visions of opening fire on the protesters cavorting behind his eyes.

11

OLIVIA OPENS HER EYES to find herself standing in a drab apartment. The smell of smoke hangs in the air, but she doesn't see anything burning. A glint of light catches her eye—broken glass on the linoleum tile. Her skin crawls as instinct tells her she is not alone, and worse, that she is an intruder. She hurries to the door but finds it locked. She backs away, looking for another exit, and gasps as the broken glass cuts into her heel.

"Who's there?" a voice demands from the bedroom.

Olivia freezes, wincing at the pain in her heel as her blood slicks the floor.

A petite woman with dark eyes stumbles out of the bedroom. "Azrael, is that..."

The woman stops in her tracks when she spots Olivia. Her light blonde hair is singed at the tips. There's red in the creases of her knuckles. Flickering light illuminates the room behind her.

"You," the woman says. The word emerges as a curse, along with a few tendrils of smoke rising from the cracks between her teeth.

An echo of recognition fills Olivia with dread.

"You did this," the woman snarls, advancing. "You took them from me."

Olivia tries to deny this accusation, whatever it means, but no sound emerges when she opens her mouth. She's trapped in a grimy apartment with an insane woman who seems to have set the house, and herself, on fire. Olivia slips on her own blood as she backs away.

The woman grins and pulls a blood-stained knife from her pocket. "Now that you're dead, we can finally be together."

"No…" Olivia says, back pushed up against the wall. The smell of smoke is cloying, suffocating…

The windows begin to rattle, and the madwoman stops advancing, staring in horror as silverware clatters off the counter and furniture rocks in the thunderous earthquake.

Olivia looks down and sees a flash of color on her own wrist. She stares at it as the world crumbles around her. It is a tattoo of a flame. Something about this, combined with the growing, crackling fire in the next room makes Olivia remember she is not defenseless.

Olivia summons the light from where it lives at the center of her and uses it to shove away the crazy woman with the knife, tearing the door behind her from its hinges,

slipping away

          to the

                 next

                      nightmare

12

THE SPIDERS IN AZRAEL'S stolen vehicle crept into nooks and crannies as Azrael, Milo, and Elijah approached the car. Azrael opened the rear hatch and lifted the base. "These are the road flares I mentioned. Will they work?"

Milo ran his fingers over them. "Yeah, these are the strontium nitrate kind. We'll need to pick up a few supplies, but I can definitely use these."

Azrael helped Elijah and Milo into the car, climbed into the driver's seat, and drove in silence as Milo's phone gave him directions to the electronics store.

"Need any help getting in there?" Azrael asked once they'd parked.

"I'd take you up on that if the two of you weren't some of the most conspicuous men in the country," Milo said. "Sit tight. I can find what I need."

Azrael and Elijah watched Milo make his way into the store. When he was out of sight, Azrael said, "I need to ask you something."

"What?" Elijah asked.

"When I go to prison, will you adopt Cade? Officially?"

"Of course," Elijah said.

"Will you do something else for me?"

Elijah nodded.

"Make sure he doesn't turn out like either of us."

Elijah's gray eyes narrowed. "I'll try."

Milo returned with two plastic bags of supplies. "Good to go."

"How many can you make with all that?" Azrael asked.

"Two," said Milo. "Maybe three, if I don't mess anything up. Elijah, I'm going to need your help identifying some things along the way. Now let's drive."

IT WAS DARK WHEN Milo, Azrael, and Elijah pulled up to the Fishers of Men facility in Denver. The drone of a helicopter mingled with the rumble of thunder.

"We're here," Azrael said.

"Any cops?" asked Milo.

"I don't see any," Azrael said. "They're all a half mile away at Robert Grayburn's house."

Arachne flipped her vision over to her spiders in and around Grayburn's house. Hundreds of protesters swarmed the street outside the gate surrounding the house, held at bay by riot police. Inside, Melinda comforted Cade, and Grayburn peered out at the protesters through a crack in the drapes.

Arachne brought her attention back to Azrael. He scanned the clouds overhead as lightning flashed across the sky. "We need to hurry. It's going to rain any second."

Milo handed Azrael one of the incendiary bundles he'd created on the drive up. He pointed to a white tab. "Pull this to activate. You'll have five, maybe ten seconds to get clear."

"Okay," said Azrael, tucking the device under his arm.

Milo went around to the back of the vehicle, pulled the wheelchair out of the trunk, and helped Elijah settle into it.

Azrael limped to the front door. "Ready?"

Elijah steered his wheels as Milo pushed the wheelchair forward. "All right, stop here." Elijah looked up at Fishers of Men and sighed pointedly. "Ready."

"You've got insurance," Azrael reminded him. "Okay, start the live feed."

Elijah held up Azrael's phone and clicked the button. "Go."

Arachne shifted her attention to Angel and Trick's Airbnb as they watched a livestream of the protest outside of Grayburn's house on Trick's laptop.

"Any mention of the cops finding bodies in the woods?" Angel asked.

"Angel, I swear I'll let you know if I see anything," Trick said.

A cry went up from a protester near the Cheshire filming the livestream. "Hey! Azrael Hatch is at Fishers of Men!"

Another protester shouted: "Holy shit, he's there right now!"

Trick's phone was in their hand in a flash. "They're right. It's him. This is live." They muted the laptop and turned up the volume on their phone.

"For too long, Fishers of Men has stood as a symbol of oppression and hate," Azrael was saying. The large front doors of the abandoned Fishers of Men facility loomed behind him. "Innocent people of all walks of life have been persecuted, and hunted, and killed. And we're not going to stand for it anymore."

Angel and Trick flinched as Trick's phone flared bright white. When the phone camera corrected for the brightness, the wooden front doors of Fishers of Men were roaring with flames.

The video swung back to Azrael's grinning face. "I staged the protest at Robert Grayburn's house as a distraction to get police away from the real target."

Angel unmuted Trick's laptop in time to hear a protester shout: "Azrael's at Fishers of Men! Let's go!"

The world in the laptop's livestream tilted and blurred as the streamer broke into a run.

"Son of a bitch!" Angel screamed, grabbing Trick's phone out of their hand and throwing it across the room.

"Hey!" Trick shouted.

All at once, down in Hell, a swarm of spiders covered Arachne. She screamed and brushed spiders from her arms as their fangs pierced her flesh, burning with poison that would not kill—

Arachne swiped spiders from her eyes and saw her.

Copper red hair, coltish limbs, flashing eyes.

The crawling, skittering, stinging sensation of a thousand spiders faded away, along with everything happening in the world of the living. She was here at last.

Arachne made her way toward Olivia.

13

"IF YOU'VE EVER BELIEVED in stopping the tyranny of religious hypocrisy, get here right now and help me *burn it down*!" Azrael shouted.

Elijah stopped the video, and the three of them hurried back to the car, Azrael grunting in pain as he settled into the driver's seat. Milo helped Elijah out of his wheelchair and climbed into the passenger seat, the side of his face illuminated in the glow of the growing fire. Azrael hit the gas before Milo's door was shut.

"Stirring," Milo said.

Azrael scoffed. "That felt ridiculous."

"I bet the Cheshires ate it up," Milo said.

"I'm sure they did," said Azrael. He glanced at Elijah in his rearview mirror as his brother watched his burning building recede into darkness.

A pair of cop cars shot past, sirens howling. Thunder growled overhead.

"This one?" Azrael asked as they pulled up to the address Elijah had indicated, a house with a FOR SALE sign in the front yard.

"Yeah, that's it," Elijah said. "The backyard connects to Grayburn's through the gate behind the house. You should be able to slip through to Grayburn's yard without tripping any lights or cameras."

"Are you sure you don't want me to set the bundle off?" Azrael asked. "I might have enough time to get across the yard."

"Not as slow as you're moving," Milo said. "We'll handle it. Now, let's do this before I come to my senses."

Azrael climbed out of the car, each step sending a bolt of pain from his ankle to the base of his skull. He hissed through his teeth as he crept past the FOR SALE house and found the rusty-hinged gate leading to Grayburn's backyard. Azrael hunkered against the fence as a spotlight swept close by, cast by a helicopter headed east, likely chasing the protesters consolidating at Fishers of Men.

Azrael hobbled toward the house, his ankle throbbing in time with his racing heart. He crouched low behind a bench beside the house and waited.

Lighting cracked across the sky directly above him. It was going to start raining at any second.

On the opposite side of the yard, in the shadows by the shed, Azrael watched as Milo trundled Elijah's wheelchair over the grass. Elijah set down the device by the shed, pulled the tab, and Milo wheeled him backward. They were barely through the gate when the device ignited with a *whuff!*

A blinding fire engulfed the side of the shed. Azrael's heart pounded as the flames grew.

Come on, come on...

14

Olivia opens her eyes.

She stands in a dark, barren wasteland stretching into what seems like forever in every direction—but it must not be forever, because sheer faces in the far-flung distance rise upward into an arching oblivion that makes her soul ache.

She's nude. The ground beneath her feet is rocky and cool. She shivers, but not from cold.

She tries to remember what happened before this place, or who she is, and draws a great big cosmic blank.

In the distance sits a golden throne. As far as she can tell, it's the only thing in this place other than a blasted landscape of rock. She starts to walk toward it, then stops when she sees something approaching her.

At first she thinks she's looking at a woman covered in an astonishing amount of hair. Long, black, cascading over her breasts, from the crown of her head to her toes...

No. Not hair. Because it's moving.

Olivia freezes in horror. The woman walking toward her is crawling with spiders.

The woman opens her mouth, and a deluge of black, squirming spiders pours out of it, flowing down her chin, neck, and breasts like a living plague, tumbling to the ground so that she leaves a trail of them in her wake. A huge black spider crawls out from behind one of the woman's eyes, and Olivia at last finds the breath to scream.

"Olivia..." the name emerges from the woman's spider-choked mouth like wind blowing through the branches of a dead tree.

She stops screaming as the name echoes in the black void of her memory. *Olivia...*

Is that her name?

The spider woman stands unmoving, watching her. "Do you remember who you are?"

"No. Why can't I remember? Where am I?"

"This is Hell," the woman rasps. "You're here because I placed a terrible wager on your soul and lost."

Olivia backs away. "No..."

"When you were alive, you had powers," the woman chokes out. "You could move things with your mind. You could hurt people. You could fly. Do you remember?"

Do you remember?

An image surfaces: footprints on her ceiling.

And it all comes back.

Her life before. Her mother. The Moloch fire. The Hatch brothers. Milo and Nancy. All the Hells she's fallen through, using her powers to break free of one only to wake in another.

Pursued all the while.

The woman claws at her throat as a cluster of spiders pours down her chin.

Olivia reaches for the woman and focuses as hard as she can.

Every spider on the woman's flesh curls up its legs and falls to the ground. The woman hacks up a knot of dead spiders and straightens.

"What's chasing me?" Olivia demands.

"Hades. Lucifer. The Devil, whatever you want to call Him. He's coming for you. But there's a way for you to return to the world of the living. There's an inscription on His throne. It's meant to drive us mad. It says: *The portal to redemption lies at the end of one of these passageways, meant for one soul for all of time.*"

Olivia looks at the throne. "So, it's a lie?"

The spider woman shakes her head. "I don't think it is. He's bound by rules older than Himself. The inscription on the throne is a contract, and if a soul ever finds their way out, He must honor it."

"But no one ever has?"

The woman sweeps her arms at the wasteland around them. "Look around. There are millions of tunnels, each of them branching out into billions more. Countless souls have gotten lost in the tunnels and gone insane, but none have found their way out. It has to be you, and you have to find it quickly, because He's coming."

Olivia closes her eyes and concentrates, letting her energy expand, searching, permeating the unfathomably enormous space, reaching the tunnels, filling each of them like blood flowing into capillaries...

In the farthest stretches of one of the tunnels, Olivia seizes on what feels like both a burning light and a door.

"I think I found it."

"Go to it," the spider woman says. "And Olivia—when you get there, go to Robert Grayburn's house as fast as you can. 498 Browning Street, not far from where your mother lives. The child needs your help."

The ground starts to rumble. Tiny pebbles hop at Olivia's feet. "What child?"

"Azrael's son, Cade. Robert Grayburn is going to kill him if he isn't stopped. Milo is there, and he may be in danger, too."

"Milo?" Olivia asks in disbelief. The thunderous sound around her grows to a roar.

"Go, now!" the spider woman shrieks, shoving Olivia off her feet.

Olivia's feet never hit the ground. She turns into a bullet.

She races across the cavernous space, past humans wandering naked and damned, over cliffs and valleys and rocks, picking up speed, and rockets into a tunnel barely large enough for her body to pass through. She speeds into its depths, chasing the bright light-door...

The walls shake with His approach. She is fast, but He is the master of this place, and He's gaining on her.

Olivia thinks of her mother. How she'd like to see her one last time.

She's close now. She can't see it yet, but she can feel the light of it, balancing the shattering darkness of the thing pursuing her, hungering for her like a slavering wolf.

What will it be like if the thing catches her? Tooth and claw? Eternal, mindless suffering?

Finally, Olivia sees it, at the end of a pristine straightaway nothing like the caverns leading her this far: a blinding light in the shape of a door.

Hope the Devil keeps His word, Olivia thinks, and barrels toward it.

15

Robert Grayburn sat in his chair by the window, sipping a glass of whiskey. It burned pleasantly on the way down his throat, the warmth spreading to his stomach and then his brain. He settled into the feeling like he would into a lover's embrace. It even lessened the ache in his leg.

As Grayburn drank, night fell, and storm clouds rolled in. Judging by the wind kicking up the leaves, rain would come at any moment, and then the gangly, sign-toting kids bellowing outside his house would disperse and go crawling back into whatever holes they'd crawled out of.

Suddenly, a cry went up among the protesters. Robert couldn't make out what they were saying over the blatting noise of the helicopter hovering overhead, but he felt the tone of the protest change from rage to surprise. He peeked through the curtains as they looked at their phones and bolted. Cop cars went wailing in the same direction, lights flashing.

Grayburn frowned as he watched them go.

Something was wrong.

He finished off his glass of whiskey and went to the refrigerator, pushing aside paperwork to retrieve the gun nestled inside the Bible at the bottom of the stack. He confirmed it was loaded, and the red dot was visible on the side. He recalled what Henry Hatch taught him about the safety when he'd given him the weapon, long ago. *Red means dead.*

He returned to his chair by the window and set the gun next to the whiskey bottle. He stared at the now-vacant street outside his house.

"Where are they going?"

Robert turned. Melinda was looking at him from the foot of the stairs.

"I don't know," Robert said.

Melinda's eyes fell to the gun on the table. "Is the protest over?"

Robert clenched his jaw. "It sure sounds like it, doesn't it? Where's Cade?"

"In bed. He's scared."

"There's nothing to be scared of."

Melinda fidgeted, biting her lip. "He says Nero stopped talking to him."

"Good," said Robert, returning his gaze to the window. "He's getting too old for imaginary friends—"

Melinda's yelp of fear cut him off.

Robert scowled. "What is it?"

"Fire!" Melinda said, pointing out the back door.

Grayburn leapt to his feet and lurched to the door. Sure enough, the side of his shed was ablaze.

"Damn fool kids," he snarled. "Melinda, grab the mop bucket from the basement."

Melinda disappeared down the hallway. Robert hurried back to the front window, grabbed the gun, and slid it into the waistband of his pants. On the way back across the room, he banged his leg on the coffee table and hollered in pain before throwing open the sliding glass door and limping to the shed. There was a tarp inside he might be able to use to stop the flames from spreading.

He reached for the door handle, coughing as smoke filled his lungs, shielding his face from the heat, when he spotted them.

Parallel lines of flattened grass, thrown into relief by the fire.

Lightning crackled overhead as Robert's hand fell away from the shed door. His gaze rose slowly to see where the tracks disappeared out the back gate to the neighboring yard.

The corners of his mouth lifted in a smile.

16

Olivia emerged from the portal into darkness, where she slammed into a wall.

Stars exploded behind her eyes. The door to freedom was a lie. Of course. She'd trusted a woman covered in spiders telling her the Devil was a straight shooter.

But then...why hadn't He captured her? He was so close behind her when she reached the door she'd felt His breath on her heels, so where was He?

Olivia's eyes adjusted, making out a few shapes in the darkness. There was something familiar about it.

The room filled with light. Her mother's bedroom.

Her mother threw off her bed sheets.

"Who's there? I've got a—"

Betty looked down at Olivia. Her face paled. "What... Olivia?"

"Hi, Mom," Olivia said.

"How?" Her eyes filled with tears as her voice broke. "They said you were dead."

"I don't have time to explain," Olivia said. "I didn't mean to come here. I was thinking of you when I passed through the door, so that must have led me here—"

"Didn't mean to come here? Where the hell have you been? Why are you naked? And how did you do that to the *wall*?"

Olivia looked at the sizable crater she'd left in the wall. "I'll explain everything, but right now I need you to call 911 and tell them to go to 498 Browning Street." Olivia ran to her mother's dresser and pulled out the first shirt and pair of pants she found.

Betty opened and closed her mouth several times. "Browning Street? Honey, you're not making any sense…"

Olivia pulled the shirt over her head. It smelled so strongly of her mother that tears welled in her eyes. "Robert Grayburn lives there. From the Colony. A child is in danger, and Milo might be, too. Mom, I love you, and I've never been happier to see another human being in my entire life, but I have to go."

"Olivia, slow down, it's like you're having a manic episode!"

Olivia's head spun. Maybe she was. Maybe this was what being crazy felt like, thinking you had magic powers, that you'd slipped through countless layers of Hell and escaped the Devil on your heels. Or maybe this was another trick, another level in Hell she had to unlock before she got devoured by a beast so old it was all but eternal…

Olivia stepped into the pants. "I'll explain later."

"Olivia, can't you please just tell me what's going on?"

"Just send the police to 498 Browning Street, now!" Olivia said, running from the room.

She waited until she got outside and launched into the air—

—and came right back down. The impact knocked the air from her lungs.

Olivia stood up and tried again. Nothing. She tried to lift one of the flowerpots on the porch. Light the mailbox on fire.

Nothing.

Her powers were gone.

"Timing could have been better," Olivia said, and ran.

17

AZRAEL WATCHED FROM THE shadows as Grayburn barreled out of the back door and rushed toward the burning shed. When Grayburn was halfway to the shed, Azrael slipped inside the open door.

He took in his surroundings. The house was laid out exactly as Elijah had described. To Azrael's left, the kitchen. To his right, a living room and a staircase leading to the second floor. Azrael made his way up the stairs, ankle flaring with pain, and opened the second door on the left—the room Elijah guessed was most likely to be Cade's bedroom.

Azrael held his breath and peered in the door. Inside was a twin bed and a scattering of toys, including Cade's toy lion, Nero. For a heart-stopping instant, Azrael thought the bed was empty. But then the sheets moved, and his son's head peeked out. "Daddy?"

The sight of his son squeezed Azrael's heart like a vice. He pressed a finger to his lips. "Hi, Button. Keep quiet and come with me. We're going to play a game."

"A game?"

"Yes. The game is running outside as fast as we can."

Cade climbed out of his bed and goggled at his father in awe. "Nero told me you'd come back someday."

"That's great Cade, now let's go. I need you to be as quiet as a rabbit. You remember how quiet rabbits are?"

Cade nodded.

"Okay, let's go," Azrael said, and took his son's hand.

He led Cade into the hallway, down the stairs, wincing at every creak, pulse thrumming in his veins. He spotted a large spider on the wall as he descended and was gripped by the sudden, insane sensation that it was watching him. His armpits went damp with sweat. He was so close to getting his son to safety.

At the bottom of the stairs, he heard a gasp and turned to see Melinda standing in the hallway, holding a mop bucket. Azrael froze. He took in her huge, terrified eyes and the bruise on her neck. Her lips trembled open, her breath coming fast through her teeth.

"Please," Azrael whispered. "Let me save him."

Melinda's eyes fell to Cade, staring up at her from Azrael's side. When she looked back at Azrael, bright crescents of tears shone in her eyes. "Get him out of here."

Azrael tugged Cade toward the front door, moving as quickly as his ankle allowed, panting through his teeth. He unlocked the deadbolt, and his hand was on the door handle when he heard Grayburn's voice.

"That would be a mistake, Azrael."

Every hair on Azrael's body lifted as he turned to see Robert Grayburn's hulking shadow standing outside the back door, illuminated from behind by the blazing shed.

He wasn't alone.

In front of Grayburn, emerging from the haze of smoke, Milo pushed Elijah's wheelchair over the threshold and into the house. Azrael gaped, not understanding, until Grayburn raised his hand, and Azrael made out the dark shape of a gun gleaming in the firelight.

18

Olivia ran down Browning Street, sweet night air rushing into her lungs. The cool pavement slapped her heels. Her mind spun with the improbability of being alive again.

Lightning snarled across the sky as black numbers on mailboxes flew past in a blur, counting down to her destination. She had no plan for what she was going to do when she arrived at Grayburn's house, but every ounce of her intuition told her she needed to be there.

Olivia arrived at number 498, which looked as normal as any other house on the block, except for the pillar of smoke rising from the backyard. She ran up to the front door and tried the handle, expecting it to be locked. Instead, it swung open, and she ran inside, colliding with Azrael.

Azrael's jaw dropped when he realized who'd crashed into him. He staggered away, pulling Cade with him until his back was against the wall. "Olivia?"

"It's all right," Olivia said. "I'm not going to hurt you."

"Olivia, is that really you?" Milo asked.

Olivia took in the room in a flash: Robert Grayburn holding Milo and Elijah at gunpoint; a terrified-looking woman by the stairs clutching a mop bucket; at least a dozen spiders climbing the walls.

"Yes, Milo, it's me."

"And who the hell are you?" Grayburn asked, training the gun on Olivia's forehead.

In Olivia's periphery, she watched the woman beside Grayburn slowly lower the mop bucket with trembling hands.

Olivia felt a rush of clarity.

She lifted her gaze to Grayburn. "My whole life, my biggest fear was that I'd turn into my father. That I'd hurt people, like he did."

Smoke billowed into the room as the blaze behind the house grew. The frightened woman knelt and set the mop bucket just out of Grayburn's sight. She reached into the alcove behind the stairs, her wide eyes telling Olivia: *Keep talking.*

"I thought I was worse than my father," Olivia said, "but I was wrong. I never wanted to hurt anybody. That's what makes me different from men like him, and men like you."

The woman near Grayburn pulled a metal baseball bat out of the shadows behind the stairs, desperation shining in her eyes.

Grayburn glared at Olivia, his heavy eyebrows gathering like storm clouds over his pitiless eyes. "Men like me?"

"That's why I'm here," Olivia said. "That's why I clawed my way out of Hell to stop you."

The smoke alarm in the hallway blared to life.

Grayburn turned toward the sound in time to see the woman beside him raising the bat over her head. He swung his gun around. It produced an earsplitting *BANG!* as the arc of her bat connected with his jaw.

The woman's head snapped back as the bullet caught her in the forehead. The bat slipped from her fingers, and she crumpled to the ground. Robert Grayburn went down to one knee, bellowing in pain as a thunderclap shook the walls.

Elijah cried out in his wheelchair, and Milo hunkered low beside him, cursing. Cade clapped his hands over his ears and screamed.

"Azrael," Olivia said.

Azrael tore his gaze away from Grayburn.

"Get them out of here," she said.

Olivia turned on her heels and ran past Elijah and Milo, coughing in the haze, ears ringing from the blast of the gun and the shrill smoke alarm. The baseball bat lay beside Melinda's prone form. She reached for it and got her hands around the peeling tape at the base of it. Behind her, she heard Azrael urging Milo to roll Elijah forward.

Olivia raised the bat over her head. She locked eyes with Robert Grayburn as he leveled the gun with her chest and pulled the trigger.

A sledgehammer of pain took Olivia's breath away. The floor rose up behind her and thumped her on the back. Olivia stared up at the ceiling, struggling to breathe. This was all right. Azrael would have gotten everybody outside by now. They were going to get away. Maybe this was enough to balance out everything she'd done...

Robert Grayburn got to his feet and loomed over Olivia. "Men like me win," he growled, aiming the gun at Olivia's forehead.

"Hey, asshole!"

Olivia turned to see Azrael run through the front door: Azrael alone, which meant Milo, Elijah, and Cade were safe.

Azrael hurled something dark through the air. The bundle struck the wall behind Grayburn and fell to the floor at his feet like a dead bird. Grayburn looked down, eyes bulging in understanding a split second before the device ignited in a blinding explosion of light.

Grayburn howled as flames consumed him. He shrieked like the souls of the damned and fired the gun wildly until it clicked. He staggered against the wall, his screams fading into moans, then collapsed into a heap and was still. Olivia heard the applause-like hiss of countless raindrops striking the house as flames from Grayburn's prone form licked the walls.

Shuffling footsteps approached, and Azrael was at her side. "Olivia, come on, let's get out of here."

"Azrael..." Olivia coughed.

Azrael stopped trying to lift her. "Yes?"

Olivia tasted blood as she smiled. "We've got to stop meeting like this."

Tears stood in his eyes. "Olivia...I..."

"It's all right," she said. "I know." She closed her eyes.

Her chest rose, fell, and did not rise again.

19

Hades's roar of fury shook existence.

Hell—at least Arachne's version of it—was breaking down. Flames burst from fissures splitting the rocky terrain. Massive chunks of rock broke free of the ceiling and plummeted, terminating in deafening crashes. Souls ran screaming in all directions.

Was this how all the other levels of Hell looked after He chased Olivia through them? Was everything falling apart?

Did Olivia *break* Hell?

Arachne's right hand blazed with agonizing, invisible fire. She looked down at it, expecting to see flesh melting from bone, but it was just her hand, pale and shaking.

She looked up to see a chunk of ceiling come unmoored above her. No chance of getting out from underneath it. She scanned her surroundings, the home she'd known for the last few millennia, and wondered what happened to souls when there was no Hell to hold them.

It couldn't be worse than how it worked when it was intact.

Arachne lifted her eyes to watch the approaching monolith of rock like a woman enjoying the soft patter of rain.

She was smiling when it crushed her.

Darkness. Silence.

But not oblivion: Arachne's breath still panted between her clenched teeth, and she felt the prickle of her spiders on her limbs, so even after being crushed by a small mountain, her torment continued. There was no escape...

Arachne opened her eyes.

Hades loomed over her, His eyes alight with inner flame.

Arachne shrieked and turned to bolt, but her feet tangled and she collapsed to the rocky earth. He'd torn countless levels of Hell apart. There was no telling what He was about to do to *her*—

She looked over her shoulder. He closed the distance between them in massive strides that shook the ground beneath Him.

"You showed her how to *escape*," Hades growled, His voice reverberating through her quivering body like the peals of a colossal bell. He reached for Arachne with His glowing hand.

Arachne squeezed her eyes shut and braced herself for the inevitable consequence of defying Him.

Instead of flaying her skin from her bones, or a thousand other tortures, she felt the pressure of a single finger, nearly too hot to stand, gently touching her forehead.

A trickling sensation washed over her, at once familiar and strange, and it took a few breaths for her to discern what she was feeling. All of the spiders on her were now moving in the same direction.

Arachne opened her eyes and watched as the spiders on her flesh trundled down her legs to the earth below. She opened her mouth and allowed the spiders inside of her to follow, slipping away from her like a living shadow.

Arachne looked up at Hades, who was glaring at her like He'd like to tear her to shreds. Her eyes continued upward, and she gasped when she saw that the ceiling above was intact. So was the rest of it. All the tunnels, valleys, outcroppings—everything was as it was before.

As the last of her spiders clambered away from her, Arachne found the strength to ask: "What's happening?"

"You won, Arachne," Hades said, His smile widening under His blazing eyes. "You found the only way you *could* win."

"But...but the collapse," Arachne stammered out. "I was buried...you were furious..."

"Oh, I was, dear Arachne. Furious enough to tear all of Hell asunder, and not just because you bested me. By telling Olivia how to return to the world of the living, you created a paradox."

"A...a paradox?" Arachne panted.

Hades gestured to His throne. "*The portal to redemption lies at the end of one of these passageways, meant for one soul for all of time.*"

Arachne shook her head. "I don't understand."

"Olivia passed through that doorway and was granted a clean slate. She died a sinless death soon after, earning herself an afterlife where I could not reach her—but because of the terms of the inscription, I could no longer free you through that same portal as promised." Hades laughed darkly. "In a single stroke, you both won our wager, and made it impossible for me to honor it."

Arachne blinked, remembering Olivia vanishing into one of the billions of apertures in a blur of movement. "One soul for all of time."

"Yes. A contradiction such as this cannot stand. Olivia's escape and redemption gave me no choice. The only way to honor our wager was to turn back the clock."

"Turn back the clock?" Arachne echoed.

"See for yourself," Hades said.

Arachne's mind filled with a sudden vision.

"There is nothing in this world you cannot accomplish if you put your mind to it."

The speaker's voice echoed over the heads of the graduate students and their families, including Olivia and Milo at their grad school commencement. Olivia glared at the program on her arm rest with an intensity that rippled through Arachne's entire being.

More visions came flooding in. Nancy, alive and well, visiting her parents in their Austin mansion. Azrael, toiling in the Colony garden. Lila, checking herself for the monthly blood that wasn't coming. Elijah, legs intact, reading the Bible in his bed at the Colony.

Arachne's terrestrial spiders bristled in astonishment. "What—they're alive! How?"

Hades's expression darkened. "The rules written by the Old One before time began cannot be broken. Thus, we have returned to the moment in time before I began meddling in the course of our wager." His lips curled in a snarl over His teeth. "I saw all of it plotted out, each stitch of tapestry, except for what happened when she got here. Bringing her powers with her...you telling her how to get out..." Hades's teeth sharpened as He spoke, His fingers lengthening into claws— His true form, the one that had leveled Hell, beginning to emerge. "I was *this* close to seizing her in my grasp. No amount of strength she possessed could have stopped what I would have done to her, had I caught her."

Arachne made a small, terrified sound as her breath caught in her throat.

In a blink, Hades returned to His glowing veneer of humanity.

"You'll have to forgive me, Arachne." He shook His head, chuckling. "I'm not accustomed to losing, and that was the first time—in all of time—I lost to someone who wasn't You Know Who. And I must admit you won in spectacular fashion. You saved not just Olivia, but the rest of them, too."

Arachne struggled to keep her voice steady. "Olivia... Milo...do they remember, too?"

"No," Hades said, "at least, not the way that you do. Their souls know the truth, so they will feel echoes of what happened to them in half-formed memories, or dreams, or moments of déjà vu. A lingering sensation of trauma or triumph. A suspicion that they're on an altered timeline, that things once played out very differently."

Arachne gaped at Him. "I won," she breathed.

"Don't think you're so clever." Hades peered up at the cavernous space above Him. "This is exactly the sort of joke the Old One loved to play on me. Your freedom may be nothing more than the punchline of a Creator with a sense of humor."

A mad hope surged in Arachne's chest. "Does this mean I get to return to the world of the living?"

Hades nodded.

Arachne swallowed. "How do I find it? The portal?"

Hades pointed to the spiders crawling away from her. "Follow them. It's going to take them a while to get there, but you've got nothing but time."

"You won't try and make her fall again, will you?"

"Not this one. I lost fair and square. Don't worry, there are plenty of other souls for me to corrupt."

"Good," Arachne said. She rose to her feet, trembling. "Will I remember all this, once I'm alive again?"

Hades lifted an eyebrow. "Only one way to find out."

Arachne drew in a deep breath. "Farewell, Hades."

"Farewell," Hades said, tendrils of smoke rising from between His grinning teeth.

Arachne turned away and followed her flowing stream of spiders. During her walk, she spotted Agon, perched on a high cliff. It grimaced at her with its horrible gaping maw but kept its distance. This struck her as a good sign, even if that was just wishful thinking.

Maybe she could get used to that sort of thinking.

EPILOGUE

LILA MONROE DREAMED SHE was a passenger in a vehicle far larger than the handful of cars she'd seen coming and going from the Colony. In her dream, it was pitch black outside. She was using the edge of a discarded postcard to dredge rust from underneath her fingernails when an odd sensation fluttered in her belly, as if she'd swallowed a live goldfish.

Lila startled awake. A frigid wind whistled through the cracks in the window by her bed. She shivered in the dark, waiting for the swishing in her stomach to fade along with the rest of the dream, but it persisted. Lila lay her cold hands on the small, taut bump of her belly, confused, until she remembered the word for what she was feeling: the quickening.

Her baby was moving.

Lila clenched her jaw to suppress the panic welling in her throat. She fought against tears, but they came anyway, coursing down her cheeks. She was alone in her room—severed from the rest of the Colony as a Shamed Woman—a fate that at least gave her the privacy to weep in peace.

It had been more than two months since Azrael fled the Colony. What if he didn't keep his promise to come back for her? What if she had to bear her child in this unspeakable place? The Colony was all she'd ever known, but she had to believe there was hope for her and her child in the outside world, no matter what horrible things the Prophet said about it.

Lila thought of her dream, the memory of it already growing faint, of her desperation as she'd dug red from underneath her nails. She shook the thought away, allowing it to descend into the dark depths of her subconscious.

Lila closed her eyes and silently vowed to the life growing in her belly that she'd do whatever she needed to keep it safe.

A sharp, splintering bang startled Lila from her thoughts, and her heart thumped madly in her chest at the sound of men shouting. A dazzling band of white light pierced her window. Moments later, she gasped as her bedroom door banged against the opposite wall, and a uniformed man stormed inside.

Lila shielded her eyes from the light trained on her.

The man dipped his flashlight away from her face. "Just one in here!" he shouted out the door. Outside, the commotion grew—doors kicked in, flashlights throwing shadows in all directions, women screaming, children crying, men hollering and cursing.

Lila lay stock still, too stunned to scream, as the intruder approached her bed. He held out a dark, gloved hand, and Lila made out a badge gleaming on his vest.

"Don't worry," he said. "You're safe now. Everything's going to be okay."

The fluttering in Lila's belly as she took the man's hand suddenly felt like hope.

Hours after learning of the raid on the Colony, Warren Young stood in his living room, staring at an envelope with wide eyes.

Azrael tore his gaze away from the news on his cell phone. "What is it?"

"It's for you."

"Who from?"

"There's no return address. There's no *address*, either. No stamp. Someone dropped this off in person," Warren said. "Who knows you're here?"

Azrael reached for the letter. "No one."

Elijah poked his head into the living room. His eyes were rimmed with red from weeping at the news of the raid. "What does it say?"

Azrael tore open the envelope and pulled out a handwritten letter. "It says to read it aloud."

Azrael,

I am sending you this letter because you've been given a second chance—a chance to be a better man than your father. You can hide from your past, or you can stand and face it. You can be a good father to a kind-souled boy. You can stand by Lila. You can be compassionate to Elijah and show him there's more to be gained from forgiving than from condemning. You can be a good friend to Warren, who has opened his home to you at great risk to his own safety. You can give the lost followers of the Colony strength so they can step into the light of the world, unafraid.

A fire burns in you—make it a fire that forges, rather than immolates.

The future mother of your child is waiting for you. She's been forced out of the only home she's ever known, and she needs you. Be kind to her, Azrael. Be kind to all of them.

Azrael swallowed hard. "It's signed, A."

Elijah wiped his nose on the back of his wrist. "Who do you think wrote it?"

A fire burns in you.

A vision of a house fire flashed behind Azrael's eyes. For the briefest of moments, he felt the steely heat of the fire on his flesh.

He shook the thought away. "I have no idea."

"Whoever sent the letter to the police about the Colony signed it the same way." Warren showed them the picture of it on his phone. "Who's doing this?"

Azrael set the letter aside. "You know what? It doesn't matter. They're right. I need to go find Lila. Will you two come with me?"

Warren said, "I...I don't know if it's safe..."

"We haven't done anything wrong. We can't help any of the innocent people the Prophet hurt if we remain silent."

Elijah scowled. "Azrael, what you're saying is heresy..."

Azrael shot an angry look at his brother for using his old name, then made himself take a breath. "That's not heresy, brother. The heresy was Father teaching us that fear and love are the same thing. Come on, Warren—are you prepared to come out of hiding and tell the truth?"

Warren took a shaky breath and nodded.

"And you, brother? Are you ready to reveal who we are?"

Elijah wiped tears from his eyes. "I never wanted to hide it."

Azrael regarded his brother and friend. "Well then... let's go."

"CAN YOU BELIEVE THIS cult stuff?" Olivia asked Milo over the phone. "Those poor women. They must be so scared."

"They're brainwashed," Milo said. "It's going to take them a long time to understand they were being abused."

"One of the pregnant girls can't be more than fifteen years old."

"At least her baby will be born on the outside," Milo said. "Maybe the kid will have a chance of being a normal, well-adjusted person."

"I hope you're right."

A knock fell on her door. Olivia answered it, but no one was there. As she started to close it, she saw a white envelope sitting on her welcome mat. Written on the front was a delicate cursive "O."

The hairs on the back of her neck prickled. She hadn't lived in Austin long enough to make friends with anyone who knew where she lived. Did she somehow already have a stalker? She scanned the street but didn't see anyone other than a couple with a stroller a block away. She picked up the letter, stepped inside, and closed the door.

"Holy shit, Olivia, they're finding bodies buried in the woods."

Olivia's heart pounded in her ears. Something about the "O" on the envelope made her think of spiders.

"Milo."

"They've found three so far—"

"*Milo.*"

"What?"

"Someone put a letter on my porch."

The line went silent for a beat. "Just now?"

"Yeah. They knocked and ran away."

"What does it say?"

Olivia opened the envelope, pulled out a single sheet of paper, and read it out loud.

Olivia Madden,

You are more powerful than you know.

You've never met me, but I've been something of a guardian angel to you for years. I've watched you struggle with the trauma of a past that was not your fault. I've watched you battle your demons and come into your strength. I am writing to let you know that the past need not have its claws in you anymore. You have emerged from everything you've been through as a beautiful, courageous soul who will be a source for good in the lives of those who know you.

I don't know what the future holds for you, but I know you're strong enough to stand up to whatever adversity comes your way. Take comfort in knowing that you once triumphed over something unimaginable.

Enjoy what I'm sure will be a beautiful life.

Oh, and make sure to introduce Milo to Nancy.

Olivia set the letter down. "It's signed, A."

"Well, *that's* fucking weird," Milo said. "Who the hell is Nancy?"

ABOUT THE AUTHOR

Risa Patterson has been many things over the years — a singer, a musician, a graphic designer, and a producer — but she has always been a writer. Born in Delaware, and raised in North Carolina, she received her B.S. in Communication at Appalachian State University, where her short story, "The White Death," was published in the *Appalachian Anthology*. In 2015, she self-published her first novel, *Author Asbury*, creating a small run to share with her friends and family.

She is currently working on another novel called *Loop, Nevada*, a story about a time loop in a remote mining settlement in 1888 Nevada.

She lives in Pittsburgh, PA, where she enjoys playing piano, hiking, driving around in her van, and relaxing with her cat, Paloma.